Efrat Eshel

Yael Hedaya is a journalist and humor columnist for the Israeli daily *Yediot Aharonot,* and the Tel Aviv weekly magazine *Halr.* She currently teaches creative writing at Tel Aviv University. *Accidents,* her first novel, was a bestseller in Israel and will be published in four languages. She lives in Tel Aviv, Israel.

ALSO BY YAEL HEDAYA

Housebroken

accidents

YAEL HEDAYA

translated by jessica cohen

acc*i*dents

A NOVEL

PICADOR

METROPOLITAN BOOKS HENRY HOLT AND COMPANY, NEW YORK

www.picadorusa.com

Picador® is a U.S. registered trademark and is used by Henry Holt and Company under license from Pan Books Limited.

For information on Picador Reading Group Guides, as well as ordering, please contact Picador.
Phone: 646-307-5629
Fax: 212-253-9627
E-mail: readinggroupguides@picadorusa.com

Designed by Fritz Metsch

Library of Congress Cataloging-in-Publication Data

Hedaya, Yael.
    [Te'unot. English]
    Accidents : a novel / by Yael Hedaya ; translated by Jessica Cohen.
      p cm.
    ISBN 13: 978-0-312-42604-0
    ISBN 10: 0-312-42604-6
    I. Cohen, Jessica. II. Title.
  PJ5055.23.E33T4813 2005
  892.4'36—dc22

                                            2005041977

First published in Israel in 2001 under the title *Te'unot* by Am Oved, Tel Aviv

First published in the United States by Henry Holt and Company

First Picador Edition: August 2006

10 9 8 7 6 5 4 3 2 1

PART ONE

Dana sat waiting on a chair in the nurse's office. The nurse sat on the other side of the desk and pretended to be busy. She riffled through her papers and tried to come up with a phone call she needed to make—something that would sound important, or at least real, because she knew the girl would easily pick up on a fake call. But she had no one to phone. To avoid Dana's look, which was directed at the floor and, being lowered, seemed all the more invasive and bothersome, she picked up a pen and started scribbling.

Half an hour later, Yonatan Luria came to collect his daughter. He was dressed in faded corduroys and the brown suede jacket he had worn every winter since the girl started in first grade, all those mornings when he was called to the nurse's office. The nurse walked Dana and her father down the wide corridor leading to the school entrance and then went back to her room, where she sat down at her desk again and returned to her papers. She was not amused by what she saw, but rather a little worried; she had written *Yonatan Luria* over and over again, like a schoolgirl, filling up half a page.

She envied the child for her daily proximity to this man. There were times, as she sat with Dana in the room that smelled of iodine and Band-Aids, cut off from the chaos of the school, taking her temperature and pressing her tongue down with a wooden stick, when she wanted to ask her about the man who was known around school as Dana's dad but whom she preferred to think of by his name, Yonatan Luria. She couldn't fantasize about Dana's dad.

He was always polite and inquired about his daughter's health. He listened quietly when she suggested treatments and wondered whether she thought they should go to the doctor to get a prescription for some new antibiotics, or whether they could make do with the supplies they had at home. She knew what was in their medicine cabinet but wanted to know more; although she did not have the authority to prescribe a particular course of action, she always tried to find ways to prolong their conversations. Yonatan would say goodbye to her at the school entrance, placing his hand on his daughter's shoulder as she stood next to him, downcast, and add: "Well, thanks, Esti, and I hope we won't have to meet again this winter."

But the nurse knew they would, because she followed the girl during recess, in the yard or in the bustling hallways, which, during winter and with the windows closed, had a sour smell of damp bread and cheese and fruit sweating in plastic bags. Then, whenever she caught Dana sniffling or if her eyes looked suspiciously shiny, she went up to her, put her hand to the girl's forehead, and asked softly if she felt well. Sometimes the nurse also found an excuse to order her, with the same authoritative tenderness, to come and have her temperature taken. Temperatures can vary, but since in Dana's case you couldn't take any chances, she would call Yonatan without hesitation but with butterflies in her stomach. She always forgot that before he arrived to pick up his daughter, she would have to spend at least twenty minutes trapped in her office with the girl.

Dana was quiet all the way to the car. She walked behind her father, who strode quickly, as he usually did, particularly when he had been taken away from his thoughts in the middle of the morning. It was as if he believed the quick striding would salvage his severed train of thought—although Yonatan knew it had long been cut off—and prevent it from being severed again. Because the routine of phone calls from the nurse had become part of his new life, he was easily able to integrate a separate track of thoughts into the noisy lanes of his existing thoughts, practically without disturbance. He no longer bothered to slow his pace as he used to, after Nira, his dead wife's sister, had commented gently but with the superiority of someone trying to sound convinced that he was acting out of ignorance and not lack of love (either way he was hurt by her words), that he walked too fast, that he looked as if he were trying to get away from his child. To demonstrate, his sister-in-law had walked quickly back and forth across the rug in the living room. She said the last thing the girl needed was to be afraid that her father might also disappear.

Dana was ten now, and she no longer tried to make things easier for him or find things to talk about when he picked her up from school with her shivers and her runny nose and sore throat, or to placate him because of these repeated disturbances which prevented him from working and meant he could not write; she knew his writing also suffered from an illness, one that had begun before her mother died and worsened afterward. When she tried to imagine what her father was feeling when he sat at his computer in the little study between his bedroom and hers, unable to write, she thought about the cramps she got in her legs after gym class, which was boring but at the same time too exhausting to allow time for thought and so she especially hated it. The pain was a familiar one but she was not afraid of it because she knew that although it appeared gradually, it disappeared at once, and she wondered if that was what he felt too, and where he felt it—perhaps in his chest, because that was where she felt fists of pain when she cried, or when she tried not to cry. She wondered what would happen if whatever he had did not go away, either gradually or at once, because she had been seeing him sitting at his computer looking cramped for a long time now. It scared her to think he might become permanently paralyzed, like the dad of a girl in her class who had been injured in army training. But with her father it would be different, a paralysis of the spirit, worse than that of the other dad, who was a happy, funny person and volunteered to do magic tricks for the class at all sorts of events.

She didn't ask him about it, because she didn't want to worry him and didn't want him to know that she knew, because that would make him even sadder. She assumed he was aware of his condition, and sometimes she told herself encouragingly that his stillness only looked like paralysis to her; it actually involved some hidden motion that she could not detect because she was too young, and perhaps because she was his daughter and was too close to him—just like he didn't notice what she was going through—and that in fact when he was not moving, the writing was raging inside his head and that he was afraid if he moved it would all escape; he was just waiting for the right moment. But she remembered that when she was little, three or four, she would stand outside his study door and hear the rapid clicking of his keyboard, and sometimes also the wheels of his office chair moving back and forth on the floor. Her mother would tell her not to play there so she wouldn't disturb Dad while he was writing, so she learned that writing was the sound of clicking and wheels; over time her mother understood that her daughter's games involved listening to her father write, so she let her stand by the door as long as she kept quiet.

Noise of any kind drove Yonatan out of his mind, apart from the noise he himself made. In addition to the sound of his writing, there was also the noise he made when he paced restlessly around the apartment between paragraphs, listening to classical music, going in and out of his study, turning the volume up or down according to how things were going for him: High decibels meant inspiration, bad days were always quieter. The noisier he was, the more confident they were of his good mood, and that made them happy too. But her mother had often said, "People change," and that gave Dana hope that perhaps things had changed with him. The fact was that he had also started speaking more softly in recent years, and she had too, and he cooked and ate quietly, as did she; everything was done quietly. Even his driving had become quieter—he didn't curse anyone or get annoyed—so it seemed reasonable to her that the book he had started five years ago would now be written in absolute silence.

When her teachers or the parents of kids in her class asked if her dad was working on a new book, she said he was, even though she knew by their tone that they were not interested in the book but rather in how he was getting along without a wife. The nurse asked several times, while examining her, if she knew what the book was about. Was it another romantic novel like the previous two? Dana said she thought it was. The nurse said, "A writer's daughter should know what a romance is," and Dana said yes, and the nurse said, "I bet he doesn't tell anyone what he's writing about, not even you."

"He does tell me," Dana replied, and the nurse said, "Your father doesn't talk much, does he?" Dana said nothing, and the nurse smiled and said, as if to herself, "Your father protects his privacy." Dana thought about the term *your father,* which on the one hand didn't sound like her father at all and on the other hand described a mood that seemed to fit his condition.

He didn't tell her what he was working on and she didn't ask, because by this point, after four years, they had reached an understanding, and she was afraid to destroy it. She had once read in an advice column that when you love someone you don't ask too many questions; it must be true because he didn't ask her questions either, except for essential things. Theirs was a two-way understanding and also a dead-end road: The widower knew he could not protect his ten-year-old daughter from what she had already endured, while the worried child wanted to understand her quiet father.

(2)

Dana got into the car and fastened her seat belt. While she had been sitting in the nurse's office she had prepared a mental list of topics to think about on the way, because over the last four years she had learned to take advantage of the silences instead of fearing them. There would be at least twenty minutes before they got home, because of the traffic, and because her father always drove slowly when she was in the car, deliberately. While he turned the engine on and pumped the pedal with his foot and cleaned his sunglasses with the edge of his sweatshirt, she tried to decide what to think about first—because the first minutes of the drive were always quieter than the final ones, when subjects would come up, like what there was to eat and what was on TV, and reminders to buy juice and go to the drugstore—how she wanted to stop her piano lessons; or the Girl Scouts, which she also wanted to quit; or the slumber party she had gone to over the weekend, which was where this flu had started.

She didn't like Lilach Kahane, but when Lilach invited her to the party, she was glad they were considering letting her join the "team." The invitations were always covert, delivered by a messenger during recess, and every girl who accepted—and they all did, including the ones who were invited out of pity and knew it—was given a long and impossible list of things to bring, written by Orit Segal, Lilach's second-in-command, who sat behind Lilach in class and played with her hair and traced things on her back while she sat erect and squirmed with delight.

After Ilana's death Yonatan, who hated groups, had forced himself to be slightly more forgiving toward these childhood rituals whose significance he had long ago forgotten and had, if truth be told, never really understood. He only realized this after he was left alone with his daughter; he had never, as his mother liked to complain and cheerfully tell Dana, been "a real child." Dana wanted to know more, as if this diagnosis had something to do with her future rather than her father's past. "But what does that mean?" she asked. Her grandmother explained willingly, saying, "If you really want to know, though it's not a nice thing to say, your dad was insufferable."

Then came the questions, which Dana never tired of asking, and which Yonatan's mother, as she grew older, increasingly enjoyed answering. "Was he naughty?" His mother said no, quite the opposite. Dana would say, "What is the opposite of naughty?" and her grandmother would say there was no word for it. Dana asked if he was rude, and his mother said that sometimes he was, when he was in a bad mood, especially to his father, who put up with a lot from his son. Dana asked whether he was often in a bad mood, and her grandmother said he was born in a bad mood. Is that why her father was insufferable, Dana asked, wondering what kind of mood she had been born in. Her grandmother said, "Not just because of that—I got used to that a long time ago." Had her father been a sad boy? As Yonatan sat quietly smoking, pretending that he also enjoyed this game, his mother gave him a wink, which in recent years was starting to seem like a nervous tick, and said, "Yes, your dad was certainly sad." When Dana asked why no one tried to cheer him up, her grandmother said, "We did. We tried the whole time, but he was a lost cause." Out of the corner of her eye, Dana saw her father blowing rings of smoke into the air and smiling to himself.

When Ilana was alive, the questioning would continue later, at home. Dana always wanted to know more, while Ilana, making light of it, going about her business, would say she hadn't known Dad as a boy but she thought that Grandma was trying to say he was special.

"Special like you?" Dana asked, and Ilana said no. "Like me?" Dana asked, and Ilana, who knew how much the girl admired her father, said, Yes, special like you. Those words, which had been so pleasing at the time, now haunted her but could no longer be taken back. Dana understood that she too, like her father, was insufferable and sad, that she was special but not real, and perhaps also a lost cause.

Before the party they had sat in the kitchen and gone through the list Orit Segal had given her. Yonatan thought the pink fluorescent writing looked violent, but he kept quiet and watched his daughter mark a check next to each item. When they got to the photograph she had to bring, one of her as a baby, alone, Dana said she had chosen the one of her in a swimming pool, floating on her stomach with two inflatable wings on her arms, looking up at the camera and smiling, her hair tied up in two wet pigtails. Yonatan had taken that picture when she was three. They had gone to visit Ilana's parents in New Jersey, where Nira and Ilana had been born. Maxine and Gerry had returned to New Jersey after a failed immigration attempt that had lasted eighteen years and left them with a hatred of Israel, leaving behind their two daughters, who were in their twenties at the time, one married and the other single, a student in East Asian studies.

Yonatan said it really was a good picture and asked if she would get it back after the slumber party or the entrance exam or whatever they called it, and regretted his cynicism immediately. Dana said she didn't know, she hadn't asked. To change the subject (because he could see the picture business was starting to trouble her), he asked what she would give the girls for the gift she was obliged to bring for every invitee. That morning he had given her fifteen shekels to go to the toy shop on King George Street after school to buy each girl—all of whom he hated by now—a small present, "but *not* a token," as Orit Segal had instructed.

Dana ran to her room and came back with a plastic bag and emptied its contents onto the table. She arranged the little items in a row, pointed to each of them, and told him how much it had cost and whom it was for. Knowing she would be happy to explain, he asked her why this particular item was for that particular girl, although the gifts looked identical to him in their plastic cheapness, and they seemed very much like tokens to him. Dana described the different girls' personalities, and he listened, amused by her insights as he recognized in them his own cynicism. But he was also worried; the eight girls now appeared to him as a field of land mines that his daughter had no chance of surviving intact, particularly Lilach and Orit, whose gifts were larger than the others', and more expensive.

He wanted to ask her why she needed this dubious package of eight friends, why she couldn't make friends with just one or two girls, but he kept quiet. Dana, as if reading his mind, said, "They won't take me anyway." He asked why not, and she said, "Because I don't fit in." He wanted to know why she was going to the party in that case, but instead asked why she didn't fit in. "It's just not that important to me," she said, adding that she didn't like those girls, except for Tamar.

Yonatan knew Tamar Peretz, whose mother was a single parent. He liked her and Rona, her mother, who was a psychologist; they lived in a big apartment on Hess Street. He wondered if Dana liked Tamar because she only had one parent. Dana said, "Tamar is the smartest, and she hates parties too." Like you? Yonatan said, and she said, "Yes." Although he was proud of his daughter, who, like him, hated groups and made friends with other group-haters, what he really wanted to know was what was going on with the Girl Scouts, because she hadn't gone to meetings for a few weeks. He guessed she was unhappy there, and then pictured what would happen to her at the party. He couldn't do anything to spare her, or even promise that these exhausting attempts to join a group would stop when she got older, when she became like him, because he knew it was a lie; she would never be like him. He knew that however similar she grew, however she mimicked him and his patterns of happiness and sadness—he could see her doing it expertly and could do nothing to prevent this either—she would be someone else, one day a stranger to him.

Dana sighed and put her baubles of bribery back in the bag and said she still had to wrap the presents in the gift wrap she had bought with the change. She took the roll out to show him: shiny blue paper with pictures of golden teddy bears in pajamas and hats. He asked if she wanted him to help, and she said, "Are you kidding? You're terrible at wrapping." He laughed but was a little hurt.

The combination of two left hands and a sense of impatience made Yonatan helpless and sometimes even harmful when it came to minor tasks such as tying shoelaces, folding shirtsleeves, pulling out splinters, or wrapping gifts. Ilana was no good at them either—she was just as clumsy as he was—but she was patient and rarely ruffled. Sometimes, when he was angry at her, he wondered if she really was just calm or whether it was something closer to passivity, the kind you see in large friendly dogs. But even when he felt irritated and compared her to animals, he knew he was jealous. Whether she had true tranquillity or a blessed simplicity, he did not possess it, and after Dana was born, but especially after Ilana died, his need to take pleasure in life had become suddenly urgent, as if joie de vivre were yet another of the new arenas of responsibility that had fallen to him.

When he was single, he used to fantasize about the woman he would eventually choose to live with. He knew it would be a female version of himself, an identical twin, if he could find such a person. He had wanted someone stormy and brilliant and unpredictable, because that was how he saw himself, but then he was surprised to discover how many such replicas there were, or at least, how many women pretended to be like him until he would get scared and hurriedly put an end to his ties before they became real relationships.

When he was thirty, a large publisher agreed to publish his debut novel based on the first fifty pages he had submitted, and out of pride and a sense of victory he shut himself in his rented apartment and wrote. He was a young author at the start of his career and he behaved accordingly: He was demanding and moody and made it clear to the women he dated that his only real commitment in life was to his writing, and in all probability that was how it would always be, although even then he knew these were lines taken from some parody of a young writer's life and not something he was really able or willing to stand behind.

A few years later, still spinning from the success of his first book, he found himself growing apart from his university friends, most of whom had married and had children, and becoming closer to aging bachelors and divorcés in their forties and fifties. Among them were two authors, one of whom had published a failed book while the other claimed he didn't write for publication anyway; a theater actor who had once enjoyed mediocre success; and a historian whose notions were too radical for any university to hire him. His new friends saw themselves as true bohemians and were not particularly bothered by the fact that there was no longer a true bohemia to belong to.

He sat with them in cafés and bars and listened to them complain about the bourgeoisie, which to him, much like bohemia, was a concept that had all but consumed itself. They mocked the married writers who had the best of both worlds—stability and the lack thereof—and claimed you couldn't be a serious artist if you had a house to go home to, kids, debts, home-cooked meals, and regular sex. Yonatan drank beers and smoked weed with them and pretended to be quietly absorbing their words and hoping for a life like theirs. He tried to persuade them that he was scornful of his own success, but his real scorn was directed toward them. He pitied them and they bored him.

Around the time he decided that misery as a permanent state was no longer for him, Ilana quietly entered his life as if she had been standing in the wings all along, listening with amusement to the usual circular conversations that hovered above his head, waiting for the right moment to introduce herself, and then, with the cunning of a seasoned saleswoman, to present to him gradually the contingency plan of a family and kids, debts, home-cooked meals, and regular sex.

She was in her final year of a BA in East Asian Studies—she had been attracted by the color of the Far East, she said, particularly the spices and the cuisine. He had started a PhD in the Hebrew literature department but was dropping out to write his second book, an act that Ilana supported. It was the first indecision he let her in on. They had only been dating for three months, but Ilana knew what he wanted to hear:

He wanted to be released from the university, which he couldn't stand anyway, and he wanted permission—not just from the publisher, who had quickly signed another contract and paid a handsome advance—to sit at home and write. She gladly gave it to him. At first he suspected she was making things easy for him so he'd like her, that she had no opinion of her own, that maybe she was a little too simple for him. Before they met, and while they were going out, he dated other women too, who impressed and exhausted him with their verbal skills. A large part of what he found attractive was the violence of their conversations. It never occurred to him that he could be attracted to someone who was so supportive.

He was convinced that his relationship with Ilana was temporary, a place to rest until he moved on to his next stormy affair. But he very quickly found himself addicted to her support, and then he began falling in love with her. His criticism turned into quiet astonishment: at the way she lived, at her rhythm—he imagined her as the left hand in a piano composition, the musical babysitter of the right hand—and at her kind of strength, made up not of elements so familiar to him, like ambition and anxiety, but rather of optimism. He was surprised to find that she was happy with him, that he wasn't able to make her miserable, but even more surprising was that from the very beginning, when she came up to him in the cafeteria and asked if she could sit down without waiting for an answer, he didn't even try to.

He remembered their first conversation, the way he had scrutinized her every word and every movement, convinced he was about to fail her. They had talked about the cafeteria food and he said it was inedible and expected her to agree with him, but Ilana said she liked the food, especially the schnitzel, which they were out of today so she had to get meatballs. He said he must have taken the last schnitzel, and when he told her she was welcome to eat it because he wasn't hungry, she reached over to his plate with her fork, speared the chicken, transferred it to her plate, drowned it in ketchup, and gobbled it up with a glee that was somehow childish and unself-conscious; it both repelled him and aroused his curiosity. Then she polished off her meatballs as well, and when he chuckled and made some comment about her appetite, she said meatballs were one of the things she couldn't resist. He said he couldn't either, but only if they were made properly, and Ilana invited him for Friday-night dinner at her sister's—"the queen of meatballs," she called her—and he accepted her offer, which was the oddest proposal he had ever received from a strange woman. And so, on a wintry Friday evening, he met Nira and Zvi and their baby boy, and found himself immediately liking Nira and detesting her husband the chemist, who shook his hand and said, "I hear you're an author. You must be a leftist." Later, happily wolfing down meatballs, he sensed himself very calmly being attracted to Ilana, who brought a cake she baked for dessert, which was a failure.

She was his complete opposite, and something in him recognized that and lashed out, but he was wise enough, and lonely enough, not to reject her up front. It took him years to understand that Ilana was not the left hand and he was not the right; they were not even playing the same composition; rather, that they were more like two musicians in a huge conservatory, separately practicing their own—different—instruments in adjacent rooms.

He missed her. He missed her voice, with its hint of an American accent, and the scent of her body, and sometimes he missed her clothes, but more than anything he missed her talent for experiencing life instead of thinking it to death. Like one organ projecting pain onto another, Ilana had spent ten years showering him with daily doses of the complete opposite of pain, the complete opposite of himself. Losing those gifts was, for him, the essence of being a widower.

(4)

He remembered the first time he went to a support group for widowers, the summer after his wife died. He spent the whole afternoon trying to decide what to wear to the meeting, and this surprised him because he had never been bothered by such things before. He did not consider himself a handsome man, although he knew there was something sexy about him. He knew it had something to do with his face, and on good days managed to convince himself that it might be somehow related to his body, but he did not dwell on his appearance—at first naturally, then later almost as policy.

That scorching summer afternoon, he found himself wondering what his clothes said about him; the question made him embarrassed, not only because he had never engaged in these thoughts before but because the audience to whom they were directed was composed of widowed men, which made him think that perhaps he was dressing not for them but for their dead wives. He was so taken by the notion of flirting with the dead that he hurried to his study and made a note to himself to work up the idea somewhere in the novel he had begun writing a year ago. Then he went back to the bedroom and continued to deliberate in front of the closet.

Dana, who was six at the time, sat near him on the bed, humming songs from *The Jungle Book,* which was her favorite movie of the moment. She started folding up the shirts he had taken out of the closet and spread on the bed, as if it were a game. She tried to copy her mother's method of folding the sleeves in half, crossing them over the front of the shirt, then folding it over twice so it always looked like a brand-new article of clothing on a shelf in a store. With great concentration, Dana managed to fold one sleeve, crawl around the shirt, and fold the other one, but when she tried to fold the whole shirt, the sleeves came undone. She repeated her crawl-and-fold act over and over again. Yonatan could hear her frustration, as well as her stubborn optimism, in the rise and fall of her humming. Eventually she gave up on her mother's method and invented her own: she folded the shirt in two, then in four, then quickly rolled it up without giving the sleeves a chance to revolt, until finally the shirt was defeated; it did not look like the shirts on a store shelf, but like an object that had just been through a tussle. Her method touched him. It was like his own.

He looked at the growing pile of shirts on the bed and at Dana, who surrounded the heap with her arms, embracing it, perhaps estimating how long it would take her to fold them all up again. He sat on the edge of the bed, took off his T-shirt, held it up to his face and smelled it, then tossed it on Dana's head. As she giggled and squirmed, he hugged her, nibbled her nose through the fabric, and asked, "Is it stinky?" When she nodded, he put it back on, muttered to himself that he didn't need this business now, the widowers would just have to take him as he was, slightly smelly, and then he went into the living room, lit a cigarette, and waited for Nira.

He didn't have a babysitter yet, back then. Before Ilana was killed they had Ziv, the teenager who lived upstairs. He used to come down to their apartment barefoot, hiding two or three cigarettes in the waistband of his shorts, intending to smoke them secretly while he babysat. But Ziv had started his army service a short while before the accident. As a good-will gesture, and perhaps in an attempt to overcome the embarrassment that struck him whenever he ran into the new widower in the stairwell, Ziv offered to look after Dana sometimes—for free, he emphasized generously—when he came home on leave. But that was during his basic training; he didn't yet know that, due to a suddenly diagnosed heart defect, he would be posted at the local army base and would spend all his evenings at home anyway, with nothing to do. Even so, Yonatan never asked him and Ziv never offered his services again, because they both knew that the babysitting contract had been terminated when Ilana died. Ever since, when they met in the stairwell, they would smile at each other politely. Ziv would ask how Dana was and Yonatan would ask about Ziv, who would always sigh and say, "It'll all turn out fine," like an old man. Then he would hurry about his business, which was undoubtedly the business of being a young man; that first summer without Ilana, when Ziv's parents went on a safari trip to Kenya and Yonatan sat on the balcony smoking at nights after putting Dana to bed—which was, in those days, a long ordeal because of the series of questions she had about death and about her mother's new place in the world—he heard Ziv having sex in his parents' bedroom, whose window faced the backyard. It was short and noisy sex, full of groaning, and here and there a young girl's peals of laughter, and a loud sigh at the end. Then there would be footsteps, the ones Yonatan remembered from the babysitting days, with the explicit sound of feet carrying a hundred and sixty-odd pounds of horniness to the kitchen or bathroom.

Nira came over to look after Dana. Her children, Evyatar and Michal, were already old enough to stay on their own, and anyway his brother-in-law Zvi, the tight-lipped chemist, was always at home, immersed in research in his study—a closed-in balcony off the living room—and sometimes Yonatan thought Nira was so generous with her babysitting not only out of a sense of obligation but also because she wanted to exchange the silence of her own home for that of another.

He wondered whether Nira was happily married, although he couldn't imagine how anyone could be happy with Zvi, who was not only taciturn but was also the only right-winger in the family. Ilana had volunteered no information about her sister's marriage, and Yonatan never inquired. When he went to their house to drop off Dana or pick her up, he exchanged polite greetings with Zvi, who, during the first years of Yonatan's widowhood, would ceremoniously get up from his desk and come over to shake Yonatan's hand or pat him on the back. He also adopted the annoying gesture of condolence of offering Yonatan a glass of local brandy from a dusty bottle he kept in his cabinet of chemistry books, even if it was morning or lunchtime. Yonatan always refused the drink, but found himself politely drawn into small talk. Their conversations sounded more like the exchange of grunts between two animals who feared each other, and they both carefully avoided talking about the accident or about politics, which was particularly difficult for Zvi because he had something to say about both topics. It was unclear whom he hated more: Israeli drivers or the left. Yonatan, who did not recoil from talking about Ilana or view political arguments as a desecration of his grief, enjoyed the diplomacy and restraint his brother-in-law imposed upon himself and never bothered, even a year or two later, to signal to Zvi that it was all right for him to go back to chatting about his favorite subjects. Conversations with Zvi had always bored him, and he saw no reason to deny himself the exemption he had been granted.

Even so, there was one occasion when Zvi was unable to restrain himself. A few months after the accident, when Yonatan came over with Dana for dinner on Friday night, his brother-in-law called him into the closed-off balcony and presented to him, shyly but with an unconcealed degree of pride, a massive diagram of the road on which Ilana had been crushed to death. It was full of numbers and measurements and arrows, and childish little drawings of the two vehicles: the truck and the Subaru, one in the lane heading south and one in the lane heading north, one red and the other green. "It's a little something I made for you," said Zvi, alternately examining his creation and scrutinizing Yonatan's face, and when he detected no signs of curiosity or protest, he considered himself at liberty to proceed. He spread the poster out on the table, placed improvised paperweights on the corners, and said, "If you don't mind, I'll explain it to you simply." He invited Yonatan with a sweep of the arm to sit down, but Yonatan remained standing.

Zvi, who was extremely methodical, had gathered data from the police and the Ministry of Transportation about accidents that had occurred on that road during the past five years. There were thirty-seven of them, nine of which involved fatalities, and one morning, he confessed to Yonatan, he had driven out there and taken his own measurements. Yonatan listened as Zvi held forth about various laws of physics, driving speeds, braking distances, and statistical probabilities, and very soon found himself losing track of his brother-in-law's voice—which, as usual, was at once enthusiastic and monotonous—but he continued hypnotically to follow his index finger, whose gnawed fingernail and inflamed cuticles stole the show for a moment. The finger traced the course of the accident with soft circles and zigzags, and the sleepiness that had descended upon Yonatan was replaced by anger. He had no idea why his brother-in-law insisted on reconstructing the accident, and the combination of his scientific explanation and its horrifying content seemed like a double dose of abuse. But then he saw the injured finger rapping decisively on the roof of the green car, their Subaru, and heard Zvi's voice saying, "No one could have survived it, Yonatan. Believe me. No one," and he suddenly realized that his brother-in-law's intent was to console him. This entire project—the poster, the rulers, the colored pens, and the secret journey up north—had a purpose besides satisfying Zvi's methodical cravings and his constant desire to prove that he was right, and that purpose was to offer Yonatan some real scientific consolation, something that could not be refuted, something far stronger than a shot of brandy in the middle of the day and yet, Yonatan thought as his eyes welled up, just as cheap.

Since that time, he learned to treat Zvi with forgiveness, because he appreciated Zvi's attempt to encourage him, much the way adults appreciate useless gifts that children make for them with their own hands. And, so as not to insult him, he had even accepted his offer to take the diagram home—in case he wanted to look at it again, as Zvi said. But he never had looked at it again, and the thing stayed in the trunk of his new car for almost a year until he needed the spare tire one day and found it, crumpled and dusty, rolled up in the rubber band Zvi had put around it, and threw it in the trash.

He was fond of Nira, though. During his first year without Ilana, she helped him overcome some of the daily difficulties he only identified later, when she saw that he was getting along and withdrew from his day-to-day routine a little. He was grateful to her for having taken control of his life and sometimes found himself missing that period, the days when she treated him as unstable and helpless. He also liked her because she was so similar to his wife. Ilana was five years younger than her sister, but their faces were almost identical: the same light brown eyes, slender eyebrows, and eyelashes that were practically translucent; the same dark-blond wavy hair and the same haircut. They both had fair, freckled complexions, very narrow lips, and little upturned noses that looked utterly goyish—they both joked about them and called them "Waspish noses"—and they both had the same figure.

Sometimes, when he looked at Nira as she walked around his apartment, especially when she was busy cooking and cleaning or hanging laundry, when she had to stand on her tiptoes and stretch out of the bedroom window over the laundry line—when she made those movements, he saw Ilana and remembered what he knew when he met her but forgot when he fell in love with her: that initially he had not liked that body.

When he first saw her in the campus cafeteria holding a tray, leaning against the counter, she had been standing up on tiptoe to see what was in the stainless steel vats, even though she knew just as well as he and all the other students what was in them, but she was an optimist. She stood then in the same pose as she did years later, when she hung laundry, and just as Nira stood when she hung the laundry during that long year after Ilana's death. Back then he had thought that Ilana was a midget. She wasn't terribly short—in fact, she was of average height—but she had the body language of a short person: something apologetic and yet full of energy. And she had a strange backside. It was flat, almost invisible, and when she stood she always tried to make it stick out, planting her hands on her hips and leaning back. When they became a couple she told him how much she hated her rear end, but it made no impression on him because he had never met a woman who didn't. Now, when he thought of it, he regretted never having told her what she must have wanted to hear, what she had tried unsuccessfully to squeeze out of him: that he loved it. It's great, he thought, when he saw her naked; how had they lived together for ten years without his ever telling her that?

He remembered saying to himself in the cafeteria that day, as he sat opposite her at the sticky table and poked his fork into a mound of mashed potatoes, that he would never be attracted to her. He looked at her, and at the other female students standing in line, and made a mental note of his level of attraction to each of them. *Very, Depends on the circumstances, No,* and *Never:* those were his categories, and Ilana oscillated between the latter two. A few weeks later, he slept with her in the backseat of his Citroën DS.

She claimed to have fallen in love with the car long before she fell in love with him. The car made her curious, and after the curiosity, she told him, came the fantasies: she wondered who owned the car. She couldn't explain why, but she was certain it was a man, and every time she walked by the charming Citroën parked outside campus, she tried to guess what its owner looked like. She was sure he was a Humanities student, or at least she hoped he was, and she bet he was either arrogant with too much self-awareness or a poor bohemian type who had no idea what he was driving and didn't much care either. Then she said it occurred to her that he could be a combination of both. It turned out Ilana had asked around long before she saw him in the cafeteria, and someone had pointed to him as the owner of the car, so when he watched her that day he had no idea that Ilana was watching him back and that all her movements were calculated to attract his attention.

The only area in which the sisters were unalike was the way they dressed. Ilana liked loose colorful clothing with distracting prints, chiffon, and Indian fabrics, and when batik came back into fashion she bought blouses and skirts with patterns that always looked like dartboards to Yonatan. Her sister treated clothing as a necessary nuisance, and in that respect she resembled him.

Nira came in and put her handbag down on the couch, complained that the apartment was too hot, told him there was a sale on air conditioners, and said that all in all he looked well, as if she had been keeping a meticulous record of his progress since that December morning. Then she went into the kitchen and put the meatballs she had brought into the freezer. She asked if Dana had eaten and said, before he could answer, "I'll make her an omelet." He said okay and stood by the fridge for a moment. "Go on, go already, you're late," she told him, and before she closed the door behind him, as Dana stood next to her, tightly grasping the collar of one of the shirts she had dragged out of the bedroom, she said he should take his time and not rush. Although he knew she was referring to the meeting, he thought about that sentence in the car and decided to use it if they forced him to talk. "Me," he would say, if the moderator asked how he was coping, "I'm taking my time and not rushing." He knew it would make a good impression because it was the type of thing support groups liked.

But how could he know what support groups would like? And why the cynicism? After all, he was going for Dana, not for himself. When he parked and got out of the car and wondered if the other cars parked outside the building belonged to its residents or to the widowers, he asked himself if that was the truth, because he knew he was not going only for his daughter, and perhaps not for her at all but for himself, only for himself (in the group they'd probably tell him it was all right to be selfish). Six months had passed since Ilana died and he felt lost, and above all he felt childish and angry, as if he were conducting a secret life, like Ziv, but without the hormones or the future.

He was the last to arrive, twenty minutes late. It seemed as if they were sitting there waiting, angry at him for holding them up; they had little kids too and they had managed to get there on time. But he knew it was arrogance to assume that the sadness in the air was because of his tardiness, as if the fact that he was an author—he assumed the moderator had informed the group members—gave him the special status of some kind of senior widower, someone who knew more about life than they did, someone who had something meaningful to say about death.

Ilana had believed in God. She wasn't religious, but her Jewish-American upbringing had given her certain habits that he found annoying: She lit candles on Friday nights, and on Yom Kippur she fasted and went to a Reform synagogue. When she moved in with him, to the massive apartment he rented on Montefiore Street, he would tease her about her "pagan tendencies" and watch with amusement as she lit candles, covering her face with her hands, and sang the blessing. Sometimes he would try to catch her eye through her fingers or distract her by making faces, blowing cigarette smoke at her or hugging her from behind and tickling her; then he would pull her to the bed and have sex with her as if that would somehow shake off the crumbs of traditionalism.

When they talked about getting married, he made it clear that a religious wedding was out of the question. But Ilana and Nira and Gerry and Maxine created a long-distance alliance with his mother—who, more than being supportive of the rabbinate, was simply bored—and they defeated him. During one particular argument with Ilana in their huge square kitchen, Nira, who was pregnant with her daughter at the time, spat at him, "Why are you such a Nazi?"

He put on his insolent look and said, "Nazi? You're calling me a Nazi? You and your sister, who grew up in New Jersey and Ramat Hasharon, do you even know what religious oppression is? I grew up in Jerusalem, so I can tell you exactly what it is. You think I want to live in Tel Aviv? I hate Tel Aviv. I despise this place, but I had no choice."

"What does that have to do with it?" Nira said.

"Yes, Yonatan," Ilana said softly. " I don't understand what that has to do with a Jewish wedding. Why do you have to be so extreme?"

"Why? Because I'm not the one who made things extreme. That's it—the days when you could be moderate and enjoy a little Yiddishkeit are over. Believe me, I'd love to be moderate, but it's no longer possible. The market has no moderate positions to offer."

Nira said it had nothing to do with religion, it was just part of his personality. Ilana said, "Don't exaggerate, Nira," and her American *r* reminded Yonatan of why he loved her and why he hated her. He thought to himself that Nira wasn't exaggerating, that he was born an extremist, that he must have inherited extremist genes from his father, who spent his whole life a fervent secularist, as he liked to call himself, and wouldn't even give Yonatan a bar mitzvah. But he had eventually given in to Yonatan's mother, and when Yonatan was a soldier, serving at a military administrative office in Jerusalem, his father had said to him, "Finish your army service and get the hell out of this city, because we've already lost this war." Yonatan never forgave him when suddenly, at the age of seventy-nine, from his bed in the old-age home where he would shoot looks of contempt at the religious orderly who bathed him and changed his sheets, that from there of all places, three months before he died, he commanded Yonatan to have a rabbinical wedding. "But why?" Yonatan asked him. "Because it won't do any harm," his father said, and that was when Yonatan knew with certainty that these were his father's final days.

During those moments, he was sorry he was an only child and had no brother or sister to support him, or at least accompany him down his father's winding path of betrayal. When Yonatan asked if he was saying it to please his mother, which was what he desperately wanted to hear, his father said, "What difference would that make now?" Yonatan swore to himself that his future child would never be lonely. He glanced at his father, who had a defeated look in his eyes, and although Yonatan knew the look had nothing to do with the war between the secular and the religious anymore, he prayed that the religious orderly would come into the room, with its greasy chicken soup odor wafting in from the kitchen, and his father would straighten up in bed and motion toward the man with his chin, rather than talk to him. But the orderly did not come in, and his father fell asleep with his sharp chin drooping onto his chest; his chin was covered with white stubble, which Yonatan thought looked like cactus.

His father died one morning in September, three months after the wedding. They had borrowed a donated wheelchair from Yad Sarah for him, and he had sat dozing in a corner at the ceremony, covered with a blanket from the old-age home; the guests would walk up to him and gently pull back the woolen blanket to shake his hand. Ilana heard the news of his death over the phone and waited for Yonatan to get back from the supermarket. When he came home, she told him to put the shopping bags down on the floor, took a Time cigarette out of her pack, lit it, and said, "Your father died." Before he could say anything, she put the cigarette out and went to him and hugged him, and he said, "I have to call my mom." She nodded into his neck and he said, "We have to call the Chevra Kadisha for the burial." Ilana tightened her grip on his back, and he said, "I don't even know who we're supposed to call." She stroked his back, and he felt that she was tense and waiting for something. She said, "Let's sit in the living room for a minute," and he said okay.

They sat on the couch and he stared at the blank television screen and then looked into her face, which also seemed tense and expectant, and asked, "Do you think they're listed in the Yellow Pages?" She said nothing, and he mumbled, "We don't have the Jerusalem Yellow Pages," and she said they could call Information. He asked her to bring him a cigarette, and she said okay but remained sitting. Then he remembered. "Actually, we do have the Yellow Pages for Jerusalem. I brought it home from my mom's once. It must be in the study. Do you think they'll be listed under C?" She took his hand in hers, predicting his imminent disintegration, held it up to her lips and kissed his fingers, and he burst into tears. She hugged him and he sobbed in her arms and all the rest could wait.

For the rest of the day he walked around the apartment in a daze, making phone calls and arranging whatever needed to be arranged. Ilana watched him quietly, and every so often he turned to her and hugged her, and at night they sat on the balcony, on the rattan armchairs, holding hands like two strange vacationers. The next day at the funeral, supporting his mother with one arm and crushing Ilana's fingers with the other hand, Yonatan looked at the Chevra Kadisha men lowering his father into the pit, and at once the fears awakened in him by the thought of spending the rest of his life with one woman dissipated, and for a moment he was flooded with tranquillity.

They were stuck in the usual traffic jam on King George Street, listening to classical music on the Voice of Music. Yonatan looked at Dana out of the corner of his eye. She was lost in thought, as always. A drop of snot hung from her nose, and he almost reached out to wipe it away, as he used to do when she was little, but instead he asked if she needed a tissue. She turned around and leaned over to the backseat and pulled a roll of toilet paper from beneath the piles of newspapers and ad sheets. Before she could tear off a piece, the drop fell on the back of the seat, and she wet her finger with saliva and quickly wiped it away. Yonatan smiled and said, "Never mind, the car's filthy anyway."

He remembered his Citroën DS fondly. The huge car, which looked like an elderly frog, had been his first and had belonged to his landlord. He was thirty years old, living in an apartment with three enormous rooms, high ceilings, and ornate floor tiles. The rent was so low he didn't need roommates.

Dana watched him driving and he took his hand off the wheel and touched her forehead, and since they were almost home he asked what kind of juice she wanted. She said she didn't care and he said, "Apple?" because he knew it was her favorite. Dana nodded, and he said after they went upstairs he'd go down to the corner store and also stop by the pharmacy before it closed. She reminded him that the thermometer was broken and he said, "It's a good thing you reminded me, I'll get a thermometer too. Maybe this time we'll finally buy a digital one." Dana asked him to buy the new one she'd seen advertised on TV, which takes your temperature through your ear, and Yonatan said he thought it was for babies. Dana said that in the commercial they said it was good for big babies too and showed the sick baby's dad, who was also sick, making a sorry face. Yonatan said she shouldn't be fooled by commercials. He asked how high her temperature had been when the nurse took it, and she said 101.8 degrees. She figured when he went down to the store and the pharmacy she'd have time to finish thinking about the slumber party. If she had any time left over, she'd think about the other things too.

When he was at home she couldn't concentrate. She was always listening to him, whether he was in his study, in the living room, or on the balcony. Sometimes he would listen to a CD from his massive collection, mostly classical music. He liked old Israeli folk music too, and he would play *The High Windows* continuously for a whole afternoon; it had been her mother's favorite album, and someone once told her she looked a little like their lead singer. Dana liked the music he liked, and when she would ask him what to put on, unless he felt like something in particular, he would say, "Whatever you want." This flattered her but also put her under pressure, so she always chose something she knew he liked but hadn't heard for a few days. When she knelt by the stereo and slowly turned up the volume, she would hear him shout out from his study or from the kitchen where he was making dinner, "I haven't heard that in ages!" or "How did you know?" and she was glad she had made a good choice. She liked his music but hated his cooking. If she could make a reasonable guess at his mood based on the music he was playing, his choice of dishes left no room for doubt: roast chicken and meatballs meant a good mood, schnitzel and pasta were neutral, and frozen hamburgers or hot dogs had the distinct flavor of sadness.

They both loved meat, and every few weeks they went out to a restaurant together to enjoy filet mignon with cream and mushroom sauce, or else they would stay home and grill steaks in a heavy iron skillet. She preferred the homemade steaks. She never saw her dad happier than when he was chatting with the butcher and choosing the cuts of meat and, later, melting butter in the skillet and throwing in the beef, and especially when he was pouring a little brandy in the skillet and lighting it up over the meat. At the butcher shop and in the kitchen, her dad had the movements of a dancer, and it seemed as if even the Voice of Music, which accompanied them from the living room, cooperated by playing cheerful compositions.

They had special wooden plates for the steaks, and serrated knives, and during those meals she would also have a few sips of very dry red wine. She was in charge of the roast potatoes and green salad; she tore the lettuce leaves with her hands instead of cutting them, because that's how Tamar's mother did it and she was an excellent cook. She was also responsible for lighting candles to add to the atmosphere—although they never turned off the fluorescent light in the kitchen—and she felt like part of a team that had been working together seamlessly for years. Since they both liked their steaks done medium, they didn't have the timing problems of people who liked their steaks done differently— especially parents and kids.

Eating steaks done medium, which came naturally to Yonatan and which Dana learned to like over time, was also part of their secret understanding. Sometimes this understanding was grating, and then Dana wasn't sure who was more pained: she saw how hard her dad tried, and knew that he saw her trying not to show that she knew, because she sensed the awareness would ruin things for the two of them and even more so for her mother. She wasn't sure about this last point anymore, but she thought that if her mother still had desires, she would want them both to be happy, although Dana no longer believed what she had just two or three years ago: that her mother saw everything from above.

The notion was fine for a six- or seven-year-old, but at ten it seemed ridiculous. It used to comfort her to hear Nira and Grandma Maxine promising that her mother was somewhere on top of a beautiful mountain, sitting by a huge window through which she could watch Dana's and her father's lives. When Dana asked what else you could see through the window, whether you could see sheep, they said no, absolutely not. After the accident she had wanted to know the last thing her mother had seen before dying, the road she was driving on or an image of her dad and herself, because as far as she was concerned, it was the road that had killed her mother, not the other driver. Nira had said, "What kind of a question is that? Of course she saw you and Dad," and Grandma Maxine confirmed this a few times in transatlantic calls. Lately, the image of her mother sitting on the mountaintop had faded, superseded by the knowledge that there was nothing up there, that her mother did not exist and neither did God.

It was hard to give Him up. Other kids her age were afraid to commit to any one position, and if an argument broke out they never dared proclaim, "There is no God," because if they were wrong they'd be in big trouble. When she was eight, a few boys wearing yarmulkes came up to her Girl Scout group and asked the girls why they wore pants. Tamar, who was in the same group, whispered to her, "I hate that kind the most, even more than the Black Hats." Dana said she did too, but she still felt a shiver when one of the boys shouted that because they were immodest and didn't observe the Sabbath and ate pork and because their parents were Jew-hating lefties, they would all go to hell when they died.

Tamar called out, "Who cares where you go when you're dead?"

The boys yelled back, "Let's see you talking when you're burning in the fires of hell!" Tamar shouted that she'd rather burn in hell than be in the same place as them. Dana was glad that Tamar talked back to them—the fact was, they had nothing to say in reply so they left—and Rona laughed afterward when they told her what happened and said they had nothing to worry about because everyone they knew would be in hell so it would actually be pretty nice. Dana asked if her dad would be there too, and Rona—who was in the middle of baking a pear tart and had asked Dana to wait till it was ready so she could take a few slices home—said, "Your dad will be CEO of the place." When Dana reported that later to her father—who gobbled down his slice of tart as well as hers because she said she had no appetite—he obviously liked it, and he also said that life here was hell so no one would notice the difference anyway. But despite that, the thought of hell still scared her for several months and she was afraid of ending up there. Since her mother had lit candles on Friday nights and gone to synagogue on Yom Kippur and had been such a positive and happy person, Dana was certain her mother would not be there, and she very much did not want to be in hell alone with her dad.

When she asked Yonatan if he believed in God, he said very determinedly that he didn't, but then he softened and asked why she was asking. She said, "No reason" and asked if he had believed when he was her age. He said he couldn't remember but he was almost positive he hadn't. Then she asked Nira, who said she believed there was a supreme power in the world who saw and heard and knew everything, and that we were not alone. Zvi called out from the balcony, "Oh, come on!" and Nira laughed and said, "See?"

At night, before she fell asleep, Dana would say a secular prayer. She asked the supreme power that Nira believed in—whom she had adopted for herself because it seemed like a good compromise between heresy and faith—to protect her from hell and not send her there, and not to send her dad and the people she loved there either, and also not to send them to heaven, which is where the religious kids would go, but to find them another place, somewhere in the middle, something between heaven and hell, somewhere like where they lived now. She prayed every night, and sometimes found herself praying at daytime too, at school or in the car or in the middle of her piano lessons. And she prayed every time she saw something that reminded her of hell, like cripples or beggars or something particularly sad on TV, and every time she visited Grandma Rachel, who was the closest person to death that she knew and who claimed she already had a place in hell; Grandpa had reserved it for her.

(7)

When they got out of the car, he could see that she was shivering. He took her backpack, took off his jacket, and draped it over her shoulders. He suddenly got a whiff of the sour damp smell of the cottage-cheese sandwich she had made herself that morning, and reminded himself to take it out of the backpack when they got home and throw it away, as well as the fruit she hadn't touched.

"What did you take this morning, an orange?" he asked.

"Persimmon," she said.

"Did you eat it?"

"No," she said. "I didn't have time. And I didn't eat my sandwich either."

"Did you feel sick when you were at Lilach's yesterday?" he asked, as he put the key in the door.

"A little. I think I started getting a fever there."

"But on the whole you had a good time?"

"Yes," she said. He knew she was lying.

The smell of cigarettes lingered in the apartment. He had promised himself he wouldn't smoke when she was at home; he had also promised himself he would give it up, but when she was at school in the mornings he chain-smoked. He apologized and said he didn't expect her home so early and he hadn't had time to air the place out, and Dana said it didn't bother her and her nose was stuffed up anyway so she couldn't smell anything. Then she lay down on the couch and turned on the TV. Unlike other children, his friends' kids, who got on their parents' case when they smoked, Dana was never bothered by it, and he oscillated between worrying that she was different—or pretending to be different—and the sense of relief it awarded him.

Ilana had smoked two cigarettes a day. If they went to a party or to dinner with friends, she had three or four and then said she felt ill and didn't smoke for a few days; he couldn't understand how you could feel ill after three cigarettes. She smoked Time, and he made fun of her and said they tasted too sweet. But every time he got stuck without any of his Winstons, he smoked hers. Her pack of cigarettes was always on the spice shelf in the kitchen. Twice a day Ilana would walk up to it almost incidentally and pull one cigarette out—once in the afternoon, when she got home from the university, where she had a part-time secretarial job in the English department, and once at night, when they watched the news together.

Months after the accident, the pack still lay on the spice shelf. He couldn't bring himself to smoke her cigarettes, just as he wasn't able to eat the leftover curried chicken and tomato soup she'd made, which sat in the fridge for several weeks until Nira threw it out. He felt that finishing the leftovers and smoking the twelve remaining cigarettes would practically make him a cannibal. He was relieved to discover, one day, that her herbal shampoo and conditioner, and her moisturizer and leg wax and boxes of tampons and pads, and the unopened purple eye shadow she had received as a gift and the one lipstick she occasionally used had all disappeared. He assumed Nira had taken them but he never asked whether she threw them out or took them for herself, because he felt that his wife's things, which were so mundane in the bathroom that he never noticed them, had become intimate and embarrassing now that she was no longer alive.

Dana wouldn't let him throw out Ilana's pack of Time. Every day she would climb up on a chair, take the pack down off the shelf, open it as if it were a picture album, and count the cigarettes. When he watched her, it occurred to Yonatan that her strange tolerance of smokers was not directed at him and his heavy smoking but rather at her mother and her two daily cigarettes. He felt as if his daughter, although she said nothing, missed not only her mother but also a certain kind of moderation, and it made him want to give up smoking again.

One night, almost a year after the accident, he had been sitting in his study trying to write, chain-smoking until he absentmindedly finished off his stock of cigarettes. He searched through his coat pockets for the extra pack he was sure he'd bought that morning but couldn't find it. Then he rummaged through the kitchen drawers, where he sometimes kept a spare pack, and his eyes lit upon the Time on the spice shelf, which he hadn't touched since the accident. He told himself this was his chance to exercise a little self-control: it was two in the morning, his daughter was sleeping in the next room, it would be mad to go out and buy cigarettes now, he should go to sleep too. He didn't have to smoke.

He went back to sit at the computer, and for a moment was happy that his lack of concentration was not his usual vacant state of mind but a simple and legitimate craving for a cigarette. He looked back and forth from the screen to the full ashtray beside him, got up and went into the living room and lifted the couch cushions to see if there might be a cigarette that had been buried there at some point. He went to the kitchen and poured himself some apple juice, hoping the vitamin-heavy drink would take his mind off the toxins he longed for, but his gaze locked on the Time, and although Dana had given up her habit of counting the cigarettes, he would never dare smoke a single one of them without her permission. Since he knew he wouldn't be able to get to sleep, he went on sitting in the kitchen, drinking juice until he emptied the bottle, and tried to decide what would be less despicable: gently shaking his seven-year-old daughter awake to get her permission to smoke one of her most precious memories of her mother, or taking a cigarette without making a big deal out of it and, if his daughter accused him some day, telling her it was an emergency.

He took a cigarette out of the pack and lit it and took a long ceremonious drag, as Ilana used to do. He tossed the burning match into the sink and slunk back into his study, where he went on staring at the computer and smoking. The cigarette tasted damp and sickly sweet. He turned off the computer and then put the cigarette out, and his heart sank when he emptied the ashtray into the trash and saw the one white-tipped butt lying among all the brown-tipped ones.

He smoked the remaining eleven cigarettes over time, whenever he got stuck without his own, always surprised by their moldy flavor but also delighting in it like a glutton for punishment. He left the empty pack in its place until it suddenly disappeared; one evening when they sat down for dinner Dana saw him looking at the shelf and said, "I threw it away."

(8)

When he went out to the store and the pharmacy, she turned off the TV and snuggled up under the wool blanket they kept on the couch, which had soaked up the smell of a hundred childhood bouts of flu. Even after the slumber party, she wasn't sure of her chances of getting on the team; she hadn't yet had time to analyze the weekend with Tamar. But now, with her shivers and her throat that was so swollen she couldn't even swallow, she didn't care and was glad they'd given her back the picture of her in the pool.

She thought about the cake she'd asked her dad to buy. She told him it had to be a good bakery, and even gave him the name of one, but the cake he'd brought home on Friday afternoon before he drove her to Lilach, whose parents were architects and lived in Jaffa, wasn't what she had asked for. She wanted a cake called Mozart, which one of the mothers had once brought to a birthday party. She had overheard Lilach and Orit admiring the cake, and the woman who brought it had declared,

"It's a Mozart," and told them how much it cost and where you could buy it. Dana fell in love with the cake, even though she didn't get a taste because they polished it off so quickly—she fell in love with it only because she knew who Mozart was, and she liked his music because her dad did. But her dad bought a different cake that looked like it had been made for a wedding: tall and colorful with little mounds of pink and white icing. It was an embarrassment, but he couldn't see why and said the bakery she sent him to had already been closed, so he had gone to another one, but they didn't have Mozart cakes and hadn't even heard of them, so he asked for the fanciest one they had.

She didn't make a big deal out of it because she knew he was trying to make her happy, then felt not only disappointed but also guilty as she sat in the car with the cardboard box on her lap, holding it so the cake wouldn't slide around and get squashed. But she wanted it to get squashed, she wanted them to have an accident, nothing fatal, just enough to flatten the cake and land them in the ER for their cuts and scrapes to be bandaged.

Instead, she said goodbye to her father next to the beautiful Arab-style house in one of Old Jaffa's alleys, holding the cake box with both hands. She had her backpack with her pajamas, the gifts, and the photo of her in the pool. Suddenly her eyes welled up with tears. She felt sorry for her dad, who was leaning over the wheel and watching through the windshield to make sure someone buzzed her in through the gate; he seemed forlorn. And she felt sorry for herself and for the cake, because she knew her mother would have preferred it to the Mozart because she always liked colorful, cheerful things and she didn't care what people thought of her. But Dana did care, and so now she felt guilty toward her mother, and toward the embarrassing cake, which she had spent the whole afternoon trying to like, opening the fridge and peeking into the box over and over again, but hadn't managed to.

Yonatan drove away and up the promenade and looked out at the water to his left. He didn't like the sea, but he tried to for Dana, who some-times asked to go there by herself and he wouldn't let her. He remembered that he hadn't asked which possession she had decided to sacrifice for her big evening—they were supposed to bring a prized item from a collection—in fact he didn't know whether she even collected anything. She didn't seem the type. It seemed dollish and unlike her, and as his mother always said in her nervous way, Dana was very much like him, and other than papers and lists and old bills he kept out of fear, he didn't collect anything. Ilana, on the other hand, had left a cruel inheritance of little items that had occupied him and Nira for many months until they were able to sort them out, rearrange them, pack up some of them to send to her parents in New Jersey, and throw the rest away. The question bothered him the whole way home and even later, when he sat down and turned on the computer: Did Dana collect anything? He was almost tempted to go into her room and search her closet and underneath her bed, or in the blue wooden chest where she kept all her discarded dolls and toys. He wasn't sure what he'd rather discover—little treasures of napkins, scented erasers, postcards with exotic animals and movie stars that would be evidence of a normal childhood, or nothing, which would bring her closer to himself.

He stared at the screen, ran his fingers over the keyboard. If in the past he had wanted Dana to be like him, to like the things he liked and share his dislikes, today he wanted the opposite, but he didn't know if he had the talent and the strength, or at least the lack of selfishness, to give her what he himself did not know—what he hated. The question of her collection distressed him again and he went into the kitchen, put the kettle on for some coffee, even though he didn't want any, and when the water boiled he poured it over the dishes sitting in the sink, drizzled some soap on the scouring pad, and started distractedly scrubbing a plate. He put it back in the pile, dried his hands, and went into her bedroom.

He turned the light on and scanned the room as if he hadn't seen it a thousand times before, went in and closed the window because the forecast had said it would rain tonight, and looked at the bed. It was covered with a piece of Indian fabric with an elephant print that Ilana had once sewn herself a skirt from. His eyes came to rest on the blue wooden chest. Its lid had a picture Ilana had drawn with gold paint, of a smiling girl with two pigtails, and under the picture it said DANA'S SECRETS. On the sides, next to peeling stickers of *Jungle Book* characters, there were now stickers commemorating Yitzhak Rabin—SHALOM,

FRIEND and FRIEND, WE MISS YOU—and an SPCA sticker that said LET THE ANIMALS LIVE.

He remembered the day Ilana painted the chest, and the rash she got from the gold paint, which they only later found out was toxic, and the young resident at the ER who gave her a cortisone shot and asked if the gold staining her fingers was stardust. He remembered Dana, who was three then, bursting into tears when the resident jabbed the needle into Ilana's arm. He took her out to the vending machine, and when he asked what she wanted she told him, hiccuping, her eyelashes soaked with tears, "Stardust." He said, "Let's see if they have any," and pretended to look in the machine. "We're in luck," he declared. She eyed him and the machine suspiciously, then he put the money in and lifted her up so she could press the button herself. She kept asking if what they were getting was really stardust, and he told her she'd see soon. They pressed the button together, he pressing down on her fingers, and a pink coconut candy covered with white flakes came down the chute, and she asked him to get one for Mom too.

Not long ago, at the supermarket, he saw they were selling the same candy in big family-size bags, so he bought some. When Dana asked him why he'd gotten all that disgusting coconut, he said it was stardust, and she said, "Very funny."

He wanted to open the chest, but went to the open closet instead. Drooping down from one of the shelves were the sleeves and legs of various jumpsuits, her winter pajamas. For the party, she had chosen the cool gray one with the hood, which Ilana's parents had sent her from the States; they had also sent one in his size. He closed the closet door, then turned off the light and went back to the kitchen, and started washing the plate again. Then he thought he'd wash the dishes later because he needed to write now, precisely when he was so restless, and he put down the plate once more, dried his hands, went to sit at the computer, and thought perhaps he had been wrong not to shelve the novel he had started writing before the accident.

It was supposed to be a great love story. *Love in the Time of Cholera* was his model, and he envied García Márquez for the restraint and maturity and patience that permeated every line of his novel, almost as a separate plotline. Sometimes he had wondered if you really had to be old and experienced and successful, like Márquez, to write like that, or whether it was enough to be forty, with a wife and a little girl and thoughts of another pregnancy. The fifty pages he had written over the past five years were hidden in his hard drive and now seemed toxic and hateful in their disingenuity, and when he turned on the computer and opened the single file called "new novel," he called it up as you summon an obdurate dog whom you never liked but do not have the courage to get rid of. He knew he did not have the restraint or the maturity or the patience—nor the fame or even the talent, and that scared him—to write a true love story. Not a tale of wild lust, like his first novel, which he had named, with manipulative simplicity, *Passion,* and of which he was ashamed precisely because it was so successful. And not an allegory about relationships with near-proverbial quips, like the second novel, *Silence,* which was less successful. Not those, but the great work he had always wanted to write.

He got up and went to the bathroom and urinated in short spurts, a staccato that reminded him of his writing, and thought maybe he should go into therapy after all. He occasionally thought about therapy after he had abandoned the support group and had almost called Tamar's mother for a referral—she knew him and would be able to match him up with a therapist at his level, a man, because with a woman he was liable to fall in love—but he didn't. Although he liked Rona, he didn't want to get too close, and as he zipped up his pants, it suddenly occurred to him that maybe Dana liked Tamar so much because she hoped they would become sisters one day.

Last week, when Dana was washing the dishes after dinner, she had said matter-of-factly, without looking at him (it scared him to see how quickly she was learning the game), that Rona was having a dinner party for some friends next Friday, and had invited her, and could she go. He said yes, as long as they walked her home, because although Rona lived on the next street over, he was afraid of Allenby Street, which connected the two. Then Dana added, "Oh, and she said you're invited too." He immediately said he couldn't go, but to tell her thanks. Dana said, "See how you feel. You may change your mind," and he realized that perhaps her pain and longing for Ilana were making way for a search for another mother, and more than being insulted on Ilana's behalf he was insulted himself. He wanted to tell Dana he would be a good dad. But how could he make that promise, knowing full well that between himself and his daughter, between her room and his, between the kitchen and the balcony and the car and the school and his study, there was something like suffocation, the kind that only the presence of another person could relieve?

He sat down on the old rattan armchair on the balcony and sipped the coffee he didn't even want and swore to himself, as he did almost every night, that starting tomorrow he would reduce his coffee intake, because it made him feel bad. He could tell that his nerves were on end and his fingers trembled a little as they held the cigarette, and although he knew the coffee was not the culprit, it reassured him to think that he had control over his life, real control and not just the pretense of it for Dana, who was improving her own pretending techniques with worrying skill.

She had always been a quiet child, but her new quietness had a frightening presence because it was a silent echo of his own. Before Ilana died the house was noisy, full of kids from Dana's kindergarten and their parents who came to drop them off and pick them up and stayed to chat with Ilana, and Nira, who spent many hours there with Evyatar and Michal, who were now too grown-up for Dana. The noise had disturbed his work, because in those days he was working rather than pretending, but he never complained; on the contrary, he was grateful for it, saw it as vocal evidence of some kind of blessed normalcy, proof that he had a family and the family was noisy because that's how families are. The truth was that the noise not only did not disturb him but was sometimes his inspiration; the breaks in his writing rhythm weren't so scary as long as he could hear the family metronome ticking outside his room.

Now he listened to the sounds of a television coming from the neighbors' windows and to a distant ambulance or police siren, and when he looked into the empty mug on the floor, he reminded himself again about cutting down on the caffeine—and the nicotine, while we're at it, he thought. Perhaps he would call Rona after all, to apologize for not being able to come to dinner on Friday. They would probably talk about Dana a little—Rona, like other parents, was always impressed by the girl's maturity and he knew it embodied implicit criticism of him: a child who is too mature does not speak well of the parents. He would say he wanted to ask her something but maybe not over the phone, although perhaps he shouldn't make a big deal out of it: He was thinking of going into therapy and hoped she could recommend someone. It would need to be a man, he'd probably be more comfortable with that, a woman is a bit of a problem; but whatever she thinks, he's not sure.

The decision never to let a new woman into their lives suddenly seemed about as valid as the decision he'd made five years ago to write his life's work; it was based more on how it sounded than on any true desire. He knew at the time he was not ready for someone else—he was incapable of it—and Ilana's death was only an excuse. Who was he to make these decisions for his daughter? Who was he to make these decisions for himself? Yes, tomorrow he would start off the day with a cup of herbal tea; they had some herbal tea in the house. Although perhaps he shouldn't make drastic changes that he wouldn't be able to stick to later, and one cup of coffee in the morning wouldn't do any harm. He'd phone Rona to help him find someone to cancel out for him all the big decisions he'd ever made. The idea of phoning Rona filled him with optimism, and he went into the living room and closed the balcony door, because although it wasn't raining it was getting cold. He put the mug on the plate in the sink, emptied the ashtray into the trash can, took a new pack of cigarettes from the box on top of the fridge, and went back to the study and sat determinedly at the computer. His fingers hovered over the keyboard. It doesn't have to be a great love story, just a story, he told himself. Let's see you do it—no great expectations. And suddenly his new plan filled him with fear that was worse than the restlessness that had preceded it. He suddenly felt like getting into the car and driving to Jaffa, flying past the sea, which he didn't really like and never would no matter how hard he tried. He would park outside the Kahanes' mansion, ring the intercom, apologize for the time, and go in and find Dana—who would probably come out with her new friends, wearing pajamas and wrapped in secretiveness—and whisper to his daughter that something had happened and they had to go home, not something serious, no need to worry. Dana wouldn't ask any questions but would pack her things and put her coat on over her pajamas, and he would throw a fake smile to Lilach's mother, who would say goodbye to Dana with apologetic sweet words, and the girls would huddle around and say in a chorus that they were so sorry, except for Tamar, who really would be sorry. And in the car he wouldn't tell her what had happened, because there would be nothing he could say, and when they got home she would go into her room and take off her gray pajamas, which she hated sleeping in (he did too, because they were warm and bunched up and the hood got in the way), and maybe before she went to bed she'd pluck up the courage to ask him what happened, and he'd know it was best to tell her the truth, that nothing had happened in fact, that he was living his life in appearance only, for her, and that he had missed her. But she wouldn't ask, she'd come in the kitchen wearing her old blue sweats, which she liked but which didn't quite fit her anymore, and would fill a glass of water from the tap, and he would beg her with his eyes to ask, to scream, *What have you done to me?* But she would stand facing him in her too-short sweats and socks, and quietly drink her water in little sips, and her eyes would watch him over the rim of the glass, and then she'd go over and give him a good-night kiss on his cheek, and he would feel that her face was a little too warm, that she was getting sick again, and then he'd collapse, fall apart, not caring that she was just a little girl. Or maybe he would keep pretending nothing had happened, that it was not her or her mother he missed, but rather the life he thought he could have had, and before she put the glass in the pile in the sink and went to her room, he would ask her, in passing, whether there was anything she collected.

(9)

When he went to pick up Dana the following afternoon, Rika Kahane invited him to come in and have some cake on the patio with everyone. He tried to get out of it by saying he was parked illegally, but Rika put her hand on his shoulder and said it was all right on Shabbat, so he followed her into the paved inner courtyard. There was a marble birdbath at its center. He had never seen a birdbath in Israel before and it looked pretentious and incongruous, both for Israeli birds and for

Israelis. Before he had time to make a mental note of yet another strike against Rika (he didn't really know why he couldn't stand her—perhaps because she was the mother of the girl who led the group that had abducted his daughter for the weekend), a sparrow landed on the rim of the birdbath, tipped its head from side to side, hopped cheerfully into the water, splashed around for a moment, then jumped back to the rim and shook off its feathers.

They entered the vast living room, which had three levels of ceramic tiled floors; at first glance Yonatan thought it looked like a furnished swimming pool. On the highest level, the smallest, there was a black grand piano with a matching bench. The middle level was a kind of sitting area with two antique couches facing each other and a low round table between them, with a copper Turkish coffee set on a tray. The lowest level must have been the living room itself, furnished with a huge couch upholstered in off-white canvas, two matching armchairs, and a low coffee table with curved metal legs supporting a thick slab of rough stone. Yonatan had seen this stylish table in other houses. It reminded him of Ilana's gravestone.

According to the carver who had helped him and Nira pick the stone out, it was considered a modest choice. Nira chose it after methodically paging through the catalog of gravestones with that special, almost delirious look on her face that Ilana used to get when she leafed through foreign fashion magazines. He told Nira that whatever she chose would be fine; he trusted her taste and knew nothing about gravestones. She looked up from the catalog for a moment to give him a look that said, But who does? Then she kept on turning the pages. He asked her to call him back when she found one and said he was going outside to smoke. He stood outside for a long time, chain-smoking, until Nira came out to him, wiping her eyes with a tissue, and said, "This is the simplest one but it's expensive." He touched her arm and went into the office and sat across from the stonecarver, who offered him some cold water. When Yonatan didn't reply, the man got up, went over to the water cooler, and put a plastic cup down on the table, next to the open catalog. Yonatan sipped his water while he wrote out a check.

Ilana's parents paid for the gravestone, and after an exhausting telephone argument they agreed to give up Our Beloved Daughter, which they had wanted to inscribe on the stone. Yonatan explained to them—and although he was used to talking with them in English, this conversation sounded extremely foreign—that Our Beloved Daughter would also necessitate My Beloved Mother and My Beloved Wife, and that seemed sentimental and too crowded. When Maxine sobbed and said, "Don't talk to me about sentimentality," and took the opportunity to accuse him of always being a cynic, he explained to her quietly that Ilana wouldn't have liked it, which worked its wonders on her parents and helped everyone compromise on OUR BELOVED.

The financial assistance had started even before the wedding, when Gerry and Maxine went all over Tel Aviv with them, looking for a home. They finally bought them a two-bedroom apartment on Bialik Street, which looked a little like the one on Montefiore, in spirit if not in square footage. Instead of floral tiles with different colors in each room, it had cracked tiles in a faded shade of orange. Ilana fell in love with the apartment immediately and told Yonatan it wasn't all that different from where they lived—after all, both buildings were old and decrepit. Yonatan explained that the building on Montefiore was built in the early twenties and the building on Bialik was from the thirties. She saw no difference, but he claimed there was one: the ceiling at Bialik was almost four inches lower than the one at Montefiore. When Ilana hugged him and asked, "What exactly are you planning to do with the ceilings?" he was a little annoyed by her lack of interest in architecture, and that she didn't seem to miss the floral floor tiles at all.

After they got married, Gerry sent them a check in dollars every three months, which Yonatan converted to shekels at the money changers. The checks came with a little note that said at the end, *And this is for you, children.* When Dana was born, the sums doubled and the notes read *And this is for Dana.* After Ilana was killed, the sums were doubled again, now reaching three thousand dollars a month. The notes, which became shorter and shorter, were signed *And this is for you,* as if his industrialist father-in-law had decided that Yonatan deserved greater support, not only because he was the beloved husband of his late daughter and the father of his granddaughter but because he believed in him as an author, which was ridiculous, of course, because Gerry Fisher, despite having spent eighteen miserable years in Israel, did not read a word of

Hebrew. But Yonatan liked to amuse himself with the idea that he had a patron; it turned his idleness, his paralysis, into an almost legitimate way of life—a full-time job.

He stared at the ugly table and Rika asked if he liked it, and he smiled an inscrutable smile. She said it was commissioned from a stone-mason in Ramallah and had cost them a fortune. He said, "I would imagine so," and Rika said they were a little sorry they had bought it because it had turned out to be a problem—it was impossible to move. Yonatan asked when they would want to move it, and she said, "When the house gets cleaned. And anything you spill on it stains."

Three large arched windows faced the patio; he could see the girls out there sitting on garden chairs at a round wooden table. Tamar spotted him through the window and waved. He couldn't see Dana and was briefly worried. He complimented Rika on how beautiful the room was and she said, "Really? You like it?" in a way that suggested she was filing away the compliment with all the others she had received, most of which were as fake as her tone. Yonatan, who was starting to enjoy their game of housewifely Ping-Pong, said, "And it's so clean in here!" It sounded like a stupid thing to say, but at least it was true. Rika smiled, and he wondered how nine little girls could have spent twenty-four hours here without leaving a trace.

They went out to the patio and Lilach said, "Hi, Yonatan," as if there was no thirty-five-year difference between them, and the other girls smiled at him like old friends. Lilach twisted around toward a little patch of lawn and yelled, "Dana, your dad's here!" and only then did he notice a swing set near the stone wall, where Dana was sitting with a little dog on her lap. The dog leaped out of her arms, rolled around on the lawn, got up and sneezed, and then rushed toward Yonatan, barking. Yonatan waved to Dana somewhat shyly. She got off the swing and gave him a strange little smile. Then she leaned down to the dog and reassured him: "Quiet, Rudy." She picked him up, but the dog leaped to the ground and started sniffing Yonatan's shoes suspiciously, grunting and sneezing.

"I'm making coffee," Rika said. "Sit down with the girls in the meantime." Before he could sit on the vacant garden chair, Rika turned back and suggested that Dana take him on a tour, if he wanted, because she knew the house. Yonatan looked at his daughter and asked, "Do you want to?" She smiled her new grin again and said, okay, and called to the dog, but Rudy, after having done his duty by making a symbolic attempt to banish the intruder, jumped back on the swing with the agility of a circus animal.

"This is the living room," Dana said, and gestured at the trilevel space like a museum docent with a broad sweep of the arm. Yonatan nodded and said it was lovely. She walked unenthusiastically to the staircase that led to the second floor and started going upstairs, her hand on the banister, and he followed her. The steps led to another sitting area, which also had an arched window that faced the backyard, and it also had two couches and a table. Instead of a Turkish coffee set, there was a series of architecture magazines in English and German. Dana said, "This is the sitting area, and here, on the right, is the parents' wing." Now she sounded like a real estate agent, and he wondered who had taught her this text.

"Is this Rika and—I forget Lilach's dad's name—is it their bedroom?"

"Amos," she said, standing in the bedroom doorway.

Rika and Amos Kahane's bedroom did not fit Yonatan's theories about bad yuppy taste, theories he was always happy to bolster with new evidence, which had been supplied in abundance during this short tour. The "parents' wing" was charming and exactly to his taste, especially the complete disarray. It seemed as if people other than Rika and Amos lived in this room, people whose common disorganization reminded him of his and Ilana's own mess when they still lived on Montefiore and had a huge bedroom like this one. He was standing in the doorway with Dana and peeking inside when they suddenly heard high heels clicking up the stairs, and Rika was saying, "Oh, my goodness! You weren't supposed to come here. I forgot to tell you; there's a terrible mess." She pulled them away and closed the door, and the remainder of the tour was conducted under her strict supervision.

"Did you sleep well?" he asked Dana, when they left Lilach's room, where sleeping bags lay scattered around the white carpet. He had asked Dana where she had slept, and she pointed to a sleeping bag that had her backpack on it; it was surrounded with shreds of the teddy-bear gift wrap. Before she could answer, Rika said, "They all slept great! They were partying all night and only got to sleep at three!" Yonatan gently squeezed Dana's hand, to tell her that he had missed her, and felt her fist burning.

Yonatan saw that Rika had laid some refreshments out on the patio table, but the girls didn't seem particularly interested, perhaps because they had already sampled them the day before and that morning. He sat down next to Tamar and asked how her mother was, and Tamar said she was fine. "Give her my regards," he said, and then Tamar went to sit with Dana, who had gone back to the swing. There was a French-press coffee-pot and a pitcher of milk on the table, and a pile of blue glass dessert plates. Savory pastries were arranged on a large platter; Rika pointed to each of them and explained what they were and where they were pur-chased. She especially recommended that Yonatan try the olive rolls and the mozzarella shells and said she'd be right back with the sweets.

The girls stopped their conversation and watched him, curious to see what he would put on his plate. He smiled and said, "What do you recom-mend?" Lilach said the olive rolls were really good, and he looked at the girl sitting next to her and asked, "And what about you?" The girl said she hated olives but the mozzarella ones weren't bad, and Yonatan asked her name. "I'm Orit," she said. "Oh, you're Orit?" he said, and immediately regretted it because he had given away the fact that he had heard about her before. He took an olive roll and reassured himself that perhaps these laws of discretion did not apply to children. Orit straightened up in her chair and smoothed her hair back with her hand and said, "You know me from school, right?" He chewed and nodded, and Orit said, "And one time you gave me a ride home." "Yeah, I remember," he said, even though he didn't. "What are you talking about?" Lilach said. "You're getting mixed up; it wasn't Dana's dad at all." Orit said, "Yes it was, it was in the third grade, don't you remember? You were with us too." Lilach said, "Me? Are you nuts?" Yonatan, who had given rides to countless children over the last four years, took a mozzarella shell and asked, "Where do you live?" Orit gave the name of a street and Yonatan said, "Yes, of course I remember," but the two girls kept arguing eagerly, while the others around the table supported Lilach's version, and then the conversation moved on to the topic of cars and jeeps and which was better.

Rika came out holding a platter with two half cakes and one whole. It was the one Yonatan had bought, and for a minute he was glad to see it was still whole and impressive, but then he realized that meant no one had touched it; he turned back to his daughter, but Dana was busy talking with Tamar. "This is the Pavlova, which Liat and I baked for the girls," Rika said. "And this is the Mozart. Hila brought it." She smiled at one of the girls. "And this beautiful cake is yours." Yonatan blushed. At the bakery, the nameless cake had seemed like a winner, but now, standing tall with its ringlets of icing, it looked ludicrous—more like a parody than a real cake.

Rika called out toward the swings, "Girls, come and eat with us," and the two walked over to the table reluctantly and both squeezed onto one chair. Yonatan tried to catch Dana's eye, but she wouldn't pick her head up. He knew that look of hers, the downcast one reserved for times when she felt trapped and knew no one would come to rescue her. He knew that look because he had invented it.

"Which kind would you like?" Rika asked Dana.

Tamar quickly answered for her. "We're not hungry." "Are you sure?" Rika checked, and they both nodded. The other girls asked for slices of the Pavlova and the Mozart, and when Rika asked Yonatan, he said, "I'll try that one," pointing to the loser cake. Dana looked up briefly and peeked at him, and he smiled at her. Rika put a huge slice of the cake on his plate and said, "Enjoy!" Then she asked, "Anyone else?" Tamar straightened up suddenly and said, "Actually, I also want some of that," and Yonatan and his little ally ate their cake obediently, down to the last crumb; it turned out to be nothing more than a flamboyant version of a dry pound cake.

(1 0)

During the moments when he was able to overcome the terror of what lay ahead for them, Yonatan managed to enjoy filling the roles of two parents. He enjoyed other things too, things he could not quite identify; they had tried to define them in the support group, but he found the definitions insulting to his intelligence, even if they were sometimes correct. The scene of eight men crowded into the living room of a north Tel Aviv apartment, with two large fans spinning slowly at their feet, turning first to one sad face and then to another like microphones, all approximately his age (except for a young moshavnik whose wife had died during childbirth and left him with a malpractice case and a fussy baby), all trying to get the most out of a common affliction: the scene made him think that this framework for talking about all the things you couldn't really talk about—what's best for the child, what's best for the father, the advantages of the new smaller family, trying to reorganize the unit like an amoeba—was supportive of nothing other than itself. And since he hated frameworks, he left after three meetings, persuading himself with the thought that he would have derived no benefit from it and that he was doing the group a favor by leaving, because not only had he never opened his mouth at the meetings, he had felt he was spreading a mood of cynicism and desperation. Even so, over the next few years, he found himself wondering sometimes what had happened to those men and their children.

Once, on the eve of Rosh Hashanah, a few months after abandoning the group, he met one of the widowers standing in line at the ATM. Yonatan couldn't remember his name but remembered he was a geography or history teacher and had been the joker of the group. The man stood behind him holding a thick wallet. He pressed up against Yonatan while he was punching in his secret code and said, "So. Getting cash, eh?" Yonatan couldn't tell if the man was making some kind of joke, so he said, "What else?" And the man, who was wearing a T-shirt and Bermuda shorts, fanned himself with his wallet and hummed.

Yonatan was suddenly flooded with the embarrassment of a chance meeting with an old fling and decided to drop the other transactions he was planning to make and just get his cash. The man said, "So. Shopping for the new year?" He said yes, and smiled, wanting to end this flirtation imposed on him by the other widower, but when he pulled out the bills from the slot and moved aside, the man examined him, scanning his green Chuck Taylors, his jeans and slightly dirty white T-shirt, lingering on his face for several seconds. Yonatan hadn't shaved that morning, and he ran his fingers over his chin defensively. The man asked, "So. Are we writing?" Yonatan sighed and said again, "What else?" He quickly shoved the bills into his pocket and said, "I'll see you around." The man nodded a little sadly as he waited for his cash and tapped the ATM screen with his fingers, one of which still bore a gold wedding band. He looked over his shoulder as Yonatan crossed the street and suddenly called out after him, "Luria! Happy New Year!" Without turning back, Yonatan raised his arm in a kind of reverse salute and walked away.

He thought of himself as an unemployed actor who suddenly gets the part of a lifetime and reads his lines for the first time. It was a huge part and filled him with a sense of power, which was sometimes replaced by confusion and helplessness, then exchanged again for power and the knowledge that he had the skill to pull it off and only he had that skill. Sometimes he wondered what would have happened, had he been in the car with Ilana when the truck whose brakes failed in the opposite lane had homed in on their Subaru like a smart bomb. He wondered whether he could have done anything, because if they had been in the car together he would have been driving instead of her. What would have happened if he had been in the driver's seat?

The summer after the accident, he drove up on his own to that road in the Upper Galilee, where Ilana had gone to visit a friend who had moved with her husband to some hilltop village. He sat on the shoulder of the road in the new Subaru, the smaller one, which he had bought with the insurance settlement, and examined through dark sunglasses the steep incline down which the truck had come. The driver, a contractor in his fifties, had called him on the anniversary of the accident, introduced himself, and burst into tears. Yonatan had listened silently to the sobs of the contractor, whose license had been revoked for eight months, and tried to understand what he was saying, although he had meant to slam the phone down on him. Apart from sentence fragments that sounded like *have kids* and *I also,* and a few words screamed hoarsely into the receiver (*family, poor things,* and *God*), he couldn't make out anything, and the contractor suddenly hung up and never phoned again.

Yonatan sat behind the wheel for almost an hour, watched the cars coming up from his left and down opposite him, and tried to imagine possible accidents. The windows were closed and the air-conditioning was turned all the way up, slamming the cigarette smoke back into his face through the ventilators. He envisioned dozens of accidents, some of them minor and some fatal, giving the drivers and the passengers various degrees of injuries, some of them crippled for life, some walking miracles. Then a semi charged down the hill and roused him from his daydreams. He merged into the traffic and climbed slowly up the hill, which was higher and steeper than he had imagined. He was stuck behind a bus full of kids and didn't dare pass it; the convoy of cars behind him reprimanded his cowardliness with flashing lights and adventurous sallies into the opposite lane. Feeling suddenly hungry, he stopped at a little restaurant with a wooden painted sign that said HOMEMADE GOAT'S CHEESE.

It was late morning, and he was the only customer. He sat in the left corner, next to one of the large windows. The waitress, who looked like a young girl, brought him a handwritten menu and cleared the extra dishes and silverware off the table, which was set for four. He asked what she recommended, and she said everything was good. When she saw he couldn't make up his mind, she said, "Hang on, I'll get my mom," and disappeared behind the bar. A woman who looked too young to be her mother came over to Yonatan, carrying the *Ha'aretz* weekend supplement in one hand and a pen in the other. She put the paper down on the table and told him about the different kinds of cheese, and Yonatan realized he had taken her away from doing the crossword. Eventually he ordered a cheese plate, which the woman assured him was very filling, and a basket of homemade bread.

He looked out the window, chewing the bread slowly. It was fresh but did not offer the bursts of flavor he had hoped for. There were kernels of something tough in it—corn—which he took out of his mouth and placed in the little clay ashtray. He went on chewing and staring at the purplish-gray mountains and the square fields of brown and green, which separated the restaurant from the highway that stretched out in the distance, and at a few little sheep that were closer and clearer. As he picked out the kernels, he suddenly noticed the road he had parked on earlier, which wound around the mountain and disappeared and then turned up again and surprised him right beneath the window. Only now—he gave up on the bread and put it back in the basket—did he realize he was sitting in the ideal vantage point for that road, and that from here, behind the double-glazed windows isolating him from the noise, he could see what he hadn't seen before: the twists and turns, the cars driving up and down, the impossible shoulders, the stone wall on one side of the road and the chasm on the other—this time as a viewer comfortably watching a movie, not someone trapped inside a three-dimensional fantasy. He wondered what you could see from the other windows. He got up and went to the one nearby, leaned on the table with his elbows, and looked out. From here you could see a gas station and the intersection connecting the little road with the highway. Then he went to the window on the right, which looked out onto the backyard of a two-story stone house that looked new and well cared for.

"Nice view," he said, when he noticed the proprietress watching him as she leaned on the bar with her newspaper.

"The nicest view is from where you're sitting. You chose the best seat."

Yonatan smiled and went back to his table.

He wanted to move to a different seat, but he didn't want to bother the girl or her mother and knew that if he moved they would think something was wrong. He was suddenly ashamed of the evidence of his dissatisfaction that he had left in the ashtray. The presence of the road distressed him. He would have preferred to look out on the yard while he ate, but he was too shy to get up.

He had never liked nature and preferred to enjoy it from a distance, but now, sitting by the large window with its polished frame, on his one side the thicket of roads and traffic, which he couldn't hear, because of the air-conditioning and the double-glazing, but whose vibrations he thought he could sense, and on his other side a little family hermeticity that was also transmitting vibrations from the bar, where the mother kept on calmly solving her crossword while her daughter sat beside her sorting through receipts, and behind him the house and the big yard, and somewhere perhaps also a goat paddock that produced cheeses— now he felt as if something was very wrong with his life and that perhaps he should take his daughter and move to the Galilee. Here he would have the quietude to write, and Dana could run around carefree in the big yards with girls who looked like the daughter, who in fact—and Yonatan glanced at her again—didn't look any different from the girls in Tel Aviv, with her nervous gauntness and the overdone makeup and the midriff shirt and overall air of hostility.

Even so, something here seemed optimistic and, if not for the modern road, which was definitely too busy for its narrow proportions and,
like any alleyway in Israel, served as a main traffic artery; and if not for
the sign in the entrance that said they took all major credit cards; and if
not for a man around his age who suddenly came in wearing tailored
light linen pants, an elegant shirt, and a tie, put his keys and cell phone
down on the bar, and went over to the girl and stroked her hair; and if
not for the girl's navel ring; and if the radio the proprietor turned on had
not broadcast the beeps signaling the twelve-o'clock news, he could have
believed for a minute that the lap of nature was the perfect solution for
his daughter and himself.

When the woman saw he hadn't touched his food she sent her husband over. The man leaned down, placing both hands on the table, and
asked, "Is everything okay?" Yonatan smiled and said, "Yes, thanks,
everything's fine," and dug his fork into a slice of cheese. It tasted familiar, like the feta he bought at the supermarket, except with a spoiled flavor. The piece next to it had a hard texture and was saltier; he tasted the
olives, hoping to find in them what he had vainly searched for in the
bread and cheese, but they were dry and salty too, and he wondered if
they were also made locally. He ignored the tomato and dug his fork into
a slice of cheese with a pepper-coated rind that looked interesting, then
tried a slice coated with sesame. One after the other, he tried them all, as
well as a few of the Israeli herbs, and halfheartedly ate a pale slice of
tomato and a couple of olives, and more than cheated he felt sad.

(1 1)

He went to the store and bought two cartons of apple juice and
two packs of Winstons. When he started walking toward the pharmacy,
he remembered that the fridge was empty and he should get some bread
and dairy products, in case Dana's fever went down and she was hungry
later. But he suddenly had a better idea: he would make her some tomato
soup, not the frozen kind they sometimes had but the kind Ilana used to

make with fresh tomatoes and cream. The recipe was still scrawled on a piece of paper, slipped between the pages of a French cookbook that was too complex and pretentious and served mainly as a file folder for other recipes. He knew he needed whipping cream and butter but couldn't remember what else, so he decided to go past the pharmacy, then back home, and go out shopping again later that afternoon. He crossed Allenby going west but then remembered the bread shop on King George and quickly crossed back again before the light turned red. He hoped they still had some of the onion bread Dana liked. He glanced at his watch and saw it was almost one. He was glad his writing day was already a loss. This time it was not his fault.

The onion bread was sold out. A young woman was standing in line to pay, holding the last loaf. The shopkeeper, who could see how disappointed he was, tried to console him with a loaf of rye. As he looked at it, trying to decide, she handed the woman her change and the woman said, "Sorry." He smiled and said, "It's all right." "It's for my dad," the woman said. "It's the only kind of bread he likes; otherwise I would gladly let you have it." He said, "I wouldn't if it were me"; when she left the store with her onion bread wrapped in a paper bag, he suddenly regretted saying that, although he knew it was true.

His father hated bread. It was a bizarre hatred, and Yonatan never really believed him. He understood his father's hatred of the religious, as well as his hatred of the extreme right wing, which over the years became an abhorrence of the right wing in general and of what used to be the center, which, like bohemia, had disbanded. Yonatan suspected him of also hating the left, because as he grew older his hatred became more sweeping and democratic—he hated everybody and hated them harshly— but Yonatan never understood how you could hate bread. When he was a child, he would watch his father closely every time he went into the kitchen, hoping to catch him in the act of slicing himself a piece of the caraway-seed bread stored in the bread bin, but it never happened. At dinner, he would take a mental picture of the length of the loaf before his mother put it back in the bread bin, and in the morning he would force himself to get up before everyone else, slip into the kitchen, take the loaf out, and measure it between his hands; but the bread, like his father, remained the same.

A few weeks before he died, his father was snoozing in his bed in the old-age home in Jerusalem, and Yonatan was sitting beside him on a plastic chair, reading the paper. The kitchen lady came in and put his dinner tray on the little retractable table attached to the cabinet. His father, who barely spoke anymore, woke automatically and sat up. Yonatan took the two slices of brown bread off the tray, as he always did, placed them on the folded newspaper, and started peeling the hard-boiled egg. Then he mashed it with a fork and mixed it in with the yogurt, but when he took a spoonful and held it up to his father's lips, his father shut his mouth and shook his head.

"What's the matter? Aren't you hungry?" he asked, and his father kept shaking his head. "I don't understand, Dad. Explain to me what you want."

His father pointed with his chin toward the tray, which held a few slices of hard cheese, a pad of margarine, a quartered tomato, and a clementine.

"Do you want the fruit?" he asked, and his father kept shaking his head and motioning at the tray. "The cheese?" he asked, and his father nodded. "Should I put it in the yogurt for you?" he asked, surprised because he had never shown any interest in cheese before. His father narrowed his eyes angrily and beat his fist on the sheet, motioning with his chin toward the newspaper.

"What is it? Do you want me to read to you from the newspaper? After dinner, Dad. Let's finish eating first." But his father's chin didn't move and his eyes, which showed a glimmer Yonatan had not seen for a long time, locked in on the bread, almost toasting it with their gaze.

"Bread? You want the bread?" The torn eyes and nodding chin told him yes.

"I don't believe it, Dad," Yonatan said in a vexed tone, and thought it might be the first moment of happiness he had experienced in that place. "I just don't believe it," he said, and spread the slice with margarine—not before receiving another nod of the chin in approval—and then put a slice of cheese on it. When he held the revolutionary sandwich up to his father's lips, waiting for him to take a bite, his father's hand emerged from beneath the sheet and grasped Yonatan's wrist. When Yonatan asked, "Don't you want it?" the fingers loosened their grip, snatched the sandwich away from him, folded it in two, and stuffed it into his mouth. Before he could swallow, his father was making that same, now intelligible, gesture toward the second slice, and Yonatan quickly spread it with margarine and put a piece of cheese on it too, and garnished it with a slice of tomato. Then he put it in his father's waiting hand, and knew he would never forget the moist sounds of chewing and the crumbs covering the sheet; he also knew he would never be able to tell with any certainty whether the memory was happy or sad.

He paid for the rye and went out onto the street. He turned right at Allenby, waited at the long pedestrian crossing light, which always got on his nerves, crossed the street, and went into the pharmacy. The pharmacist came out of the back room and smiled at him like an old acquaintance, which he really had become, considering all the medicine he bought there every winter. "How's it going, Luria?"

"Thanks. How are you?"

"What will it be for Dana?" the pharmacist asked, and they both smiled.

The pharmacist's elderly mother, who always sat in the back room, called out, "Who is it, the writer?"

Yonatan said, "Hello, Mrs. Gorman, how are you?"

"Is the girl sick again?"

"What can you do?"

Yonatan heard her click her tongue and say, "Poor child," at which point the pharmacist said, "Enough, Mother."

Yonatan said, "That's the way it goes, Mrs. Gorman—children get sick."

"Yes, but not like this," she replied, and the pharmacist—who was no longer a young man himself—rolled his eyes.

Yonatan gave him a forgiving look. "I'm making her some soup."

Mrs. Gorman peered out of the room. "Soup is good. What kind?"

"Cream of tomato." He couldn't understand what possessed him to let the pharmacist's mother in on the menu. Perhaps he hoped she would have a tip or a recipe.

"Cream of tomato is no good, it's too heavy. She needs broth or chicken soup."

"I think tomato soup is all right; it's what Dana likes."

Mrs. Gorman said it didn't matter what Dana liked, Dana had to get better, and the pharmacist said, "Mother, will you please stop meddling?"

Yonatan smiled shyly and Mrs. Gorman pursed her lips, insulted, but she soon perked up and asked, "And how is your mother? Still with the high blood pressure?"

Yonatan had once consulted with her about his mother's health, wrongly assuming that a woman who spent most of her life in a pharmacy would have some medical inside knowledge. "She's fine," he said.

"Is she being careful with the salt?"

"Not really."

Mrs. Gorman said he needed to watch her, and he said he tried, but it was difficult because she cheated. Mrs. Gorman said, "Elderly people like to cheat, but you mustn't let them." Yonatan thought about how Mrs. Gorman and his mother were roughly the same age, and the old lady said, "And you must watch Dana too."

"I do."

"Children cheat too," she told him.

He said he was doing his best, and could tell that the pharmacist was losing his patience, so he said, "I hope you feel well, Mrs. Gorman."

"There's nothing wrong with me."

He asked if the new thermometer from the commercials was worth anything, and the pharmacist, relieved that the small talk with his mother was over, said it certainly was but that it was expensive. He took down the box of thermometers from one of the shelves and put it on the counter, and Mrs. Gorman peeked out from the room again and said there was no reason for that thermometer to be so expensive, and it was only because of the commercial that everyone was buying it now. She ordered her son to show Yonatan the other thermometers, which were also fine and much cheaper, and Yonatan said there was no need and that he was in a bit of a hurry. He picked up the package, which was wrapped with a brochure showing the sick man with the sorry face, glanced at the price, which was much more than he had intended to spend, and said he would take it.

PART TWO

1

There was something lonely and yet, at the same time, comforting in the short walk from Borochov Street to Hess Street on a Friday night. She couldn't pinpoint exactly what it was but thought it had something to do with crossing Meir Park, which at this time of day was populated mainly by dogs and their owners and a few homeless people sleeping on benches, unlike the daylight hours, when the same benches were inhabited by mothers with their children or by nannies rocking strollers with mechanical indifference. During this changing of the guard and especially at wintertime, the park seemed different to Shira: quieter, wilder, open to interpretation.

She strolled down the pathway, which was wet from the rain that had fallen all day, and the yellow leaves stuck to the soles of her shoes. She was carrying a plastic bag containing a bottle of Chilean wine, a container of vanilla ice cream, and an umbrella. She walked slowly, deliberately, taking steps that looked almost artificial, so as not to be the first guest to arrive for dinner at her friend Rona's. Friday-night dinners at Rona's were always a culinary event and sometimes a social haven; Shira viewed her friend's home as a lighthouse that transmitted quiet flashes to call in boats full of weekend refugees like herself. She had no idea who else would be there tonight but knew that, despite her delaying tactics, she would still be morbidly punctual.

More than punctuality, she was driven by restlessness. She had inherited from her father a chronically fast internal clock that prompted her to leave home too early, spurred by an acceleration she was unable to control. She would then find herself trapped in a cage of idleness for fifteen minutes or sometimes more—time that swelled into huge proportions and which, like any monster, was hard to kill. Sometimes she tried to be late, but she was never successful. If she was walking, she walked slowly, choosing the longest route, scanning shop windows with an intrigued look but without truly seeing their contents, and if she took the car she slowed down as she approached lights, hoping they would change to red, and prayed for traffic jams or a wrong turn that would lead her astray and waste another ten minutes. But the trips always turned out to be quick and smooth, as if to aggravate her, and at the end she had to stay in the car a little longer, listening to the radio and staring at the digital clock flashing above the glove compartment, waiting for the green digits to indicate a reasonable hour, taking into account that she still had to get out of the car, lock the door, and perform her check to make sure she hadn't forgotten to put on the steering wheel lock, all the while telling herself she could have passed this time at home; but at home she had told herself the minutes would go faster if she went out. She envied people who were always late, who tried to buy time, because sometimes she felt like a wholesaler with an embarrassing quantity on her hands, unable to get rid of it.

Now she thought that if the benches were not wet she would sit down and smoke a cigarette, join the bench dwellers who had nothing to be early or late for, and pretend she owned one of the dogs running around on the lawn. But she knew she would never have the courage to sit down in case someone, another of Rona's guests, walked through the park and saw her. If they knew each other, they would strike up a conversation. Hey, what are you doing here? he would ask. Nothing, she would say. He would say he was on his way to Rona's, and she would say she was too, and he would glance at his watch. What time is it now? she would ask, as if she had no idea. He would say, It's almost eight, and she would say, We'd better get going, then.

Or perhaps the person who saw her in the park would be a stranger, one of the men Rona was always trying to set her up with. He would walk past her as she sat smoking and watching the dogs, also carrying a bottle of wine or a bunch of flowers, and later, when Rona opened the door for her at ten past eight, he would be there, sitting at the round table in the kitchen. She would look familiar to him and Rona would introduce them, and in order to save herself she would say, quickly but calmly, "I saw you before in Meir Park." "Really, when?" he would say, as if he were the one with something to hide. She would say, "I was sitting there earlier," as if it were the most natural thing in the world to sit alone in the dark on a Friday evening with wine and ice cream on a wet bench in a public park.

She walked through the gate to Tchernikowsky Street and glanced at her watch: still seven forty-five. It had taken only three minutes to cross the park. But in fact there was nothing wrong with being the first to arrive. She could help Rona set the table, or make a salad, or chat with Tamar, who was one of those children who were great conversationalists without pretending to be adults. Fridays were always difficult for Shira. If she wasn't invited somewhere, she would stay home and watch television or read the papers, solve the crosswords, and leave at least one—usually the cryptic crossword in *Ha'aretz,* which took up more time—for Saturday morning. Or she would go and visit her father, whose restlessness was also worse on Friday nights, when routine and its side effects reached their climax, ebbing slightly the next day—Shabbat, with its laziness, was somehow more tolerable—and gaining momentum again on Sunday. Sometimes a distraction came along: a dinner invitation, a housewarming, or an evening spent watching TV at a friend's house. Shira found it strange to think that she was her father's distraction, that he looked forward to her visits as she looked forward to Rona's invitations, that a whole hierarchy of distractions were at work; she wondered who was at the top.

Shira was always surprised at how calmly Rona organized these big dinners. Rona never knew in advance how many guests would show up, if any, because there were people who refused to make a commitment in the morning for that evening, and Shira wondered how she knew what to cook and how much to make if she didn't know who was coming, and why even bother. On the other hand, she thought, that was probably it: Rona Peretz and her daughter Tamar's home always went about its business, whatever happened. It was a home that could easily take in people, but it also remained a home without them; in that respect it was modular, but it was more stable than any other home she knew; above all, it was a home that didn't need any favors from anyone.

2

She had met Rona ten years ago, when she translated an article into
English for her. Rona was about to finish her PhD in psychology at the
time and was pregnant with Tamar. Shira had finished her BA in philosophy and was making a living doing odd translation and editing jobs. She
was twenty-six, and Rona was ten years older. A common acquaintance
had introduced them.

They met one winter afternoon in Rona's apartment on Hess Street.
They sat in the huge open kitchen that faced a backyard full of tangled
growth; the tops of a few palm trees peeked out, and Shira thought they
looked out of place, like the other palms scattered around the center of
town. She was impressed by the large windows, squares of glass set in
light-blue-painted iron frames, and said she'd always dreamed that when
she had her own house it would have that kind of window. Rona asked
if she wanted a tour, and Shira followed her from room to room, enchanted and full of envy: there was something that transcended Rona's
excellent taste and the massive spaces that contained it; the apartment
had a tranquillity that Shira had never encountered in any of the homes
she'd lived in. She knew that she took her uneasiness with her each time
she relocated, and like a piece of furniture it had survived every move.

Even the Voice of Music, which was on the radio in the background, sounded different. She recognized the piece, a Mozart clarinet
quintet. She told Rona that when she turned the program on at home
they were always playing some screeching modern composition, and
Rona said that Saturday afternoons were always a gamble. When Shira
sat at the large round wooden table in the kitchen and looked at Rona,
who was bending over her huge belly to take a cake out of the oven, she
was suddenly overcome with hunger, not necessarily for the pear tart—
although she did have two slices—but for something in the air and in

Rona's movements, which were heavy and slow, and even in the way she dressed. She wore gray sweatpants and a white undershirt under an old banana-colored sweater with buttons, only the top two of which were fastened. Shira suddenly became aware of her own clothes: a black miniskirt, with black tights and a black polo-neck sweater, and boots, also black, whose heels made too much noise on the kitchen floor.

They talked about renovations, and Rona told her how difficult it was to find a contractor, and about the delays and the hitches along the way, and how much it cost, and she said that in fact the work wasn't over and there were still things to do, but she would probably never do them; she didn't have the patience for it. But Rona did not look like someone who didn't have the patience for things, and the tone she used when she said it was soft and soothing, like the taste the tart had left in Shira's mouth. Shira asked when she was due.

Rona looked at her stomach and said, "March second."

"Wow, that's in three weeks!"

"Yes," she said, in that same contemplative tone.

Shira asked who would be with her at the birth, and Rona said she didn't know yet; two girlfriends had volunteered, but one of them was supposed to go overseas for a conference. Shira asked if the friend was a psychologist too, and Rona smiled and said no, not at all, she was a dentist.

"And the other one?"

Rona smiled and said, "That's the thing. The other one is due to give birth too, at the end of March. Only her last two came early."

Shira asked what the other friend did, curious to know more about her life, and Rona said, "She's a math teacher, but now she's on sabbatical at home, painting."

Shira was jealous of Rona for having real friends with real professions, whose lives were full of conferences and sabbaticals and hobbies and pregnancies, and although she was younger than Rona and her friends, she felt as if the ten years that separated them had already gone by; she sensed that what she was feeling now were not the little jolts of great plans for the future but premature disappointment over things that would never happen. "So you won't know until the last minute?" she asked.

Rona sipped her tea and said, "I guess not."

"Are you scared?"

"No. Whatever happens, happens."

Shira wanted to volunteer to be at the birth with her, but they had only met half an hour ago, so she said nothing.

Rona said, "That's how it is when you don't have a partner," but she said it without any resentment, and then she offered Shira some coffee and said she herself was only drinking tea now. Shira said herbal tea sounded great, and then Rona, with the same calm with which she had shown Shira the apartment and just made her herbal tea, told her about her decision to have a child and about the sperm bank.

Shira, briefly embarrassed by Rona's frankness, asked, "And do you know if it's a boy or a girl?"

Rona looked at her stomach again, where all the answers must have come from, and said, "Girl."

"I've always wanted a girl."

Rona showed her the article and asked if Shira would be able to finish the translation before she gave birth. Shira said she would, she didn't have much work at the moment, and when Rona asked how much she charged, she gave a price that was much lower than her usual rate.

"That's not much. I thought it would cost more," Rona said.

"You're not supposed to bargain up."

"Okay, but I'll have you over for dinner sometime." Shira asked if she cooked a lot, and Rona said, "All the time. It's my hobby. Are you hungry? I could heat something up for you. There's some roast beef in the fridge."

"Really? Did you make it?" She didn't know people who had roast beef in their fridges.

"I had guests yesterday. I can carve a few slices for you and heat them up."

Shira said she liked it cold too. She wanted to taste the roast beef, not because she was hungry but because she wanted to linger in this apartment, but she refused and said she was full and had eaten too much tart. She got up and asked if she could use the bathroom, and Rona reminded her where it was.

The bathroom window had little diamonds of blue glass set in it;

this window also looked out onto the yard with the strange palm trees that must have been planted, decades ago, by someone dreaming of another city. She sat on the toilet and wanted to keep sitting there, smelling the laundry softener, which was the same kind she used at home but here it had a completely different scent, and the smell of the clear bar of soap that lay in a little dish on the counter, and the shampoo on the windowsill. From the moment she had entered the apartment she felt assailed by a barrage of soft scents: the kitchen and bathroom smells, the smell of the pears and the dough, the tea aroma, the fresh whitewash on the walls. And there were hidden scents: the conversation smell, the pregnancy smell, the smell of the day when she too would have roast beef in her fridge, and the smell of her fear that the day would never come.

When she came back to the kitchen, Rona asked if she wanted some more tea, and Shira said she would, that herbal tea really was calming. Rona smiled, and Shira asked where she bought it. It started to rain. Instead of the clarinet quintet, the radio was now playing Brahms's first piano concerto, which Shira especially liked because it was the first piece of classical music she had heard, when she was eight, on her mother's old gramophone. It was a winter day just like this one, in their apartment in north Tel Aviv, whose windows did not overlook a courtyard but looked into other windows, into their neighbors' lives; Shira always wanted to trade places with them, or at least be able to stand sometimes at their windows and look in on her parents. Their apartment had three rooms, a long narrow kitchen, and a bathroom and toilet with a little window that opened onto an air shaft, into which sounds poured from the other bathrooms—funny sounds, sometimes disgusting or scary, but all preferable to her parents' silence.

No one was at home that day she fell in love. She came home early from school because she had the flu. She let herself into the apartment with her key and lay down on the couch in the living room and watched the educational programs on TV until it was time for the math program, which she couldn't stand. Then she went into the kitchen to make herself a cup of tea. She had a fever and was shivering a little, and as she stood waiting for the water to boil, her knees suddenly felt weak. But it wasn't just the flu; there was something adventurous, something airy and cheerful, about being in the empty apartment during the late morning hours.

She took her tea into the living room and dragged her comforter over to the couch from her bedroom. She thought about calling her dad at his office, or her mom, who was probably at her sister's, and letting them know she'd been sent home early. She had promised the school nurse she'd call as soon as she got home, but now it seemed unnecessary. She didn't feel that bad. In fact, there was something pleasant about this weakness, and one of them would be home soon to make her lunch anyway. She wondered who it would be today, him or her, because you could never know, and she was curious as to whether they coordinated it, and how, in the middle of mutual anger, which the three of them woke up to every morning, they remembered that someone had to come home at lunchtime. Two or three years later she was no longer impressed by her parents' sense of responsibility and their excellent memory, but as she lay on the couch, huddled up in the comforter, and stared at the black-and-white TV screen and at the math teacher who reminded her of a big goose, she felt protected.

Next to the couch was a little cabinet with a gramophone on top. There were rows and rows of records stuffed into the shelves below. She turned down the TV volume, sat on the rug with the heavy comforter around her shoulders, and pulled out the first record she could extract. The cardboard cover was faded and slightly stained and showed a bearded old man with a penetrating look, whose large hands hovered over a piano. The record collection was one of several of her mother's belongings that Shira could never imagine her using, because they didn't fit the woman she knew at all: the sewing machine that sat in the porch off the kitchen, covered with a thick sheet of plastic; a big old food processor that stood on the counter, also covered, looking like a minia-turized replica of the sewing machine; and large philosophy and poetry books that lined an out-of-reach shelf in the bookcase. It was as if her mother had a previous life that she had frozen when she got married, or perhaps these items belonged to a life she had planned to have, when she married, but that had never materialized.

Her mother did not sew or cook or listen to music. On Fridays she would buy fancy expensive cakes with foreign names at the bakery; Shira's friends were always impressed by the cakes. In her spare time, she read one mystery after another, and Shira sometimes thought she had abandoned the things she loved as a form of protest against her father, who wanted a normal family but lived, like a reclusive camper, in a tent of anxiety set up in the middle of the house, which he folded and carried if ever he went anywhere. Over time, the protest turned into apathy, which her mother fought to combat with the courses she signed up for, the lectures she attended at the university, her ever-expanding fields of interest, the long-standing pool membership, and the hours she spent at her sister's. When she came home, her mother returned with her suspect energy and an exaggerated joie de vivre, which she sprayed over them as if she had opened a bottle of champagne. She would stand in the living room, telling Shira and her father where she had been and what she had seen, and Shira could detect two languages in her speech: the minor scale, which was meant for her father, and the strained major scale, which was for her. Nonetheless, or perhaps because of that great strain, her mother seemed even sadder than her father at those moments.

Shira didn't know that the elderly pianist on the cover was meant to be Brahms, but the minute she placed the needle on the record, the moment she heard the first demanding chords, serious and threatening like her mother's big books, and then the piano, which seemed to have no intention of surrendering to the threat, she fell in love with him.

She listened to the concerto over and over again, chilled by her fever, with shivers running through her. She turned the volume up a little higher each time she played the record, so she didn't hear the key turning in the door and her father's footsteps as he hurried into the living room. He was alarmed to see her lying on the couch with her eyes closed, her hands floating above the blanket mimicking a conductor's gestures. When she heard him call her name, she opened her eyes, leaped onto the rug, and turned the volume down. He asked what she was doing home, and she said she was sick. He asked why they hadn't called him from school, and she said she had promised the nurse she would call as soon as she got home, but at home she felt better.

Her father picked up the album cover off the floor and asked why she was suddenly listening to classical music, and she said she didn't know, she was bored. "Brahms of all things?" he said, and she quickly filed the name in her memory. Her father handed her the sleeve and said, "Your mother likes him too." Then he bent over and touched her forehead. He asked if she was hungry, and she said she wasn't, and he offered to make her a salad or an omelet anyway, but she said she wanted to sleep for a while.

Her father phoned her mother, and half an hour later she came home and he went back to his office. Her mother looked tired, but she smiled and asked Shira how high her temperature had been when the nurse had taken it, and Shira said she couldn't remember. "I'll get you some juice," she said, and went into the kitchen, and Shira quickly put the album back among the other records. She wanted to listen to it again, with her mother, but she suddenly felt the need to protect her new love with a coat of secrecy. When her mother sat opposite her on the armchair and turned the TV up so they could watch it together, a sense of guilt diluted her excitement.

But her love of classical music survived, and when she found herself alone at home again, she looked for other records with the illustration of the bearded man with the penetrating look; she couldn't find any, although there were many Brahms albums in the collection. Since she couldn't read English at the time but could recognize the letters, she always chose the albums with a large *B* on their covers, so by the time she grew up, she had fallen in love with Bach and Beethoven, too, and with the Berlioz requiem. Eventually, she moved the album collection into her room, where she listened to the records on a new stereo her parents bought for her bat mitzvah. Her love was diminished somewhat by the sense that she was continuing some struggle on her mother's behalf, and the battlefield was the earphones, through which the sounds flowed in full volume; still, the silence on the other end always trickled through.

(3)

Rona stirred a teaspoon of honey into her tea. "I hear you write," she said, and the conversation abruptly took on an ominous tone.

"A little," Shira said.

"Prose?"

"I wouldn't really call it prose yet. It's at a very embryonic stage. Preembryonic, even."

"I envy creative people," said Rona.

"I don't know if I'd call myself creative. So far I haven't really created much of anything other than expectations."

"But you're getting there."

"Yes, I suppose so, but I have no idea *where* I'm getting," Shira said thoughtfully, and suddenly wished the psychologist in Rona would answer her small cry of distress as promptly as she had earlier offered her the roast beef.

Rona asked, "So, do you write on a computer or on paper?"

"Computer," Shira replied. "It's impossible otherwise."

"And do you work every day?"

"I try to. But lately I'm really not into it. I can't concentrate."

"I know what that's like," said Rona.

"You do?"

"I haven't been able to concentrate on anything either recently."

"Well, you have good reason," she said, and pointed to Rona's belly.

Rona smiled and said, "Yes, I suppose I do."

"Have you chosen a name yet?" Shira asked.

"Tamar."

"That's a lovely name."

"I like it too. I thought of Shira at first, but then I decided on Tamar."

"Tamar is definitely nicer."

"They're both nice, but I wanted a name that would sound different from mine. Rona and Shira sounded wrong somehow. Like Sally and Molly."

"And Tamar ends with an *r* and Rona begins with an *r*," said Shira.

"That's true. I never thought of that."

"It's as if you continue each other."

"Yes," Rona said. "I pick up where she leaves off. But shouldn't it be the other way around?"

"I'm not sure," Shira replied, fearing she might be wading into a swamp of symbolism. "Don't you sometimes feel like our parents are more an extension of us than we are of them?"

Rona took her time to reply. She wasn't the type to answer quickly or feel compelled to show off her conversational skills, agility, or wit. Shira envied her, the way she sat there, stirring her tea, resting her other hand on her belly as she considered—not because she wished to prove anything but rather out of curiosity—whether or not she had anything to say.

"I don't know," she said finally. "But it's interesting, what you said."

"I'm not sure it's all that interesting. Maybe it's not really interesting at all."

"No, no, it is," said Rona.

"Well, perhaps."

"Are your parents still alive?" Rona asked.

"My father is. My mother died two years ago."

"I'm sorry."

"It's been quite a while."

"Two years is not such a long time," said Rona. "How did she die?"

"She had a brain aneurysm. It was very quick and sudden, and fatal."

"How old was she?"

"Fifty-nine," Shira said, and looked outside at the palm trees' fanned branches thrashing about in the rain. She remembered the day her mother had died. It had been scorching hot. But she did not need to call the day up from memory because it was always with her, expanding and contracting like an accordion, sometimes taking up only the polite space of a reminder, other times, if it caught her at an especially bad moment, taking control and transporting itself into the present.

On such days she would wake up with the same feeling she had had that June morning when she took the bus to the university for her final exam in logic. She knew she would flunk it, so she hadn't bothered to stay up all night trying to make sense of the material. She'd gone to bed early and slept well, and when the alarm clock rang at seven she had sat up feeling very calm. On the bus, she stared out the window, without taking even one last obligatory peek at the highlighted lecture notes prepared for her by Nurit, her classmate. She sensed the calm that precedes a foreseen failure, a pleasant surrender of the brain, suddenly free to deal with other things. But her head was empty that morning—which was odd for her, because one way or another it was always full of thoughts—completely empty, as she sat in the café on campus and drank a latte and chain-smoked. It remained empty as she walked into the building and went up the stairs and looked at the groups of students huddled outside the exam room, exchanging frantic last-minute information. She liked the emptiness so much and she wondered whether she'd ever feel it again or whether this was perhaps the first and last empty moment of her life borrowed from someone else—someone whose life was more tranquil and didn't need it.

But when she sat down in one of the rows in the middle of the auditorium, pen and watch laid out in front of her, and when the proctor laconically explained the exam rules, she suddenly felt as if she was not supposed to be there just then, and not because she had no chance of passing but because something fateful was happening elsewhere; her mind, which had been empty all night and that morning, flooded with a torrent of anxiety.

The proctor handed her the exam sheet and Shira picked up her pen and began filling in her personal information in the answer booklet, She looked back at Nurit, who was sitting two rows behind, smiling. The exam was in fact very easy, she found out later, but she was incapable of grasping the questions. She turned back again and Nurit smiled and signaled various numbers with her fingers, some of which Shira managed to take in and jot down on the margins: two, five, six, and ten. But suddenly the numbers were replaced by others, the digits that made up her parents' telephone number, and they stubbornly hummed inside her head and flashed in front of her eyes, and her lips began mouthing the figures in a silent mantra.

Shira glanced at Nurit again, but she was engrossed in the exam. She looked around. Everyone seemed calm, scribbling in their answer books. She tried to solve the second question, which began with: "X is a black cat," and remembered how amused she had been by this image when she first heard it in class; in her mind's eye she had seen a black alley cat with a big X on its back and someone trying to catch it so they could put it in a logic problem. She made an effort to read the question again but went on to the fifth one, which had no black cat, but there was no point because her body had become her parents' phone number and she suddenly understood that the pleasant emptiness she had felt before was not true emptiness but the incubation of the fear that now overcame her, and she was then convinced that the black cat with the X was a sign that something terrible had happened.

She put her watch and pen into her bag, got up and went to the front of the auditorium, placed her empty booklet on the desk, and told the proctor she had to leave. The proctor asked if she was sure, because there was still time left—there was something maternal about her—but Shira shook her head and said, No, there was no point. As she walked out she saw Nurit watching her questioningly, and Shira waved and hurried out to the pay phone and called her parents.

Her Aunt Malka answered the phone. Shira asked where her mother was and Malka said, "Dad's here. You'd better come over."

"Tell me what's happened," Shira insisted.

"Mom didn't feel well," her aunt said, and Shira recognized the words and the tone because she'd heard them dozens of times from her father when she was little and used to come home from school to find him in the kitchen making her a sandwich for lunch. When she'd ask where her mother was, he would lean heavily on the roll and squash it down with both hands and say, "Mom didn't feel well. She went to rest awhile at Aunt Malka's." For a moment Shira hoped that this *Mom didn't feel well,* uttered by her mother's younger sister, who had now begun to cry on the other side of the line, was that same *Mom didn't feel well* intended to blur the truth for her as an act of kindness. But she knew this time it was both a lie and the truth, because this time her mother really hadn't felt well and she wasn't alive anymore.

"You'd better come home," said Aunt Malka firmly.

"But what happened?" Out of the corner of her eye she saw two students she knew; as they left the exam hall, they laughed with relief and lit up cigarettes. They waved to her.

"Come home," her aunt said, in a broken voice. "Things are not good."

"Is she dead?"

"She had a stroke," Malka continued. "She had a very bad stroke."

"When?"

"This morning, at eight. It happened as soon as she woke up. Dad found her in the bathroom. We tried to call you."

"I had an exam. I'm on campus now." The two students walked by and cast her a *How was it?* look. Shira made a face that said *very bad* and thought of the life she had had five minutes ago and the one she would have from now on. She missed her old life.

"Come quick, Shiraleh," her aunt sobbed.

"Where is Mom now?" she asked, and dug around in her purse to see if she had enough money for a cab.

"They've taken her away already," said Malka, and blew her nose. Shira asked who took her, but her aunt broke into tears again and said, "Come quick, Shiraleh. Your father needs you here with him now." She thought it sounded strange for Aunt Malka to say *your father* rather than just *Dad,* and the word *your,* which had been absent from *Mom didn't feel well,* was now very present and demanding. At that moment Shira understood what she had always known: that the death of one parent would instantly turn her into the parent of the one who remained.

(4)

She stood on Tchernikowsky Street and considered crossing the park again, in the opposite direction this time, and walking along King George, then turning right onto Allenby and right again onto Hess, which might buy her a few minutes of tardiness. But she kept standing where she was. She knew that to go back the way she'd come, something she'd never done before, would constitute an escalation of the endless preoccupation with killing time, a low point that might well conceal even lower points, and she wondered if she might not find herself, one day soon, walking back and forth across the balcony of her apartment on Borochov Street, waiting for someone—a partner, even a delivery boy— as her father used to do when she was a child.

She used to see him from a distance, leaning on the railing with his elbows, looking down at the street as if he were bored rather than anxious. From afar she would catch him retreating into the apartment as soon as he spotted her, and when she was with her girlfriends she quickly distracted them so they wouldn't see him. Sometimes she saw her mother too, motioning with her hands, trying to persuade him to come inside, not to embarrass his daughter in front of her friends. She would see him follow her mother inside, but not before throwing another glance at the

sidewalk, and when she neared the building she knew he was still scanning the street in his imagination, as he shifted uncomfortably in his armchair until he heard her come in. When he asked how it went at the
Scouts meeting or visiting her friends or later, at parties, his voice was
full of feigned indifference, like her mother's eyes.

To tell him how it went, how it really went, was impossible, because
even when she spent time out of the house, she was still in tune with him,
with his waiting, and when she was a child, something told her he was
not only waiting for her to get home safely but for something else, something greater, as if her father was waiting for the moment when his current life would be over and a different one would begin. When he stood
on the balcony, looking down and to the sides, and sometimes also up,
perhaps he was expecting a miracle, maybe even the very same miracle
she was expecting: to be like everyone else.

Everyone else had younger fathers, athletic men who wore jeans
and T-shirts and looked like boys next to her father, who always wore
suits. These fathers smelled of sweat, not aftershave, and the mothers
always looked in love with them. Families who went away on Sukkot and
Passover, went camping in the Sinai Desert, families who talked about
sports and politics and gossiped about other people. But what typified
them more than anything were the smells: the smell of the soap the other
fathers used to wash their cars on Shabbat—her father had a car too, but
he hated driving and usually preferred to take the bus—and the smell of
the other kids' laundry, but mainly the smell that to this day prompted in
her a sense of longing: the waft of cheesecake that hung in the stairwells
in her friends' buildings on countless Friday afternoons, heavy and soft
and disapproving, as if the baking of cheesecake was a neighborhood
scheme the other mothers had concocted after seeing *her* mother leave
the expensive bakery.

When Rona had called that morning and invited her for dinner, she
had asked what to bring. Rona said nothing, but she was already planning to buy Rona's favorite red wine and the ice cream from the Italian
gelateria that Tamar liked, and her day suddenly took on structure and
meaning and had a beginning, a middle, and an end, like a good writing
day. She had not had such a day for a long time, because since her novel
had been published, three years ago, she hadn't been able to write, and

when she did the words behaved like chromosomes, forming the wrong combinations or not connecting at all. She forced herself to write every morning, if only to prove to herself that physically she was still doing it. There were mornings that started out promisingly, and mornings when the sentences crawled along the screen and created a lazy paragraph or two, but because they were written out of desperation and alarm, she knew even before she saved them that the defective creature she had birthed would not survive to the next day.

Her computer was full of files containing no more than a page or two; when she opened them, she did so with the distance of a pathologist interested only in his subjects' cause of death, not their lives or the lives they could have had. During the time that had passed since her first novel came out and climbed to the top of the bestseller list, there were mornings when she treated these writing attempts—no longer intended to be a new book but rather a kind of writing reflex—not as failures, necessarily, but as the loyal representatives of her talent. Her novel's success, she sometimes thought, was what had been the mistake, the true mutation. The dozens of files with promising names, containing words that refused to cooperate and fragments of pages and paragraphs that kept their distance from one another with disgust—these were her true genetic makeup.

She enjoyed the success but was unable to feel it. People knew her name, readers sent her letters saying how her book had changed their lives, which was strange because it had not changed *her* life at all. Sometimes she thought her success had only made life seem even more miserable, deepening the chasm that lay between what others thought of her and what she knew about herself—so much so that on particularly bad days she thought that the chasm was not what separated these two things but was the only thing that truly existed.

But there were more forgiving mornings too, when staring at the screen and typing a few apologetic keystrokes did not seem like punishment for her success but like waiting. And although waiting was also a form of punishment, and although she did not know exactly what she was waiting for, these mornings were colored by a certain pathos, like a little boy who suddenly appears in his pajamas in a living room full of people in the midst of a fervent argument about politics or sex or money or justice: When they notice him standing there, rubbing his eyes and yawning, they fall silent.

She had had one of those mornings today. The rain had begun to fall at night, and by early morning it was pounding down in her bedroom balcony. Shortly after sunrise, when the rain turned to hail, she heard in her sleep a familiar and beloved sound, as if a truck were unloading gravel, and she got out of bed and raised the blinds covering the door to the balcony and looked at the frenetic stuff covering the tiles, and the stones of ice jumping off the railing and the potted plants. She went back to bed and got under the covers and listened to the other melodies of the storm, which had joined the hail in harmony—gutters ringing, the window shuddering, thunder, and a car alarm set off by the hail—to her, this was the most wonderful way to wake up.

She got up and went into the kitchen and turned on the electric kettle, and when she got back from the bathroom and the kettle switch flipped, she decided this was a morning that should be celebrated with real coffee. She took the mocha pot off the shelf; it had been a gift from Eitan, and she had only recently started using it because for the past three years, since they broke up, she hadn't been able to. He bought it for her, like his other gifts, after they had visited friends who served coffee made in a mocha pot, and Shira said it was about time they also started drinking good coffee at home. She never gave it another thought, but Eitan, who kept a mental list of ways to make her happy because he believed in the cumulative power of little details, called the friends the next day and asked which model it was and where they had bought it. As it turned out, the pot was simple and cheap, and that same day he went and bought one and had it gift-wrapped, and at night he hid the box in his side of the closet beneath a pile of sweaters.

Then, when Shira woke up—she always woke up before him, especially during those days when their breakup was hovering above them like an ugly chandelier—and went into the kitchen, the electric kettle had disappeared, and in its place on the countertop was a box wrapped in colorful shiny paper. She opened the box and smiled, and for a minute she wanted to shake Eitan awake and give him a grateful hug, but she knew there would only be embarrassment and guilt in the hug, because she knew she was going to leave him, and she knew he knew too, but as usual he was also clueless. In any case, she couldn't be bothered to start fiddling with the pot. She guessed where Eitan had hidden the kettle, as she had been guessing things he would do and say for months, and she took it out of the cabinet under the sink and made herself a cup of instant coffee.

Eitan woke up and came into the kitchen in his underwear. He saw her sitting at the table and the pot in its box on the countertop. He looked at her with sleepy wonderment that quickly turned to sadness, and she hurried over to him and kissed him on the cheek and said, "Thanks! What a surprise! But I didn't know how to use it, so I waited for you," which softened the insult a little. He said it was easy and he'd show her soon, and she asked if he wanted some instant coffee in the meantime and he nodded and rubbed his eyes and his underwear suddenly looked several sizes too big for him. He went to the bathroom, and she listened from the kitchen as the short bursts of urine turned into a steady stream, and heard him flushing the toilet and turning on the tap in the bathroom sink, which made the kitchen pipes vibrate. She heard him splash cold water on his face and pat his cheeks, then the little scrubbing sounds of his toothbrush, which sounded like a small animal munching. Then she heard him spit into the sink, and when the kettle switch flipped and she poured boiling water into his mug, she knew they would never drink coffee together from the mocha pot.

They broke up a few days later, the morning after the surprise party Eitan threw for her at a club in south Tel Aviv. He invited everyone she knew and all their common friends. There were dozens of people there, some of whom she hadn't talked to for years, but they came, which both touched and annoyed her. She walked into the dark club, whose walls were shaking from the force of the bass, believing she had been invited to a surprise party for someone else. Eitan hugged her as soon as she entered and shoved a plastic cup of beer into her hand, and then she saw all those friends and acquaintances and imagined Eitan locating everyone and introducing himself, and telling everyone about her book, expecting them to be as excited as he was, inviting them to the party and asking them not to say anything if they talked to her. As she stood blinking, holding her beer, she realized that during all those weeks when she was busy with herself and the book, Eitan had found himself a project that, as usual, was connected with her and with ways to make her happy.

On the bar, next to little dishes of snacks, was a stack of her books; they looked as if they didn't belong, not just to the place but to her. In the corner, next to a bathroom sign that was spray-painted with graffiti, behind a massive speaker, she saw her father sitting straight up on a chair, his brimmed hat on his lap, his hands folded on the hat. On the floor next to him were a cup of beer and a plastic plate with some pretzels. Eitan whispered to her, "Your dad's here; come and say hello to him." She made her way through the crowds of people, who touched her and kissed her and congratulated her and said, "Mazal tov! Mazal tov! You're great! Way to go!" and she thought about Eitan, who had driven several hours earlier to pick up her dad from his house. He had escorted him down the seventeen steps, with the natural patience she herself never had, especially lately, when her father had begun having dizzy spells and sometimes rocked on his feet when they walked down the street together, falling and fearfully grabbing hold of her arm. Although he was very thin and light, he transferred a huge weight into her body as he grasped her, as well as sadness, which was replaced by anger that melted into compassion. With him gripping her arm she imagined a kitten clinging to her sweater, because there was something kittenish about her father and his touch was fragile, and when they stood like that she tried to picture herself rocking that way, one day, on some street, and wondered whose arm her fingers would grasp, and both hated herself ahead of time for the burden she would be and feared she would have no one to burden. During those moments when she steadied her father on his feet and said, "Oops!" with a kind of artificial cheerfulness, in a tone reserved for babies learning to walk, or when she said, "Let's rest for a moment," and watched him standing on the sidewalk, staring ahead, his fingers loosening their grip on her arm—during those moments she did not yet know that these terrible scenes would one day seem even more terrible when, in the evening in the kitchen, or in front of the TV, or in bed, she would have no one to report them to.

She looked at her father sitting behind the speaker and imagined Eitan opening the car door for him and gently helping him in, fastening his seat belt and driving carefully, looking for a radio station appropriate for the journey, constantly trying to strike up a conversation with her father, whose hat—which he wore in winter and summer, because his head was always cold—was squashed against the Fiat Uno's roof and who had no idea where he was going.

They had arrived first, and Eitan had sat him behind the speaker so the dancers wouldn't step over him. He went to the bar and came back with the beer and pretzels, although her father didn't drink and at that time had also lost his appetite. He put the refreshments down on the floor and said, "It's here, Mr. Klein. See?" Her father nodded without looking and mumbled thank-you-very-much, and then people started to arrive, and Eitan expertly maneuvered between them and the old man, who only a few months previously, when he was still capable of liking anyone, had liked Eitan very much and asked why they didn't get married. (Shira had said there was still time, and Eitan had said everything would be okay.)

Her publisher and her editor were also there, and they came over to her as she knelt by her father, shouting something in his ear. She stood up and shook their hands and they each gave her an awkward embrace. "This is my father," she said. The two men, who were both around fifty, shook his hand ceremoniously, and the publisher said, "Well, so what do you think of Shira?" Her father looked at him vacantly and said thank you, and the editor smiled embarrassedly and stared at the floor. Shira bent over and said, "Dad, this is Eli Davidoff, my publisher, and this is Reuben Tamari; he's the one who edited the book. You remember I told you about them?" Her father held his hand out to be shaken, and the publisher and the editor shook it again, and the three of them stood there silently, the publisher moving to the sounds of the music and Shira staring down at the cup and the plastic plate, which looked as if they had been placed there for a dog or a cat, until Eitan came over, sweating and laughing and dragging two teenage girls behind him whom Shira did not recognize. They asked her to sign the book they had just bought at the bar with a 50 percent discount. One of the girls gave her the book to sign while she held her change in her other hand, and Shira asked if she had a pen. The girl said she didn't, and apologized and said she felt bad. Eitan dug through his pockets, and the other girl said, "Whoa, what a nuisance," and the publisher and the editor also looked through their pockets for a pen and couldn't find one. The first girl said, "No big deal, then," but Shira turned around and leaned down to her father and gently pulled out the Parker he always kept in the coat pocket of his brown jacket. The girls stood dancing in their spots, waiting for their inscription. Shira asked for their names, and when they told her she wanted to ask who they were and how they had even ended up here, but she wrote on the inside jacket, *For Noga and Meital, with much love from Shira, and may you have a beautiful life.* They thanked her excitedly and disappeared into the crowd, and Eitan held her arm and said something, but the noise drowned out his voice. Shira yelled, "What?" He leaned over and shouted into her ear, "Those are your first buyers!" Shira said, "No. You're my first buyer," but Eitan couldn't hear her and yelled, "What?" Shira said, "Never mind," and followed him to the dance floor.

Eitan had bought a hundred books at full price and sold them at half price. She tried to figure out how much it must have cost him, how much money he had lost, and in the smoke and darkness she suddenly noticed a cardboard sign hanging behind the bar: SHIRA KLEIN'S BOOK WEEK. All around her, people she didn't know were dancing and smiling at her, and some of them held books in their hands and waved them at her as if they were part of the dance. She smiled back at them and suddenly felt closer to her father, who sat staring into the darkness, than to the man who loved her in a way that always made her love him less.

(5)

They had met on a blind date. Shira's upstairs neighbor, Dalit, who would occasionally invite her to the student apartment she shared with two roommates, and who was bothered by the fact that Shira didn't have a boyfriend—she herself was planning to move in with the guy she had been dating since her army service—set her up with him. "Why can't you go out with someone who isn't an intellectual for once? Try it, just for fun," she pleaded with Shira one evening, when they were drinking coffee in her room. They were sitting on a mattress on the floor covered with dozens of dolls and stuffed animals, which Shira found both charming and alarming.

"Okay," Shira replied feebly, "but he has to be smart."

"Of course he's smart. Would I set you up with a dumb guy?"

"But he's not brilliant, is that what you're saying?" Shira could already taste the rejection, and it was not as sweet as it had been when she was younger. But not bitter either, just bland.

"He doesn't read philosophy."

"Me neither, but does he read books?"

"I don't know what he reads, I've never asked him."

"But you've been to his house; have you ever looked at his bookshelves?"

"No, but he has books. I'm sure I've seen a few books there."

Eitan suggested they meet at his place. He was sick of cafés and pubs, he said, adding, "But if you're uncomfortable with that, we can meet wherever you like." She wondered if he was a cheapskate but agreed, and just to be safe she arranged for them to meet on a Saturday afternoon, before dark, so the meeting wouldn't have any romantic undertones.

When he opened the door for her, she saw the snacks he had prepared on the coffee table in the living room: a dish of sweet pastries, a plate of *borekas,* a bowl of cashews and pistachios, two bottles of beer, and a bottle of white wine, still sweating from the fridge. He said he didn't know what she liked; there was also some orange juice. The coffee table was so loaded with good intentions that for a moment it seemed as if it were all these refreshments that had been waiting for her rather than Eitan, who stood next to her shyly and asked her to sit down. She was already imagining this man, who had pretty eyes and strange hair, rushing to the store after their phone conversation and buying food for the date, along with the weekend newspapers that were arranged in a pile on the floor, and she hated herself because, instead of enjoying the refreshments laid out on the table for her, she was seeing her host buying them, and it was not him she was seeing but his endeavor, as if it were a separate human being—one she didn't like.

She sat down on the couch and put her bag on the floor. He asked what she wanted to drink and she asked for coffee; she regretted it immediately—the other drinks waiting on the table looked suddenly abandoned. She said she would actually like some beer instead, but Eitan said he'd be happy to make her some coffee, and he was going to make some for himself anyway. He said there was instant and Turkish, and she said instant would be great, and he asked if she preferred a mug or a cup, and she said it didn't matter. He went into the kitchen and emerged a few seconds later, asking, "Are you sure? Because some people have preferences." She said that as far as coffee was concerned, she had none, but to make things easier for him, she said, "I'll have a cup." He went back into the kitchen and came out carrying a tray with two cups of coffee and a little dish with flower-shaped biscuits with jam filling, covered with powdered sugar, which reminded her of her childhood and made her smile.

"What is it?" he asked.

"Nothing. I used to love those biscuits when I was little."

Eitan looked at them worriedly. "I don't know why I bought them. They just looked good. There are other things if you feel like it."

Shira leaned over and took a biscuit. "No, I love these."

She ate two biscuits and sipped her coffee, and he asked if it was all right, and she said it was great and could she smoke. He said he didn't smoke but it didn't bother him, and he looked a little disappointed. He went into the kitchen again and came back with a huge glass ashtray that looked like crystal. The ashtray must have belonged to someone else, perhaps the previous tenants, perhaps his parents, much like the old china cabinet in the living room; behind its glass doors Shira noticed a set of the *Encyclopedia Hebraica* and a book of photographs from the Six-Day War.

Eitan sat down opposite her on an old armchair, leaned forward, and took a biscuit. He held it gingerly between his fingers, and when he put his hand down on his knee a little cloud of powdered sugar scattered over his jeans.

He was thirty-four, four years older than Shira. He was a computer programmer and was very excited, he told her, when their common friend had told him Shira was a writer. He had always admired creative people, he said, and had always wanted to write. Shira asked why he didn't, and he said it probably wasn't enough of a burning passion with him, and besides, he had no talent. Shira asked how he knew that if he'd never written; she could already feel the first tinglings of the aggression she sprayed like tear gas in the faces of men she found either very smart or not smart enough. Eitan replied, "I just know."

"I haven't really written yet either," Shira said.

"But you will," he asserted. When she asked how he knew, he said again, "I just know," and he really did, in much the way that he turned out to know other things about her. Two weeks later, when they slept together for the first time, he knew what she liked and that she was surprised because she was expecting it to be bad. And in the morning he knew to tell her, "I know I'm not your type," and he knew it would make her look at him differently, because there is something winning, even for a moment, about someone who amazes you in bed at night and in the morning tells you he knows he's not your type. He knew everything he needed to in order to form a relationship and stay in it long enough to gather more knowledge, but he never managed to compile all that knowledge even into the frame of a puzzle, while to Shira it seemed she had finished his entire puzzle within seconds. The more he tried, straining with loving violence to force the wrong pieces together, the more he hurt them both.

But that Saturday afternoon, among the overwrought refreshments and the restrained conversation, something normal developed between them.

Eitan told her about his old girlfriend, who had left him two years ago and got married in the meantime. "And how about you?" he asked. He was referring to her past, and she didn't know what to say, because she knew her past wouldn't be a past until someone became her present. For five years now, since she started studying at the university, she had been having an affair with a guy who was having three such affairs at the same time. Idan had studied history and was already a lecturer now and kept complaining that he didn't want an academic career. He was good-looking and brilliant and awful in bed. Every time he slept with her he led her to understand it was the last time—not just with her but with them all, all the other women whose existence he never hid from her. He told her about his other women as if she were a disinterested party—as if he himself were a disinterested party. He was sick of everyone wanting something from him, even sex, because there was no warmth to speak of. "I'm a cold person," he claimed. His love of himself was enough for him, until he felt like celebrating something or needed consolation, two situations that were identical for him. Then he would phone Shira, or Ravit, who was an eighteen-year-old dancer, or Karin, a married pediatrician, and say, "I'm depressed." Then he would ask, "So, what are you doing tonight?" Shira didn't know what the other women said, but she always

replied, "Nothing." She assumed Ravit worshiped him and that he himself was in love with Karin, and from what he told her she knew that the
dancer played hard to get, and the doctor was unavailable anyway, and
she didn't know exactly who she was in this quadrangle, which seemed
more like a pyramid to her, with her at the bottom. When she asked herself what she saw in Idan and what the other two saw in him, she had no
answer. She knew, in fact, that the question itself was irrelevant; there are
those, like Idan, who tend to take and accumulate—loves and crises,
homemade dramas, and people like her—and there are those, like her,
who tend to give and lose in silence.

Even now, as she sat with Eitan, who kept holding the biscuit
between his fingers and looking as if he had forgotten about it or perhaps
regretted taking it, sensing that if it crumbled, their entire afternoon
would disintegrate, Shira felt she wanted to lose him. The generous
refreshments and the perfect hosting seemed suddenly like an attempt to
distract her from what he was incapable of giving, and she was impatient
to get home and phone Idan and ask how things were and hear him complain that he was busy. "I'm beat," he would say, as he always did when
he didn't want to see her. "How are you?" he'd ask, and she'd say she
was fine and would be about to ask him if he wanted to go see a movie,
but he would quickly say, "So listen, let's talk later, I have to make some
calls. What are you doing tonight?" She would say, Nothing, and he
would say, "Aren't you writing?" She would say she wasn't and would
ask, "So what are *you* doing tonight?" He would say he didn't know; he
might watch TV or read some articles or maybe go to sleep early because
he was exhausted. She would ask if he wanted to meet, and at that second Idan would have a call on the other line, and even if he didn't there
would be the air of a bothersome third party between them, and he'd say,
So we'll talk later, but they wouldn't.

Idan always pretended to be interested in her writing; when they met,
he made her swear she'd let him be her first reader. When she gave him a
few pages she'd written, he left them sealed in an envelope on the backseat
of his car. A few months later, on the way to a party, she leaned over and
took the envelope and said, "I'm taking this back, 'cause I've changed
everything now." He had said okay and asked if she had a cigarette.

Eitan asked what she was thinking about and she said, "Nothing."

"You look as if you're someplace else."

She smiled. "No, I'm completely here."

"It's embarrassing, these dates."

"Yes, kind of." She thought about other blind dates she'd had, and about a few one-night stands, and about Idan, and they all seemed like a terrible discord in her life—or perhaps not discord, she now thought, but part of her routine, like this afternoon.

Eitan looked at her as she floated away from him on the couch, and when she took another cigarette out he quickly leaned over, took her lighter, and lit it for her. She smiled and thanked him and imagined what he would be like in bed. He asked if she wanted some more coffee, and she said, "Why not?" even though she was already planning to leave. He got up and went into the kitchen, happy to have a task, and she looked at the clumsy ashtray and thought: He'll be bad. She heard a glass shatter in the kitchen, and Eitan hurried through the living room to the balcony to get a broom and dustpan. She asked if she could help, and he said he was used to it, he was always breaking things; not a day went by when he didn't break something. He went back into the kitchen. She got up and followed him and he said, "Don't worry about it," but she stood in the doorway and watched him sweep up the fragments and gather them into the dustpan with one expert sweep. When he bent down, his shirt climbed up and she looked at the small of his back. He had a nice skin tone. She said she also broke things all the time. As he knelt, he looked at her standing at the door, smoking, and said, "You don't look like you do," and now in his voice there was something less effortful. She asked what someone who broke things looked like, and he said, "I don't know, maybe more clumsy." She was flattered because she *was* clumsy and broke things all the time. She thought about Idan; although she had been sleeping with him for five years with a regularity dictated by him, she had never seen him break anything. They were always in the living room in front of the TV or in bed; the kitchen did not exist in Idan's life, and the kitchen was her favorite place.

She examined Eitan's kitchen, which was long and narrow. It had a little table with two folding chairs, and on the table was a white tablecloth with a print of two black dogs, and salt and pepper shakers, utility bills, and crumbs. The old cabinets were painted yellow and blue, and there was a half-covered pot on the stove with a ladle sticking out. Eitan filled the kettle and took another cup out of the cabinet, and Shira asked what was in the pot.

"Chicken soup. Are you hungry?" She said she wasn't, but she was always curious about what people were eating, and he said he was too. "I always think everyone else is eating better food than I am." She said, Me too, and suddenly they had something in common. She wondered if he was also constantly hungry like she was, and she went over to the pot and lifted the lid and peeked in. Eitan said, "It came out pretty well." She asked who made it, and he leaned on the counter and said, "I did. Are you sure you don't want any? I've got some crackers as well." His voice now had a tone of seduction, and Shira smiled and said she'd like some crackers, without any soup, and Eitan took a glass jar out of one of the cabinets. He opened it with a pop and gave it to her, and she took a handful. He put the jar on the counter and said, "Take as many as you want. I have more." He threw a cracker into his mouth, and when the water had boiled he made her some coffee. She leaned against the counter and ate one after another of the crackers, watched him go to the fridge and lean down to get the milk, pour it into the glass, put it back into the fridge, throw the teaspoon into the sink, and turn around, holding the glass, ready to go back into the living room. But she didn't want to go back, she wanted to stay in the kitchen—she no longer saw effort but just the movements of his body, and she was attracted to him. There was something so clean about him, as if he had just come out of the shower, unlike Idan, who reeked of cigarettes and smoke. She suddenly noticed the biscuit lying on the edge of the counter, and she was happy for him because he'd finally managed to get rid of it, and she said maybe she would try a little soup after all.

(6)

After they broke up, Eitan would call her every so often and ask that they meet and talk. She usually refused, saying it wasn't a good idea to reopen wounds that hadn't yet healed; she meant his wounds, because she herself did not feel wounded at the time. Sometimes, when he insisted, she agreed, and he would turn up at the new apartment she'd rented on Borochov Street.

They talked about the good reviews her book got, and Eitan said how happy he was for her and asked if she felt different now that she had accomplished what she'd always wanted. She said she didn't, that she probably still hadn't grasped the accomplishment, and that perhaps in fact there *was* no accomplishment. He said he understood her, that the truly great and critical things in life were difficult to grasp; he meant their separation. They sat in a kitchen where they both felt alien, and she thought Eitan looked strange in her new landscape, like a beloved armchair or bureau that suddenly seems smaller in a different space.

During the first weeks after the breakup, they had a few sexual encounters that were full of guilt and blame, and in the mornings Eitan would get up and leave with a look on his face that said he could not understand why he had to go. On every morning they both wondered, separately, how to say goodbye: with the kind of kiss they had at night, or with a little kiss of the kind the morning dictated, or perhaps a symbolic caress, because a handshake was out of the question. All this made the doorway partings a sad circus, with Eitan leaning in to her face and kissing the cheek turned to his lips, or Shira embracing him as he stood frozen, his arms at his sides between hers, and the second he acceded and lifted his hands to hold her face he encountered an elbow accidentally raised. This went on until the great separation abruptly swallowed up all the little ones, and Eitan stopped calling.

The novel was the kind of love story she wished she could have. A man and a woman meet one night in the ER, after being injured in separate motor accidents. They both have only scratches and bruises, but as they wait for hours for a doctor to examine them, they have a long slow conversation—a DNA conversation, she called it, like two children showing each other cards from some collection and discovering they both have the same ones.

She started writing the book when she and Eitan moved in together. It happened quietly, without warning: One morning, after having their coffee in the kitchen, Eitan kissed her, promised to cook dinner, and left for work, and Shira sat down at the computer and started to write. It happened the next morning too, and the next day, and went on for three years, with a continuity and naturalness that seemed strange and even slightly disappointing after so many years of planning. She had always pictured the moment it would occur as a dramatic instant of shock, but the writing was not dramatic or shocking—it did not change her life but simply became a part of it, shirking the great responsibility with which it had been saddled.

Every morning, after he went to work, she felt she was betraying Eitan, because the story she was writing was about her but not about him. When she gave it to him to read—he always waited impatiently for pages each time she finished a chapter—he was impressed by her writing and sometimes, in bed, before he fell asleep, he hugged her and said he liked her characters, that they reminded him of her and himself.

They lived in an apartment with two bedrooms, one of which was her study. Every so often she worked on translations she was given, but most of the time she wrote, riding a long wave of lack of sensations, which was sometimes pleasant and sometimes scared her. Eitan worked twelve-hour days at an IT company in Herzliya, and when he came home he sprawled on the couch and asked her to come and sit with him and tell him what she'd done all day and how her work was progressing. She told him, but in her mind she always conducted other dialogues, more interesting ones, with a different man whom she didn't know. When she finished writing, she realized that the novel was, in some ways, her farewell letter to Eitan.

The confidence she had then that she'd done the right thing— confidence she now thought she'd never again have about anything—was the fuel that drove her in the months following the breakup. She was busy with the novel and its success: she gave interviews to the press, made occasional appearances on TV, and closely followed her book's position on the bestseller list. One day, a few days after her thirty-third birthday, which passed without the little gifts Eitan used to scatter around the apartment to stretch her birthday out over a whole week, her book climbed to first place.

She walked around the apartment holding the newspaper, until her happiness turned to paralysis, then to disturbance. The phone rang and Rona was on the line to congratulate her, and Shira heard Tamar shouting in the background, "Mazal tov! Tell her mazal tov from me!"

Rona said, "Can you hear your fan?"

"Yes, tell her thanks."

The seven-year-old Tamar grabbed the phone from her mother and said, "Please accept my happiness."

Shira smiled. "You say, 'Please accept my condolences.'"

"What do you say when you're happy?"

"'I'm happy for you.'"

"Then I'm happy for you," Tamar said. "So when are you coming over? You probably won't come anymore. You'll probably be busy with guys, now that you're so famous."

Rona took the phone back and said, "We really are so happy for you."

She pictured them sitting at the kitchen table, across from each other, the girl swinging her legs, her mother perusing the literature supplement, scanning the bestseller list as she ate, with the radio and the TV on in the living room, blurring the National Geographic Channel or the kids' station together with the Voice of Music. It was an impossible and yet reassuring combination, the music of home. She imagined them eating a light dinner, maybe an omelet and salad and cream cheese—things that always taste so good at other people's houses—without it occurring to them to invite her to join them, certain that their home was the last place she would want to celebrate her moment of glory.

Regretting it already, she phoned Eitan. He was surprised to hear her voice, even a little alarmed. She asked if he'd seen *Ha'aretz* today and he said he hadn't had time yet. "Guess what?" she said, as if months had not passed since they last spoke.

"What?" he asked. She told him that the novel had landed in first place. "Mazal tov!" he said with a grand voice. "Wow, I'm so happy for you!" and in the background she heard someone asking who he was talking to.

"Do you have someone over?" she asked. "Am I interrupting something?"

"No, not at all," he replied. She heard the voice again, getting closer and breathing into the phone. "Why mazal tov? Did someone have a baby?" Eitan said, "I'll tell you in a minute."

"Well, I just wanted to let you know," Shira said. "I thought you'd like to know."

When the other voice wafted away, Eitan asked softly, "Are you all right? Is everything okay?"

"Everything's fine," she replied, more excited than she thought she would be. "I thought maybe you'd like to go out to celebrate together."

After a long silence, Eitan said, "I'd be happy to go out for a drink sometime. I'd really like to, but I'm living with someone now."

"I understand."

"Wow, I'm embarrassed."

"Don't be."

"We've been together for almost two months. We just moved in together this week."

"She moved in with you?"

"Yeah. There's more room here. You've never been to my new apartment, have you?"

"No. What does she do?" she asked, because an interview seemed like the least painful type of conversation.

"Who, Ayelet?"

"Yes. Ayelet."

"She's finishing up a master's in psychology."

"Sounds good."

She wanted to ask him what she looked like, but Eitan said, "So listen, I'm really happy for you. Honestly. I'm really proud of you. I'll go and have a look in the newspaper, I hope Ayelet bought one." Shira said it wasn't that important, and Eitan said it was. "Ayelet!" she heard him yell. "Do we have *Ha'aretz*?" *What?* she heard a voice from the other room. "*Ha'aretz!*" he repeated.

"Never mind, Eitan, it doesn't matter."

"I'm sure we have it, but worse comes to worst we'll get it from someone." He promised to call soon so they could go out and celebrate, the three of them. "She liked your book a lot," he said.

"Really?"

"Yeah. She even bought it as a gift for someone."

"Wow." She didn't know what else to say.

"So lots of best wishes. And hugs."

"To you too."

"What for?"

"For the apartment, for Ayelet, for everything."

He thanked her and said, "So we really should go out someday, the three of us. Ayelet would really like that. She's doing exams now, so we're not going out much."

"Okay, we'll be in touch, then."

He said he was happy for her again and when she put the phone down she felt an urgent need to go out; she folded the paper up and put it in her bag and walked to her father's.

(7)

Up until a few years ago, her father had owned a small architectural firm that carried on practically by force of inertia. The two young architects who worked for him were always encouraging him to computerize the office, to modernize, to bid on large contracts, but her father kept working with a couple of old contractors who gave him little projects that made the office archaic and superfluous and depressed and bored the two young men. A short while after her mother died, they resigned and left her father alone in his huge office, in an old building on Yavneh Street.

When she was little, Shira liked to stare at the geometrical patterns on the office floor tiles, which had a hypnotizing power. Or she would sit on the deep windowsill and look out onto Allenby Street, which always fascinated her and which she still loved; something in its madness and filth reassured her. A few times a week, when her mother went to her courses or to the pool and left her with her dad in the office, they would go down together and sit at a café whose name she could not remember. At the time it struck her as a very brown place, with four Formica-topped tables that looked scratched, although her father said that was just their pattern. There were silver-colored ashtrays and a counter with an espresso machine, behind which stood a woman with gray hair and bitter brown eyes. Her father would order a Lungo and soda water, and Shira drank chocolate milk and ate napoleons.

She remembered how her father would try to engage her in conversation, taking an interest in what happened at school and who her friends were. She always gave him the same reports, spreading a wide net of little details, sometimes negligible ones, designed to prevent the penetration of silence. She knew he wasn't listening, even though he looked as if he were, because she recognized in him a lack of concentration—a combination of anxiety and contemplation—that resembled her own lack of concentration at school and with her friends, one she had learned, over time, to camouflage beneath a serious mask of attention.

She thought that if she could find a way to engage him, she would be able to rescue him from his usual condition, the one her mother so hated and which, she claimed when they fought, was destructive and morbid and harmful, mainly for the child. Shira envied her mother for being able to hate his condition so much without feeling guilty. To her, the condition was part of who her father was; it was one of his limbs, like the brown jacket he always wore, and his hat, and the clean handkerchief he kept in his trousers pocket, and the little pair of scissors he used to cut his fingernails when he sat at his drafting table, and the checkbook whose register he always filled out meticulously, and his reading glasses. To hate his condition, she thought, would be to hate him.

Her father liked Allenby Street too. He always had errands to run there—banks, stationery stores, a tailor he visited every few months—and when she accompanied him to these places she spent an hour or two with a different father: busy, energetic, sometimes almost happy. When he retired, his restlessness turned to apathy. He spent his days at home, sitting on an armchair on the balcony that overlooked the street, listening to the morning shows and the hourly news on the radio with great anticipation, as if he were expecting to hear some message for himself in the broadcast. On rainy days he sat in the living room and watched TV, and after the late-night news he dragged himself to the bedroom, took off the robe he wore all day over his clothes, put on the pajamas he kept folded beneath his pillow, made sure several times he had locked the doors properly, left a light on in the hallway, and went to sleep.

When Eitan started coming with her to see her father, the trips almost seemed like normal visits children make to healthy parents. There was no pity, and above all they did not have the alarm that arose in her every time she saw how from day to day her father was becoming a kind of sideways-walking crab; it was unclear whether he was retreating or advancing. Eitan did not see these mental zigzags, and everything that bothered her about his approach to her became a kind of solace regarding her father. Eitan, with his practicality, was like a great wave that erased the marks her father left in the sand.

Each time they visited, Eitan would fix a broken blind or a leaking tap or do some other odd job. Her father looked very pleased when he stood next to Eitan, who was a head taller, and handed him a hammer or screwdriver, or when he walked him to the fuse box in the stairwell. When Eitan had finished the repair jobs, the three of them would sit and watch TV, her father in his armchair, Eitan alongside her on the couch, and everything seemed very normal. Sometimes they even ate dinner together, and her father seemed to enjoy the food. Later, while she washed the dishes, she listened to their conversation in the living room, which kept coming back to the topic of computers; Eitan tried to explain the basic concepts to her father, but he never understood. From the kitchen, she listened to their voices: Eitan's was confident and calm while her father's voice, despite the hoarse roughness of old age, sounded suddenly clear and curious. At those moments she felt as if they were almost those other people she had wanted to be when she was a girl—they were almost the same as everyone: a man and a woman and a father, who was their child.

(8)

Eitan's parents were in their fifties and had young names: Oded and Leora. They lived on a kibbutz in the south. They were lively and energetic people who went on organized nature hikes on Saturdays and every so often came to visit Tel Aviv, bringing Shira and Eitan crates full of fruits and vegetables; they always remembered to bring a little parcel for Shira's father too.

Once Shira and Eitan took her father to Eitan's parents' kibbutz for Passover. He didn't ask where he was going, and he sat in the car the entire way humming songs that might have been his own inventions or distorted versions of old tunes he liked. He kept humming to himself as they sat down for the seder meal, and when his turn came to read from the Haggadah, Eitan, who was sitting to his right, pointed at the lines in the book for him, but he had forgotten to bring his reading glasses and Eitan read the paragraph instead, as her father sat staring ahead, crumbling a piece of matzo. She watched Eitan's parents as they gave her father warm glances, and she looked at all the other people she didn't know, sitting at the long table with their children and grandchildren, and she envied Eitan's parents for having this place to grow old in, although they seemed to have no intention of growing old. For a moment she wanted to rush over to her father, put a sticker on his lapel that said MAX KLEIN: AVAILABLE FOR ADOPTION, kiss his cheek, and abandon him there.

At night, after Eitan's parents walked them to the guesthouse where they were staying, she sat outside on the front porch, smoking a cigarette, and let Eitan help her father put his pajamas on and get into the little cot, as if he were putting a doll to bed. She did not yet know how much she would miss this moment and how she would miss the two of them: her father, a minute before his depression metastasized to his internal organs, and Eitan, who came out to the porch and leaned over her and hugged her shoulders and said her father was asleep and asked if she wasn't cold.

They broke up a few months later, in August, and at first she didn't know what she would tell her father when he asked where Eitan was and why he didn't come around anymore. But her father, who had started falling asleep in his clothes in the living room armchair, with the radio and the TV and all the lights turned on, didn't ask.

That evening, when she arrived at her father's apartment with the bestseller list, she found him lying on the floor in the hallway that led from the living room to the bedroom. She didn't know how long he'd been lying there, and when he saw her standing over him shouting "Dad!" he looked at her gratefully. She helped him up carefully and walked him to his armchair, next to which, on a little table, was a cup of coffee that was still hot. He sat down heavily, his flannel robe falling open to expose a pajama top soiled with fresh food and coffee stains and some older, more faded spots—as if the top were snitching on her father, as if it were the true mirror of his life.

She tried to find out what had happened, how he had fallen, but her father couldn't explain it. "Did you get up to go to the bathroom?" she asked, and he nodded, still grasping her hand, his palm transmitting alternating currents of old age and childhood, both his and hers. "But how did you fall?" she asked. "I fell," he said. She realized there was no point in interrogating him, and since her father seemed indifferent, she concluded it was not the first time it had happened.

She sat at his feet on the rug, still holding the folded newspaper, and asked how many times he had fallen. For a moment he looked as if he were concentrating on the question, but then he repeated, "I fell," and looked down at the newspaper. "You brought the paper?" he asked, as if he had forgotten that a moment before he was lying on the floor in a fetal position, and asked her to bring his reading glasses from his bedside table.

She brought his glasses—they were old-fashioned ones, with square brown plastic frames—and he glanced at his watch and said the news was on soon. "Yes," she said distractedly and went back into the hallway, still trying to figure out what had happened and whether there was an obstacle of some sort there. But apart from a crumpled pink tissue that had fallen out of his pocket, she found nothing.

She went into the kitchen, opened the fridge, and threw out everything that had accumulated since her last visit, a few days earlier. There was a blackened avocado with only one wedge missing; a glass dish with a mound of yellowish rice and lentils, which her father would sometimes make from a packet; one apple that still looked all right; a carton of eggs; and a little container of low-fat UHT milk. She went back into the living room and found her father immersed in the paper, reading the headlines, with the literary supplement tossed on the rug at his feet. She asked if he'd eaten and her father nodded.

"What did you have?" she asked.

Without looking up, he answered, "Some yogurt and a pear."

"My book made the first place in the bestseller list," she said, with the same dryness with which he had previously said, *I fell.*

He looked at her happily for a moment, but still slightly perplexed and lost. "Really?"

"Yes. Today. Here it is." She pointed to the supplement.

"Well done," he said. He stared at the TV screen and the news anchor and asked her to turn the volume up. She asked if he was sure he didn't want anything to eat—she could make him an omelet—and he shook his head and took off his glasses and put them in his lap. She took the literary supplement and put it in her bag and took out her cigarettes and lighter and sat on the couch smoking, watching the news with her father.

"It's not good to smoke," he said.

"I know."

As they watched the news, he mumbled every so often, "Well done, really, well done." Just before the weather forecast, he fell asleep.

She was afraid to leave him sleeping, worried that when he woke up, still sleepy, he would forget about the dizzy spells and the instability and leap out of the armchair as if he were a healthy man but collapse after a few steps like a wind-up toy.

She watched a talk show—she didn't have anything to do at home anyway—but she was restless and wanted to leave. She looked at him sleeping. His head drooped forward onto his chest, he snored slightly and looked very tranquil, and she wondered if he was miserable in his sleep too, or if sleep was a time of grace for him. When she was little, she sometimes used to hear him walking around the house in the middle of the night, turning taps on and off, coughing, rustling the newspaper. In her half-awake state she had wanted to get up and join him on his nocturnal journeys, but she always fell back asleep, and her sleep was full of his insomnia.

Her father woke up suddenly. His head snapped up, his eyes looked frightened for a moment, as if he didn't know where he was, but they emptied out instantly. He glanced at his watch instinctively, then saw her sitting on the couch smoking and asked if she hadn't just smoked a cigarette. She said, "Did you sleep a little?"

"A little."

She asked if he felt well, if he wanted her to help him into bed. She pictured the day when he wouldn't be able to live on his own anymore and wondered whether they were both denying that the day was already here.

Her father yawned and said, "Shiraleh."

"What?"

"Well done," he said, and put his hands on his reading glasses and said he would watch TV for a while longer and then go to sleep, and she should leave the paper for him.

On the way home she stopped at a pay phone and called Rona, hoping she would sense the distress in her voice and invite her over, but the babysitter answered and said Rona had gone to a seminar and would be back late. She went home and got into bed and, surprisingly, fell asleep immediately, but she woke up again a little after midnight and sat up in bed. Three new facts flickered in the dark: Eitan would not be coming back, her father was slowly dying, and her book was a success.

(9)

She rang the bell at Rona's apartment at exactly eight o'clock. The bell, followed by the sound of little feet running and Tamar's singsong voice, "Come in! Come in!" on the other side of the door—the way kids used to call out "Come out, come out, wherever you are!" when they played hide-and-seek—and finally the quiet turning of the lock aroused her from what suddenly seemed like a very long and exhausting journey. All at once she felt the cold stabbing her cheeks and ears, and the moisture in her hair, and the heaviness of the plastic bag with the wine and ice cream, its handles wrapped around her fingers. It was one of the longest short walks she had even taken, and although she had still arrived on time, she was relieved that the voyage was over.

Tamar took the plastic bag and jumped with joy when she saw the ice cream. Shira saw Dana, Tamar's friend, leafing through a cookbook. She asked Dana how she was, and the girl looked up and smiled and said okay. Shira asked if she was learning to cook, and Dana nodded and went back to looking at the book. She went and looked over her shoulder at a photograph of a filet mignon in cream sauce with fresh asparagus, and said, "That looks delicious!"

Rona said, "What does?"

"The steaks," Shira said.

"My dad makes ones exactly like these," Dana said.

"He does?" Shira exclaimed, and the girl nodded again and flipped to the next page.

Shira sat down at the round table. Nothing looked ready yet. Rona took a large cut of meat on a tray out of the fridge. "Veal. I'm making stuffed veal." Tamar turned her nose up.

"What's the matter? Don't you like veal?" Shira asked.

"I hate it."

Dana said, "I like it, actually."

"You should learn something from your friend, little princess," Rona told her daughter.

"I'm not a princess. I'm allowed to develop my own taste in food, aren't I? You're always encouraging me not to be like you the whole time. Well, then, here I'm not like you."

"Whoa!" said Rona, as she rubbed the meat with butter. "Will you listen to that? I've created a monster!"

Tamar hugged her mother around the waist and tickled her. "*You're* a monster!"

"From now on, you'll eat nothing but falafel," Rona said, concentrating on the wine she was measuring into the pot.

Tamar kept holding on to her mother's hips. "Yuck!"

"Don't tell me you hate falafel too?" Shira exclaimed. Tamar nodded excitedly, and Shira looked at Dana, who was now standing in the corner holding a garlic press. "You too?"

"No, I like it."

Tamar said, "She's like a dog. She eats everything."

Shira looked at the two girls. Tamar was very thin, dark-skinned with smooth black hair, and Dana was fair, with brown wavy hair, hazel eyes, and a roundish body. She reminded Shira of herself, especially in her lack of pickiness about food, something that always touched her in children, while in adults it seemed like a delayed reaction to some kind of orphanhood.

Tamar started making barking noises and biting her mother's back lightly, and Rona squirmed a little but stayed focused on measuring the ingredients. "Think twice before you have children," she told Shira.

"Yes, think three times; otherwise you might get one like me!" Tamar said.

Rona asked where the garlic press was, and Dana gave it to her and sat down at the table and opened the *Ha'aretz* supplement to the crossword page. Shira asked, "Do you like crosswords?"

"My dad does," the girl said.

"Arik and Ruti are coming," Rona said. "You haven't met them yet, have you?"

"No." She had heard about them from Rona and although, like her, they often came for dinner, she hadn't met them. "Who else is coming?"

"No one. Tonight we'll be a small party."

"Yes, we don't have a date for you today," Tamar said, and burst out laughing.

"Thank God." She was happy but also somewhat disappointed, because although she had never liked the blind dates Rona sometimes invited for her, there was something appealing about this brief period of sitting at the table anticipating the new man: the ring at the door, his entry. The expectation always filled her with the adrenaline of optimism, but as soon as the guest recognized the role he had been cast in, he would either reject it—deliberately talking more with the other guests and with Tamar than with her—or else delve into it with desperate enthusiasm, staring at her all evening, pouring her wine, and lighting her cigarettes, and the adrenaline of expectation would turn into a cynical heaviness. As she walked home on those evenings through the park, without lingering, she would sense her body mocking not only the candidate and the entire candidacy but itself too, as she dragged it along the path, listening to its rapid breaths, a few centimeters shorter than when the evening began, a little fatter, compressed.

When she reached home after these dinners, she felt she needed compensation, or at least a form of repair: so much hope and desperation had been crammed into such a short time—and the transition between the two was so rapid—that she would sit on the couch for a few minutes, staring ahead, trying to reset herself, although nothing had occurred that evening to throw her out of balance; and perhaps that was why she felt this way.

The girls were running around the kitchen now, throwing cherry tomatoes at each other, and Rona turned to them, brandishing her wooden spoon, and said, "You're fired!"

"You can't fire me. I'm your daughter."

"Oh, really? You don't say!"

"I do say!"

Rona grabbed her daughter's shoulders, leaned over her, and rubbed her nose against her cheek. "Well, then, let me tell you the truth, because you're old enough to hear it now. I'm not your mother!"

"Very funny! Who do you think you are then?"

"Who am I?" Rona asked with fake innocence, and it was clear this was part of a regular act.

"Yeah. Who are you?"

Shira looked at Dana, who stood by the fridge watching them expectantly, her mouth slightly open and an amused but slightly troubled look on her face.

"I'll tell you who I am!" Rona said, as she squeezed the girl against her body. "I'm the boss!"

"Yuck, gross! You spat in my ear!" Tamar jumped out of her arms, and Dana ran over to Rona, who was still squatting on her heels, as if she wanted to squeeze her way quickly into the embrace Tamar's body had left vacant, but instead she leaned over, picked up a tomato that had rolled into the corner, and threw it in the trash.

The smell of butter and garlic spread through the room. The Voice of Music was playing a Schubert quartet, and in the living room the TV was tuned to the National Geographic channel with the sound turned off. Shira looked at the girls. They stood beside each other at the counter chopping vegetables and chattering: Dana, the shorter of the two, on a plastic footstool. Then she looked at Rona, who was at the stove with her back to the room, stirring something in a pot. Her movements were slow and precise, like the other things she did in her life—Tamar, for example—and she embodied no haste and no yearning, no incidental relationships, with men or with the world. Her life was full and busy and replete with the troubles of making a living, but it was not frenetic. Rona is a family, Shira thought, and families can't make any sudden movements. She looked at Rona and at the girls and at the huge window, which was steamed over, and for a moment she no longer heard the sounds around her. The kitchen seemed like a kind of air pocket, and she was struck with reverse claustrophobia: the suffocation was on the outside.

PART THREE

1

He sat in the kitchen with the pile of dishes in the sink, the challah peeking out of the bag, and the sections of *Ha'aretz* scattered everywhere, in that domineering manner of weekend newspapers, and reminded himself there was a book review he wanted to read. He looked in the magazine to see what was on TV, although he had promised himself he would really try to write this evening. Then he got up, opened the fridge and peered inside, closed it, sat down again, and regretted having turned down Rona's invitation. He wondered why he had automatically resisted, whether it might be a holdover from his bachelor days, when he was fierce in protecting his wolfish routine. He wondered whether this resistance was still relevant to his life, to the routine that was no longer wolfish but canine, full of worry, restlessness, and a constant hunger.

Rona had said he could make up his mind even at the last minute, he recalled, but it was already nine and the last minute seemed to have passed. He couldn't show up for dinner now without receiving a second, insistent, last-minute invitation, and he made up his mind not to think about it—it was just dinner, after all. He gathered up the newspaper sections and took them into the living room, where he sprawled on the couch and looked for the review he had wanted to read. But when he found it, he wasn't able to concentrate and his thoughts wandered to the literary critic, whose name he recognized but whom he had never met. He tried to imagine what the critic was doing now and whether he was having dinner with his family, because it was clear to him, at least from the tone of his writing, that the critic was a family man. For a moment he thought of himself and wondered what conclusions a stranger might draw upon reading his own writing, and it flattered him to think there might be someone in the world who envied him without knowing him.

He tossed the newspaper onto the rug, picked up the remote control, and switched on the TV, but he turned it off immediately and got up abruptly, almost pulling a muscle in his back, and went to turn the radio on. He meant to go into the kitchen and tear off a piece of challah, spread it with mayonnaise or store-bought hummus or chocolate spread, and then hole up in his study for a few hours and try to write until Dana came home. Then he would ask her how it was and what they ate. But he skipped the kitchen and went straight to his study, where he flipped through his phone book and dialed Rona's number.

Tamar answered the phone, and Yonatan could hear in the background the sounds of dinner: silverware and glasses chinking and lively conversation. He said, "Tamar? It's Yonatan. How's it going?" The girl said, "Okay. So, are you coming over?" She sounded so natural that he almost said yes, but instead he said, "You mean you haven't eaten yet?" She said they hadn't, and he said he needed to ask Dana something. Tamar said she'd call her and added, "So, are you coming? You should, we're having stuffed veal." Not wanting to appear as if he were wangling an invitation out of a little girl, he said, "I don't think it will work out for me tonight, but thanks anyway." During the seconds that passed until his daughter picked up the phone, he listened through the earpiece to the same music playing in his own living room.

When Dana picked up, he asked, "What's up? Aren't you eating yet?" She said they weren't, and he asked if she happened to know where the can opener was; he couldn't find it anywhere. She asked if it wasn't in its regular place in the drawer. "I've looked there," he said. He got up and walked with the phone into the kitchen and said, "Here it is. It was here all the time. I didn't see it before." Dana asked what he was eating, and he said, "We'll see. I haven't decided yet." She asked if he was sure he didn't want to come over—Rona would like it—and he said, "I don't think so. I want to do some work tonight." "Okay then," she said, "don't worry. Rona will walk me home afterward, and it will probably be late because we haven't started eating yet." "So how's Rona?" he asked. "Fine. Do you want to talk to her?" He said, "No, no, there's no need." In the background he heard Rona yell, *Tell him he's still invited!* "Rona says you're still invited," Dana said. Yonatan said, Yes, tell her thanks, another time, and knew he was in trouble; only a direct invitation from Rona could save him now. Dana said, "So you're not coming?" He could see how the dinner that was within reach a moment ago was again becoming unattainable, and he said, "I don't think so." Dana said, "Wait a sec, Dad, Rona wants to talk to you," and Yonatan was flooded with happiness.

"So what do I have to do to convince you to come?" Rona reprimanded him from the other end of the line, and he said he would really love to come, but he had to work a little; he purposely emphasized *a little,* so she would realize this was not a genuine obligation. Rona said, "So what's the problem? Eat and leave; we don't stand on ceremony." And because he was afraid to seem like someone waiting for a last-minute invitation, he said he wasn't all that hungry. He felt like a gambler risking an entire evening's winnings, and Rona said, "So just eat a little." "You really haven't started yet?" "No, but come now. Let's go. We're waiting for you!" And he set the phone down, put on his jacket, and left the house, feeling equally victorious and defeated.

The girls opened the door. They stood on either side of him as he went into the kitchen and told Rona, who was at the stove, stirring something in one of the pots with a long wooden spoon, "I came empty-handed."

"Nonsense," she said. "The main thing is you came."

Yonatan smiled at the people sitting at the round table. Dana took his coat and hung it on a hook in the entryway. Then she stood by the counter and shredded lettuce leaves. Yonatan noticed she was wearing a large apron that was tied around her neck and reached down almost to her ankles. It said SUPER MOM, and he wanted to hug her but was afraid to extract her from the busy happiness that radiated from her as she stood there on a plastic footstool and cautiously tore lettuce leaves into small pieces.

"Yonatan," Rona said, and went up to him and kissed his cheek. "Meet Ruti and Arik, and this is Shira."

The people sitting at the table smiled at him and he said, "Nice to meet you."

Rona said, "This is Dana's father."

Arik said, "Oh! So you're the writer?"

"Guilty as charged," Yonatan answered, and thought that although the phrase he used belonged to a different type of man, not his type, he actually enjoyed being that man for a moment—more pathetic, less sophisticated but far more alive.

Ruti said, "So we have two writers here tonight."

"We do?"

Rona gave him a glass of red wine and said, "This is Shira Klein; she wrote *Accidents*."

"Oh, of course, I know the name, but I haven't read your book." He didn't know why he said that, whether out of a desire to apologize or to jab at her or, as usual with him, some combination of the two.

Shira said she had read his books, and he sat down in one of the empty chairs and Arik said, "We read your first book."

"We really liked it," Ruti said, "but we haven't gotten around to the second one yet. What's it called?"

"*Silence*."

"*Silence?*" Arik repeated.

Yonatan nodded, inexplicably afraid of him.

"And the first one was *Desire,* right?"

"*Passion,*" said Ruti, and Yonatan smiled.

"Passion, desire, what's the difference? They're both the same thing."

"Arik!" Ruti scolded him.

"Well, they are, aren't they? What's the difference?"

"There is a difference, isn't there?" Ruti looked at Yonatan.

"I have no idea," Yonatan said.

"You have no idea about that either? Then how can you write that kind of book?"

"Oh, Arik, really."

"Really what?" he grumbled. "Shouldn't a writer know what he's writing about?"

"There's no rule against inventing," said Ruti.

"Yes, all right, but he should have some basic knowledge, don't you think?"

He looked at Yonatan, and Yonatan—the same Yonatan who had earlier said "Guilty as charged"—said, "You're right; of course you are." From the corner of his eye he saw Shira smiling to herself, or perhaps to him.

"Well, then, we have a lot to read in the near future." Arik sighed and looked at Shira. "We haven't read your book either."

Shira said, "That's all right," and Yonatan looked at her and saw in her eyes the same blend of embarrassment and impatience he knew in himself.

"So what's your book about, traffic?" Arik asked Shira.

Ruti said, "Oh, come on."

"I know, I know, I was just kidding. But really, what's it about?"

"It's hard for me to say," Shira said. Yonatan commended her silently for not answering the question he so hated.

"Come on, give it a try," Arik persisted.

"Yes, give us a little hint," Ruti said, "so we'll know what we're buying."

"It's a little complicated to explain," Shira said. "And you don't have to buy it."

Yonatan hoped she would keep up her resistance, but Rona interfered. "It's a book about relationships."

"Oh, relationships!" Arik said. "That's an important topic."

"Yes," Shira said.

"And a very interesting one. I have a lot to say on that topic."

"Don't we all," Ruti said. "Your book was about relationships too, wasn't it?"

"Yes," Yonatan said, and looked at Shira. She took a pack of cigarettes out of her bag and offered one to Ruti and Arik, who refused, then to Yonatan, who drew one out of the pack. When she leaned toward him with the lighter, he looked briefly into her eyes, which seemed sad and exhausted, although her face looked young, and there was something childish and eager in it, as if she were running through the rain. She suddenly looked familiar to him: he remembered the orange corduroy pants from somewhere, and the leather jacket hanging by the door next to his.

"We've met before," she said.

"Really? When?"

"Monday, in the bread store on King George."

He remembered the woman who had bought the last loaf of onion bread, and what he had told her when she'd said if the bread weren't for her father she would give it up. "Are you sure? When was that? I don't remember."

"You wanted an onion loaf and I had taken the last one, and you were about ready to murder me."

"Really? Was I that bad?"

"And I said I would give it to you if it wasn't for my dad."

Yonatan chuckled and said, "Oh, it was for your dad?"

"Yes, and you said *you* wouldn't have given it to me."

"Way to go," Arik said.

Rona said she was surprised. "Very ungentlemanly of you."

Yonatan said again, "Guilty as charged." After all, the evening had begun with a lie, and now he felt the lies becoming part of the menu and was afraid he would no longer be able to enjoy the meal, because with each bite he would taste a little lie.

Arik said that after the age of forty our brains stop working and we don't remember anything. "I meet people on the street and they talk to me and I have no idea who they are," he said. Yonatan smiled at him but felt embarrassed and turned to look from Shira to Rona, who was stirring the pot and looking at them, smiling to herself. Then he looked at his daughter, who was busy chopping a red onion, sniffling and wiping her eyes on the sleeve of her sweater. He thought of how in a few years she would have him over for dinner at her place; he would find himself calling her up on a Friday evening, hoping she would invite him over so he could spend the evening with her and her children and her husband, with whom he would conduct clumsy small talk, like his conversations with his brother-in-law. With one ear he listened to Ruti and Arik arguing about the price of bread, Dana looked at him with teary eyes, and he smiled at her and was struck by the alarming thought that his son-in-law might be a young Arik. He heard Ruti say she loved bread stores, to which Arik replied that it was all a scam. "As if we even have a culinary culture. Look what's happening on our roads."

"What does that have to do with it?" Ruti asked.

"It has everything to do with it! We're barbaric. Fundamentally, we are a barbaric country, and no amount of ciabattas and focaccias will change that."

"We're not barbaric. Not all of us."

"But most are," Rona said, leaning with her back against the counter, sipping her wine and watching Shira, who seemed disconnected from it all, distant.

Arik said, "Let's ask the writers what they think; they're supposed to be our watchdogs."

Yonatan turned to Shira and said, "I believe that's the role of the media, actually."

Arik said, "And what are you? Aren't you the media?"

Yonatan kept looking at Shira and said, "Not at all." He wanted to form an alliance with her.

"Well, what are you then?"

Shira said, "I don't think we're even *we*—there's no *we* here."

"Exactly!" Yonatan exclaimed.

"We're too preoccupied with ourselves to be able to talk about ourselves in the plural."

Yonatan said, "Yes, that's exactly it. We're too busy hating ourselves."

Rona protested. "Here we go again with the lack of self-confidence."

Shira looked up from the ashtray to Yonatan and said, "Self-hatred is a daily condition for us."

"Yes, precisely." He smiled and felt it was important for him to agree with her now, because he felt guilty about denying their meeting in the bread store.

Rona said, "Don't tell me you hate yourself too. You're a little too old for that sort of thing, aren't you?"

Yonatan looked at Shira and said, "You're never too old to hate yourself."

"And just what's wrong with loving yourself?" Arik asked. "What's wrong with that?"

"Nothing, it's just less interesting." When he looked at Shira he wasn't sure if she agreed with him. She was staring at the table, her fingers caressing the shiny wood.

Ruti said, "Our son, Gilad, has this self-hatred thing going on now. He's sixteen."

"He has a parent-hatred thing going on too," Arik said. "Is there any more wine?"

Rona quickly put another bottle in front of him and said, "How is Gilad doing? Why didn't he come?"

"He does his own thing on Fridays," Arik replied.

"But he said thanks for the invitation," Ruti added.

Rona ladled soup into bowls and said it was an experiment, a new recipe, and Yonatan said it looked great and asked what kind of soup it was. "Sweet potato," she replied, and sat down next to him. The girls sat on either side of them. He passed the bread basket around, and when he offered it to Rona she grasped his hand and squeezed it and said, "I'm glad you came." He felt embarrassed again, because it occurred to him that perhaps, when she had stood at the stove watching them, she had somehow seen in him the entire path he had taken that evening, from the challah, in the bag on the table in his kitchen, to her kitchen and her soup—one taste of which confirmed what he had already known: that it was wonderful—a path that was twisted and paved with lies. Her hand, which still held his, was very warm. She looked at Dana and said, "We dragged your dad here by force today, didn't we?"

Dana nodded and sipped her soup quietly.

"Making out like he's some busy guy, your dad."

Dana smiled, and he wondered who had taught her to eat so delicately, because he always wolfed down his food. He put his spoon down in the bowl and wondered if his daughter knew, or at least guessed the truth, and whether after they had put the phone down half an hour earlier, she had imagined him scurrying about the apartment happily, looking for his wallet and keys, putting his coat on, bounding down the stairs and taking the shortcut from Bialik to Hess Street in a jog, but then slowing down his steps so as not to seem too enthusiastic, and even standing for a moment on the corner of Allenby to smoke a cigarette before coming into this beautiful, comforting house, reeking of cold and cigarettes and lies. He put his hand on the back of her neck, as part of the dialogue he had been having with her in his heart, but Dana flinched and said, "Stop it, Dad. You're strangling me."

Shira thought Dana resembled her father. She liked her. Shira and Dana were both regular guests here, and sometimes, although they were separated by more than twenty years, she felt as if there were no age gap at all, and they had both been annexed to this house for the same reasons, except that the girl didn't have to pretend she had other options. She looked at the stuffed veal and at Rona. As Rona carved the veal expertly into thin slices, she leaned over Yonatan, who shrank back so as not to get in her way, but she still rubbed her arm against his shoulder every time she cut a slice.

Ruti put her hand on her stomach and said, "Wow, I'm stuffed from the soup, how am I supposed to eat veal now?"

Arik said, "You'll eat it like a champ, I have no doubt."

Ruti said she had tried out a recipe for sweet-potato soup last week and it hadn't come out this well. "Gilad said it looked like camel vomit."

"Yes, and tell them what he said afterward, your son," Arik said. "She asked how he would know what camel vomit looked like."

"What did he say?" Tamar asked.

"He said he's been living here long enough to know," Ruti said, and the girls burst out laughing. "Why is it that everything you make turns out incredible and everything I make is a catastrophe?"

Arik sighed—"Here we go again"—and smiled at everyone as if he were proud to present their show. "What do you think? You think only you authors hate yourself? My wife has a patent on self-hatred!"

They were in their late forties. Ruti was Rona's best friend, also a therapist, and Arik was CEO of a telemarketing company. Shira watched them teasing each other; she liked them. Then she looked at Yonatan. What did he think of them? Was he measuring his level of belonging to this conversation much the way she was? She wondered whether he would also have preferred to be less self-aware at this moment, less aware of his observations and gauging, whether he missed a certain naturalness that always seemed so close and yet unreachable. So this is Yonatan Luria, she thought. She had heard a lot about him from Rona and had wondered if Rona was interested in him. She had asked her once, but Rona had said, "No way. He's lovely, but he's problematic."

She tried to conquer the attraction she felt. He seemed disheveled, but there was something soft and clean in his dishevelment. His brown curly hair, peppered with gray, his long thin face with slightly sunken cheekbones and hazel eyes, the faded green jeans and gray sweatshirt he wore, with a white T-shirt poking out from beneath the collar, and mainly his movements, clumsy and lazy—all these gave him a shy but confident look, full of contradictions. Or perhaps, she thought, it was not his appearance but her gaze that was full of contradictions.

She thought, So this is Dana's father. She saw him taking her in, too, and could tell he knew that, more than listening to Ruti and Arik's play of couplehood, they were listening to the tense silence that had closed in on them. She told herself it was a dangerous invention, to think that he was connecting with her in the same way she was connecting with him, from that injured and arrogant place, from the loneliness that searches for potential partners, because perhaps she was wrong and he was actually entirely present at this meal, not partially, as she was. He leaned over and asked if she was working on anything, and she was glad he had removed himself from Rona's arm as she passed around plates piled with slices of veal alongside dried fruit stuffing.

She said, "Not really. You?"

"Same."

"I'm stuck."

He smiled and said, "Me too."

She tried to overcome the attraction he aroused in her again, because she wanted his *same* to be expanded. She wanted him also to say, *I'm not writing because I'm restless, I'm here to escape the restlessness and I can't; and I look at you and wonder if you're here for the same reasons.* And she wanted to say, *Yes, exactly the same reasons; let's go.*

"I've been stuck for a long time," she said.

"Me too."

"Is it driving you crazy?"

"I don't know if it's driving me crazy," he said, suddenly more moderate and calmer than she, cautious with his choice of words. "But it makes me restless. You know that feeling?"

"Absolutely." She wanted to say, *Let's not talk about writing.* She said, "I know it well."

"So you know what I'm talking about."

"Yes, I do."

"You look a little restless too."

"Really?"

He nodded and she wanted him to say, *I also tend to fall in love in an instant*. He said, "Yes," and she thought that in fact every time she had fallen in love it had only been in retrospect.

"Is it so obvious?" She remembered how Eitan had always been surprised to discover who she was.

"To a well-trained eye, it is."

She thought of how she had fallen in love with Eitan only after someone else moved in with him. She said, "I thought I was hiding it so well," and her attraction to him was suddenly flooded with a sense of nakedness.

"Why hide it?"

She felt that although her clothes had been peeled away she still wanted to keep undressing, and she said, "Habit, I guess."

"I know that habit. It's a terrible one." She wanted him to say, *I look at you and I see your restlessness and it is the most attractive thing I have ever seen.* But he leaned back in his chair and said, "Shall we eat?"

She felt embarrassed when she saw how completely absorbed he was in his food, with a look of delight on his face that had nothing to do with her, with their conversation. Now he was the one who grasped Rona's hand and said, "Amazing!" "Really?" she said. He nodded with his mouth full. Then he shook his head from side to side and said, "Simply amazing!" He turned to Dana to see if she was enjoying the food too, then turned his attention back to his plate. Shira tasted the veal, which really was amazing, but she couldn't delight in it the way Yonatan had, because she felt betrayed—not by Yonatan, who was eating like a famished soldier home from basic training, nor by Rona, who sat next to him, casting a maternal look first at her daughter, then at his daughter (that's the look, Shira told herself; that's the look I don't have)—but by the automatic, childish, indefatigable hope, the hope that does not even know what it wishes for but always finds an anchor of air to hold on to: the hope that ruins the moment because it always skips beyond it.

Yonatan ate three slices of veal, then wolfed down the potatoes au gratin and served himself more and more of the fresh asparagus, which was one of his favorite things and which he never bought for himself and Dana, not because it was expensive but because he thought asparagus would be wasted on the kind of meals he made, coincidental meals, cooked quickly and eaten in haste, except for the few occasions when he grilled steaks. I haven't made steak for ages, he thought to himself, and made up his mind to get some asparagus the next time he bought them. He took some more, and reached out his fork to the big dish of veal, and speared two more slices.

He saw how much Dana was also enjoying the food and made a note to get the recipe from Rona. He would take the opportunity to ask her how she cooked the asparagus, and on Friday he'd go to the butcher's and buy a breast of veal and would cook up a meal like this. Maybe he'd start inviting people over too, and in time their house would become the kind of house that invited people and cooked for them. But whom would he invite? he asked himself, and he scanned the list of possible guests. Rona and Tamar were on the list, although that would seem almost too familial. He could invite Nira and Zvi, but he didn't want to. He wanted to invite Arik and Ruti and Shira, but that would be ridiculous; they weren't his friends. In fact, he wanted to *be* Rona, and he took another helping of veal, and piled some more potatoes on his plate, and was sorry to find that the asparagus was gone. He poured himself another glass of wine.

Ruti and Arik continued their argument, and although they were starting to bore him, he was relieved that he could be quiet, thanks to them. Every so often he asked Dana if she was enjoying the food, and Dana nodded and smiled with her mouth full. He could see that Shira kept looking at him from the other side of the table, and he briefly felt the pleasant shiver of someone targeted for observation, someone who is somehow being flirted with, although it was hard for him to say how, because her look was both attentive and disconnected. It reminded him of his own—that, at least, was how he perceived his look from inside.

Ten years ago he could have told himself with certainty that she belonged to the "depends on the circumstances" category. There was something wild about her; her hair, for example, was somewhere between curly and wavy and looked like the hair of a child who has just got out of bed. And her face appeared slightly angry and dreamy. When she got up to help Rona clear the table, he saw that she was fuller than he had thought, or perhaps the corduroys made her look broader, and the way she walked revealed a certain self-consciousness and lack of confidence, the walk of someone who would prefer to remain seated. He liked that.

He couldn't decide if he was attracted to her. He lit a cigarette and focused on Arik and Ruti but kept following Shira out of the corner of his eye. The categories he used to assign to women had long been erased, or perhaps had merged into one indistinct category, which was related not to attraction so much as to fear, because, since Ilana's death, the first thing he saw in women was not their face or their breasts or their backside or their legs, but rather his own reflection in their eyes.

He recalled the first woman who had hit on him, a few months after he was widowed. He met her in a home-improvement store, where he was looking for bookshelves for Dana's room. She walked around the store behind him, pushing a huge shopping cart, and he suspected she was deliberately following him. Every time he turned around she was there, and her cart, like his, was still empty. Finally, he stopped and asked, "Can I help you?" as if he worked there.

The woman said, "Yes," and told him she didn't really know what she needed but she wanted to build a closet.

"Then you need the lumber department. Come on, I'm going there anyway."

"I'd love to. I've been following you anyway."

He smiled and kept going, and heard the wheels of her cart rattling behind him. A pleasant shudder went down his back, and when they reached the lumber area and the woman studied the planks of wood and the shelves, she said she couldn't be bothered after all, and that it would be easier just to buy a closet.

"I'll never be able to put a closet together myself, I can hardly hammer a nail," she said, leading Yonatan to believe that she was alone. For a moment he wanted to volunteer to build the closet for her, but he didn't know how to do it either; he could barely put up shelves and didn't even own a drill. The woman said, "I need a man to help me," and Yonatan suddenly felt both impotent and aroused.

"I need a man to help me too," he said. Alarmed at what he had said, he explained. "I have two left hands."

"So where does one find such a man?"

"I imagine they hang around this type of store," Yonatan said, and they both laughed.

"I'm Idit. Pleased to meet you."

"Yonatan."

They shook hands—hers was a little sticky from holding the shopping cart handle—and they pushed their empty carts around the massive store and chatted. When they went out to the parking lot together, Idit asked if he wanted to get some coffee somewhere. He said he did, and she said she thought there was a café in the area but not a very nice one. Yonatan said he didn't mind, so they went into the nearby mall and up the escalator, and this time he stood behind her and found himself staring at her behind and sensed her embarrassment. She turned to him and smiled, and tried to stand so that her back wouldn't be facing him, and he still kept staring at her behind. There was something weak about it, and he noticed the two lines her panties made in the thin shiny fabric of her slacks. The escalator moved slowly, and Yonatan felt his penis rousing a little in his own pants and grew alarmed; he turned away to look at the stores above them and at the domed glass roof. Idit said, "Here it is. I think it's on this floor."

By the time they got off the escalator he had managed to subdue his threatening erection, and they sat on two lawn chairs beneath a striped umbrella. A ray of sun shone through the dome and illuminated Idit's face, which he now saw was covered with a thick layer of makeup; her mascara looked very sticky in the sunlight. They both concentrated on the menu and Idit said, "What do you feel like?"

He wanted to say, Nothing, actually, but he said, "I'll have a coffee."

"That's it? Don't you want anything else?"

"That's it."

She worked in a bookstore and knew his name. She had read both his books and had loved them and was waiting for the next one. He said he was too. She told him she was recently divorced, no children, and that in the meantime she was partying.

"Partying?"

"All the time."

"What do you mean, partying?"

"Partying! Don't you know what partying is?"

"No."

"Seriously?"

"You mean going to parties and bars?"

She laughed and sipped her coffee and tore off a tiny piece of the croissant she had ordered; her fingers were long and her nails were painted with silver nail polish. She put the piece in her mouth and said, "That too."

Although he knew exactly what she meant, he kept interrogating her, because he refused to believe she was really hitting on him in this way that seemed both disgusting and exciting and because there had never been ease in his life, and this seemed to be his opportunity to finally experience it.

She said, "I go out all the time. Blind dates and that sort of thing. And sometimes I sit at a bar, just for fun."

"Alone?"

"Yeah, sure. Why not?"

"And don't people hit on you the whole time?"

"They do; that's why I go."

Yonatan, who had never picked up a woman in a bar, suddenly felt his life to be terribly lacking, and asked, "How do people hit on you? What tactics do they use?"

Idit laughed. "Oh, there are all kinds. Do you really want to know?"

He nodded and lit a cigarette. He offered her one and she took it with the same delicacy with which she had torn off pieces of croissant, and told him about the pickup methods of men in bars, and Yonatan again felt that combination of aversion and excitement.

"I'm thirty-three," she said, when he asked how old she was. "I'm supposed to be in my prime, aren't I?"

Yonatan imagined her sleeping with a different guy every night and asked what her ex-husband did.

"He's an electrical engineer."

"Interesting job."

"Not at all."

"At least it's a job." He tried to picture himself in bed with her but couldn't.

"What about you? Are you married?"

"My wife died." The words sounded sterile; their sound reminded him of the way the lawn chairs and the stripy umbrella looked, and the whole mall.

"How did she pass away?"

Yonatan had never thought of Ilana as someone who had passed away, but rather as someone who had died, and he said, "Motor accident." Idit was quiet and he added, "I have a six-year-old girl," because he urgently needed to transmit all the relevant information about his life to Idit, and he did not know why or what, in fact, *was* relevant to this occasion or what this occasion even was.

When she got up to go to the bathroom, he followed her behind again, which was now an independent entity, uninterested in this conversation and unaffected by Yonatan's dilemmas, because he really could not imagine himself sleeping with her, not with someone like that, not so soon after losing his wife. Although, on the other hand, maybe it had to be with someone like her, because it would have no meaning from the get-go. But Yonatan knew he had never been able to enjoy the advantages of meaninglessness—on the contrary, it was meaninglessness that always took on a double meaning for him—and the behind moved farther and farther away and Yonatan briefly recalled the little erection he had had fifteen minutes ago on the escalator, and pictured Idit peeing in the bathroom, and thought, That was the first erection since Ilana died. For four months he had been unable to think about sex. He hadn't even been able to masturbate, although he had tried, one afternoon in the shower, more out of desperation than horniness, but he couldn't concentrate, even though Dana was out.

He had stood in the stream of water and thought, It's all right, you're allowed; Dana's over at Nira's. But that knowledge only intensified the girl's presence and her mother's absence, and although he was able to arouse himself, he was overcome with lethargy as he soaped his penis and started rubbing it with an automatic, almost bored motion. He stood that way for a few moments until the lethargy was replaced by anger, and he tried urgently to call up a fantasy, the one he especially liked: a replay of his sexual encounter with a woman who had gone to school with him during his BA, a kibbutznik named Hagar. She was particularly wild in bed, and the memory of their sex was always wonderful fantasy material. He had run into her on the street not long ago. She had found religion in the interim and was wearing a long dress and a head covering, and her eyes escaped his look to the sidewalk. When he told her his wife had died, she clucked her tongue, the same tongue that had once scampered over his body, and said, "Hashem gives, Hashem takes." He had felt like slapping her but had said, "Yes, I suppose so." That day in the shower, he started the replay, but suddenly, as if the reel had been torn in the projector, the picture was cut off and he couldn't see anything. He kept standing like that with his eyes closed, his rubbing turning to desperate little tugs, until he let go and washed off the soap and got out of the shower.

When Idit came back, he decided he would sleep with her. He imagined them leaving the café and going down the escalator and standing in the parking lot, embarrassed by the anticipated parting. Idit would start to give him her phone number, but he would stand close to her and put an unequivocal hand on her shoulder and ask if she was busy right now. Maybe they could go and have lunch somewhere? Idit might be disappointed for a moment, because she had hoped for a nighttime encounter, but she would realize that late morning was when Yonatan operated and would say she was free—why not?—and would suggest that they go over to her place and she'd make something to eat. Yonatan would say, If it's not too much bother. And she would say, It's no bother at all. And he would say, Then I'll follow you. He tried to guess what kind of car she drove and thought it was probably something compact, a Subaru like his car, or even a Ford Fiesta. He would follow her car the whole way, as he had followed her backside, and she would drive slowly so she wouldn't lose him, and it would be a kind of foreplay on the road.

When Idit sat down across from him again and put the last piece of croissant in her mouth, he wondered if she would look so made up when she was naked. When he tried to picture himself naked, the notion was not frightening so much as it was impossible, and he consoled himself with the thought that he didn't have to undress or undress her; on the contrary, this was a quickie, a onetime exchange between two strangers who had nothing to say to each other, so there was no point in pretending and undressing. The idea encouraged him, and he thought about fucking her fully clothed, standing up, in her kitchen, and his sleeping erection stirred, and Idit asked, "What are you thinking about?"

"Nothing. My mind was just wandering for a minute."

He asked if he should get the check, and she said she felt like some more coffee and called the waitress. She said she'd never met an author in person. She really liked reading, she said. "I love books. I devour everything, in huge quantities."

"Yes, I like to read too."

She told him she read interviews with authors and watched them on TV and always tried to find a connection between what they wrote and the way they looked and spoke. She said she was always surprised to discover that there was no connection and that the authors, when compared to their books, were disappointing.

Yonatan asked, "So are you disappointed?"

"Goodness, no! Goodness, no! I saw you on TV a long time ago, and I read the interview you gave, that time, when your second book came out."

"In *Ha'aretz*?"

"Yes. And I'm not disappointed at all. Quite the opposite!"

"So you knew what I looked like. It wasn't a coincidence that you followed me in the store?"

"No. Actually, yes, it was a coincidence. A sort of coincidence. I mean, I recognized you, yes. It's embarrassing."

Yonatan was momentarily flooded with a sense of power he had never known: not when his first book was a success, not when the second gained a respectable position on the bestseller list—not first place, which still saddened him a little; like a stubborn koala bear, *Silence* had stuck in sixth place for weeks until it dropped off—he had never felt as powerful as he did at that moment, sitting opposite this woman with her heavy makeup and long fingernails and jet-black hair that suddenly looked dyed, this woman who had hunted him down in the store and chased him with her cart to fulfill the fantasy of meeting a writer and sleeping with him.

"I don't want you to think . . ." she said.

"Think what?"

"You know."

"No, I don't." But he did. This woman—who had surprised him by saying she read a highbrow newspaper like *Ha'aretz,* and he hated himself for the prejudice but was still surprised—had seen him wandering around the home-improvement store and realized this was her big chance. The fact that she was so excited at this prospect seemed sad to Yonatan, and he pitied her, and she seemed pathetic, as she had for a second when he had seen the lines her panties made in her slacks, and he suddenly felt cheated, and the sense of power gave way to insult, and he tried to reassure himself with the knowledge that she was the kind of woman who hunted down men in bars, that she had liked him anyway, regardless of the fact that he was an almost-famous author, but he didn't believe it, and he felt it wasn't him that she wanted but the fleeting, relative fame that sleeping with him could offer, and he felt pathetic himself, for being the object of a fantasy for someone like this, and the ease he had wanted to experience turned finally into depression.

"Are you okay?" Idit asked, and used her fingernails to tear off the corners of two packs of sugar.

"I'm fine," he said, but he could no longer look at her and he turned aside, to the escalator.

"Yoo-hoo!" She waved at him. "I'm over here!"

"I'm sorry. I was just looking at something." He waited impatiently for her to finish her coffee.

"Were your thoughts wandering again?"

"Yes." He smiled.

"Where?" she asked cloyingly, and leaned her chin on her hand.

But the magic was gone—it had never been there, he realized—and her voice sounded demanding, and he glanced at his watch and said, "Listen, I have to run, but you drink your coffee. I just noticed the time."

Idit sat up straight and said, "I see. That's a pity."

"Yes, I think so too, but I have to pick my daughter up from school."

"Already? It's only eleven."

"Yes, I forgot they're finishing early today, the teachers have some seminar or something."

"Oh, a seminar."

"They're always having seminars, those teachers; you would think they'd all turned into professors."

"My sister's a teacher."

"Really?" He called the waitress.

"I have to go too, actually."

During the minutes that passed until the waitress came with the check, he politely asked her about her sister the teacher; then he paid the check and Idit did not object, and he said to himself, At least she can tell people that an author bought her a cup of coffee, and he hated her and himself, and they got up and went down the escalator. This time she stood behind him, and he turned to face her but her eyes were focused on the stores passing them by.

When they got to the parking lot, he said, "It's been a real pleasure."

"For me too," she replied, and hesitated briefly.

He was planning how he would refuse when she offered him her phone number, and he said, "Where are you parked?"

"Here, just nearby. I got lucky."

"I didn't; I'm over there on the other side." He took his key chain out of his pants pocket and said, "It's pretty hot today."

"That's it, winter's over."

"Yes. But at least we *had* a winter this year, for a change."

"I hate winter."

"I like it."

"Really?"

Yonatan thought he detected a hint of hope in her voice—perhaps a conversation about the weather would take them back to the starting point?—and he said, "Yes, my daughter likes winter too."

"Okay. You should really get going." She held out her hand to be shaken.

He shook it feebly, and her hand felt nice, and he said, "Bye, then," and turned away and started walking to his car. When he felt he was far enough away, he turned back and saw Idit getting into a white Fiat Uno.

2

Shira walked home with quick, disappointed steps, wishing she could go back to the beginning of the evening, to the time when she could have acted differently—could have been more friendly and flirted more, or at least more unequivocally; could have worn something else, something sexy instead of corduroy pants that made her look fat— because she felt she had looked old and bitter tonight. She could have smiled more and asked him about himself when they sat at the table on their own—Rona and the girls were washing the dishes, Arik and Ruti sat watching TV, and the two of them found themselves again within a circle of silence—but they were both quiet. She wanted to go back to that time she had tried to kill, the endless moments in the park, the slow walking, that time now seemed precious and so wasted, the time before she fell in love with him.

Or perhaps she hadn't fallen in love with him. But it didn't make any difference. The sense of falling in love, the air it brought with it, sud- denly became an internal conversation, something to talk about with herself, familiar and yet very new. It was emptying and filling and exhausting, she thought, as she climbed up the stairs to her third-floor apartment. So exhausting, she said to herself, and lay down on the couch, but in such a refreshing way.

When she saw Yonatan gobbling his food, heaping more and more of the veal and potatoes onto his plate and finishing off the asparagus practically single-handedly, she felt close to him, in the same way that people can feel close to themselves, but with more compassion, but she knew there was something in him that rejected closeness, something that awakened compassion and at the same time disdained anyone who pitied him.

She picked up the newspaper off the floor, looked at the cryptic crossword, but couldn't concentrate. Why him? she asked herself. You could feel compassion for anyone, and closeness too. She got up and went to the kitchen, distractedly opened and closed the fridge, then took a cigarette out from the pack on the table and thought, Because he looks unattainable. Even his body looks fortified.

She remembered the first time she had slept with Idan, after many months of watching him in the cafeteria on campus, convinced he didn't know, long months during which he tipped the scales in his favor without even realizing it, or so she thought, because he later confessed that he had purposely ignored her because she seemed too enthusiastic and a little scary. She remembered the sense of challenge that accompanied their first sex like background music.

The pub they had gone to, on Allenby, was a tourists' pub. She had encouraged him to get drunk. Only later did she realize that he always got drunk before sex—not so he could perform but so he could be raped, which was the only thing he knew how to do. As she stroked his fingers, which gripped his glass of beer, and looked at him giggling like a girl and turning aside—far away from her, far from her passion, far from any passion—she believed that, the minute she managed somehow to penetrate him, he would penetrate her back, and the insult of his ignoring her would be erased, along with the insult of the drunkenness he needed so he could be with her. In the car, when she drove him drunk to his apartment, she imagined the moment when he would lunge for her, but the lunge never came, and she slept with him for five years without his truly wanting her even for a minute.

And then there was Eitan, who was all lunge. After the first time with him, she was stunned by the way he loved her body, which over the years, especially the years with Idan, had become a cynical lump of desire. She walked around naked in front of Eitan on their very first night, something she had never done with anyone, and she didn't like to do it even alone. She had got out of bed and gone to the bathroom and then to the kitchen to get them both some cold water, and had come back to the bedroom, then to the living room for cigarettes and an ashtray; her breasts and stomach and ass and hips hung around his apartment with an ease that practically bordered on reproach, and everywhere they went they found Eitan waiting for them, missing them, lunging at them.

For a moment, when Yonatan got up and went to the bathroom an image flashed through her mind, flicking back and forth, of Yonatan naked. She pictured narrow, boyish hips and a broad torso, and his nakedness was hairy, without Idan's eel-like slipperiness or Eitan's yearning bearness; Yonatan's nakedness, unlike any other because she had not yet seen it, aroused intense attraction, but mainly compassion. When he came back from the bathroom, she saw that he was thinner than she had thought, that his sweatshirt and the T-shirt he wore beneath it made him look bulkier but the jeans gave him away, and she knew that the compassion he aroused was misleading because it was so sexy.

Now she told herself that her attraction to him, like the falling in love, was also fake, and that even if it was real it was circumstantial. She knew it wasn't his body language, lazy and supple, or his body, which she saw as being split in two, or his face, which radiated soft cynicism—although you couldn't say that cynicism radiated, in his case it did—or his tone of voice, which held a mixture of seduction and indifference. It was Dana, because there was something in him that clearly said, I'm lonely but not completely. That was his strength, she decided, and his power over her. I'm lonely, he told her wordlessly, but you are far lonelier.

Apart from the moments when he was entirely engrossed in his food—and perhaps that was why she had fallen in love with him precisely then, because he belonged to no one, not even to himself—it seemed that his daughter was constantly within his field of vision, even when he wasn't looking at her, when he was talking to the others or listening or smoking or being quiet, and she could not help being slightly afraid for the girl. But she also envied her for having a constant spotlight shining on her, even if its heat singed her wings a little. She asked herself if that thing could also exist between men and women, that the thing should exist: that each possess a copy of the other, a backup of their being.

Everyone had looked so backed up this evening—Arik and Ruti, Rona and Tamar, Yonatan and Dana, Rona and the girls, Rona and the girls and Yonatan—until at a certain point it seemed that her bothersome attraction to him was not passion or compassion or a combination of the two but a longing to join the group, any group, even Arik and Ruti's, who didn't stop arguing the whole evening even when they were watching TV, leaving Yonatan and her to sit by the table.

They sat that way for almost an hour, exchanging a few words that she now could not recall, until Yonatan suddenly got up and told Dana it was time to go, and the girl protested a little but he said he would still like to try and get some work done tonight, and Dana took their coats off the hooks and he said goodbye to everyone else, including her, in the same tone. After he left, she wanted to go too. Arik and Ruti said they were also leaving, and the three of them went downstairs together. When they walked out onto the street, they asked if they could give her a ride. She said no, she lived nearby, and Arik asked if she was sure, it was late, the streets were unsafe. She refused again and said goodbye and started walking, quickly this time because she needed this walk to digest everything that had not happened this evening, and everything that had.

She went into her bedroom and started to undress, purposely standing far away from the large mirror in the corner, because she knew that her body's appearance would sadden her now more than usual; bodies, like children, can never hide their disappointment. Still, she found herself passing by the mirror in her underwear and stopping there, smoothing her stomach, examining her thighs, which clung to each other; they looked like the thighs of a big chicken—and her breasts, which now looked very heavy and sad.

(3)

The whole evening, especially when she watched him gobbling his food, Dana had thought that she would have had more fun if he hadn't come. She was sorry for the thought and was flooded with guilt as they walked home together along Bialik Street. But she persuaded herself that she was entitled to be angry at him because he had invaded territory that didn't belong to him; it didn't belong to her either, but at least she worked hard to be part of it. His last-minute arrival meant she could no longer behave as a different girl—someone else's daughter—as if she too, like Tamar, belonged to this kitchen, to the center of the world. As soon as he walked in, so embarrassed and embarrassing, she sensed the way everyone attached her to him with their gaze, even though she stood far away, by the counter, and she felt how her father was a magnet that drew her to him, into the margins.

She knew that if they didn't feel sorry for her for not having a mother, the other girls would have been jealous of her. They had often said, on various occasions, "Your dad is cute" or "Your dad is lovely." They asked what it was like to have a dad who was a writer, and she said, "It's really fun." At Lilach's party that night, when they were lying in their sleeping bags, the girls started talking about their fathers: how they looked and how they dressed and which of them was cute. Tamar, who was lying next to Dana, had something bad to say about all of them. Dana kept quiet, listening to the girls as they agreed that her dad was all right. When Tamar said, "Yes, he really is okay," Dana felt proud for a minute but thought that it wasn't true, and that in fact the cutest dad was Amos, Lilach's father, who was very tall and broad and went to a gym and always looked so calm. When Orit said, "Dana's dad does look good, but he's not perfect," Tamar had propped herself up on her elbows and said, "As if your dad is." Orit, who was a little insulted, said obviously her dad wasn't perfect, no one was, but at least he dressed better than Dana's dad. "Maybe he's not your type," Tamar said. "He's my type. I mean, he's not my type now, but when I'm into men he'll definitely be my type." Lilach said her mother said Yonatan was a bohemian type, and there were women who liked that. Tamar said she did. Lilach said her mother said Yonatan's scruffiness was part of his sex appeal, and Orit asked what sex appeal was. Hila said it was physical appearance. Another girl, Naomi, said, "No, it's not. Sex appeal is if you're attractive or not. It's a characteristic, like intelligence or a sense of humor." No one argued with her, because Naomi was born in England.

The girls kept on talking about Yonatan and whether he would be their type when they had a type, and Tamar leaned in and whispered to Dana, "They're such retards." She nodded, and Tamar said, "You should be happy they didn't accept you." Her heart sank and she asked Tamar how she knew. Tamar said, "Before, when you were in the bathroom, they said you didn't fit in." She asked why, and Tamar said, "What difference does it make? You should be happy and that's that. I'm leaving this horrible team anyway." But Dana still wanted to know what they said. With one ear she heard Orit whispering, "Are they finally asleep?" She saw Tamar shut her eyes tightly, and she closed her own. Lilach whispered, "Naomi, go and see if they're awake." Dana felt Naomi's breath as she leaned over them and then turned around and said, "They're asleep."

"Did you see what she brought?" She heard Orit's voice.

Lilach answered, "I can't believe it!"

"Me neither!" Naomi whispered, and Dana felt the skinny English girl's back against her legs. She dared to open her eyes for a second, searching for Tamar's eyes in the dark, but Tamar was really asleep and her breath was rhythmical and serene.

"But you saw how I didn't say anything," Lilach said.

"Me either," Orit said.

"Me either," Naomi said.

Dana heard Hila yawn and ask, "What didn't you say?"

"Shhhh!" Orit hissed at her. "Don't wake them up."

"What didn't you say anything about?"

"About what Dana brought."

"Oh," said Hila. "It was really awful. She has some nerve, don't you think?"

"But what are we going to do with it? Do we keep it?" Orit asked.

"No way! Are you crazy? We'll give it back to her," Lilach replied.

"Yeah, we'll give it back to her," Orit said.

"When?" asked Naomi.

"Tomorrow morning?" Orit asked.

"No," said Lilach. "We'll wait a week or two, after we tell her she doesn't fit in."

"You're right," said Orit.

"Even though we're the ones who should be insulted," Lilach said.

"That's true," said Orit. "That's absolutely true."

Dana heard another few sleepy whispers of consent in the room.

All week she had been bothered by the request for "an item from a collection," because she didn't collect anything. She wondered whether she should ask Orit to ask Lilach if they would agree to drop the item and let her bring something else instead, but she was afraid that if they found out she didn't have any collections, they wouldn't accept her. She didn't tell Tamar either, because Tamar collected everything. In the desk drawers in her room, and in her closet, were shoe boxes full of dried leaves, smooth stones, lighters, greeting cards, feathers, sugar packets from different cafés, pens, and broken watches, all mixed up in one mess. When she was considered for the team a few months ago and they had invited her to a slumber party like this one, she took a bag full of different items, as well as two cakes her mother had baked.

Dana had sat in the kitchen two days before the party and looked at the list. The only thing missing was the item taken from a collection, and now, in retrospect, as she lay in her sleeping bag, she realized she could have gone down to the kiosk and bought a pretty lighter or two; she had enough money in her pocket. Or she could have called Tamar, confessed, and asked to borrow something of hers. But the worry had paralyzed her. Finally, she remembered her mother's cigarette pack. The Time package was pressed between the pages of an *Encyclopaedia Britannica* volume, where she had hidden it three years ago after her father had smoked all the cigarettes and it was empty.

Like a dried flower, the pack was waiting between the encyclopedia's pages, and it still had a distant scent of tobacco. When she placed it carefully between the pages of a notebook and wrapped the notebook in her gray sweatpants so it wouldn't get crumpled, something told her she was making a mistake, not by parting with a precious souvenir, because she had long ago parted with it, but by taking to the group this thing she had parted with, the addiction itself.

She noticed the first indications of her unfitness early on in the evening, when everyone sat on the rug in Lilach's room around two large pizzas they had ordered, and she gave them their little gifts. They all looked disappointed, apart from Tamar, who loved her banana magnet. But they all thanked her politely and smiled at her and smiled at each other knowingly. Then they put the gifts on the rug and devoured the pizzas. Every so often they each looked at one another's gifts and said, with their mouths full, "It's so cute," or "How sweet." Tamar picked up Lilach's key chain, which was attached to a fake fur tail of some animal that looked like a raccoon, stroked it, and said, "It's so nice. It feels really soft; touch it." The girls reached out and stroked the tail, and Lilach pulled the slice of pizza away from her mouth and stretched out a string of melted cheese in the air, and said, "It's too bad I don't have any keys."

Then they asked Dana to show them her photograph she had brought. Dana wiped her hands on a napkin and took the photo out of her backpack and they passed it around and said, "You were so cute," and no one noticed her mother's foot.

They got carried away with talking about their childhoods, as if they had been left long behind, and there was another half hour of tension until Orit asked her to show them the collection item. Tamar looked at her expectantly as she took out the cigarette pack from her notebook. The girls were quiet, but their eyes darted from one to another, then to Lilach, and back to the piece of cardboard, which sat on the rug between the two empty boxes full of crumbs and bits of congealed cheese, until Tamar said, "Wow! That's so original! A collection of cigarette packs!"

"Yes, it's really original," Lilach said, and looked askance at Orit, who was stifling a giggle.

"I would never think to collect something like that," Orit said.

"I have them from all kinds of countries," Dana lied. "But they're rare, so I didn't bring any others."

"Your dad smokes, doesn't he?" Lilach asked, in a medical tone of voice.

"Yes. But this was an old pack that belonged to my mom."

"Oh, it was?" she asked, and they all looked down sorrowfully.

"Yes. But she didn't smoke much."

"And does your dad smoke a lot?" Naomi asked with her British accent.

"Kind of."

"Not that much," Tamar said. "Don't exaggerate."

"How much does he smoke?" Hila asked.

"I don't know," Dana said.

"More or less," Lilach said.

"Maybe five cigarettes a day. Maybe four."

"That's really not a lot," Lilach said. "We're not allowed to smoke in my house."

"Us either," Orit said.

"Us either," Naomi said. "My big brother has asthma."

"My parents really hate smokers," Hila said. "They really hate them."

"We're allowed," Tamar said.

"Your mom smokes?" Orit asked.

"No way!" Tamar said. "But she doesn't mind if other people do."

For a minute Dana hoped the conversation would distract the girls' attention from the flattened square of cardboard that was making her miss her mother. It also made Dana angry, because for the first year or two after she died, her mother had still seemed to be making an effort to protect her daughter, as if she were a road sign pointing the way. But lately she had become more and more of a memory—a living memory, but with limited abilities. Sometimes it was a relief, because in return for her mom's protection Dana had felt she had to be like her, and since she didn't always like the things her mother liked, there was a certain freedom in not always knowing what those things were. So her mother went from being someone who continued to maneuver her to a memory that could be maneuvered, from a road sign to a gravestone. Although Dana liked this freedom, the most painful freedom she had ever known, she didn't want it now. Now she wanted her dad. She had started feeling unwell that morning, but she didn't know if the chills and the burning throat and the weakness in her limbs were because of the flu or because of the trap she had fallen into. The idea that she still had to spend a whole night and day with the team scared her, reminding her of a time when she was four, when she had begged to spend a weekend alone with her grandmother in Jerusalem and then began aching for her mother and father even before they had left Tel Aviv.

She lay awake in her sleeping bag and listened to the girls chattering. They had changed subjects long ago and forgotten about the cigarette pack, but even so she felt they were still talking about her. She wondered what time it was, how many hours were still left until the next day, and then the door opened and Lilach's mother whispered, "Aren't you asleep yet?"

Lilach hushed her and said, "Soon, Mom."

"It's almost two," Rika whispered.

"So what?"

"So nothing. I thought you'd want to know what time it was. Do you want something to drink? Do you want some juice? Or something hot? Should I make you some hot chocolate?"

"No!" Lilach whispered for everyone. "We don't want anything. We want to be left alone."

Dana was sorry that because of Tamar she had to pretend to be asleep, because she was suddenly very thirsty and her throat was burning. But there was nothing to be done until morning. Nothing to be done, she told herself, and wondered if her dad was still awake.

(4)

He looked at her now as she walked beside him, struggling to keep up, and only when he saw how hard she had to try, and that she was still short of breath due to her recent flu, did he realize his pace was too fast. It was a getaway pace, but what was he escaping? He knew the answer, and it flooded his body with warmth and anxiety: something had happened to him this evening, and he felt his skin stretched out like a crispy crust of dry earth, slightly cracked, both outside and in.

Women were always hitting on him. Even when they weren't, he felt they were treating him as if they would like to hit on him if he would let them, if he would only signal his approval. But he always made sure to signal the opposite, even when he was no longer sure that he wanted them to keep their distance. He was reminded of those drivers who forget to switch off their turn signals long after passing; he hated them. He always wondered, as he drove behind them, what they were thinking—those daydreaming, irresponsible drivers who didn't hear their turn signals ticking away. Perhaps they had the quiet kind, unlike his, which you couldn't ignore even if you wanted to. Then one day, two or three years ago, a little after Latrun junction, when he was taking Dana to visit his mother in Jerusalem, his daughter told him he'd been signaling for fifteen minutes. "It's really annoying," she said. I must have been daydreaming, he told her, but ever since then Latrun had become a junction of insult.

Shira intrigued him but, more than that, she made him curious about himself. He had not felt that way for a long time, that old sensation of arrogance and fear tied up together in a pleasant emotional tickle: How do I look, how do I sound, what do they think of me, who am I winning over now, who's winning me over, who wants to sleep with me, where is all this leading?

Maybe it was her relentless gaze. When he got up to go to the bathroom, he suspected she was staring at him, sending X-rays that prowled his body, radioactive and nosy. All evening he felt trapped and flattered by her gaze, and while he ate he felt she was devouring him with her restlessness, her sadness, and even though during those moments a voice told him he should eat slower, calm down, not finish off the asparagus in front of everyone, there was also another voice that urged him to wolf it all down, because he wanted her to see him that way, not any other way, so hungry, always, so she would know what she was getting into, if he ever let her in. And since that was not an option—after all, he would never ask Rona for Shira's phone number, much as he had never called her for a referral to a therapist—he began to amuse himself with the idea of letting her in and stood waiting for Dana as she stopped to tie her shoelaces, sitting tiredly on the sidewalk. He turned back and said, "We have to get you some new shoes."

"I don't need any," she replied.

"Yes, you do."

"You're such a pain!"

What would it be like if a new woman entered his life? The idea that not only the woman would be new but his life, too, seemed enchanting. There was fear though, because she would have to come into his bedroom. It had been more than four years since he'd slept with a woman, and even the memory of the last time he had sex with Ilana, just a week before she was killed, was becoming dull, like the sex itself. It had been an uncharacteristic morning encounter. Neither of them had enjoyed it, and later, during the day, they gave each other apologetic looks. It occurred to him that perhaps he should have read into it some essence of separation.

After a few years together, every time they had bad sex there was the consolation that next time would compensate for it, although they no longer needed the compensation. Even so, they always both tried harder the next time, which came sooner than usual, sometimes even the same night or the next day. But the last correction never came, and it left him bitter for many months, longing to compensate her and himself for his miserable morning performance, for having pressed up against her back and felt her sleeping body tense up, drowsy but full of willingness. Without caressing her, without kissing her, without touching her, he had entered her while she was still half asleep and felt he was hurting her; he knew he would always remember the way she turned her head toward him and opened her eyes and then closed them immediately in pain, because a ray of sun that shone through a crack in the blinds lit up her face, and she said, "Good morning," and reached around to caress him. But he grabbed her hand and put it back, and wouldn't let her touch him, and did not answer when she asked him something—he couldn't remember what she asked for a long time—but moved quickly inside her, with strange matter-of-factness, and looked at her cheek with its pillow creases, and came and pulled out quickly, not because he was afraid of pregnancy but because he felt guilty. Ilana turned to him and smiled, fully awake now, and he lay on his back and looked at the ceiling and felt that another man had just fucked his wife, and she took his hand and placed it between her legs, and that other man, the stranger, who was a bad lover, let his hand lie there like a stone while his wife squirmed beneath it. And that man wished she would come already because he wanted to get up and pee, and every movement of hers distanced her from him, from his paralyzed hand, and finally—Yonatan didn't know how he had allowed the man to abuse his wife that way—she climbed onto him and pressed her thighs against his, and rode him until she came, lonely and tired, uncharacteristically silent, as if she didn't want him to know, as if it were none of his business. She got up and hurried to the bathroom, perhaps because she didn't want to see his face, and a few minutes later they met in the kitchen and he said good morning and kissed her cheek, and she asked him to wake Dana, and they both acted as if they had just woken up.

A few weeks after she died, when he was lying in bed alone, with his hand, motionless, in his underwear, he remembered what she had asked when he had been moving inside her. "Is it good for you?" She had never asked that before—she had never had to—and the question echoed in his mind like a terrible accusation.

The thought of sleeping with a different woman frightened him. He knew he would have to invent a new, conciliatory sexuality to suit his forty-five-year-old self. Each time a sexual memory was erased from his body, it simply made way for a fresh dose of fear: Who would be the man who would sleep with this woman? What kind of man would he be? How much of a stranger? He was terrified by probability that the next time would be self-aware, postmodern—like the literature he couldn't stand—perhaps it wouldn't be sex at all but a paraphrase of sex, even a parody. He could imagine mocking himself and his own performance and feeling guilty toward Ilana, convincing himself that he was guilty of nothing, constantly anxious about his erection, which had never betrayed him before but would probably start now. And when he came, if he even did—and he had no idea if he would come in a condom with the new woman; it had been more than ten years since he'd seen a condom—he wondered what would come out of him, whether it would contain the baggage of everything he'd been through all these past years, whether bitterness and stifled tears or relief and happiness, or perhaps just great nothingness. The more he considered it, the more he understood that he was distancing himself from the moment when he would lose his second virginity, this middle-aged virginity.

Now he felt a little short of breath as they walked upstairs like two old people: he was huffing because of the cigarettes and Dana, half a flight below him, grasped the handrail tightly and dragged behind him as she wheezed a little; perhaps she was also angry at him for walking so quickly and leaving her behind.

He asked if she had had a good time at Rona's, and she nodded, and he said, "You feel very much at home there."

She didn't know what to say, because she was afraid to hurt his feelings, so she said only, "Yes. I like it there."

"Rona really is lovely."

"Yes."

"And Tamar too, she's a great kid."

"She is."

"It was nice tonight," he summed up, as he locked the door behind them and threw his keys on the kitchen table as usual. They took their coats off and Dana hung them up on the coatrack in the hallway, the one she had needed to stand on a chair to reach only a few months ago, which also held two scarves and a girl's wool hat, from much colder winters.

He sat down at the kitchen table and lit a cigarette. "Put some water on," he said, and Dana filled the electric kettle. "I really feel like mint tea, all of a sudden. It's too bad we don't have any mint."

"We could grow some on the balcony."

"That's an excellent idea." He yawned. They would never grow mint on the balcony. They weren't those kinds of people; he wasn't that kind of man. Then he asked if she was tired, and she said a little and asked if he was going to write now, and he said he would try. Yes, he would try. He wanted to be a man who grows mint on his balcony.

"So are you going to sleep?" he asked, and she nodded and filled a glass with tap water and stood leaning against the counter, sipping it. "Should I tell you a story?" he joked, because they had given up that bedtime habit long ago, and she smiled at him cynically. And yet each night an accounting occurred between them, a forceful report of what they had done all day and what they had thought and felt, and tonight, more than usual, they both knew it was time for a new story.

(5)

That night, Shira dreamed about her father. They were talking on the phone. She had just come back from overseas (when she woke up, she couldn't remember where she had been) and had called, expecting him to complain about how hard it had been for him while she was gone and to ask her never to go away again. But her father sounded unusually excited and vibrant, except that his speech was garbled—it sounded dim and slow, like a record played at the wrong speed. She tried to figure out what he was saying and was able to extract a few names of medications out of the jumble of words. Some were familiar, the pills he took, and some were new, but their names made sense, and then suddenly he became lucid and asked her to come and eat fish cakes with him. She wondered where the fish cakes were from and who had made them, but before she could ask, her father declared, almost joyfully, "I got the most awful case of jaundice." She was overcome by a wave of fear, because at that moment she remembered she was pregnant, only in the third or fourth week, but still pregnant, and her father asked when she would come and she said she wouldn't come at all because she was afraid he would infect her and the fetus, and in fact, she thought, he was supposed to be setting the table for three . . . and then she forced herself to wake up.

She lay in bed, and the relief at waking gradually mingled with sadness over the loss of being pregnant and having an excellent excuse not to eat with her father—dreamy moments in which her priorities were clear, nonnegotiable, and she had not even a single pang of conscience. She knew that in a few hours she would visit him, as she did every Saturday, and they would sit quietly together for a couple of hours, and occasionally they would exchange a few vague words, and the apartment would have the usual air of disease—not jaundice, but something gray and nameless—and before she left she would go into the kitchen and empty the fridge of everything that had gone bad in there over the past week, and when she left she'd throw the bag into the trash can—as if she were putting a period at the end of a sentence—until next weekend.

She went into the kitchen and filled the pot with water and coffee and put it on the gas stove. Then she sat at the table and waited for the bubbling to signal that she should get up and turn the heat off. Every morning, the bubbling sound echoed a different mood: Sometimes it sounded like lava rushing to the mouth of a volcano, and sometimes like stifled laughter or a stomach rumbling. This morning it was the coffee's aroma, rather than its sound, that got her up, and when she poured it into a mug she realized she had been cut off from herself for a few moments, cut off from the usual stubborn morning rituals. How rare are these moments outside of time, she thought, and how pleasant.

When she sat down at the table with her coffee, her father's voice started echoing in her mind again, asking when she would come. But now it was no longer a record playing too slowly, as it had been in the dream, but a scratchy record, and the knowledge that her father, like her, was awake now, so early, and that many other elderly people were awake, made her sad. A ten-minute drive separated them, separated the house she had grown up in—which was now his house, and where nothing remained, of her or of her mother, and which a sour density had now overtaken, like a weed—from her rented apartment, with its warmness and airiness, not the beauty or the stability of Rona's house, but still: something healthy.

She imagined her father dipping a sesame cookie in his instant coffee, as he had always done since she was a child. She thought of the cheap instant coffee he liked, and how he always rejected the jars of imported coffee she brought him. She tried to impose a better quality of life upon him, as if finer coffee could somehow tip the scales on which her father stood, thin and fragile and yet so heavy, with her on the other side, jumping up and down with the things she brought him: foreign architecture journals he wasn't interested in, books she had read and liked, the onion bread he sometimes ate, and jars of imported instant coffee, which always remained sealed on the top shelf in the cabinet, the coffee turning to a lump behind the tempting label. She sipped her coffee, seeing before her his freckled hand—which had remained strangely large in comparison to his shrunken body—dipping a cookie in the cup as if it were fishing. She thought about the crumbs she always found at the bottom of his cups when she washed them, the way they disgusted but also fascinated her, as if they were crumbs of her father, bait at the bottom of the sea.

She tried to reconstruct the dinner at Rona's, as if the replay would compensate for the bad dream, and wondered what Yonatan was doing now. She wondered if he was awake yet, if he was one of those people who slept late on Saturdays, and if Dana was tiptoeing around the apartment so as not to disturb him. Maybe she was asleep and he was awake. When Shira looked at the clock she realized it wasn't even eight yet and assumed they were both still sleeping, unaware of her stealthy infiltration into their lives, into their as-yet-unbegun morning.

She took the coffee over to the computer, sat down, even though she knew she would not be able to write a word. Her first novel no longer seemed relevant, as a book or as a fantasy. She wanted her next book, if she could ever write one, to be completely different, even contradictory. She started typing the day's first lines with the usual hesitation. Although she didn't yet have actual characters, she knew this book would also involve a man and a woman. She thought she should make up a woman's character that was not an invention but an enhancement, and perhaps also a simplification, of herself, the character now sitting at the computer or perhaps somewhere else, somewhere similar in the desperation it inflicted. Where would she locate the new character? Where was she sitting now? Perhaps on a bench in Meir Park, a park weighed down with so many of her steps. Perhaps in a café or in a car, or perhaps the character was still asleep in bed, and soon she would shake her shoulders gently and help her wake up into her banal morning, both their mornings. The fingers flitting over the keyboard were suddenly alive with desire, and she was filled with great admiration for this character about to be born: she herself. This was the moment when she said goodbye to Aya, the protagonist of the last novel—who was the woman she had once hoped to be—and created a new, still unnamed person.

She thought of Aya, how she had loved her once and had tried to promote her interests, as if she were her agent. She remembered how easily she had fitted the character of Uri to her dimensions. From the moment he was born on the screen, he was a twin, identical to her, as if she had been turned inside out like a shirt. Perhaps that was why it had been easy to write their story. She realized she had never written a real man (or a woman either), and the love story she had written now seemed fake, especially the scene of their meeting in that ER, with their instant love and their DNA conversation. Nonsense, she thought, there's no such thing, and for a moment she thought of reconstructing Rona's dinner on the screen, along with Yonatan's silence and her own, which suddenly seemed like the most profound conversation she had ever had with a man.

She walked around the apartment restlessly, as she always did when ideas came to her. During these moments, which had become rare, she would jump up from her chair as if something had burned her, go in and out of the kitchen without knowing what she was looking for, put a load of laundry in the washer or go down to the store, turn the TV on and then quickly switch it off, feeling guilty about the wasted time, and go back to the computer. She liked this agitation because it contained excitement and optimism to which she might have been afraid to admit, as if this inspiration, always sudden, was a pipe that could leak or burst at any minute and so needed to be handled gently.

She glanced at the clock and saw it was ten and thought, He's probably awake now, and maybe he's also trying to write. She put the coffeepot on again, wanting to keep sitting in the kitchen and missing him, but she thought, I should be missing my writing, not him; who is he anyway? And why him?

She went back to the computer with a cup of coffee, an ashtray, and a pack of cigarettes and started quickly typing an encounter between a man and a woman. They were still nameless; she didn't want to give them names yet. There's plenty of time, she told herself; they may not get names until they fall in love. The scene was a dinner at a mutual friend's. But how could they fall in love? And was there any justification for their existence if they did not?

She wrote for almost two hours, until the phone rang and her father asked when she was coming. "Soon," she told him softly, distracted. She went back and finished their first meeting, which concluded not with desperation but with hope. Then, still distracted, she got dressed, returned the coffee cup and the full ashtray to the kitchen, and when she went downstairs to the street and got in her car, she was sorry, for the first time in a long while, to leave the computer. She started driving north, and the streets were quiet Sabbath streets, and she drove slowly and turned the radio on, and the songs were Sabbath songs, but the Sabbath struck her as less interminable than usual.

"What do you want to do today?" he asked Dana, who was sitting on the balcony, leafing through the newspaper.

"I don't know."

"Did you make any plans with Tamar?"

Dana shook her head. "Are you going to work?"

"Yes. I think so." But since waking up he felt like getting out of the house, away from the restlessness that had stayed with him through the night. "Do you want to go somewhere?" he asked hesitantly, as if afraid of rejection.

"Where?" She looked up from the newspaper.

"I don't know. We could go and have lunch somewhere, sit at a café."

"Are you hungry?" she asked, and suddenly she sounded like Ilana, because she had used that same tone of voice, interested and yet indifferent at the same time.

"A little. You?"

"Also a little."

"So do you want to?"

"Where should we go?"

"I don't know. Let's go out and see where we feel like sitting."

"Okay." She put the paper on the floor. "I'll get dressed, then."

"Me too. I'll meet you at the door in five minutes?" He tried to pump some enthusiasm into the outing, which seemed already to have exhausted them both, and they each disappeared into their rooms.

He changed his socks and underpants but put on the same clothes he had worn the day before, which had been tossed on the floor, leaving off the undershirt because it was warm outside. Then he went into the bathroom, looked in the mirror, and tried to decide whether or not to shave. Brown and white stubble covered his chin and cheeks. Dana came in and stood beside him while she brushed her teeth. "What do you think, should I shave?"

She glanced at his reflection, reached out to touch his cheek, and said yes, he was prickly.

"Later, then. When we get back. I can't be bothered now." He put deodorant on.

When they went downstairs, Dana wearing her cousin Michal's old clothes—a pair of red jeans and a pink sweatshirt with a print of white clouds—she told him the clothes were a little too small for her, and he said he'd buy her some new ones. "I gained weight," she said.

He was filled with sadness because she spoke like an older woman in miniature, and her voice sounded like her mother's again. Sometimes, before they went to sleep, Ilana used to stand in their room in her underwear with her back to him, turn her head back, pat her bottom, and ask if she'd gained weight. When he looked up from the newspaper or book he was reading in bed and mumbled no, she would sigh. "Liar."

"I want pants like Shira was wearing yesterday," Dana said.

"Shira?" he asked, because although she had haunted him all night, she had appeared in his imagination as a nameless entity. "The one who was at Rona's yesterday?"

"Yes."

"What was she wearing? I don't remember." But then he recalled the orange corduroys, which he had seen before.

"Corduroy pants, kind of wide ones."

"Oh, yes." He wanted to say, They might make you look fat, but he kept quiet. Maybe if he had been her mother he would have said something, but maybe not. Dana had very few years left to be a child, but she would have plenty of years to torment herself over a couple of extra pounds. And she would have good friends—Tamar, for example, who would probably be tall and thin, like the father she didn't have—to go shopping with her and look her over when she came out of the fitting room and twist their faces and shake their heads and veto the purchase because it made her look fat. And there would be men she would face, at nights, in a room lit only by a reading lamp, and she would show her back to them with a shy, flirtatious half turn and ask if she'd gained weight, full of hope that they would lie. "But it's almost spring. Isn't it too hot to wear corduroy?"

"So what? We'll still have cold days, and I'll have them for next winter."

"Whatever you want. Buy them in a few different colors, even." He suggested they go to the mall some day this week to shop for clothes, because he needed some new things too.

They went into a café on Sheinkin that was too busy. Dana chose it. She said she didn't mind the crowds and preferred somewhere full to somewhere empty; an empty place was like sitting at home, only with a menu and waiters. He thought she was right, but then he was sorry that they'd even left home and that he hadn't shaved.

They got a little table near the restrooms. An irritable waitress handed them menus, smiled at Dana, and disappeared. It seemed to him as if the place was full of people he knew and that everyone was looking at him. At the table by the window he recognized the journalist from *Ha'aretz* who had interviewed him a few years ago, when his first book came out, but the reporter didn't see him. He was practically a kid back then, nervous and perspiring through the interview, and he had chain-smoked and not stopped complimenting Yonatan on his book. Now he was eating lunch with a beautiful woman, a three- or four-year-old girl, and a baby in a plastic high chair pushed up against the table. The journalist was talking loudly on his cell phone, and with the other hand he was shoving little pieces of focaccia into the baby's mouth.

Yonatan thought back to the days when he used to sit with Ilana in cafés, when Dana was a baby, each of them busy reading a different section of the newspaper and both busy with Dana, who had loved bustling cafés since the day she was born. He remembered the mornings when Ilana went to her job at the university while he was working on his second book. He would take Dana out in her stroller and wander around Sheinkin with her, sometimes going into a café or sitting outside if the weather was nice, reading the paper and smoking, stirring his coffee, feeding her little pieces of croissant or toast or a teaspoonful of froth. He would look at her as she watched the world from her stroller, and the world would watch her back, leaning over her, smiling, responding to her gurgles with a gurgle. How calm he had been as they sat in cafés, this one too, although they had seemed friendlier back then, and he had enjoyed the attention he received via his daughter as she sat in a crumb-filled stroller, waving her little fists.

Now she perused the menu, concentrating, thinking out loud, mumbling different possibilities to herself—she did feel like meat, she didn't feel like meat, maybe she'd have pasta, perhaps she wouldn't. "What are you getting, Dad?" She roused him from his nostalgic day-dream. He took a menu and started murmuring to himself too, and the waitress came over and asked if they wanted to hear about the specials. They both nodded, and she recited the names of different dishes and pronounced them all incorrectly, and he said they needed another minute. She said, "Take your time," with a look that begged them to hurry. Yonatan knew there was no need to agonize; he should take a gamble. But he had lost his appetite and felt his stubble growing quickly and turning into an ugly beard that drew everyone's attention. He told Dana he thought he'd go for the fettuccine Alfredo, but he pronounced it the way the waitress had: *pettuccine*. Dana smiled and said, "Then I'll get the veal *masala*!" She burst out laughing at her deliberate mispro-nunciation. Yonatan said, "Nice! Two points!" and was proud of her. He remembered that when she was little and had just started learning to read and write, he used to play a simplified alphabet game with her, which involved coming up with names of food beginning with each let-ter. Every time they got to *C,* Dana would say, "*C* for *cesame,*" and he would say, "That's with an *S.* How about *carrot?*" And when his turn came he would say things like *coq au vin* or *crème caramel,* just to make her laugh.

The waitress came back and took their orders. Within the surround-ing chaos, he heard organ music playing over the speakers and was in-sulted for Bach to be heard that way, in the tumult of children shouting, the noisy espresso machine, and fragments of cell-phone conversations, and with smells of deep-frying, too much rosemary, and fashionable an-drogynous perfumes. He remembered the organ music he used to listen to sometimes at the YMCA in Jerusalem. He had discovered it by chance, a little after his bar mitzvah, when he was walking home from the center of town. He liked to find new routes, little streets he didn't know, shortcuts and alleys between buildings, and he always found them, excited each time and pleased with himself and in love with his city, which offered endless opportunities for getting lost as well as a comforting familiarity. Strangely, getting lost gave him a sense of power, because the city suddenly seemed as if it belonged to him and played games with him, long before it had lost its sense of humor.

One Sunday, coming back from sports practice, he made his way down through the old Mamilla neighborhood and started going up King David Street. He knew the YMCA building from when his father used to take him on Saturdays to eat ice cream at the snack bar. It was locally made ice cream and tasted different from the other kinds he knew, and they both liked it—he because it always had little slivers of ice in it, and a yellowish color, and his father because he derived satisfaction from sitting in a busy snack bar on the Sabbath, licking ice cream made by Christians.

That afternoon he decided to go into the YMCA through the rear entrance, so he could walk down the hallway with the high arched ceiling that led from the concert hall, whose acoustics everyone always praised, to the large square in front of the building. As he passed the concert hall's heavy wooden doors, he heard sounds that reminded him of the music that accompanied the old horror movies he watched with his mother at the Smadar cinema, in black and white, movies that never really scared him. But as he stood outside the doors and listened, he began to feel true fear: not the fear caused by vampires or lonely distorted creatures who lived in church basements and bell towers but fear of an emotion that paralyzed his body and fueled his mind, a deep and metallic fear, like the sound produced by the organ.

He stood there for a long time, holding his breath, until he dared open the doors a crack and peek inside, afraid they would creak, but they opened silently. The sun was shining in through the tall windows, illuminating the front of the hall with what struck him at the time as the light of a foreign religion. Yonatan could see the back of an older man, bent over, his hands spread to the sides and his feet hitting the pedals as if he were riding a celestial bicycle. Without the dimming effect of the wooden doors, the notes sounded even more dangerous and inviting, and Yonatan found himself inside the hall, leaving the banality of Sunday afternoon behind. Entirely captivated, he leaned against the doors and followed the man's movements. From behind, he reminded Yonatan a little of his father, bent over his books at his desk across from the window that looked out onto the garden where his mother always puttered around— an amateur gardener dressed in work clothes and rubber boots. His mother had once offered him his father's antique desk, but he had refused, convinced he would not be able to write at it.

His father taught medieval history at the university, but when Yonatan was a boy he retired and delved into research. He was a poor teacher and his students never liked him. When he lectured, they thought he was talking to himself, and when they came to consult with him, he would insist on lecturing them eagerly. Every so often the students would be courageous enough to visit their professor at his home. They would give a short buzz on the bell, smile at his mother, who welcomed them quietly and led them like a receptionist into the garden, where the consultations were held during summer, or to the study in winter, and offer them coffee or tea with homemade cake.

His mother was an anthropologist. She met his father a few months before she was to begin her PhD, having returned, bronzed and enthused, from a research trip in Africa. She got a grant and was about to go and study in London, but his father was offered a position at Hebrew University. In love but reluctant to give up her trip, his mother, who was thirty-three at the time, suggested to his father, who was five years younger, that they postpone their marriage a year or two and, in the meantime, meet every few months. She promised to come to Israel for the summers. "We'll miss each other," she said, as they sat together in her rented room in Rehavia. "It will be good for us," she said, in a voice that tried to sound clinging but did not succeed because she was too independent and strong and different from the handful of women his father had loved before he met her. "We'll love each other even more," she promised, in a tone that faked neediness, and sat on his father's lap. He was not a handsome man, but something in his eyes, the same something Yonatan had inherited, won women over in an instant, particularly women who had been on their own for too long and who saw in the eyes both a challenge and a type of salvation. Only when Nathaniel Luria gave her an ultimatum did Rachel Levin realize that her neediness was not fake but real.

"I'm sorry," he announced in his distant tone, "but two years is too long. Even a year is too long." He held her hand, which was stroking his chest. "And to tell you the truth, Rachel, I don't know what you're waiting for. I want to marry you now, but if you have time to spare, you'd better find someone who does too; I'm sure it won't be difficult for you."

She was hurt that he threw her age at her but recognized what she had forgotten during her year of studies, delegations, travels, and sleeping in tents: She was old, almost too old. She got off his lap and sat on the floor.

"You can get your doctorate here," he said, trying to appease her. "There's nothing preventing you from getting your doctorate here." Then he got up, made a pile of the books he had left at her place over the months, loaded them in his arms, and said, "I'd like you to think about it." He stopped by the door to kiss her cheek coldly. He ignored her lips as they tried to divert his from their calculated course, and when she said she would give it some thought, he said, "I would really like you to." Three months later they were married in the courtyard of the King David Hotel.

She started her PhD studies at Hebrew University and tried, unsuccessfully, to get pregnant. The first doctor she saw advised her to give up her studies. "Emotional stress has a negative affect on fertility," he said, and sent her on her way. Another doctor conjectured that it might be caused by the malaria she had suffered years ago, but a third doctor said, "Nonsense. It's not stress and it's not malaria. You're just too old." In the end, after having abandoned her studies because they no longer interested her, and having begun to accept the fact that she would never be a mother, and after they had signed up for adoption, she got pregnant and gave birth to Yonatan. There were labor complications that almost cost her her life, and she had to have a hysterectomy.

Yonatan listened to the organ playing. Shivers ran up and down his body, but not just his body; he felt as if his entire being were shivering. It was pleasant but also something of a commitment, because he knew, after he tiptoed out and closed the wooden doors behind him and went on walking down the hallway as if nothing had happened and out into the sunlight flooding the square, that he would be a different person. He would be someone who had been through something, who would spend his whole life searching for ways to feel that shiver over and over again, because the organ had heralded a sense of great gravity in his life, as if its sounds announced a struggle against death as well as the very touch of death itself.

(7)

Max Klein had a guest. Emmanuel Herman was an elderly construction engineer who had been widowed at the age of seventy. He was as happy as a child and full of plans for the future, despite the recent amputation of his left leg at the knee because of diabetes complications. He visited Shira's father sometimes, without calling ahead, and spent an hour or two on the couch in the living room, sipping instant coffee and nibbling sesame cookies, chatting happily and overriding the silence and the frightened glances her father stole at his stump.

He was her father's last remaining friend, and like a mother worrying over her unpopular son, grateful for any boy or girl who came to visit, Shira was glad whenever her father told her, grumblingly, that Emmanuel had stopped by, or when she found him there on Saturday afternoons—his favorite visiting time—sitting in the living room, cheerful and flushed and covered with crumbs.

Every time he left, moving slowly to the door on his crutches, they would both watch him from the balcony as he got into the old Volvo he had owned even before he became handicapped. Then her father would go inside and sit down grumpily in his armchair and turn on the TV or the radio. She would take the coffee cups into the kitchen and rinse them, sit across from him in the other armchair, which was still warm from Emmanuel's visit, and ask why he didn't invite Emmanuel over more often. Her father would say he didn't invite him at all, he came without calling, just like that, in the middle of the day, at a time when people wanted to rest—especially on Saturday. He claimed it was annoying and added that he might say something about it one of these days. Shira asked why, but her father continued the private conversation he had been having with the world for many years and said that if he could tell Emmanuel not to come anymore he would gladly do so, but cultured people didn't do such things. Shira, who always felt insulted on Emmanuel's behalf and angry at her father for letting himself be picky when he was so lonely, asked, "But why do you hate him so much?" With no fear in his voice, simply stating a dry fact, her father said, "Just because. He's the angel of death."

For years, she had mocked him but lately she had come to understand him better. Galia, an old high school friend whom she hadn't seen for eighteen years, had called her out of the blue one day. Shira remembered her as a very beautiful confused girl who wanted to be an actress. In high school Galia had taught her how to smoke weed. They would slip out during recess to the park across the street, where, on a bench hidden among overgrown shrubbery, Galia would reach into her bra for a little fabric purse with cigarette papers and marijuana leaves and would roll a joint for them, wetting it with her lips in a movement that was both skilled and panicked.

They talked mostly about sex. Galia described her sexual encounters with young actors and students at the drama school. Shira talked about the flings she longed for as if they had already happened. "You'll be a great writer," Galia would say to her, leaning back on the bench, turning her head up to the sun and closing her eyes. "I can tell just by your descriptions." Shira would look at her and know even then that Galia would never be an actress; she would fail before she even tried.

When she was seventeen, in the winter of the eleventh grade, Shira lost her virginity to a boy her age whom she met in a creative writing workshop. When she told Galia about it the next day, as they sat on their folded coats on the bench, still wet from the night rainfall, Galia told her it was a pity she had wasted her first time on someone so young and inexperienced. Shira found herself defending Ariel, even though she agreed with Galia and envied her because her first time had been in the ninth grade, with a twenty-five-year-old actor who had a small part in a movie. By the time she reached the eleventh grade, Galia had slept with twenty-two men, she claimed, and she gave each of them a cruel nickname afterward, like Tiny, The Moaner, Black and Decker, Red Chest, and Honeysuckle.

She was very thin and seemed to shed a few pounds every time she went from one man to the next, from nickname to nickname. She was pale, with sunken cheekbones and greasy strands of black hair that dropped over her beautiful eyes. Her advice to Shira about sex was, "Men like you to tell them when you're coming, it excites them." When Shira asked how she was supposed to tell them, Galia said, "Just say you're coming."

"Just say 'I'm coming'? Doesn't that sound kind of funny?"

"No," Galia said with extreme gravity. "It's not funny at all. It really turns them on."

When Shira asked how you could tell if sex was good, Galia said that good sex should always feel like the last time you'd ever have sex in your life.

Shira and Ariel used to make out in his bedroom. He lived alone with his mother, who owned a little café on Ibn Gvirol and was out at nights. They would lie on his firm youth bed, under a comforter that smelled of teenage sweat and weighed on their hasty hand movements. When he came on her inner thigh before being able to penetrate her, she was surprised by the sticky warmth of the semen, which burned her throbbing skin slightly as he lay over her like a corpse, his face in her neck, wetting her cheek with tears.

When she asked why he was crying, he shook his head and said nothing, but after a few moments he murmured, "Because I wasn't able to pleasure you; because you didn't even come; because I'm lousy." At that moment she understood that true maturation did not occur the first time you had sex, as she had always thought, but the first time your body was flooded, soiled like her inner thigh, with compassion and with the knowledge—still distant then, merely fluttering like a moth around a lamp in the room—that within the tenderness she summoned up to console this boy who had failed between her legs, a tiny computer had just been switched on.

She stroked his hair and his forehead and wiped the tears from his cheek, then put her hand on his back, beneath the thick sweater he hadn't had time to take off—they had both only taken off their pants and underwear—and ran her fingers up and down his spine, feeling his breath relaxing and his sniffles subsiding. His heart kept beating against her, and beneath him her hips throbbed like a metronome that keeps ticking even after the music has stopped.

She knew what an orgasm was, but thought that to have an orgasm with someone else was a completely different experience, a climax in and of itself. That's what Galia had told her. "You have no idea what it's like," she said, as they sat on their bench, her face turned to the sky, thin wisps of smoke coming out of her nostrils. "You just have no idea what it's like, to come at the same time with someone, together!" She opened her eyes for a minute, her eyelids were almost transparent in the sunlight. "You'll see, you'll see," she said, almost to herself, and handed the joint to Shira; there wasn't much left of it.

She had discovered masturbation when she was eleven. One morning, as she was waking up, she rolled over on her stomach onto one of the big stuffed animals she slept with, a beloved gray teddy bear. She started rubbing up against it, hesitantly at first and with a sense of guilt, because the bear was a childhood friend, but then she moved faster, without being able to stop and without wanting to, until she was surprised by her first orgasm, brief and stingy. She had not yet lain under someone and waited, with painful anticipation, for his movements, feeling so strong and yet so helpless.

From Ariel's diminishing tears came another erection, and without exchanging a word, without lifting his head from her neck, as if afraid that if he moved or said anything it would all go wrong, he entered her with an ease that contradicted the stories they had both heard about losing one's virginity, and they both uttered surprised sighs. She ignored the dim pain and the burning sensation and moved her hips quickly and whispered, "Don't come yet." Ariel nodded seriously into her neck, and as she moved beneath him she felt his body straining to remain frozen. In those seconds she could no longer feel his penis or the pain or the burning, only the weight of his body on her like the weight of her body on the teddy bear, and she whispered, "Don't move." Ariel nodded briskly again, and emitted a whimper of effort, and perhaps of sorrow at discovering that it was not he who was pleasuring her now, that he was a weight for her, not a lover. As she came, she notified him matter-of-factly. He whispered to her, "Yes," and tried to sound excited, even though he was disappointed that she'd abandoned him like that, inside her. But the currents from her dying orgasm thought otherwise and, free from constraint, he began moving inside her quickly until he came, suddenly straightening up, throwing his head back, closing his eyes, and arching his back authoritatively.

Three years later, he was killed in Lebanon. A sniper hit him in the rearguard of a convoy, his friends from the unit told Shira and the other girls who met at a memorial evening at his high school. Shira, who had slept with a few other guys since then, remembered that movement of his: his closed eyes, his arched back, and his face that looked distorted in pain.

They had stood at the door and kissed for hours when she went home that night. He called her early in the morning and asked her to come to his place again, as if he would ask her over every night from now until eternity. He said his mother would bring home some lasagna and a salade niçoise at lunchtime. She asked herself if she was his girlfriend now and told herself she was, she must be, and after they ate cold lasagna and salad they got into bed, and this time they did it slowly, naked, on top of the comforter that was still full of the night's smells and stains. Ariel moved as if his first experience had turned into years of practice, and this time she didn't come, nor did she when they did it again the next day, and a week later she went to Galia's gynecologist and got a prescription for birth control pills, and they met almost every evening and sat naked on his youth bed and read each other the short stories they wrote. Within the unripeness of those stories there was also a huge certainty, like the certainty of their being a couple as soon as they had slept together, simply because they didn't know any different. She missed both those things now: both the certainty and the lack of knowledge.

In the twelfth grade, roughly around the time she broke up with Ariel, Galia dropped out of school, and despite mutual promises to keep in touch they didn't see each other. Here and there Shira heard things about her: She had gotten married; she had left Israel; she had gotten divorced, had come back to Israel, and was hospitalized in a mental institution. Once she saw a picture of her in the paper, holding up a sign at a rally protesting cruelty to animals. She looked even thinner than she had as a girl, her hair still fell over her eyes, but she wasn't as pretty.

A few months after Shira's novel reached first place on the bestseller list, the phone rang very late at night, and Galia was on the line. "Remember me?" she asked, and before Shira could say yes, Galia said, "I've been looking for you for ages. You're not listed in the phone book."

"I'm in a rental apartment."

Galia ignored her reply. "I've been looking for you forever. You're hard to find, but you were hard to find back then too; you were always kind of slippery; that's why I liked you."

Groggy from sleep and a little embarrassed, Shira took the phone into the kitchen and put the kettle on. "How's it going, Galia?"

"I read your book, and I wanted to tell you that I really liked it. I was very moved. I thought of us. I remembered our talks."

"Yeah?"

"Do you remember?"

"Yes, of course I do."

"I thought we could get together."

Shira heard her lighting a cigarette. "Do you live in Tel Aviv?" She didn't want to meet her but didn't know what to say.

"I live on a moshav, not far. I run a cat shelter."

"That sounds nice."

"So I thought we could get together, if you're not too busy or too famous."

"Of course not. We should definitely get together."

"What are you doing now? Are you going to sleep? Did I wake you?"

"Kind of."

"What time is it?"

"One forty-five."

"And is that late for you?" she asked, instead of apologizing.

"Yes, sort of."

"Because I thought I might pop over to see where you live, see how a famous writer lives. But you probably want to go back to sleep."

"Yes. Why don't you give me your number and we can talk tomorrow?"

"You won't call."

"Why wouldn't I call?" She felt herself being assaulted. "Of course I will."

"I'll call you, okay? I'll call tomorrow morning. What time do you get up?"

"Nine or ten."

"Then we'll talk. Good night, sleep well."

"You too," Shira said, although she knew Galia wasn't planning to go to sleep. She imagined her sitting in her garden on the moshav and smoking, with those nervous movements of hers, surrounded by darkness and cats.

The next day at lunchtime they met at a café. Shira was a few minutes late, and when she walked in she saw Galia sitting at one of the tables. They hugged, briefly; Shira could feel Galia's ribs beneath her transparent chiffon blouse, spiky and brittle, like the embrace itself.

"You haven't changed at all," Galia noted, in a tone that sounded more accusatory than flattering.

"You haven't either," Shira lied.

She now looked like the roughness her voice used to have. Her hair was no longer black but dyed an eggplant shade and looked very dry, almost flammable. Her eyelashes were coated with black mascara that had smeared on her eyelids and pooled in the corners of her eyes. It was the same makeup she had worn eighteen years ago, but the black circles around her eyes had an aura of mystery back then.

Instead of the cheap Noblesse brand, she now smoked long brown cigarettes, and when she moved her hands her bangles chimed. She ordered soda water and a latte, then a beer, then another, and talked incessantly. She told Shira everything she had been through since leaving high school. Oddly, the story of her chaotic life was very organized and told in a businesslike fashion, and she never took her panda eyes off Shira for a minute, as if she were examining her, as if she expected that when the speech was over Shira would tell her things that would erase everything she had said, or at least rearrange them and offer revisions, as if what she had said was just a bad text and not her life story.

"Wow, you've been through so much," Shira said, when Galia finished talking, and finally turned her head away to face the window. Shira noticed a fleshy scar on her neck and asked what it was.

"That's from a long time ago," Galia said, and ran her fingers over the scar. "It happened in Paris. Someone I was living with. He cut me."

"Why?"

"He was crazy, forget about it."

They were silent for a few minutes. Shira was fascinated by the scar, but Galia called the waitress and asked for the menu again.

"I was pregnant with his child," she said, and crushed her cigarette out in the ashtray. "He wanted the baby, I didn't. I had an abortion behind his back and he found out. That's it."

"Wow," Shira repeated.

"I don't regret it," Galia said, as if answering an unasked question. "I want you to know that I'm not sorry. It was the right thing to do, period."

"Of course. You have nothing to regret."

"I got pregnant lots of times after that."

"Lots of times?"

"Twice. Another time in Paris, by him."

"The same guy?"

"Yes." She smiled. "He had good sperm."

"You mean you stayed with him after he cut you?"

"I left him, I went back to him, don't ask."

"And then?"

"Then in Israel, by some married guy. And I'm not sorry, I'm telling you. First of all, I'm not meant to be a mother, and second, if I want to there's still time, isn't there? We're still young."

"Young enough."

"It's good material for a book, my life, isn't it?"

"Absolutely."

"So maybe you can write about me?" Something in her panda eyes lit up again.

"Maybe," Shira said. Was that the purpose of their meeting—to turn Galia into a character in a book?

"Because I have lots of fascinating material," Galia said, as if she hadn't just been talking for a whole hour. "Don't ask, the pregnancies are peanuts compared to the other stuff."

"I can imagine," Shira said, and wondered why Galia had said pregnancies rather than abortions. She suddenly felt tired and wanted to get up and leave. When she looked at Galia she was filled with pity, wondering why the weak always manage to deceive the strong, how their weakness turns into a trap. "So what's up with you now? You're taking care of cats? Is that how you make a living?"

"I don't make a living from it. It's volunteer work. My dad left me some money; he died three years ago."

"So you're set."

"You could say so."

"At least you have that."

"Yes, at least I have that."

They were quiet. Galia ordered another beer. When she saw Shira restlessly shredding a napkin, she said, "You know? I always knew you'd make it. I always knew."

"Really?" Shira looked up from her heap of paper shreds.

"Yes, really. Something in you really wanted to be successful."

Shira nodded but couldn't remember herself that way.

"Some people are like that." This time Galia didn't pour her beer into a glass but drank straight from the bottle. "You can just see it in them."

After saying goodbye and promising each other they would keep in touch and knowing they'd never see each other again, Shira felt as if *she* had now met the angel of death. There was something so demanding about Galia's failure, something that made her feel so healthy and happy with her life, that when she walked into her father's apartment and saw Emmanuel sitting in the armchair, she was struck by how relative everything was: in her eyes, her father's house was full of illness and Emmanuel was a healthy breeze who sometimes entered it, but to her father the situation was reversed. And the guest himself, she thought, as she leaned over to kiss his cheek, had no idea what role he was playing here, with his one leg and his boundless cheer.

She kissed her father's stubbly white cheek too and offered to make them some coffee. Her father said he'd already had some, but Emmanuel gladly accepted. In the kitchen she thought it was unfair what she was doing to her father, thinking of him as handicapped, as someone for whom one despised friend was better than none. She opened the fridge and took out disposable plastic containers with lentil soup, cooked beets, and stuffed cabbage, all of which her father had bought at the delicatessen across the street. She put the containers out on the counter, gave them a sniff, and threw them in the trash.

(8)

It was two and the café was packed. Yonatan was convinced people were watching him and his daughter while they waited for tables in the long line stretching from the bar out to the street. The waitress was going down the line taking people's names, scanning the tables with her eyes, trying to guess who was about to finish and who was not yet done, throwing desperate smiles at Yonatan as he drank his espresso and smoked a cigarette with faked serenity. He signaled to her and she hurried over with the check. He paid and got up and made his way through the crowd with Dana until they came out into the early spring sunshine. "Crappy place," he said, and his daughter concurred. "Home?"

"Home," Dana said, and Yonatan told himself that in the end he really did like his apartment—*their* apartment. The morning's adventurous restlessness, the night's troubling thoughts, and above all the sudden longing for change, or at least renewal, had been nothing more than a passing anxiety attack.

They walked down Sheinkin, the street that for Yonatan had turned from friend to foe; he hoped they wouldn't meet anyone they knew. But then, at the intersection with King George, he spotted her. She was standing at the pedestrian crossing with her back to them, her bag slung over her shoulder, wearing jeans and an old gray sweatshirt, just like the one he had on. He thought it was her, but he wasn't sure; he didn't know if he hoped it was, but before he could decide, Dana shouted out, "Dad, there's Shira. Shira!" The woman turned around, and he felt the blood rushing to his head and then draining out, and Dana waved, although she was only a few steps away. Shira smiled and waved back.

For a moment Shira thought they looked like twins, she and

Yonatan. They were wearing the same sweatshirts and similar jeans, and when she looked in his face, which seemed paler than it had last night, it reminded her of the skin tone her own face took on after a sleepless night. She touched Dana's shoulder lightly and asked, as if she were addressing her and not him, "What are you doing here?"

"We just had lunch," Yonatan said, then looked at his daughter and touched her shoulder too. "And you? Just hanging out?" He thought he sounded like an annoying old man again.

She said, "I'm on my way to buy some cigarettes."

"I need some too." The light changed, and the three of them crossed over toward the kiosk.

Only then did she begin to feel her heart racing and her brain trying to catch up. She mustn't miss the opportunity she thought she had missed yesterday. She could already see the café on the corner, which she didn't like because it was too noisy, and the kiosk a few yards in front of it, and she thought that if it weren't for Dana she might have been bold enough to ask if he wanted to get some coffee somewhere.

The shade of Yonatan's face stabilized, but something inside him kept changing colors. As he stood next to Shira at the kiosk, leaning slightly against the stainless steel vats of nuts and snacks, he was suddenly struck by the thought that he was not interested in a relationship—interested, perhaps, but incapable. He asked for a pack of Winstons, then decided he wanted a lighter. He told Dana to pick one out, knowing she would take a long time to decide, and a new thought shot the previous one off course—the fixed course that was so familiar it didn't need Yonatan as a pilot—he had to buy time and not let this minute get away. In the sunlight he saw things he hadn't seen yesterday: that she had good skin and a few gray hairs hiding in the mass of curls. They both waited for Dana, who examined the lighters, picked up two of them, told the shopkeeper, "This one," and then, "No, wait, wait a minute, this one," and then changed her mind again, and then, "Dad, which one do you guys think is prettier?"

The phrase *you guys* was so intoxicating that Yonatan chose a transparent lighter with ducks on it, looked at Shira, and asked, "What do you think?" And she, without even seeing what he was showing her, said, "Pretty." He paid the shopkeeper, and Dana skipped ahead, then stopped and waited for them. Something had filled her with energy, and Yonatan wondered if she felt his excitement now, transferred to her, as if by dialysis. She hopped a few steps, then waited again, then skipped ahead, and suddenly he thought he heard Shira say something, but he wasn't sure. He heard his daughter's pleading voice, "Dad, please! Please!" "What?" he asked.

Shira, who suddenly looked embarrassed, said, "I asked if you felt like going somewhere for coffee." As it turned out, she had taken courage from the girl's presence, because she had realized that it would be easier to say *you guys* than *you*.

Yonatan said, "Yes, sure, we'd love to!"

The new café turned out to be empty and quiet, and they wondered whether to sit inside or out. Dana eventually decreed, "Outside." Yonatan looked at his daughter sitting on the iron seat, swinging her legs under the table. She looked at the menu and hummed to herself but was focused solely on them. He kept quiet.

He tore the cellophane wrapper off the pack of cigarettes he had just bought, even though there was another pack in his pocket that he had opened just before they left, and offered one to Shira. She said, "No, thanks. Do you want one of mine?" and offered him a Camel Light.

He said he hated light cigarettes, they seemed like an oxymoron to him, and Dana asked what that was. They both tried to explain, and Yonatan said, "It's something and its opposite."

"Like a clever idiot?" Dana asked.

Yonatan said yes. He thought about himself: he was being something and its opposite—a clever idiot. He was on the verge of suggesting they call Rona to see if she wanted to join them with Tamar, but instead he said, "So what's new? What have you done since yesterday?" as if she gave him such reports every day.

"Nothing. Really nothing."

Dana asked the waitress for hot apple pie with ice cream and whipped cream, to compensate herself for the bad panna cotta they had shared just a few moments earlier. "You're both wearing the same thing!" she said. They looked at each other and at themselves, and smiled. Dana bent over and checked their feet beneath the table. "Look, you're even both wearing running shoes." They leaned over to look, and

Dana said, pointing to each in turn, "You could be twins, except that you're wearing a bra and you're not."

"Why are you so sure I'm wearing a bra?"

Dana pointed at Shira's shoulder. "I can see the strap."

Shira looked down at her shoulder and quickly pulled up her sleeve. She regretted having worn an ugly old bra that day, already gray from so many washes.

Yonatan, suddenly embarrassed, said, "And why are you so sure *I'm* not wearing a bra?" Dana made a face at him and he made one back and said, "Haven't you ever seen my bra collection? Don't you know that at nights I perform in all kinds of clubs in women's clothing?"

"Yeah, sure, we know all about that," Dana said.

Yonatan whispered, "You didn't know your dad was a transvestite?"

"What's a transvestite? Is it the same as gay?"

"No," Shira said, and tried to explain.

Dana said, "Yeah, right, Dad, a transvestite would kill himself if he saw what kind of underwear you wear." She turned to Shira. "Do you want to know what kind of underwear he wears?"

Despite the barriers that had been crushed beneath their feet, Yonatan and Shira both said, "Yes," as if they were two children who had suddenly discovered their sexuality during a game of doctor–patient. They wanted someone else to lead them to the place where strange and forbidden secrets are revealed, but for that they needed a third child, smaller and more innocent.

Dana said, "Well, then," and told Shira about the old baggy underwear her father liked to wear, and how they always bought him boxers because he fell for the models in the commercials and was convinced they would look good on him too, and how he never wore them because they were uncomfortable; he only liked his ugly cotton ones with fraying elastic.

Yonatan leaned back in his chair and listened and pretended to be horrified, but he knew his daughter was doing his dirty work. He was letting her take the new woman down that corridor to his bedroom, opening his closet doors for her, and emptying his drawer of ugly underwear onto the bed so she could see exactly what she was getting into. Then he said, "Now you have to ask her what kind of underwear she wears too, because it's not fair that she only knows about mine."

He felt like a child on the verge of his first orgasm, and Dana, who took her role seriously, asked, "What kind of underwear do you wear?"

Shira looked deep into Yonatan's eyes—he thought he saw an invitation to bed—and said, "The same as your dad's."

As he stirred his latte and watched Shira empty two packets of sugar into her coffee, and heard Dana sucking lemonade through a straw, something moved in him—not in his underwear, although he was a little turned on, more alive than turned on; not in his insides, because he was not afraid; not in his heart or his mind, which was now finally empty of bothersome thoughts; but in his hands, which suddenly wanted to caress his daughter's sun-flushed face, the face that was dotted with his wife's freckles, and also the shoulder of the woman sitting across from him, just in the place where the gray bra strap had left a reddish line, because something in him knew that this encounter would soon be over: The check would be ordered, he would offer to pay, she would refuse, he wouldn't have the courage to say *you can pay next time,* and in the end they would split it.

He caressed himself with words, his hands resting on the table. "Calm down." His daughter, who had suddenly become mischievous, was scattering sugar from a packet on his hands. This is what people do in the world, he thought. They sit in cafés and flirt, with or without excited children keeping their fingers crossed.

They talked a little about their writing problems, and Shira said she had been quite successful that morning, and then she talked about her dad and asked if his parents were still alive. He said his mom was and told her about her house in the German Colony. Shira said she had always envied Jerusalemites, because she thought they had different childhoods, more mysterious, more wintry. Dana asked if she also liked winter, and Shira said she did. Dana ran her fingers over her father's sugary hands and said, "We do too."

Then they talked about computers and Yonatan complained about the software he used, which was slow and old-fashioned, and Shira told him she'd recently been given a new program. Yonatan enthused and said it was an excellent program but very expensive.

"I could copy it for you, but I don't know how."

"It's easy. I can show you. Do you have any blank diskettes?"

"Yes, sure. Do you want to come over now? I live just here, on Borochov. Want to come over?"

"We could." He turned to his daughter and, without meaning to, said, "Do you want to go over to Tamar's in the meantime?"

Dana said no firmly, but then added, "Actually, yes," as if she had remembered something, or only just learned it, absorbing it from her father's look, which seemed so hopeful and desperate to her.

"Then let's call Rona. I think there's a phone here."

"There is," Shira said. It felt as if she were promoting a little scheme whose essence was unclear.

"Here," he said to his daughter, handing her a few shekels. "Go call her and say hi to her."

"From both of you?" Dana said, and jiggled the coins in her hand.

"Yes, from me too," Shira said.

They watched her through the window as she dialed the number and talked, putting one coin after another into the slot. They were as quiet as they had been when they sat together the night before, but this time it was the silence of people recovering, resting after a big achievement, the silence of anticipation of the next accomplishment.

When Dana came back, she said that Tamar was waiting for her and Rona said they were both invited for leftovers that evening. "Okay, I'm going," she said, as if she wanted to disappear quickly.

But her father caught her hand. "We'll walk you."

"It's daytime, it's not dark! It's right here, two doors away!"

"We'll walk you," Shira said, and Dana huffed and said, *ugh!* Not only was she not wanted now, she wasn't independent either.

Yonatan gestured to the waitress for the check, and Shira took her purse out, and he protested, and she said, "What's the big deal? Can't I buy you coffee?"

"I didn't have coffee," Dana said.

"Lemonade then."

"But I had cake too."

"Oh, well, in that case—"

"Then next time I'm paying," Yonatan said. "I mean it." He sounded like an old man again with the *I mean it* and he reminded himself that he'd better start learning how to control this man who insisted on emerging and talking in a language that gave away everything Yonatan didn't even know he was trying to hide.

(9)

He fell in love with the coffeepot as soon as he saw it. He stood in the kitchen, examining it, and said he had to get one for himself.

"Should I make some coffee?" he said, and waved the pot in the air. He looked around at the walls, which were painted in an old shade of yellow, the high ceiling with two large damp spots spreading out from the corners as if they were going to meet in the middle, and the long narrow window that was open and looked out onto the wall of the next building and into another window, from which a little boy was watching them. "I want to learn how to use this thing," he said, and she asked how it was possible that he'd never come across one before. He said he often had, at friends', but he'd never bothered to watch when they made coffee. "It didn't interest me. I enjoyed the coffee and didn't ask any questions."

"Then why are you so interested now?" She hoped she didn't sound hostile and suddenly felt as if a nosy stranger had invaded her lowly empire.

"I have no idea. Don't you sometimes find yourself suddenly fascinated by something you've never noticed before?"

"No."

"Me neither, to be honest. So what do you do with this?"

"Leave it. I have to clean it first."

"I'll clean it," Yonatan persisted, and started unscrewing the two parts.

"You seem technically inclined."

"Yes. I've just discovered that for the first time."

"This must be your day of discoveries," she said, and immediately regretted it. How trivial she seemed, betrayed by symbols. When she had written about them, they had filled her readers with excitement, but when they came out of her mouth now they melted into thin air, leaving a cloud of cheap perfume trailing behind.

He smiled at her. Over her shoulder his eye caught sight of her lettuce spinner, which was standing, unused, on a high shelf. "That's a great thing. Simple but ingenious. I need to get one of those too."

"I never use it; you can have it." Again she regretted her words: he seemed embarrassed by her generosity. They had only met yesterday and would probably never see each other again.

"No, that's all right. I'll get one at some point."

"Or not."

"Or not."

"It's the kind of thing you want to buy but never do."

"Yes, I know those things." He thoughtfully scanned the shelves, searching, perhaps, for other things he would like but would never buy for himself, things he might get as a gift from someone one day, from someone it was okay to take things from, not her.

This kitchen looked like his own. It was long and narrow, with wooden cabinets that had never been changed and a sink that was too small and was, like his, full of dishes. There was a table big enough for two or three people, and the *Ha'aretz* supplement lay on it, open at the crossword page. He could see she'd only done half of it but couldn't tell if she'd solved the same words he had found yesterday evening, before being struck by the restlessness that now took on an almost celebratory significance, because without it he would not have wrung the invitation out of Rona. Without it he would not be here now, leaning on the counter in the kitchen of a young woman, a new woman, a woman, period. He felt comfortable in this kitchen.

He emptied the damp coffee grounds from the filter into the trash and rinsed it and the two other parts under the tap. Then he turned to Shira, who was standing beside him, watching him and looking a little worried, and asked, "So what do I do now?"

"Here's where you fill it with water. I'll get the coffee out of the freezer." She felt as if it were not the parts of the primitive little machine he was handling but those of her body, and she grew embarrassed as she watched him empty the old coffee into the trash can, tapping the filter against the sides, then running his finger through it to clean out the greasy remnants—as if he were touching her own refuse, emptying out incriminating evidence of a lonely morning, the grounds of a way of life she was suddenly ashamed of.

She put the jar of coffee down next to him and he examined it and said, "This is excellent coffee. Where do you get it, at the supermarket?"

"Anywhere. They have it at the little grocery—at least the one where I shop." He asked how much to put in, and she said, "That depends if you like it strong or not."

"Strong. I like it strong."

"Then fill the filter up all the way." She gave him a spoon and he dug it into the almost-empty jar. She felt embarrassed again. "I have to get some more. Is there enough in there?"

"Yes, I think so." He scraped the bottom and filled up the filter.

She stood next to him, following his movements, and when he screwed both pieces back together and said "That's it," and turned to her, his elbow bumped her arm.

"I'll put it on the stove," she said. When she took the coffeepot from him, her fingers touched his. She didn't want him to see that the stovetop was stained with oil and tomato sauce, every splatter like a crystal of its genetic material. "Let's sit down in the living room," she said, after turning the gas on. "It'll take a few minutes."

In the living room, without the toy that had both brought them together and partitioned them, her embarrassment increased. She sat down on the couch and briefly regretted the uncharacteristic spontaneity that had spurred her to invite him. She looked at him standing in the doorway, scanning the room, and hoped he would not stand in front of the bookshelves and examine her books. So many had done that before him and it had ended badly with all of them; with him, there was now the fear that it wouldn't even begin.

He ignored the books, said the room was nice, that it had good lighting, and sat opposite her in the armchair. He felt calm with her, without knowing why. Perhaps because she seemed so tense, tenser than he was, and he found that strangely comforting. He lit a cigarette and she got up to empty the full ashtray that was on the table, but he said, "Don't worry, I'm used to it. I hate empty ashtrays." She smiled and sat down again, but was still bothered by the full ashtray, as if the cigarette butts were further evidence.

He liked her furniture. There was something messy and warm about it, something heavy and slightly Jerusalemite that reminded him of his bachelor's pad on Montefiore Street, except this apartment felt like home rather than a set. The couch was big and old, like the armchair he was sitting in, which was very comfortable—he had the strange idea that his body was setting off on a spying mission for him—but the coffee table was the most beautiful piece of furniture. It was made of rough, scratched old lengths of wood joined together with huge copper screws. It reminded him of a loft floor. He asked where it was from.

"The flea market."

"I keep meaning to go down. Dana really likes hanging out there, but somehow we've been too lazy to go."

"Me too. Parking's a nightmare."

"That's true."

"And getting there without a car is a pain."

He nodded and blew out a thoughtful ring of smoke, and she wondered whether this sort of conversation could engender anything greater, or anything at all, and how long they would spend talking about parking and tables and coffeemakers and lettuce spinners, and whether they even *had* anything else to talk about. Then she got up and said, "I think it's boiling."

He walked with her to the kitchen and they both listened to the percolation, which sounded more energetic than usual to her, and she turned the gas off and poured them both some coffee. She handed him his mug and said they could sit at the computer. She was wary of more small talk with the echo of the previous trivial conversation still lingering in the room.

"Good idea," he said, even though he wanted to chat a little longer. He asked again if she had any blank diskettes, and again she said she did and led him to a closed-off balcony that connected the living room and the bedroom. It had a big old desk, very similar to his father's, and on it was her computer.

She told him to sit down, put the mugs on the desk, and went to get another chair. Through the open door to her bedroom he could see a bureau and the edge of a bed, newspapers scattered at its feet, and wondered if her life was like his. He suspected it was, and that suspicion filled him with joy. She came back and gave him a plastic box with diskettes and sat next to him, and he smelled perfume he hadn't noticed before in the kitchen.

When he started working on the computer, he became a different person. Confident, almost violent, he moved the mouse around, opened and closed files, put diskettes in and out, and gave her a running commentary on what he was doing, step by step, like a doctor letting a patient in on a complex medical procedure. He did not look at her for a second, and she didn't take in anything he said because she was busy planning her next move. What will happen, she wondered, when he's finished copying the program he was so excited about, and once he has explained how wonderful it is? What will we do when the copying is over?

"It'll be done in a second. There, see? Now it's telling me how long it has left."

She almost hoped for something to go wrong, like a power outage, so that everything he had done so far would be erased and he'd have to start from scratch. Because during those minutes it seemed as if copying the program was not an excuse but the true purpose of his visit. He was utterly engrossed in the job, talking to her computer as if it were a pet. "Yes," he said to the screen, "Great, excellent, good job!" He turned to her suddenly. "This is an excellent computer. Really good, and fast too. I wish mine were like this."

"Yes, it's pretty good, knock on wood."

"Are you superstitious?" he asked, as he rapidly clicked on the keyboard.

"Very much so. I'm like those old ladies. And you?"

"Not really, but talking about old ladies, my mother's like that. She knocks on everything that moves."

"I can relate to that," she said, and suddenly his mother was in the room—in some ways more present than her son. He sat next to her, typing quickly, and bent over to put the last diskette in the drive, and his arm kept bumping her elbow, and his knee jolted hers when he moved back and forth on the chair, but he seemed so disconnected, so lost in the computer, that even if she had stood behind him and wrapped her arms around him and kissed the back of his neck, as she wanted to do, he wouldn't have noticed.

She got up and asked if he wanted some more coffee, and he shook his head. "Something cold, then, a beer?" He nodded as if he hadn't heard but agreed, and she went to the kitchen, took two bottles out of the fridge, and opened them. She went back to the study and asked, "Do you drink it in a glass?" He shook his head again, and she stood behind him and put a bottle down by the keyboard, on his right side. He murmured, "Thanks," and took a short sip.

She looked at the back of his neck. All men, she thought, have something childish about their napes, the spot where the hairline meets the back of their ears, something forlorn and defenseless.

He took the last diskette out of the drive and stretched. "That's it, we're done. Do you have Solitaire?"

She said she did.

"I feel like playing a round." He turned his head around and smiled at her. "Do you play?"

"Sometimes. But I try not to, it's addictive."

"I know, that's why I uninstalled it." He was already displaying the cards on the screen. "Do you mind if I play?"

"No. No problem." Within seconds he became engrossed in the game, his hand covering the mouse, his eyes penetrating the screen.

"If you're sick of this, just let me know," he said, when the computer beat him for the third time straight, but she said it was all right, she would wash dishes in the meantime and he should make himself at home.

"Play as much as you want," she said and, again resisting the temptation to touch his nape, went into the kitchen.

She stood slowly washing the dishes, lathering each one with exaggerated thoroughness, trying to kill time, to calm herself: *He feels com-*

fortable here. Through the window, over the rooftop of the next build-ing, she saw the sky growing darker. She glanced at the clock and real-ized it was already after five, it was evening already, and she hadn't had anything to eat all day except a few biscuits at her father's. She thought about the invitation for leftovers at Rona's and was filled with optimism, because she now had plans for the evening, and they included the two of them.

She went back and stood behind him again, drinking out of her bottle and staring at the soft spot behind his ear, as if another man could be found there, not this man who seemed as if he would never finish playing. Then he asked what time it was and she said, "Five-twenty."

"Wow," he said.

"Why?"

"No reason. It's kind of late." She was worried that he would get up and leave and forget that Rona had invited them over. "I'm finishing this game and that's it, I swear."

She stared quietly over his shoulder at the screen and noticed that he'd changed the pattern on the back of the cards—instead of her dia-monds there were now fish floating there—and she felt her heart con-tract again, felt the soft spot behind his ear grow and broaden and turn into Yonatan in his entirety, a Yonatan who awakened new longings in her: to sit with him on the balcony and drink more beer, together this time, slowly this time, not with these huge gulps that tried to silence the fearful mumblings of her ego as it darted, with her, back and forth from the kitchen to the balcony, noticing on the way that today too, like last night, she was dressed horribly, that her hair looked wild, as if it too were afraid; since she couldn't change her clothes or wash her hair, she had slipped into the bathroom earlier and sprayed a little perfume on herself.

Now she wanted not to be the person who wants so much and is afraid to end up with nothing. Now she wanted not to be afraid and not to ask and not even to achieve. Now she wanted to be quiet with him and to silence herself a little, not to do anything, to like him without falling in love with him first, because she had once known only passion or repul-sion, not what lay between them.

"I got a little carried away," Yonatan said, and stood up suddenly. "My foot fell asleep." He hopped on one leg. "Wow, it's dark already."

He looked outside and gathered up the three diskettes. "Can I pay you for these?"

"Are you crazy?"

"Well, I don't know. I don't want to feel like I'm taking advantage of you." He gave a big yawn. "I came, I copied, I drank, I played."

"Big deal. At least I finally did the dishes."

"You should come over and play on my computer, maybe I'll finally do the dishes too. Should we call Rona? Ask her what time she wants us?"

He said *us* so naturally it seemed obvious to her that he wasn't interested in her; the thought hadn't even crossed his mind. If he had wanted *her,* he wouldn't have dared tie them both together in the same sentence. "I think she said we should come whenever we want. It's leftovers, nothing formal."

"It's a little early to go now, though, isn't it?"

"Yeah. We could have another beer in the meantime."

He agreed, and as she went to get them he said he would just call to check on Dana and say they'd be over soon. "What do you say, in an hour?"

"Something like that!" she yelled from the kitchen.

"What?" he shouted. "I can't hear you."

"Tell her we'll be there in an hour."

Feeling like a wife—and liking the feeling—she took two bottles of beer out of the fridge. She didn't really want one. She was a little tipsy from the first beer, on an empty stomach, but was afraid that if she didn't drink another, he wouldn't either, and if he didn't drink he might decide to leave and tell her they'd meet at Rona's. So she stood by the counter, hesitating, her heart saying beer but her stomach begging for tea.

She went into the living room and saw him standing by the bookshelf. For a moment she felt a chill and said, "I'm making some herbal tea, I don't feel like beer."

Yonatan took his fingers off the book he was about to pull out and said, "Me too. Great idea." When she asked what kind he wanted, he said, "Whatever you're having."

They sat on the balcony that faced the backyard. He asked if she visited her father every Shabbat, and she said she did. "And you? How often do you go see your mother?"

"Not as often as I should. But Dana is very attached to her, so we go once a month or so."

"Doesn't she come to visit you?"

"Hardly ever anymore. It's hard for her, she's almost eighty." He paused for a while. "Wow! My mother will be eighty this year! I just realized it."

"When was she born? Which month?"

"May."

"Same as my father. He's a Taurus." She suddenly didn't mind sounding like someone who was interested in astrology, although it was obvious that Yonatan was not one of the people who, like her, turned to the horoscopes in the weekend paper before reading anything else.

Yonatan sipped his tea. "It's tasty. What is it?"

"Raspberry and grapefruit. So your mother's a Taurus?"

"Definitely. And your father?"

She said he was becoming less of one every day, and more of an "I don't know what."

"A creature of some kind?"

"Yes. A creature of some kind. Something from outer space."

"I know. My father also turned into a kind of extraterrestrial in his final days." He corrected himself quickly and said, "Not that your father is in his final days or anything."

"He is." She thought about how, even when she was a little girl, she had always thought he was going to die.

She told him about her father, and as she talked she heard soft sounds in her voice that she had not known were there. She felt as if she were talking about someone else, not her father, or perhaps someone else was talking about him—someone who loved him more than she did—because the man being described to Yonatan, as he sat smoking on the balcony, listening to her thoughtfully, was someone with a personality and not just fragments of qualities. She told Yonatan about a different man, parts of whom she knew and parts of whom she was sorry she would never know, someone whose remnants were now fighting for recognition, even in retrospect, and who was shouting out, This is not how I want my daughter to see me: an old man dipping a biscuit in instant coffee. I'm someone else!

As she talked, her voice hypnotized him and he thought about his father: first the cactus chin, then the rest of his face. He could hardly remember his body, because at the end he was always covered with a sheet or a blanket, and Yonatan had preferred to ignore the outline beneath because it hurt his eyes. He remembered blue eyes, which always looked so watery, one moment begging for something, then indifferent. And thin lips, that turned as white as his face at the end, completely merged with it, as if he no longer needed them once he stopped talking. He saw his father's large nose, reddish and covered with purple blood vessels, the nose that right up to the end had looked independent and full of life. Yonatan smiled and Shira asked, "What?"

"What?"

"You were smiling."

"I was just remembering my dad."

"What did you remember?"

"No, you go on."

"No, tell me."

"Someday I'll tell you." She was happy to hear him say *someday*, because that meant there would be another opportunity. Or maybe he was saying, This is not the last opportunity. Or, in fact, that this was not about opportunities at all; that's not how it worked.

She went on talking: about her father's architecture office, about the trips down Allenby.

"I hate Allenby," Yonatan said.

"I love it," she said, and felt like a PR agent representing Max Klein, architect, the man who, according to her mother, was once a sought-after bachelor and not the old man dozing in his armchair with the transistor radio humming in his lap, the TV flickering in front of him, and every single light in the house turned on, as if his life depended on the electricity around him.

She remembered the Shabbat when he had rescued her from the military youth camp they were supposed to do in high school. She was sixteen and didn't want to go, but she gave in to pressure from her friends, who promised it would be nice and scolded her that it was important to do that kind of thing, to contribute. They were the same ones who were no longer her friends after that summer and were replaced by Galia, who never even considered going to the camp, which made everyone happy, particularly the teachers, who didn't even ask to hear her excuse.

When she got on the bus early in the morning, she realized she'd made a mistake and that she wouldn't survive the week with her classmates. The drive out of town frightened her. The city always gave her protection from the frameworks she hated so much and allowed her a sense of freedom; mainly, it meant she could be alone. Tel Aviv, she told Yonatan, especially North Tel Aviv, was dotted with beloved stations along her escape route. The little grocery across the street from school, for example, where she would buy a sandwich with cheese and pickles during recess, and a pack of cigarettes that she hid deep in her backpack.

"Time, Nelson, or Noblesse?"

"Noblesse, how did you know?"

"How many choices did young smokers have back then?"

"I don't really remember." She smiled. "God, how I miss that sandwich! It was so simple."

"Simple and perfect."

"But you know what? I don't like it anymore, that combination."

"Me neither."

"Sometimes I really feel like eating it, so I go and buy all the ingredients and put a lot of effort into making it, but as soon as I take the first bite I don't want it anymore."

"I wonder what changed, our taste or the sandwich?"

"The context."

He nodded in agreement and suddenly wanted to touch her, a little touch of identification, a caress of consolation for the loss of things that were perfectly simple, for the palate that never stops looking for them but will never find them again, because the search, by breaking the thing down into separate components and insisting on identifying each one precisely, ruins the perfect simplicity.

She told him about the other stations near her school, little everyday places that protected her because they gave her the security of knowing there was another life, outside of school, outside of home, perhaps even outside of adolescence. There was a certain bookstore, for example, that no longer exists. "Do you remember it?" she asked, convinced he would.

"No," he said apologetically, "I'm from Jerusalem."

"That's right," she said and envied him again for being a Jerusalemite—now he seems foreign again, she thought.

The camp, she told him, cut her off from her daily route, and even before they got onto the highway she started feeling the claustrophobia of a social unit and missed the freedom of being alone. She almost faked a last-minute illness, but the joy of her classmates, who for some incomprehensible reason treated their confinement to the bus as the ultimate freedom, paralyzed her. She promised herself she would try to have a good time, but after four hours of driving that were full of laughter and unruliness that infected even the driver, who started telling dirty jokes over the microphone, the effort became depressing in and of itself.

"I can so relate to that," he said, almost to himself, and he wanted to touch her again—a simple caress. But he knew there was no such thing. "So? What happened? I'm on the edge of my seat." He sipped his tea.

"I broke down. That's what happened. I just collapsed."

The evening before leaving, she had fought with her father. At the time they were fighting constantly, but this row was so bad that in the morning, when she left early—it was still dark—she was happy about not seeing him for a whole week. He didn't like the way she looked, she told Yonatan. He objected to her choice of clothes. "You look like a tramp," he said, and called her a bag lady. He claimed she looked derelict, as if she didn't have a home, as if she were an orphan. That evening, she had slammed back at him, "What do you mean, *as if*? I *am* an orphan."

Yonatan smiled. He said he was the exact opposite as a kid: a complete nerd, neatly combed, dressed like a refugee from Europe. "All I was missing was a beat-up leather suitcase," he said. And what was strange, he admitted, was that he didn't even have anyone to blame, because he chose his clothes and that style himself—professorial, he thought it then—in an attempt to be like his father, who did in fact look like an Oxford professor with his soft sweaters, some of which had elbow patches, and the pipe he smoked in his study or in the garden, scattering a scent of distant elegance into the air.

"But I interrupted you," Yonatan said, and she smiled as she looked at this man—who seemed so self-assured and unattainable in his jeans and gray sweatshirt and his green Chuck Taylors with loosely tied laces, sitting with his legs crossed, smoking—and tried to imagine him as a boy who didn't know what a sexy man he would be; perhaps he still didn't know.

"What else did you fight about?" he asked, and she said they fought about everything. When she was fourteen, she had started trying to drag him out of his silence and his sadness, turning it into a duel, a kind of daily workout, whether over clothes or school or his demand that she come home early at night so he wouldn't worry about her, or his stake-outs on the balcony. She said she was embarrassed to come home, that her friends made fun of him. "There's your dad," they would say, when they turned down her street after a party or a youth group meeting and caught him slipping into the apartment like a lizard as soon as he saw them. "He moves so fast!" they said. "Like the rabbit in *Alice in Wonderland*. One minute he's there, the next minute he's gone."

The fights would begin as negotiations, but they quickly turned, she realized years later, into a kind of communication to which they both became addicted. They waited for it like a meal or a favorite TV show. "I would love to fight with him today," she said. "Not that I enjoyed it then, I really didn't; I hated it. You know? I hated him with a passion, like only a sixteen-year-old can hate someone, especially her father. It was a prin-ciple, you know what I mean?"

"Yes." He knew that hatred well. To this day he was not completely weaned off it.

"But there was something so alive in our yelling and screaming, something happy, even. It was like breathing for me—as long as it was there I knew he was okay, that he was healthy, that at least there was a little action at home. And I think . . ." She paused, and their eyes met in the dimness, softened by the yellow light of the lamp in the living room. "I think he liked those fights too. He enjoyed them."

Yonatan sat quietly while she smoked for a few moments, and in their quiet there was a certain foggy appeal. He wondered if she felt it too, or whether she was so involved in the story that she could have told it in the same way to anyone, with the same calm hypnotic strength. In the night air, in which the smoke from their cigarettes lingered until a breeze blew it away, on the balcony, where they sat very close, in the yellow light that suddenly looked like the light of a second chance—in this air, on this balcony, in this semidarkness, he felt he was falling in love.

She had spent the first night at camp listening to her tent mates whispering and gossiping. They fell asleep long before she did. The next day she started planning her escape. It was obvious that she wouldn't survive a whole week; it had only been twenty-four hours since leaving Tel Aviv, and she already felt as if she had been gone for a month. She felt even worse because it was Friday, and on Fridays she used to cut gym class and sit with the weekend papers in a café on Jabotinsky Street, watching people, feeling like her own person in a big city, not a high school student or somebody's daughter. "It's strange the way today I would actually love to feel like someone's daughter."

"Maybe you need to have a child. Sometimes I feel like my daughter's child."

"Really?"

"Yes. It's a kind of second childhood. Except this time you have no one to hate."

She smiled and turned to him, wondering if the melancholic lines of his profile were true, particular to him, or whether anyone sitting in the dark on a balcony would look that way.

"So what happened?" he asked, and she wondered whether she'd ever see this face hovering above her own, see his eyes shut, his lips open slightly to let out sighs of pleasure, murmurings of love.

The depression of the first morning at camp turned to panic by lunchtime. She knew it was irrational, but she couldn't control it. In the afternoon she went to the clinic, and when the doctor asked what the matter was, she burst out in bitter tears. "The tears were real, by the way. I wish I could cry like that today."

"What do you mean?"

"No, nothing. I find it a bit hard to cry now."

"Don't you cry?"

"I do sometimes, but not that kind of sweeping, crazed, purifying weeping."

"Ilana was a crier," he said, and immediately regretted having summoned his dead wife to this conversation.

"Really?"

"Yes. But tell me what happened with the doctor." He quickly banished Ilana's shadow from the balcony.

The doctor was worried. She asked if Shira didn't feel well, and through her unrelenting sobbing she said she felt awful. When the doctor asked if she wanted to go home, she said she did. The doctor said, "Okay, sweetie, but how are you going to get there? It's almost Shabbat."

Suddenly there was a new enemy, Shabbat, formidable but not invincible. She wanted to hug the doctor, who sat staring out the window as it grew dark, as Shabbat came in, and she said, "My dad will come and get me."

"It's nighttime already. Do you think he'll drive now for four hours?"

"No, not tonight, tomorrow morning," she said quickly.

"And will you make it to tomorrow if you feel so bad?"

Shira could tell that the doctor knew the truth, so she said she'd make it; she'd call her father now and go to bed early.

The doctor asked if she wanted to use the office phone, and Shira said she didn't; she had tokens and would use the pay phone. She didn't know what she was going to tell her father and didn't want any witnesses.

He picked up the phone with his mouth full of Friday-night dinner, which was probably more enjoyable without her, without her constant agitation and complaining. She heard him say, "Hello," still chewing, and suddenly she missed him so much that the tears came again, and her voice broke as she said, "Dad?"

He asked what had happened and she heard him swallow quickly. In the background, her mother asked what was wrong; on TV, Rabbi Shlomo Avidor HaCohen was reading the weekly Torah portion. She said she was miserable. Her father asked if she was sick—she heard her mother say, "Shira's sick?"—and she said she wasn't, she just hated it here; she was crying the whole time and she wanted to come home. She wondered if she should also apologize for what she had said to him the night before leaving, but her father said, "Just a minute." She heard him ask her mother to bring him a paper and pen, and she stopped one of the counselors who was passing by and asked him to give her father directions. He did so gladly, and when he handed her back the phone, she said, "Dad?" He asked if she could hold on til tomorrow; he asked matter-of-factly, the way, as a child, she had often heard him asking clients if they would prefer windows of this kind or that. She sniffled and said she would, and he said he'd leave early and get there before lunchtime. She knew how he hated to drive, and said, "Are you sure?" He said, "What choice do I have?" and she couldn't tell if there was true anger in his voice, because they weren't accustomed to having these normal businesslike conversations, the conversations of people simply making arrangements.

She slept like a baby that night, she told Yonatan, and in the morning she ate breakfast and repacked the few things she had unpacked, and watched her friends sitting in a circle in the tent, planning the evening activity, which no longer concerned her, and at exactly eleven she saw their car on the road leading to the mess hall, like a fata morgana.

"What kind of car?"

"A Studebaker." The word hurt her mouth because she hadn't pronounced it for so many years—the car was long ago sold to a junkyard—and saying it was to remember the man who now fell asleep in his clothes in his armchair, after eating stuffed cabbage or peppers from the delicatessen; that man had once owned a Studebaker.

"My dad had a Volvo," said Yonatan, as if they were two kids boasting about their parents' cars.

"Do you like old cars?"

"Yes. I had a Citroën DS when I was a student."

"Really? That's a lovely car. You see them in old French movies."

He thought about his old Citroën and how he had to sell it, shortly after getting married, to a student who collected old cars, because it was too expensive to maintain. He looked for the car on the streets for years afterward, growing excited every time he saw one like it, looking carefully to see if it was his. But he never saw the car again, and over time its look-alikes also disappeared.

The Studebaker had glided slowly down the dirt road looking foreign and snobbish, until it stopped by the mess hall. She saw him from afar getting out of the car, dressed like someone going on safari: a beige shirt with sleeves rolled up over his elbows, and white shorts, the same ones he used to wear when they went to the beach. He had on his oxford shoes with black stretchy socks pulled up over his ankles, but this time she wasn't ashamed of the way he looked: He had come to rescue her, and you couldn't be ashamed of your savior.

On the contrary, she recounted, she remembers enjoying the curious, gossipy looks her friends gave her as she shouted "Dad!" and ran to him, listening to the backpack rattling on her back and her heartbeat mingling with the deadened sound her work shoes made on the dirt path.

He didn't open his arms to embrace her, and she stopped a yard or two away from him and looked at him, then looked down. But today, she said, it was clear to her that there, in that dusty moment, they shared an embrace, "the greatest hug we ever had."

He helped her put her backpack in the trunk, and when they sat down in the car he pointed to a plastic bag in which, he said, there were sandwiches Mom had made for the journey and washed fruit. The checkered thermos she hadn't seen for years was propped in the gap between the two seats, smaller than she remembered it, funny and touching in its sudden comeback. They didn't talk about what had happened. As they drove, her father pointed out places they passed and told her about them, stories linked with his childhood. Then they turned the radio on and listened to the Saturday sketch comedy. There was a series of Shaike Ofir sketches that her father loved, and she began to love them too that morning. To this day, when they played him on the radio or showed an old movie of his on TV, "especially the one with Abu el-Banaat," she said, she became flooded with nostalgia for her father driving his American car, the look of his profile, his lips moving with the words he knew by heart, his thin freckled leg stretched forward on the gas pedal, both hands clasping the wheel; every so often he would reach one arm out over the back of her seat, barely touching her shoulder.

In some ways, she said, it was an enchanted Shabbat. Not only because it had the presence of a father she did not know, or was not capable of knowing then, but because she was also a different girl on that

Shabbat, one who from one moment to the next, as they approached Tel Aviv, longed to get home—not so she could leave it to wander around town but so she could stay there.

And indeed, when they got home, it seemed to her as if her mother also loved her father more. From her room she listened to her mother phoning her girlfriends to tell them about his heroic act, how he drove all the way to rescue Shira from the camp. What happened to her over there? they asked. And her mother said, "How would I know? Just a mood." Shira listened to her describe, amused but also completely serious, how Friday night, before they had gone to sleep, he had meticulously planned his route, pored over an old road map he kept in the glove compartment, and marked the roads with a red pen as if it were a complicated rescue mission. She described how they both got up at five and she made food, and then she walked him to the car and stood next to him while he checked the oil and water by the light of the streetlamp and kicked each tire to check the air; before saying goodbye she gave him a supply of phone tokens, in case he got lost or, as her father used to tell Shira when he handed her a stash of tokens before she went off to a party, "so you can let us know if there's a delay."

The drive was uneventful, and they arrived in the afternoon, both starved, even though they had eaten the sandwiches and fruit and drunk the coffee, passing the thermos cup back and forth. At home a festive dinner awaited them, as if her mother had sensed that this event, the heroic father going to claim his unhappy adolescent daughter, as ordinary as it might be in other families, was no trivial occurrence in this one.

"Of course, the next day we went back to our usual routine and found something to fight about."

"Obviously," he said, and wondered what she was like in bed.

"It's seven. I've talked for so long. We should get going, shouldn't we?"

"Yes." But he didn't want to get up. He felt so calm, sleepy even, that he was alarmed. As he had listened to her, impressed by the way she managed to interweave so much compassion into such great anger, he wondered if she was like that in her writing too. He thought about himself, about the fact that his father had been dead for more than ten years and he didn't miss him, whereas her father was still alive and she was missing him to distraction.

She asked him about his parents. "So tell me what you wanted to say before, about your father." But he felt like talking about his mother. And he felt like seeing her too, driving to Jerusalem to visit her. He never felt such an urge, and almost asked if he could use the phone just so he could hear his mother saying, "Yonatan!" when she heard his voice—Yonatan! with an exclamation point.

He said he couldn't remember what he had wanted to say, and Shira kept quiet. She held her mug, smiled at Yonatan, and then looked at the floor. She seemed disappointed, even cheated, as if she had kept her end of some bargain of intimacy and he had chickened out. But what could he tell her? he thought. What could he say about his father that wouldn't be said with injury, with the teenage rebellion of a middle-aged man? He had become very aware of his anger, of his continual desire to settle accounts even when it was too late, even when there were no accounts left to settle—or perhaps, with his father, just some general amorphous account. Whenever he tried to define the essence of the conflict, he knew that as the years went by the conflict itself—which was in fact no different from any other between father and son and was essentially both the fear of becoming his father and the fear of not doing so—was losing force, but he was still addicted to the anger.

Shira got up, took his mug, and said she was going to change and they should leave soon because she was starved; what about him? He said he was too, even though he had pigged out at lunchtime.

"What did you have?"

"Fettuccine Alfredo, referred to by our waitress as *pettuccine*." Shira smiled and stood leaning against the balcony wall, both mugs in one hand. "And listen to what Dana had," he said, and hated himself for testing her. "Veal *masala*." Shira burst out laughing and raised her arm to scratch her nose, and her sweatshirt, the one that was identical to his, lifted briefly. He saw her stomach for an instant, white and full, and the elastic band of her black cotton underwear, and he felt more affection than attraction—friendly affection, like he felt toward Rona, toward women who didn't want anything in particular from him.

They took their time walking to Rona's. They crossed the park, then walked up the steps to the square on Bialik and admired the old buildings there, as if seeing them for the first time. "So where do you live?" Shira asked. He pointed toward Allenby. "You mean in that incredible building?"

"No, the one behind it."

They turned onto Idelson Street, and when they reached the intersection with Hess he motioned to the left with the sweeping gesture of a tour guide and let her walk ahead of him; she smiled shyly, consenting to be a tourist with him on a route she had taken alone hundreds of times.

"We were getting worried," Tamar scolded when they arrived. "We thought something had happened to you."

Shira said they had got carried away in a conversation and hadn't noticed what time it was. "Yes," Yonatan said, "we got completely carried away." He waited for her to take her coat off and took it and hung both their coats on the hook in the entrance. Rona came out of the bathroom, drying her hair with a towel, and kissed Yonatan on the cheek—a practice she had acquired since last night's dinner. Then she kissed Shira and said, "What a lovely skirt!"

Yonatan looked down for a moment at the skirt's hem and said, "Yes, it really is lovely."

Rona said, "I've never seen you wear a long skirt," and Shira said she hardly wore it because she thought it made her look religious.

"No, not at all," Yonatan said. "Not religious at all." He found himself closely examining the skirt as if this debate had entitled him to stare at Shira's belly, and at her backside, and her ankles, and it was suddenly important to him that the skirt not look religious—not for Shira, who stood motionless as if awaiting the pronouncement of a top fashion designer, but for himself, because once, years ago, before Ilana, it had mattered to him how his girlfriends dressed. Later, with Ilana, he had at first regarded her merry circuslike wardrobe with amusement and forgiveness, then stopped noticing it, and then missed it, and now—this scared him but also gave him pleasure—it was important to him that this woman, whom only fifteen minutes ago he had cataloged in his mind as a friend, should dress according to his taste. He gave a final glance at her behind, which was curvy like her stomach, and said, "Absolutely, definitely not religious. On the contrary!"

"What do you mean on the contrary? Secular?" She giggled.

"No. Yes." He wanted to say *sexy,* but instead he said, "You know what I mean."

She said she did and let her eyes linger on his for one long moment, almost too long, because he saw its length reflect like the glare of a dagger's blade in Rona's eyes as she stared at them both, and from the corner of his eye he imagined he also saw a little smile spread over her lips, the satisfied smile of the successful matchmaker, and perhaps a smile of jealousy, and perhaps both. The modest excitement he had felt a moment ago at the sight of Shira's full behind suddenly intensified; he liked those eyes. Even yesterday he had observed that she had sad relentless eyes and that he enjoyed their roaming over his body. He liked the eyes and the curves and the stomach, he liked what she had been wearing before, like his twin, but he also liked the skirt, and he especially liked the idea of liking things, including Rona's look, the look of a person on the outside—except this time it wasn't him.

"I'm starved," Shira said.

Yonatan said, "Me too. Where's my daughter?"

"In my room," Tamar replied. "She's making something for Shira."

"For me? What is she making for me?"

"I don't know. I think it's a surprise."

"Dana! What's up?" Yonatan called.

The girl came out of the room holding a large sheet of paper.

"What's that? I heard you were making a surprise for Shira."

"It's not a surprise. It's nothing." She was embarrassed. "I drew something for you." She came closer to Shira, who was sitting at the table.

"For me?"

"I drew my dad's wardrobe for you," she said, and presented Shira with the paper.

Along a laundry line hung a pair of blue jeans, a gray sweatshirt, two white T-shirts, a pair of green Chuck Taylors, and at the edge a pair of clumsily drawn, shapeless underpants.

"Do you draw?" Shira asked, because she didn't know what else to say.

"No," Yonatan answered. "I think she just started today."

"You draw wonderfully," Shira said, and Dana pointed to each of the items and needlessly explained what it was. Shira felt the congested breathing against her cheek, the girl's body touching her, and asked, "Can I give you a thank-you kiss?" Dana shrugged and looked embarrassed, and Shira kissed her on the cheek. "It's a lovely picture. I'll put it on my fridge."

"That makes me worried," Yonatan said, and smiled at her. Shira wanted to hug Dana, who had already moved away and joined Tamar as she took a stack of plates out of the cabinet, because it touched her to think that all these hours since they had left the café, while Yonatan sat on her balcony and became, for a short while, a family man without a family, his daughter had continued the waning afternoon for them, preserved it, given it new life as she sat on the floor with paper and colored pens and tried to promote their interests.

Yonatan found the leftovers even tastier than the food had been the day before, perhaps because he ate slowly this time, perhaps because the sweet potato soup and the veal had been supplemented by a few new things: pasta salad, green beans, cheeses, and sliced challah, which seemed like the most homemade, delicious thing he had ever eaten.

Rona asked how things went with the software, and he talked about Shira's speedy computer as if it were an accomplished child he was proud of.

"And then he played Solitaire for two hours," Shira said.

"I'm sorry," he said.

But Shira smiled. "It's okay, I enjoyed watching you."

"We used to have that at home," Dana said, "and he took it off the computer because he kept playing it."

"I'm the only one without a computer," said Tamar.

"I offered to buy you one, but you didn't want it," her mother said.

"I don't."

"You're a very strange child," Yonatan said. "Has anyone ever told you that?"

"I don't want a computer either," Dana said.

"You're strange too." He poured some more wine into his glass and Shira's and motioned to Rona with the bottle.

"No, thanks," Rona said.

"I'd like some," Tamar said.

"Wine?" Yonatan asked, and the girl nodded eagerly.

"May she?" He looked at Rona.

"Give her a little."

"I want some too," Dana said.

"What's going on with you two?" He poured a little wine for his daughter as well. "Little alcoholics."

"What's the big deal? I've been drinking wine for ages. Don't you remember?"

"When exactly do you drink wine?"

"When we eat steak. Have you forgotten?"

"That's true. Wow, it's been so long since we've had steak."

"I've been walking around with a hankering for a steak for weeks," Shira said. "I don't know what's come over me."

"Maybe you have an iron deficiency," Tamar said, and took a huge gulp of wine.

"Well, then, we can grill some," Yonatan said.

"Yes, Dad, let's do it, we haven't made steaks for ages!"

"Do you all want to come over to our place for steaks?" he asked, without looking at Shira.

"Yes!" the girls shouted in unison.

"But we'll make something too," Rona said.

"Yes," Shira agreed. "I'll also make something."

"So when?" Dana asked.

"I don't know," he said, sensing familiar panic creep into his voice.

"Next Friday, Dad?"

"Yes, next Friday," said Tamar. "We're free. Right, Mom?"

"Let Yonatan decide when it's convenient for him," Rona said.

"No, no, Friday sounds good. I think. Well, we'll talk about it during the week."

They came as a couple and ate as a family, and then they sat Rona down in the living room and ordered her to rest. They would clear the table, wash the dishes, and make coffee, because they felt bad about being her guests for two days running. "Oh, come on," Rona protested from the couch.

"No, really," Shira said, and handed a pile of dishes to Yonatan, who stood by the sink.

"Then at least put an apron on," Rona shouted out to him, "so you won't get dirty."

"Yes, yes, put on my mom's apron," Tamar said and gave him the apron Dana had worn yesterday, which had reached her ankles but looked like a miniskirt on him. The girls stood behind him and giggled, trying to untie the apron, and he turned back and gently snapped his wet hands on their busy little fingers.

Shira finished clearing the table, emptied the scraps into the trash, and piled the plates and bowls in a neat stack next to Yonatan on the counter. "Can you manage?" she asked, looking for a towel, and when she couldn't find one, she grinned and wiped her hands on his apron. Then she sat on the couch next to Rona, who was watching *National Geographic* on TV with the dish towel in her hands, and the girls joined them.

"Dad!" Dana called out, "come quickly, there's a program about penguins!"

"I'll be there in a minute."

"It's his favorite animal," she told Rona and Shira.

"Really?" Rona asked.

"What?" Yonatan shouted, almost dropping a large glass bowl. "I can't hear you."

"You like penguins?" Shira asked.

"Says who?"

"Your daughter," Rona said.

"Yes, sort of. They're cute."

He did like penguins. He liked them and felt sorry for them. Every time he saw them on TV he couldn't help smiling, but at the same time his heart shrank with pity. They always seemed so lonely, especially in the way they walked, eternally waddling toward nowhere.

He came into the living room, the apron still tied around his waist, and stood between the two girls on the rug and the two women on the couch. Shira looked at the SUPER MOM printed across his loins and smiled to herself.

"What?" he asked, embarrassed.

"Nothing. It's funny that you like penguins."

"What's wrong with it?"

"Nothing. I like penguins too."

"Did you know they're much smaller in real life?" he said, and reached for Shira's pack of cigarettes.

"Yes," she said, "like us."

They watched the program, making comments and joking around; the girls compared the penguins' walk to the way one of their teachers walked. Shira and Rona gossiped about a common acquaintance and told Yonatan about her when he took an interest. He listened and contributed his own biting comments here and there, his eyes constantly glued to the screen, watching the penguins disappear into the distance in a row as they migrated across a vast glacier. He listened to the narrator talk about their community life, about complex social structures, about mutual dependency on each other's body heat on this exhausting voyage they made every year before winter, a voyage that seemed suicidal but was apparently essential for their existence, and he took his eyes off the screen and looked at the girls as they sat whispering at his feet and then at Rona and Shira, who chatted on the couch and asked him what he thought about the woman they were discussing. He threw out a particularly nasty comment and they both burst out laughing, the girls too, although they didn't know the woman in question, and he smiled, pleased with himself, and put out his cigarette in the ashtray and looked back at the screen, at the penguins migrating on the ice; although the way they walked still prompted a certain sadness in him, they did not look so lonely.

(1 1)

The next day, he bought her book. Without knowing exactly how it happened, he found himself going into a bookstore just before noon and quickly scanning the shelves until he found the only copy in the *K*'s. Her name on the cover moved him briefly because it seemed strange without her, as if it belonged to another woman, in whom he had no interest. Then he searched the *L*'s for his own books, but they weren't there and he hoped they had sold out, that they still had buyers. When the sales clerk came over and asked if he needed assistance he replied firmly, almost chidingly, that he didn't.

He lingered awhile longer by the shelves and then went to the checkout and placed the novel on the counter. The clerk asked if she should gift-wrap the book and he said he would like that and thanked her with exaggerated friendliness, to compensate for his earlier aggression and perhaps in order to pretend that he was purchasing it for someone else and that he, personally, had no interest in a book whose dust jacket read *A sweeping love story*. Then he went out to the street, into the rain that had started drizzling hesitantly again, after the blazing spring weekend, and hurried home.

He hoped the book would be bad. He hoped she had no talent. Then, he thought, it would be easier to sleep with her. Yesterday, after dinner, Dana and he had walked her halfway home, even though she said they didn't need to. They said goodbye to her at the King George exit from Meir Park, the three diskettes in his coat pocket and Dana's drawing rolled up in her bag, like souvenirs from a short trip overseas. They shook hands curtly, and she said Rona would probably update her about the steak meal, and he said, "Yes, I'll be in touch with Rona, sometime this week, I hope; we'll see how the week goes for me," and knew he was wasting too many words on a totally empty time. She said, "Okay, so

Rona and I will coordinate what we'll make and all that." He said, "Excellent," and when he turned with his daughter to walk back through the park, he glanced at Shira as she crossed the street and disappeared down Borochov and knew he wanted to sleep with her.

When he walked up the steps holding the new book, he heard the phone ringing in his apartment. He went in quickly and picked it up, out of breath. It was Esti, the school nurse, and he was alarmed for a minute. She said she was calling to report that Dana had looked much better on Friday, as if he hadn't seen her all weekend, as if they didn't live in the same house. "So what did she have in the end?" she asked, and he said it was probably the flu, but whatever it was had gone away. He tried to steady his breathing.

"So you didn't go to the doctor?"

"No," he said, slightly embarrassed, as if he had neglected his daughter. "It didn't seem to be anything serious. She's fine now, just a runny nose; she hasn't had a fever for a few days; since Tuesday, I think."

"Yes. She really looks well."

"Yes, she's fine." It occurred to him that the nurse never called to report to him about his daughter's health once she was well.

"Did I wake you? You sound as if I woke you."

"No, not at all. At this time of day?"

"Well, I don't know, one can never tell with you artist types."

He tried to laugh politely but started coughing instead.

"It sounds like *you're* sick now!"

He said he was perfectly healthy, and asked how she was.

"Me? Great."

He walked into the kitchen with the phone, put the kettle on for coffee, and sat by the table and put the plastic bag from the bookstore on it. He lit a cigarette and found he could not remember what Esti looked like. He had seen her dozens of times, and even her voice, which he knew well from all the mornings she had summoned him to school, sounded normal and natural, as if he talked with her every day, but he couldn't reconstruct her image.

"I'm doing really great," she repeated, perhaps because he was silent.

"Good. I hope you're not working too hard."

"No. How about you? Are you working? Writing?"

"Yes," he lied. "Doing my best."

"Great. I'm happy to hear it."

He heard the school bell ring in the background and imagined kids bursting into the hallways with near-violent elation, and teachers walking toward the staff room with relief. "Bell ringing?" he said, and she said it was the bell for the long recess, and he thought about how the bell hadn't changed since he was a kid.

"So I guess I'll see you at the meeting?" she said.

"Meeting?"

"The parent-teacher meeting. On Tuesday."

"Oh, yes. Sure. You'll be there too?"

"Yes. They asked me to talk to you about the equipment fee."

"Oh, right." He had no idea what she was talking about.

"Some of the parents are pretty worked up about it."

"Really? How come?"

"They claim the Ministry of Education should finance it, and in principle I agree with them, but what choice is there? We can't wait until the ministry deigns to hand over the money. Do you know that we haven't replaced the equipment in the nurse's office since the sixties?"

"Really?" He couldn't even remember what equipment there was in the nurse's office.

"Yes," she replied. "Well, I don't want to bore you. I'm sure you want to get back to work."

"Yes. No, you're not boring me."

"So I'll see you Tuesday."

"Yes. When exactly is it?"

"Eight."

"Okay. So I'll see you then. And thanks for calling."

He took his coffee and the plastic bag and sprawled out on the couch. He slowly removed the gift wrapping, being careful not to rip it and sabotage the gift he had bought himself; then he held the book up to his face and sniffed it. He didn't know which he liked more, the rich mildewy smell of an old book or the neutral chemical scent of new paper, untouched by human hands. He read the blurb on the back again and hoped once more that as soon as he read the first lines it would become irrefutably clear that she hadn't an ounce of talent.

He started reading and suddenly remembered what Esti looked like. She appeared before him, clear and sharp like the energetic voice that still echoed in his ears: her fair, freckled skin; her spiky cropped hair of a color somewhere between blond and red; her chubby, slightly squashed body; her eyes, always framed by round glasses—she reminded him of a little bee.

He closed the book and looked once more at the back cover and held it up to his nose again and thought she was actually quite attractive, Esti, if you liked the kind of women who were entirely—their body and their smile, their tone of voice and their words—a busy hum whose only concern was you.

Chauvinist, he told himself; he sipped his coffee and opened the book again to the first page, but he still couldn't concentrate. After all, there was always the possibility that she was talented, more talented than he was, even, and then what would he do? He had never slept with any-one more talented than he was. If she was more talented, he decided, he wouldn't sleep with her. He wouldn't even try because he'd never get it up, of that he was sure.

He put the book down on the couch, took the plastic bag and the gift wrapping, went into the kitchen and stuffed them into the trash, and decided he would go down to get some falafel because he was suddenly very hungry. He took his keys from the table, put his coat on, glanced outside through the window, and saw that the drizzle had turned to a downpour. This made him happy, and he wondered if it was making her happy now too. He took the umbrella off its hook but lingered by the door, unsure. He felt like a kid avoiding his homework. He wanted to read the book and get it over with, but he was unfocused and hungry. He would go downstairs, eat some falafel, come back full and energized, and still have two hours before Dana came home; she had a piano lesson in the afternoon.

She hadn't practiced all week, or the week before. In fact, he hadn't heard her play for a long time, although it had seemed to him that she was making progress during the last few months. She had even started playing Bach's Inventions, and her teacher, Irma Gutt, said that if she continued that way she'd be playing preludes and fugues within a year. It pleased him to think that his daughter would play such complex pieces, and in order to infect her with his enthusiasm, he played her "The Well-Tempered Clavier" in different renditions, explaining to her lovingly about the differences between Glenn Gould and Dinu Lipatti in his final recording at Carnegie Hall, after which he collapsed and died, and about the recording where you could hear Lipatti dying and his fingers sliding off the keys, trying so hard, so lost.

He liked sitting in his room or in the kitchen listening to Dana as she strained to learn a new piece in the living room, tackling a short section that Irma had marked for her in pencil, playing each hand separately. He would hear the pedals tapping, and every so often there would be long pauses, and he wondered what she was thinking in those silent moments. Sometimes he would hear her turn the pages restlessly or sigh and then attack the keys again with all her might, even if it was a piece that should be played softly; Irma said she lacked tenderness, that she was too stormy. Dana preferred composers like Brahms and Chopin, who were still too difficult for her—perhaps in a year or two, Irma promised; "First we'll make a lady out of her." In the meantime, she made her play lightweight pieces by Haydn and Mozart to learn restraint.

The piano was Ilana's idea. She grew up in an unmusical house, even antimusical, she said, and she wanted Dana to be more like her father, who had absorbed classical music from both sides: from his father, who was obsessive about his album collection with its rare recordings that made dim, scratchy sounds, and his explanations that always struck Yonatan as threatening, and from his mother, for whom classical music was a background for everything she did at home, and who didn't really care what or whom she was listening to.

Gerry and Maxine Fisher sent a check and Yonatan chose the piano—a beautiful old Russian one—at the used piano store. It arrived a few weeks before the accident. Now he stood at the door, trying to decide whether to go out and eat or stay at home, and he thought about that November evening when the movers had arrived with the piano and carried it up the three floors, quietly cursing and grumbling about invisible bends in the stairwell, claiming that in such an old building, with such high ceilings, this apartment was actually on the fourth floor.

It arrived like a newborn baby, wrapped in blankets, and received the same attention. Dana was so little at the time that for one frightening second he couldn't remember what she had looked like, until the image came back. She had her hair cropped short like her mother's, because she used to imitate her mother in every way back then. She came out of the bathroom with her hair wet and combed, wearing pajamas with baby-blue feet that her grandparents had sent from America.

The sound of her padded feet running across the floor came back to him now. She watched the movers strip the piano of its robes, clutching Ilana's hand as she walked back and forth across the room, trying to decide where to put it—the piano turned out to have a presence that was greater than its actual dimensions—until she finally instructed the movers, who were making their anger very clear and giving Yonatan looks intended to double their tip, to put it by the wall, right in the entrance to the living room, by the door, across from the couch, perpendicular to the balcony doors.

He had stood in the stairwell fighting with the movers for a long time, not over the tip but about the fee they demanded for delivery, which was far higher than he had negotiated with the piano store owner. As they yelled their way through the argument, which concluded with the movers' indifferent victory, but not before they had filled the stairwell with a stench of cigarettes and well-staged insult, he heard the first hesitant notes produced by four inexperienced hands, and when he finally sent the movers on their way and shut the door, he went into the living room and stood behind them, watching. The image of their backs, their one merged back—Ilana's slender, with birdlike shoulder blades that rose and fell like the keys she played, and Dana's, furry and playful as she sat erect like her mother and looked alternately at the keys and at Ilana's profile with great admiration—that picture, their shared back, which had become one in his memory, as if it were his wife who had been wearing the baby-blue pajamas, was so alive but so silent, like the picture on a muted TV, that it gave him the chills.

He zipped up his coat, hooked the umbrella over his arm, went out, and locked the door behind him. He was no longer hungry so much as in need of distraction. The last time they had sat together in the living room and he had played her Gould and Lipatti, consecutively, playing one of his favorite preludes and fugues, Dana said she'd never be able to play like that.

"Of course you will," he said.

"But not like them."

"No, of course not, maybe not at first, but who knows? Maybe in a few years."

"No way," she said, and asked which pianist he liked better.

"Gould," he replied, in a tone so decisive it sounded like a reprimand. "Can you hear how precise he is? Can you hear how clean? Listen to that cleanness! Nothing in the world is that clean!"

She said he sounded like a laundry detergent commercial.

"Then who do you like better?"

"The other one," she said.

"Lipatti?"

"Yes, him."

"Why?" he asked, disappointed but a little curious.

"Because he makes more mistakes. I don't like perfect things."

"No?" he said, trying to overcome the insult. "Then how come you like me?"

"Who says I do?" she said with a poker face. Then she sat down to practice one of the little pieces she was playing, which now sounded silly next to the prelude and fugue they had just heard twice.

She was the one who wanted, a few weeks after her mother's death, to learn how to play. Irma Gutt said perhaps they should wait a year, but Dana insisted, so, once a week, on Sunday afternoons, he would drive her a few blocks to the teacher's home, or walk with her and wait at a café on Bograshov until she was finished. When he listened to her practice or watched her skip down the steps from her teacher's apartment, clutching her music case under her arm—an old leatherette case that used to belong to him—it never occurred to him that she was suffering.

As he bit into his falafel, he told himself that when she came home from school today he would talk to her about it; if she didn't want to keep going she didn't have to. He polished off the falafel and ordered another half-portion and finished that one in a few purposeful bites, leaning against the falafel counter as drops of rain slid off his umbrella and wet his nose and hands.

(1 2)

Shira spent Sunday in the ER with her father. When she sat down at the computer in the morning and tried to distract herself from the past two days with Yonatan, tried to redirect the frenzy in her heart to her writing, the phone rang. She let the machine answer and listened, hoping it was Yonatan or at least Rona—someone who would turn the fantasy, which this morning had shed its final remnants of tentativeness, into reality. If it was Rona, she decided, she would pick up. If it was Yonatan, she would resist. Then she heard the beep.

An old man with a Hungarian accent introduced himself as the owner of the delicatessen where her father bought his weekly supply of plastic containers which she later threw out, full or half full, on the weekends, and she hurried to pick up the phone. Her father had passed out in the deli half an hour ago, the elderly man reported in an accusatory tone—no one likes a fragile old man passing out in his deli, even if it is a loyal customer, even if he himself sounds like a fragile old man—and for a moment she hated him for his lack of empathy, but then she thought perhaps this was his usual tone, an accusing tone, like the one her father had also adopted lately, reminiscent of crying.

He said her father had come in that morning and stood in the line, which wasn't long—two or three customers at most, he insisted, absolving himself of any responsibility—and when his turn came they greeted each other as they always did, and he could see that her father was swaying a little, "but that's normal," he said, and the word *normal* suddenly sounded irritating, as if the bleak swaying reality of her father, the one she had grown accustomed to, had now been replaced by something else, and from now on the old form would arouse not sadness or anxiety but nostalgia.

"And then, down he went!" the man said. "Collapsed on my floor!" Again she thought she heard grumbling in his voice, as if her father's fall had permanently stained his deli—after all, he could have fainted somewhere else, in the bank or the post office or on the street, somewhere that didn't belong to anyone and was dirty anyway, or at home, quietly. But she knew he did pass out at home sometimes, and it was quite possible that he had collapsed outside too, dozens or even hundreds of times, but no one was there to see and he would wake up and find himself slumped on a park bench or sitting on the path leading to his building. It was a good thing he no longer walked around Allenby, because there he would have been mistaken for a drunk and ignored, and maybe, she thought, this was not really new, but an old, secret routine, from which she had been protected until this morning, until there was someone to report it to her.

She asked where he was now, and the man said they had taken him to the hospital and that her father, who had woken up when they wheeled him into the ambulance, had asked that she be called and had given the number, so here he was calling—doing his duty, as they say—and she thanked him. "I hope he gets well soon," he said in his accusatory tone, and she thanked him again, and when she put the phone down and went into her bedroom to get dressed, she heard the rain, which had been only a drizzle a few moments before, slamming down on the balcony floor, and for a moment she was flooded with the automatic joy that rain always brought her, but the joy turned to anger: This morning could have been perfect, with winter restored and her writing renewed and the possibility of Yonatan hovering over it all, if not for her father passing out in that grumbling Hungarian's deli, reminding her of possibilities she knew only too well, of fear and illness and great responsibility.

She was in such a hurry that she forgot to take her umbrella, and by the time she reached the car, which was parked on the next block, she was completely soaked. She could see herself sitting for hours in damp clothes drying on her body, sealing in the hospital smells of urine and disinfectants.

In the ER, after she had peeked behind a few screens, looking apologetically at the families surrounding other patients, she found her father lying on a bed at the far end of the room near an exit. He was awake and seemed slightly bored. He appeared neither happy nor sad to see her. He looked as if they had long ago agreed to meet here.

"I passed out," he said, when she came up to him. "I passed out at the ready-made food."

She took his hand in hers and asked, "Did you not feel well?"

"No, I felt well."

"Do you pass out a lot, Dad?" He sighed. "Do you, Dad? Tell me the truth. Does this happen often?"

"It happens," he said, and the dryness of his words was like the white crust on his lips.

"Has a doctor seen you?"

"Yes. He'll come soon."

She turned around and saw the doctors rushing among the screens in a chaotic sort of way which, their sealed faces conveyed, involved a logic and order that would never be comprehensible to the patients or to their families, who looked at the doctors urgently, imploringly, and she knew that no doctor was coming soon, because *soon* in the ER was a concept that transcended time.

Suddenly the doctors rushed to a bed near the front, and the woman sitting in the line for X-rays—which extended almost all the way to her father's bed—said, "There was a bad accident. They just brought the casualties in. I heard there were some people killed too."

Shira wanted to take her father home, smuggle him out of here, because what good would the doctors be now? But as if reading her thoughts, or perhaps having seen her look worriedly at the distant doctors, her father said, "You have to be patient." So she smiled and stroked his hand as if she had all the patience in the world.

She watched people in the hospital using cell phones, despite the signs prohibiting their use. They talked loudly with their relatives— husbands with wives, wives with husbands, brothers and sisters with each other, parents with their children at home and vice versa—and it struck her that great clans were crowded at the other end of these phone lines, their sole duty to hear news and arrange and console; and the loneliness she always felt with her father, the claustrophobic bitterness that could be navigated or forgotten when they were in his home—because despite the plastic containers of rotting food, she could pretend, as her father did, that this was a relatively healthy way to be—that loneliness now became intolerable.

She wanted to cry but couldn't imagine crying now. She stood over her father's bed as he dozed peacefully, as if the very fact of her arrival had tranquilized him, and studied his body, beneath the hospital sheet, and his face. He did look a little like an alien, as Yonatan had described his own father—that head with the sunken cheeks and prominent eyes, so large in comparison to the withered body, and especially the ears, which if not for the soft tufts of hair sticking out of them would have looked like little satellite dishes—and you could really imagine that her father came from outer space, if not for his shoes, which peeked out at the bottom of the sheet. He wore his black shoes, old people's moccasins, and gray stretchy socks pulled up to his ankles, which he always bought in packs of six and threw away when they wore out, but today he was wearing a pair that looked as old and tired as he did, with frayed elastic.

Seeing the shoes and ankles peeking out beneath the sheet, Shira remembered the Saturdays when her parents used to take her to the beach. It was a short walk, but they always arrived exhausted, silently fuming at each other. Her father would tread through the sand, holding in one hand the big basket containing towels and the sheet they always took to the beach, and two thermoses, one for juice and the other for coffee, his knuckles whitening from the weight of the basket, and in the other hand carrying his brown rubber sandals. Her mother walked ahead of them in slender flip-flops that filled with sand and emptied out with each step she took, holding a plastic bag with sandwiches and fruit, already wrinkling in the heat, and sunblock and a book. She would examine the beach, sheltering her eyes with her free hand, seeking out the ideal spot to set up their tired camp.

But they never found that spot, and every place they chose turned out to be problematic, whether because of proximity to or distance from the sea, or because of noisy paddleball players, or a smelly trash can overflowing, or the angle of the sun. But Shira, who was six or seven at the time, was determined to have fun. After they spread the sheet out on the sand and her mother and father put their sandals down as weights on the four corners, she stood with her back to her mother, who sat cross-legged on the sheet, so she could slather her with sunblock. Then she ran to the edge of the water and splashed around, under her parents' watchful eyes but far away from them. She would come back every so often to eat or drink or put a handful of shells she had found on the sheet— "Look after them for me," she would order, and her parents would nod, but when they came home the little treasures were always left behind.

Unlike her father, her mother loved the sea. Sometimes she would get up, smear sunblock over her arms and legs, and walk to the water, and the two of them would swim out to the point where her mother could no longer reach the bottom. Her father never went in the water. "Jerusalemite," her mother called him, even though he was born in Tel Aviv. He sat on the sheet with his legs outstretched, ankles crossed, leaning back on his arms, wearing white shorts and a button-down short-sleeved shirt, beneath which he always wore an undershirt. He never wore swim trunks, even though he had a pair in his closet: they were wide and made of wine-colored shiny nylon, and reminded Shira of a balloon. Her father seemed sadder than usual at the sea.

Once, when she and her mother returned from the water, breathless and laughing with their hands full of broken shells, they discovered that a little dog had adopted her father. He had a wet black coat, spotted with grains of sand, droopy ears, and a very dry snout. He was sprawled out beside her father with his head resting on his lap and his tail slowly, hesitantly, beating the sheet, as if he knew his host disliked dogs and feared the moment when his error would be discovered and he would be banished. Her father sat stiffly with his arms behind him and looked back and forth from Shira and her mother as they dried themselves, looking questioningly at each other and to the dog, who shut his eyes tightly and pretended to be asleep. Shira's heart filled with hope. She had always wanted a dog, but her father had refused. For years, she and her mother tried to convince him, making all sorts of promises, but in vain. One summer, when he went to a conference in Italy, her mother brought home a tiny puppy she had taken from a friend whose dog had had a litter, telling Shira that her father would just have to learn to accept a done deal. They spent a guilt-ridden week of happiness together, she and her mother and the puppy, but two days before her father's return, her mother got scared and told Shira they had to take the dog back. It wasn't

fair to Dad, she said; it was a hasty act and she was very sorry and promised to make it up to her. She suggested they go to the pet shop and buy a
rabbit, even two, but Shira quietly refused, without crying, and said she
was afraid of rabbits.

The dog napping in her father's lap looked like a rabbit. Shira sat
down carefully on the sheet and stroked the back of the dog's neck. He
couldn't resist wagging his tail, with open joy this time, like someone
who knows he has nothing to lose. Her mother also sat down and started
rummaging through the plastic bag, and the smell of hard-boiled eggs
and salami teased the tense quiet, and the dog's dry snout shuddered.
She dug through the bag very noisily but did not say a word, afraid, like
Shira, that the moment she said something, the moment someone
acknowledged the fact that a dog was sprawled between them with his
head resting on hostile hips, her father would cast him out.

"What do we have to eat today?" her father suddenly asked, and
shook his thighs as if they were full of sand, and the dog perked up his
head and sat up.

"Salami and hard-boiled egg, and there's also one with feta cheese
for Shira."

"I'm not hungry," Shira said angrily. The sandwiches had broken
the spell, but she suddenly had an idea. "Let's give the dog something.
Maybe he's hungry?"

"Why not?" said her mother, and turned to her father—"Max, what
do you say, do you think we should feed him?"—as if it were his dog.

"No. Absolutely not. We'll never get rid of him if we do."

Shira's eyes filled with tears. Her father and mother ate heartily, but
she refused her sandwich with a shrug. She swore to herself that she'd
never eat again in her life; the food had ruined everything. She wouldn't
even have juice. She couldn't understand how her parents could eat their
sandwiches—from the corner of her eye she saw their profiles as they
chewed and she despised them both—how could they have appetites
after the chance to become a happy family, or at least a normal one, had
been taken from them? The dog sat sniffing the air, his velvety ears
perked up halfway, drooping with each sniff. He was a beautiful dog,
even though he looked like a rabbit.

"Dad," Shira said, when her father had finished his second sandwich and was opening the thermos, "why can't we take him?"

"You know very well why," he said, and poured coffee into the thermos's plastic top, which was also a cup. "I don't want a dog in the house. When you grow up and live on your own, you may have as many dogs as you like."

"Max," her mother said, "he looks nice, actually. He looks trained."

"I'm asking you," her father said. "Naomi, I'm asking you, please." And her mother stuffed the used napkins into the plastic bag and took out a bunch of grapes, and with that the discussion was over.

As if he had been waiting for the verdict, the dog got up, walked off the sheet, stretched his legs, turned his head back for a moment to see if someone might have a change of heart, and then shook himself off, shedding the remains of their petting, and ran across the sand until he disappeared.

"He probably belongs to someone," her father said, and took a sip of coffee, the smell of the plastic cup blending with the aroma.

"He doesn't have a collar," her mother said.

"He doesn't belong to anyone," Shira said. "He's a street dog."

"An ocean dog," her father joked, and she hated him. "He probably has diseases," he added, as he shook the last drops of coffee out on the sand. "And ticks."

"Oh, Max, really," her mother said, and opened her book and started reading.

"Then why did you let him lie on you?" Shira asked, and the sob she had stifled cracked through her voice. "Why did you even touch him? Why did you get his hopes up?"

"I'm not a bad person. He came over here and acted as if he'd known me forever, so I thought if he wanted to rest here a little, let him rest. I'm not a monster!"

"You are!" she shouted, and ran to the water. She turned her head back and saw him sitting cross-legged, staring at the ocean. He had an old-fashioned white bucket hat on his head, because the sun was high, and her mother sat with her back to him, lost in her book. From that distance he still looked like a monster, but a pitiful monster, and when she came back from the water and sat down beside him, he draped a towel over her shoulders; shivering slightly, she took the sandwich he handed her.

Now she watched him sleep and her eyes filled with tears. She thought they were the same tears that had streamed from her eyes that Saturday at the beach, the Saturday with the dog, which was how she had thought of it for years. These same tears had dropped from her cheeks into the water as she sat in the wet sand, drawing circles of hatred and self-pity and guilt, but the tears too seemed to have grown old and turned heavy and slow, barely able to squeeze out of her eyes. Now when she watched him sleeping, his head drooping to one side and his mouth open, his shoes pointing in different directions, he looked like a pitiful monster again. She tried to remember when exactly she had become the stronger one, when the tables had turned, and knew it wasn't any one moment but a series of moments that had accumulated and would go on piling up until the day he died. Then the wheel might turn again, when her longing and guilt would make him stronger than her, and she thought how odd it was, how unfair that dying restored a parent's authority and infallibility.

Her father suddenly opened his eyes, confused. "Did I sleep?" he asked.

"A little." She resumed stroking his hand. "Sleep some more, until the doctor comes."

He nodded obediently and fell asleep again.

She moved back and forth between her sleeping father and the exit from the ER, where she went to smoke or buy a can of soda from the vending machine. People sat there with cell phones, delivering their reports, and when she sat next to them on the bench and listened to their conversations, she imagined the phone call she would have with Yonatan from the ER, what she would tell him—what he would ask, how he would comfort her, what they would arrange for later—and the ordinariness of the dialogue covered the glare of the fluorescent lights like a soft rain cloud.

Three hours later he was discharged without diagnosis. "Exhaustion," the doctor called her father's illness, the illness that wasn't a real illness, for a patient who wasn't a real patient, just elderly, a kind of chronic fainter, a permanent ER nuisance, and she thought he seemed a little disappointed and had wanted to be in hospital because he felt protected there.

She thought about the word *exhaustion* the whole way home, while her father, who had recovered somewhat, sat beside her and listened to Channel One on the radio. When she climbed the seventeen steps to his apartment, supporting his arm and simulating great patience, she grasped that what she felt for Yonatan was more complicated than a longing for shared banality and more dangerous than falling in love.

Her father would sleep alone that night. She thought about him getting up to go to the bathroom. She thought about him falling down. If only they could pad the floor of his apartment with something soft, the kind of material they used in children's play areas; if only they could upholster the entire floor with some absorbent and comforting material.

Exhaustion, she thought, *dependency and exhaustion.* Strange how easy it was to develop a dependency on a person you had only met twice. She had never needed someone so badly. She had never needed someone this way before she had even slept with him. As she helped her father up the last flight of steps, she decided to call Yonatan that night or the next day—she would find an excuse—and the sexual encounter suddenly became urgent, because although she had wanted him the previous day and the day before, today she wanted him differently, and, holding her father's arm and reaching into her bag for his keys, she thought, My father will never have sex again. The thought was chilling, both because she had never thought about him as a man—with lightning speed he had turned from a man with a little girl to an old man—and also because it occurred to her that a man always recognizes the first time but never the last.

(1 3)

The book was amazing. All afternoon, until Dana came back from her piano lesson, he lounged on the couch unable to stop reading. He loved her. He hated her. Each time he turned a page he loved and hated her. When Dana walked in and saw him reading Shira's book—he heard the key in the door but was too exhausted, too riveted, to hide it— she put her music case on the piano bench and sat quietly at his feet on the rug, waiting for a response.

"I'm reading Shira's book," he confessed immediately.

"What's it like?"

"Very good. Really good."

"Can I read it when you're done?"

"Yeah, sure." He asked how the lesson was, and she said it was all right.

He hadn't made time yet to talk to her about the piano lessons, and now he felt guilty. When she had come home from school he had heated up the falafel he'd bought her in the toaster oven, taken out the tahini and pickles and salads from the fridge, which he had asked them to wrap separately, and arranged them in the pita.

He sat across from her while she ate and told her Esti had called to tell him she looked well. Dana said, "She's such a drag," and told him how the nurse kept following her around. She mimicked Esti's sugary voice. "How are you? How do you feel today? Has your temperature gone down?" Dana said she was sick of the way she kept touching her forehead and looking at her with motherly eyes.

"Motherly?" he asked, somewhat amused.

"Yes," Dana said, and sank her teeth into the pita, which tore and spilled its contents onto the table. "Who does she think she is?" She picked up tiny squares of cucumber and tomato and stuffed them in her mouth.

"She's just concerned about you. There's no need to get worked up about it."

"I'm not getting worked up, I'm annoyed. She isn't worth my getting worked up."

"You're covered with tahini," he said, looking at her face. He was feeling elated—a mood to be viewed with suspicion, he thought. Only that morning he had sworn he wouldn't get involved with her if she was talented, but for several hours now he had been turning pages, hating her and loving her and mostly fantasizing about the sex they would have: a sexual encounter between two great writers.

Later, when he sent his daughter to her piano lesson and went back to sprawl on the couch, reading, a small cloud of fear entered the living room, casting a shadow over the plans he wasn't making but keenly sensed in his every limb: at dinner, the day before yesterday, she said she had read his books but hadn't said what she thought of them. He comforted himself with the thought that if she said she had read them she must have liked them but had been embarrassed to comment, because if she hadn't liked them, she probably wouldn't have confessed to reading them, out of fear that she would have to say what she thought. That was how he behaved in such situations; he had often told authors that he hadn't had time to read their books, so he wouldn't have to admit to not liking them.

But the comfort soon evaporated. To say she had read his books and not say anything more, he thought, was tantamount to saying with cruel politeness that she *hadn't* liked them, and he suddenly wanted to come up with an excuse to phone her—something about the steak dinner—and mention in passing that he was reading her novel and enjoying it very much, hoping she would say something in return. But then he would be taking a double risk: if she said she liked his books, he would never know if she was only saying it to return the compliment, while she would know with certainty that he was interested in her.

He tormented himself awhile longer, until he got up and chose a CD; he suddenly had a strange urge to listen to Arik Einstein, whom he had stopped liking after Ilana died. He looked for *Drive Slowly,* which was their favorite album, and couldn't find it. He put on *The High Windows* instead, and when he heard the voice of the lead singer, whom Ilana had resembled a little, he closed his eyes, laid the novel on his chest, and thought about Shira's apartment and how comfortable he had felt there, the way the rain had sounded through her window, the awkwardness, the quiet, the conversation, the yellow light, and he suddenly remembered he hadn't taken the diskettes out of his coat pocket and they could get damaged there. Then he fell asleep, and when he woke ten minutes later he picked up the book and went on reading from where he had left off, asking no more questions, allowing himself to be carried away into the *sweeping love story.*

Irma Gutt was a bit like Grandma Maxine. She also used to be American, but a different kind. In her apartment, which was much smaller than Dana's grandparents' house in New Jersey, there was furniture that looked a lot like theirs: heavy, with thick upholstery. Dana especially liked the cups and plates, which were white with blue prints of flowers and birds. Her teacher always served her milk and homemade chocolate-chip cookies.

She was sixty-five and had white hair tied up in a way that looked like cotton candy and smelled of hair spray. She spoke softly, with a heavy accent that wasn't entirely American; it was, as Irma herself said, a Polish Jewish accent. Dana liked watching her hands, which were dotted with brown marks, as she demonstrated a piece that always sounded much better when Irma played it, better even than all the pianists her father played for her. She liked the apartment and the cookies, which had a distinctly American flavor, she liked Irma Gutt and the pieces she played, but she hated the piano: She had no talent, that much was clear to her. She was not musical, and this presented a double-edged sword. To hate the piano was to betray her mother; to be untalented, unmusical, was to betray her father. And she couldn't betray him now, of all times, when he was in such a good mood. Nor could she betray her mother, now that a sort of collusion was being formed around her, around the place she had left, and Dana felt that if she had to betray someone, it should at least be gradual.

She herself had fallen in love with Shira in a crushing and desperate way. Her day at school had gone by quickly because she was lost in daydreams—not the usual ones, which were drawn out like bubble gum and grew tiresome quickly, but new dreams, in which she saw her father and Shira sitting together on the couch watching television, and her lying between them with her head on his chest and her feet on Shira's lap. Or she saw Shira and herself standing together in the bathroom brushing their teeth, in the morning or the evening, it didn't matter; what mattered was that Shira's full body, her stomach and her butt and her chest, which was bigger than Dana's mother's had been, now gave her new hope. She hated her own body. She had gained some weight recently; she could tell by the way her cousin's hand-me-downs didn't fit her, because Michal was taller and more slender, like Tamar. Shira seemed accepting of her body, and relaxed, and Dana knew that if she stood beside her long enough, absorbing her and her movements, rubbing up against her here and there, she would be able to become like her.

In these daydreams they stood by the sink and brushed their teeth and laughed as if they were on a school trip together, and Dana looked at the little fold of fat that emerged from beneath Shira's shirt when she leaned over to rinse her mouth, and also stole a guilty but extremely thirsty glance at her thighs, hoping there was no space between them, like there was between Tamar's long thin legs and her mother's, and when Shira straightened up she noticed that they stuck to each other like a girl's thighs, just like her own.

Now she sat on the chair next to Irma Gutt, who wanted to demonstrate a little section. They sat so close that she thought she could feel her teacher's birdlike ribs tickling her right side, and her rhythmic breath fluttering over Dana's cheek, dry and cold like a demon's kisses. She watched the keys being caressed by skilled fingers, unlike her own, which pinched the keys hurtfully, vengefully. She watched the droopy bags of skin on Irma's arms, and for a moment she wanted to confess: I hate the piano.

But instead of confessing, she nodded when Irma asked if she understood now, finally, how the piece should be played, and she tried very hard when her teacher went back to her chair and listened to her, tense and hopeful but routinely disappointed. Then Irma glanced at the clock and pretended, as usual, to be surprised the lesson was over. She went to the bathroom to get Dana's umbrella, which she had put there earlier to dry, and walked her to the door, and on the steps Dana met the girl who always came after her. She didn't know her name or who she was, but she thought she was Russian, and once she had stood behind the door after leaving and heard wonderful, sweeping playing, which went on without being interrupted by Irma's rhythmical cries of "No!

No no no!" She wondered if the Russian girl also got milk and cookies, or whether that was a consolation prize.

(1 5)

Shira went down to the corner store to buy her father some groceries, and on the way she passed the deli, which was still open, a sickly white light spilling out onto the sidewalk, but she didn't go in. She hated the food he bought there, hated it without having tasted it. She sensed a chill—her usual aversion was now intensified by what had happened there that morning. She knew that from now on she would find it hard to enter the place, because she would always see an imaginary chalk line on the floor marking her father's fall, the people crowding around him with their whispers and their clucking, and the panic, the Hungarian's anger, the ambulance double-parked outside—all these joined into a small and not particularly complicated puzzle: An old man faints in the morning hours in a North Tel Aviv delicatessen.

Exhaustion. What was the young doctor trying to tell her when he discharged them from the ER? Her father had low blood pressure, which might explain the fainting, but only when the patient was young would the condition be given a medical name. With Max Klein it was exhaustion. She took the doctor aside and tried to explain that her father's nutrition was deficient, and he nodded understandingly, recommended they see a dietitian, and said she could get a referral from the nurse at the desk. Then she snitched on her father that he was depressed, and for a moment this piece of information seemed to make an impression on the doctor, and her hope was restored.

"Is this new?" he asked.

"The depression?"

"Yes."

She briefly contemplated whether she should lie. "No," she said. "It's been that way for years, but recently it's gotten worse."

The doctor asked her to wait a few moments, and she said she would and thanked him warmly, not knowing exactly for what, perhaps for the solution he was about to return with. She went back to sit with her father, and with her eyes she kept monitoring the doctor, who stopped by another bed and listened with the same nods to the complaints of an elderly lady whose Filipina caretaker sat next to her, also nodding. Then he disappeared and came back half an hour later with her father's discharge sheet. He signed it, gave it to her, and asked her to go to the reception desk. She looked at him questioningly and he smiled and said, "Okay?" She said yes and wanted to ask, But what about the depression? What about the solution? but she said nothing. "Feel better, sir," the doctor told her father heartily, and her father mumbled his thanks and looked defeated.

Now, as she filled the basket with healthy, comforting groceries, she realized what the doctor had been telling her: you're alone. Completely alone in this dubious business of *exhaustion*. She bought eggs, milk, cottage cheese, whole-wheat bread, and chicken breasts to make him some schnitzels, as she sometimes did when she wanted to spoil him, and also to prove to him that there was nothing like home-cooked food. But today she didn't wish to prove anything.

When she got back she found him sitting in the armchair opposite the TV, drinking coffee, dipping a sesame biscuit in the cup, watching cartoons. "Are you hungry?" she asked.

"So-so," he said.

"I'm making schnitzel," she said, and he thanked her, and she took his empty cup and asked if he minded if she opened a window because it was stifling, and he said he didn't mind and stared at the screen. When they finished eating, she washed the dishes, put the leftovers in the fridge, which suddenly looked bare without its plastic containers, sat with him a little longer, and got up to go. She promised to call first thing in the morning to find out how he was.

"Promise me you'll call if you don't feel well, at any time, even in the middle of the night, okay?" He nodded and said he promised and asked her to lock the door behind her; he was going to bed now.

"Aren't you going to brush your teeth?"

"Not today. I'm tired."

"Okay, we'll let it go today, then," she said, hating herself for the patronizing nurselike plural, "but it's not a good habit."

"I know. I know, Shiraleh." He got up from his armchair and went into his bedroom and crawled under the covers and pulled them up to his chin, and she kissed his cheek and felt his stubble scratching her lips.

"And you didn't shave today," she said, and he said he hadn't had time.

"Close the window, it's getting a little cold," he said, and she shut the window and drew the blinds, then looked around and said they should get a phone extension next to his bed. He murmured, "Someday," and she went out and locked the door behind her, and knew that all this talk about tooth-brushing and shaving and phone extensions was an attempt to turn the huge monster, his approaching death—and, worse, the days that would pass before it arrived—into a few harmless pets, domestic and well trained.

On the way home, she drove down Bialik Street, slowing as she passed Yonatan's building. It was old and neglected, covered with yellowish plaster, far less attractive than the other buildings on the street. Its entryway was dark, and she could easily guess at the smell that lingered in the stairwell, that same smell that stood in her stairwell and in all the old buildings in town: a damp odor that in summer was mixed with the stench of cockroach spray and in winter had traces of rain and frying. All the front windows were dark, and she wondered which side of the building he lived on and whether he was at home. She had conducted so many imaginary conversations with him throughout the day that it seemed natural to go up and continue where they had left off. She would call him tomorrow, she assured herself, when she got home and started looking for parking. She would ask about the steak meal, which he'd probably long forgotten. It was too late today and she might sound desperate.

(16)

Yonatan was surprised to hear her voice on the answering machine when he got back from the grocery store, inviting him to go with her that evening to a gallery opening in the south end of town. As long as he had been reading her book, which he had finished that morning, despairing at how much he liked it, Shira had been an entity that hovered between the pages, a possibility with which he amused himself in his mind, a talent, a lay, a threat, or a promise but not a human voice.

She sounded hesitant, as if she was sure he wouldn't be free, that night or ever. She sounded as if she regretted even making the call, and in her voice he heard himself. He felt none the stronger at the discovery of these power relations but, rather, just as vulnerable as she was—vulnerable together with her. He listened to the message several times. *Hi, it's Shira Klein,* she said, as if she were afraid he wouldn't remember who she was if she didn't give her full name. *It's Monday morning, and I was calling to ask if you felt like going to a gallery opening tonight—if you're not busy. I mean, if you feel like it.* Then she paused. *So call me,* she said, and hesitated again. *If you want to.* She left a number and said *Bye,* and the *bye* sounded sad.

He wondered what she thought when she heard Dana's childish voice on the message they had recorded two years ago and never bothered to update—*Hi, we're not home, leave a message and we'll call you, bye*—in the cheerful squeak of an eight-year-old, which might give a stranger the impression that he'd phoned a very busy household, in which his call was one of many, and that the parents would return it at some point after they had finished their thousand daily tasks, and in the background there would always be a television blaring and children screaming and a blender or food processor running and a dog barking—so many lies in one short message.

He didn't want to go to the gallery, but he wanted to see her. This intensity scared him, but on the other hand there was something normal about it—as if they were old friends and it was natural for them to see each other so frequently. Still, he decided to wait two hours before returning her call, so as not to sound too enthusiastic. While he killed time on the balcony, he wondered what to tell Dana, because he felt he owed her an explanation; he had hardly ever gone out at night for the last few years. But what explanation could he provide? He could tell her the truth, but the truth was too vague and unclear even to him, so he decided to give her the momentary truth, the one without any further meanings: Shira, Rona's friend, had invited him to an exhibition. She didn't need a babysitter anymore, did she?

A little after two o'clock, before Dana was due back from school, he dialed Shira's number. "Hi," she said, when she heard his voice. "How are you?" He said he was fine. "So do you feel like coming?" she asked, without wasting any time, as if she feared that small talk might distance them from a meeting.

He said, "Yeah, why not? But what is it exactly?"

"It's the opening of an exhibition by some press photographers. Someone gave me an invitation. It's something to do with Tel Aviv. I didn't get exactly what the subject is."

"Sounds interesting."

"I'm not sure. There'll probably be all kinds of celebrities there. Another reason not to go."

"Come on, let's go, we'll see some celebrities. What time does it start?"

"Eight. Should I pick you up, or do you want to pick me up?"

"I'll pick you up."

"Then I'll wait downstairs at eight, so you won't have to look for parking. My street is a nightmare."

"Mine too," he said, and lingered for a moment.

"So I'll see you later?"

"Yes. At eight," he said, and they hung up.

That was simple, he thought, and the simplicity insulted the turbulence of the past twenty-four hours. Where did this leave the Friday-night dinner? Yesterday, while he was reading, he had made a mental shopping list, trying to remember where to find fresh asparagus, wondering if he should go by the butcher and ask him to keep him a few choice cuts for the weekend. His reading was accompanied by the aromas and sounds of frying, by thoughts of place settings and which wine to serve. What did it mean that they were meeting tonight? Who knew what would happen between them by Friday?

He decided to cook Bolognese sauce to spoil Dana, both because he felt guilty and because he was looking for something to do for a couple of hours. He thawed a packet of ground beef in hot water, and as he stood in the kitchen sautéing it, crumbling it forcefully in the pan with a fork, he felt so nervous and restless that he turned the gas off, locked the front door and left the key in the lock, went into the living room, rolled the blinds down, put on The Doors, whom he used to worship but hadn't listened to since he was a student, sprawled on the couch, and, to the sounds of "Strange Days," masturbated quickly, roughly, surprised at an erection which, he felt, did not belong to him at all. His head was void of fantasies or pictures, void even of words. He came with a moan that he stifled out of habit—after Dana was born, Ilana and he had learned to be quiet—and then he got up, washed himself off in the bathroom sink, buttoned up his pants, pulled the key out of the door, went back into the kitchen, and turned the gas on again. He kept on listening to the CD, as if it were playing in a different apartment.

When Dana got home, they sat down to eat and he told her in an incidental way, as he twirled spaghetti on his fork, that he was going with Shira to an exhibition that evening.

"Awesome," she said.

"What do you mean, awesome?"

"It's about time you went out. You're always sitting at home like some old woman."

How quickly your daughter became your mother, he thought, like a sophisticated machine programmed to start operating on a particular date, and that day had arrived.

"And I think you can also start going out with girls," she said.

"What?" he asked, slightly stunned.

"You heard me."

He tried to kid around. "Are you trying to get rid of me?"

"This really isn't a joke, Dad."

He felt as if it weren't him who had abandoned her over the last three days, but she who had abandoned him. Her eyes pierced him over her plate of spaghetti, her eyes that were his eyes, because everything else was Ilana's, except for her build: a mold made from the two of them that was neither Ilana nor himself.

"I'm just going to an exhibition, I'm not exactly going out with Shira."

"Pity. I think she's lovely."

"She *is* lovely, but that has nothing to do with it."

"Now you're just trying to change the subject," she said, and got up to put her plate in the sink. "Are you done?" She pointed to his plate.

"Yes," he said, and reached for his cigarettes.

"And you smoke too much."

"It didn't used to bother you."

"It doesn't bother me now either, but you can barely get up the steps."

"That's because I'm an old woman." He smiled at her, searching her eyes for the little girl who used to love his jokes.

"Very funny. Your lungs are burnt out."

"What's up? Have you started working for the Cancer Prevention Society?"

"Stop it, Dad, it's not funny." She turned to him, and he saw her fat little tummy peeking out beneath her sweater and he wanted to pinch it, as he used to do when she was little, but he knew he couldn't do that now and perhaps he'd never be able to do it again.

"Did you know that a girl in my class's mother died last month from cancer?"

"Who?"

"You don't know her."

"Breast cancer?"

"No, liver."

"Wow, that's fatal. You don't get over that."

"Lung cancer is also fatal," she said.

"That's true." He stared at the lit cigarette in the ashtray.

"But I want you to know that I'm not against smoking at all." She went back to washing the dishes.

"You're not?"

"No, I'm going to smoke too."

"You will not smoke!"

"I will, but not like you. I'll smoke like Mom."

When she washed the dishes she looked painfully similar to Ilana: the way they both arranged the dishes on the drying rack, with the plates at the right end and the pots and bowls at the left, glasses and cups on the lower part—he had no method at all—the way they first soaped all the dishes and laid them on the counter and then rinsed them all—he did exactly the opposite, wasting water, soap, and time, they claimed—and the way their backsides danced as they scrubbed.

"Dana, sit down for a minute. I want to ask you something."

"What?" she said with annoyance, sure she was about to be dragged into a serious conversation.

"Nothing. I just want to talk to you about your piano lessons."

"What about them?" she asked, and went on scrubbing the frying pan he had burned.

"You don't really enjoy playing the piano, do you?"

She was quiet. He could hear her trying to make up her mind.

"Come on, leave the dishes for a minute," he said. "Come and sit down."

"I'll just finish this pan."

"Dana?" he said, and lit a new cigarette.

"What?"

"You don't have to pretend you like playing, and you don't have to pretend to be happy that I'm going out with Shira."

"I'm not pretending."

"You are."

"I'm happy that you're going out with Shira."

"Are you really?"

"Yes."

"And what about the piano?"

"I don't know," she said and put the pan on the rack, but she didn't turn the faucet off, as if there were still dirty dishes in the sink.

"Turn around for a second?" he asked softly.

"I don't want to," she said, and used the little squeegee to wipe the water off the counter.

"Come on."

"In a minute. I'm busy."

He got up and went over to her and put his hand on her shoulder. He thought she had grown a little taller in the past few months, but he wasn't sure. "Have you gotten taller?" he asked.

"I don't know," she said, and he felt her shoulder shrinking away from his touch.

"I think you have. When was the last time your height was measured?"

"I don't remember."

Her shoulder, which was still small but had lost its birdlike quality, started squirming away from his hand and he turned her toward him and realized her face was covered with tears. He was surprised but not entirely, and lifted her chin, but she looked away so he hugged her. They stood that way, embracing, while she tried to reach back and shut the faucet off; when she couldn't, he told her to let it go. She worried about too many things at once; she was too responsible. "What a responsible daughter I have." He kissed her hair and turned off the faucet with one twist, and for some reason the word *responsible* brought on a new wave of sobbing. Only later did he remember that Ilana used that word a lot when she was trying to educate Dana, and there had been stubborn remnants of an American accent in it.

He rocked her in his arms and said, "Let's take a break with the piano, okay? Take a vacation. We'll tell Irma it's temporary."

She nodded into his chest.

"And for your information, I'm not really going out with Shira. Not yet, anyway."

"But will you?" she asked, in a choked voice.

"Do you really want me to?"

"I don't know," she whispered.

"I know you don't," he said, and felt proud of himself for his sudden intuition, after three days of being so focused on himself and thinking he had forgotten how to be a father. "I don't know either. We're alike that way, aren't we? We should be proud of it, like we should be proud of our beautiful eyes."

"Proud of what?"

He released her from the embrace and wiped her eyes with the back of his hand. "Of the fact that we don't know what we want. It's hereditary."

She smiled.

"So should I call Irma today?" he asked, and she nodded. "Did you wash the frying pan well, you lazy thing?" She nodded again, and he wrapped his arm around her stomach and squeezed her, ignoring the new rigidity that pushed his hand away from the puppyish softness.

She sat down in the Subaru Justy and smiled as she put her seat belt on, and he said, "You're punctual." She felt as if she had been caught red-handed in the act of being prompt. She had been ready at seven-thirty, so she sat watching TV, planning to be a few minutes late. She wanted him to double-park or drive around the block and wait for her, but at seven-forty she found herself standing outside the building in case he was early, leaning against the fence, hugging her bag. He arrived exactly at eight.

"Yes, I'm punctual," she said. "It's a pretty serious problem."

"Why? I think it's great."

"Because most people aren't like that, and I always find myself waiting."

"I know. I'm one of the people who are always late."

"But you got here on time."

"Because I made an effort. I didn't want you to wait outside in the cold."

"It's not that cold," she said, and thought about the chasm that stretched between the conversations she'd had with him over imaginary cell phones, and this one, which offered nothing comforting but rather a kind of banality struggling against itself.

"So where are we going?" he asked, and she took the invitation out of her bag and told him the address.

"Which way should I go?"

She said she wasn't sure. "Down Allenby, maybe?"

"I'll go via Yehuda Halevi," he said. "So what's up? How are you? What's new? What did you do today? How's life?"

For a minute, she thought she had got into the wrong car. This was a new man, this man with the small talk, neither the morose person she had met at Rona's nor the one who had sat with her on the balcony and hypnotized her with his silence. He was cleanly shaven, his hair was wet from the shower and smoothed down on his scalp, and he had changed the flattering gray sweatshirt to a sweater with a diamond pattern that was too small for him and looked prickly. When she looked at him sideways, she couldn't help comparing him to some of her worst blind dates, the ones who tried too hard and invested their efforts in the wrong areas: in the small talk that always sounded like a parody, in their dress, in an irritating cheerfulness, and especially in the way they tried to seem nonchalant as they drove.

Yonatan drove as if he were sitting on the couch in his living room and there happened to be a steering wheel and a stick shift in his hands. He sat with his legs spread, and the car, like the sweater, looked several sizes too small for him. How quickly one could go from attraction to rejection, she thought. From terrible longing to quiet revulsion, as if an automatic transmission were shifting the gears. He looked older, too. She tried to force herself to sound cheerful, but a sense of grief was taking over inside. She hadn't done anything special today, she told him; the truth was, she had slacked off.

"Didn't you write?" he asked.

"Not a word. You?"

"Me neither."

"I rested a bit today," she said. "My dad was in the emergency room yesterday."

"Really? What happened? Is it serious?"

"Yes and no. He passed out in some deli."

"Oh, no, that's not good." He honked angrily at someone who cut him off on the right. "Did you see that shit?" he hissed.

"Idiot," she said.

"So what does your father have?"

"Exhaustion," she said and felt as if the real conversation not only did not compare to the imagined one but was making a mockery of it— and not just of it but of her father, whom she suddenly felt she had to protect from this chitchat, from this date with his tight sweater and his flattened-down hair. "Never mind that," she said. "I don't know what's going to happen with him."

"Do you think I can park here?"

"Yes. I don't think they ticket at this time of day."

"You'd be surprised. On my street you get tickets at one A.M."

"Really?" she asked, and was suddenly worried about her father.

"Yes. Well, the parking people are right down my street, to my horror."

"Oh, yes, in that building by the square, right?" She thought perhaps she should call to make sure he was all right, because when she had called today at lunchtime to ask how he was, he had only answered after eight or nine rings and had sounded alarmed, as if someone were chasing him.

They got out of the car and walked toward a group huddled in the entrance to an old building. They were standing smoking and holding plastic cups with wine, looking hostile. "Come on," he said, and put his hand on her back, possibly protecting her, possibly pushing her into the stairwell, which was crowded with more people, leaning against the walls and the handrails, chattering.

She felt that, as usual, her choice of clothes had been wrong, that in the black miniskirt she hadn't worn for years, and the black polo-neck pullover, she looked as if she was trying too hard, as if it was right for her to hang out with this man in the green sweater with yellow diamonds, as if she deserved it. From the second they walked into the building, she lost interest in the exhibition and thought only of the moment when they would leave. As they made their way up the steps to the second floor, she hoped he wouldn't linger too long over the works of art, which in any case were blocked by the crowds. She hoped they could go and sit somewhere empty, quiet, unfashionable, and talk as they had talked the day before yesterday on the balcony, so she could restore the passion she had felt for him, and the compassion—not the kind from this evening, which had turned to scorn.

Restore the passion. She contemplated the words as she pressed against Yonatan's back while he tried to squeeze into one of the rooms. You could restore a ruined building, an injured body, a connection, anything built out of parts, but passion? Then she noticed that although there was barely any room to move in the room they had entered, he had still managed to light a cigarette and was holding it loosely between his lips, and he suddenly looked like a cross between an Italian movie star and a complete nerd. Someone pushed her from behind and her nose banged into his woolen sweater, which smelled like something from childhood, and she felt like wrapping her arms around his stomach so he could lead her inside like a train engine. But more than anything, she wanted him to turn to her and say he wanted to leave, that it was hot and suffocating and crowded and he was claustrophobic and you couldn't see the art anyway—and she suddenly felt his hand reach back and feel around for her own, and his hand changed everything.

She held it hesitantly at first, but the deeper they went into the room, toward a wall hung with small black-and-white photographs, the more she felt like someone to whom this hand belonged and that it was giving her a sense of belonging to the crowd, which looked as if its only purpose was to be a breathing lump exhaling foreign bodies. When they finally reached the wall, they stood side by side, looking at the pictures, with their fingers interlaced simply, wholly, and her clothes became sexy again, as they had been when she tried them on at home, in front of the mirror, all afternoon. Yonatan was interested in the photographs. He examined them seriously, making comments to which she responded without hearing what he had said. Here and there he waved at someone with his free hand, and she smiled at people she knew, but around her everything became a hum, one picture, because all her sensations, all her thoughts, all her plans for the future—everything was focused on their interlaced fingers.

A woman who was standing on the balcony, which was also full of people, shouted *Yonatan!* and he looked away from the photos to see who it was. When he saw her, he whispered to Shira, "Oh, no."

"Who is that?" she whispered, putting her lips close to his ear.

"Just a journalist. Her son goes to school with Dana." The journalist called his name again, *Yonchik!* and waved excitedly. He said, "Should we go and say hello for a minute?" and she nodded and hoped he wouldn't let go of her hand, and he pulled her after him, paving a way for them again through the crowds until they were spat out onto the balcony.

"Hi, baby," the journalist said and kissed Yonatan on both his cheeks and wiped her lipstick marks off them with her fingers.

He said, "Ziva, this is Shira. Shira, this is Ziva," and they both mumbled *Pleased to meet you*. Yonatan asked if she was going to some meeting, and Ziva went into a tirade about having to pay for equipment for the nurse's room and said she had already alerted people in the media and there might be an item about it on one of the radio magazines. A new kind of happiness flooded Shira when she saw Ziva's eyes piercing their joint hand, which swung between his right thigh and her left.

She remembered how Eitan liked to walk down the street with their arms around each other and hold hands in cafés or at friends' houses, and how she always got out of it and said she hated people who touched each other publicly. And now it turned out she was one of them.

She suddenly heard Ziva's excessively curious voice. "So what do you do, are you also a photographer?"

"Shira is also a writer," Yonatan said, and she felt his fingers tighten around hers.

"Oh, really? Do you write for the paper?"

"No, I write prose."

"Well!" Ziva said. "I see you two are cut from the same cloth, aren't you?" She looked at Yonatan. "Be a sweetheart and give me a cigarette." And suddenly the grip let go and his hand reached into the back pocket of his pants to take out the pack. He offered one to Ziva, then to her, and lit both of their cigarettes. After taking a puff or two, Ziva lost interest in them and hurried over to another acquaintance she spotted in the room. "So I'll see you at the meeting, Yonchik?" she shouted back to him, and he nodded and waved.

They stayed on the balcony, which felt more pleasant than the room but still was crowded with people, and Shira wanted to suggest that they leave but she didn't dare, so she said, "Sounds mysterious, this meeting."

"It's nothing mysterious. Just a parent-teacher meeting."

She looked at his hand, which now gripped the old wooden handrail, and envied little kids for the way they were able to arrange hugs and hand-holdings: the way they took the hand they were interested in and put it in theirs, or attached themselves to a parent sitting next to them on the couch by lifting the parent's arm and wrapping it around their shoulders, expecting with innocent and demanding certainty that the adult would know what to do. As he stared into the street she thought she would like to have a child with him. The thought shocked her, not only because he was the first man she had ever wanted a child with, but because she herself had never thought about children the way she did now, on this balcony, which, she thought, needed only one more person to come out before it collapsed.

Once, a few months before she broke up with Eitan, her period was late. At first they joked about it, as if it was obvious that she couldn't possibly be pregnant, not because they were careful but because it was impossible for a new life to begin precisely when their relationship was dying. Then Eitan started asking, "What should we name him?" and she said she didn't know, it didn't interest her, but he would still suggest different names, for girls and boys, and said he would prefer a girl. She thought it was typical of him never to consider the possibility that this child, boy or girl, would not have a name, because she would have an abortion. She had been late before, but this time it was three weeks. Eitan pressured her to have a blood test, even use a home pregnancy kit, but she refused, convinced she was pregnant but unwilling to know. They had sex all the time those three weeks, sometimes twice a day, mostly at her initiative; she hoped it would make her miscarry. Eitan accepted enthusiastically, because he thought their relationship had been saved. And one morning, after he went to work, she opened the medicine cabinet and took out the home pregnancy test he had bought for her at the pharmacy a few days before, read the instructions over and over at the kitchen table, until finally she went into the bathroom, peed on the stick, placed the test on the floor, and walked out.

She went into the bedroom to get dressed, sat on the bed, and stared at the running shoes he wore for his evening jogs along the beach, one facing right and the other left, and thought maybe she *wouldn't* have an abortion. Then she walked quickly down the hallway, opened the bathroom door, and looked from above at the stick, which only had one stripe. At first she laughed with relief and almost called Eitan at work to give him the good news, but her body suddenly felt empty. That afternoon she got her period. She went to see a movie on her own, and when Eitan came home in the evening and went to the bathroom, he saw the box of tampons she had left open on top of the toilet like a message for him.

The diamond-patterned sweater, which he had decided to wear for a change during a moment of foolishness and which had now become a torture device, reminded him of the cold winters of his childhood, when his mother would dress him in clothes she had just taken off the laundry line in the yard, some of which were still damp and held the remnants of a chilly Jerusalem night. The wool sweaters were agonizing.

He stood on the balcony, staring down at the crowd, and felt himself perspire and prickle as if the rows of woolen stitches were a beehive; for the first time in his life, he felt fat. He glanced down at his stomach, and it seemed to be swelling in front of his very eyes, threatening to unravel the sweater. His hips too, which had never been a problem, and which on good days seemed muscular and trim, now looked spindly and odd in his jeans, which were fairly new and still stiff. The only thing that reminded him of his former more comfortable self were his green Chuck Taylors. He wanted to go home, change his clothes, and start over again.

Shira, standing beside him, looked too fashionable for someone like him, too casual, too sexy in her black clothes. She saw him looking at her and asked, "What?"

"Nothing," he said, and after a long pause he said he thought they'd done their bit for the local art scene.

Relieved, she said, "I agree."

"So should we leave?" he asked, and she quickly broke away from the railing and this time she led him, paving a way through the crowd until they emerged from the building as if out of a vacuum and got into the car. She asked if he wanted to go and have a drink, and he said, "Yes, we could do that," forgetting how uncomfortable he was. "So where should we go?" he asked, once they had started driving, and she said she didn't know, she didn't get out much, and he said he didn't either. "All those places are pretty disgusting," he said, as they drove north on Allenby.

"Which places?"

"You know, the ones everyone goes to."

"We could go to my place then," she suggested. "I still have some beer in the fridge."

He said nothing, and she grew alarmed.

"What?" she said.

"We could also stop and pick up a six-pack," he said, and she felt relieved.

"What for?"

"I feel bad, I've been drinking all your beer."

"Nonsense," she said, but he stopped at the kiosk where they had bought cigarettes on Saturday—their kiosk—and got out of the car and asked if she wanted anything.

"Nothing," she said.

"Cigarettes?"

"No, I have some."

"Nuts or something?"

She laughed and shook her head and watched him as he pointed to the stainless steel vats, went inside, and then came out with a six-pack in one hand and, in the other, a plastic bag full of brown paper bags, a pack of cigarettes, and two candy bars. As they drove to her apartment she felt that things were far simpler and easier than she had feared, and the desire to have a child was replaced by a simpler and easier desire: to take off his ridiculous sweater, which she had actually started growing fond of for its woolliness, its Jerusalemness, and to sleep with him.

He sat down in the armchair he liked and, after she poured the nuts into little dishes, he asked where her CDs were. Feeling like a high school student, she pointed to a little wooden box beneath the bookshelves, and he got up, sat down on the floor, and started rummaging through the box. He was disappointed by her meager collection. She had some excellent recordings of classical pieces he liked, and a few wonderful jazz albums, but the selection seemed random, careless even, compared to his own.

"Find anything?" she asked, leaning over him. "I don't have that many CDs."

"No, but you have some good ones. What do you feel like listening to?"

"Whatever you feel like. You're the guest."

He pulled out a Stan Getz and Astrud Gilberto album he hadn't heard for years.

They sat across from each other in the room, which was lit with a yellow-orange glow from the floor lamp in the corner, sipped beer, reached out every so often for a handful of pistachios or cashews, and listened to Astrud Gilberto encouraging them in heavily accented English to fall in love, and Yonatan scanned the room over and over again and thought it was perfect. But soon the satisfied purring he could sense in his heart was disturbed by a shiver of the kind that runs down your back when you see something frightening or touching: What he saw was himself, lounging in an old armchair with his thin thighs touching each other and his new circumstantial potbelly rounding out each time he leaned forward to grab some nuts or toss the shells. It was a picture of his toadish unphotogenic self, moments before he had sex of near-historical dimensions.

He tried to fight it, but the effect gained rapid force, because now when he glanced around again, the room looked ridiculous, like a Hollywood set for a cheap love scene, and Shira too, as she sat across from him with her legs crossed on the couch and smoked and smiled at him when she saw him look at her, was suddenly a temptress, just as pathetic as he was. Attempting to calm himself, he reasoned he was simply misreading the situation: the golden light, which had a presence as thick as perfume, came just from a lamp, and the music, which he had chosen himself, was simply the backdrop for a conversation between friends. Shira was an attractive, talented woman he had met. That was all. And she was possibly the first woman he had met whose restlessness and sadness intrigued him so much that he wanted to explore them from the interior, to turn her inside out like a piece of clothing that, something told him, had similar stitches to his own.

"There's such tension in the air," she said suddenly.

"What?" he said.

"Tension. Don't you feel it?"

"A little. I don't know. What kind of tension?"

"I don't know."

"Come on, what? Tell me." He tried to simulate subtlety and maturity.

"We've been sitting here for how long, fifteen minutes?"

"Yes. Something like that." He was glad to grasp onto the minutiae.

"So what?"

"I don't know. Never mind."

"We've been sitting here for fifteen minutes and what?" he asked.

"Nothing. It's just . . . I don't know. Nothing."

"We're shy like two little kids," he said, and lit a cigarette.

"Like two little adults," she said.

"Two big kids."

"Do you want another beer?"

"Are you having one?"

"I haven't finished this one yet." She held up her bottle. "But I'll get you one." She got up and went to the kitchen, escaping the odd moment that stood between them, hoping it would dissipate by the time she returned. But Yonatan got up and followed her, as if he knew, as she did, that the kitchen was a safer place, that the tension, which had now turned to embarrassment, would not catch up with them there. "Would you like some coffee instead?" she asked.

"No. I'd like another beer actually, even though I'm kind of in love with your coffeepot."

"Have you bought one yet?"

"No. I haven't had time."

"My ex bought it for me," she said, and handed him a bottle. They went back to the living room, and he sat next to her on the couch.

The CD finished and she got up to change it, but he grabbed her hand and said, "Leave it," and pulled her to him. She stood opposite him as he sat there, her knees touching his, her hand in his, her stomach at his eye level, motionless, waiting. She tried to concentrate on his hand, an old acquaintance, tried to restore the confidence it had infused her with earlier, at the gallery, but now she didn't know what to do. They were no longer surrounded by a crowd from which she needed to protect herself, in front of which she could show off. There was no road to chart, no noise or suffocation, only silence and the claustrophobia of their awkwardness. She stood still, as if she were standing on a land mine.

He imagined himself lifting up her sweater and gently kissing her stomach. He saw himself grasping her ass with both hands and pulling her closer and closer to himself, until she put her hands on his shoulders or on his head, pushing and pulling him. But then he clearly saw the other things that awaited him, as present as her waiting body: the awkwardness that would follow, worse than the one they had just endured, the moment when he bent down to pick his clothes up off the floor, knowing he would take even less time to get dressed than he had to undress. He saw the afterward as a photomontage of this moment, of the room, of the furniture and the objects that would look different, and he disliked it and could already picture his walk home, to Dana, who was probably sprawled in front of the TV now, watching something stupid. He saw himself going to sleep, his body relaxed but his mind racing, and above all he saw himself getting up tomorrow and not knowing whether anything had changed in his life—he had never conducted such a harsh negotiation with himself over sex—and his definite sense that no, quite the opposite: that his routine had been shuffled like a deck of cards but it was still the same routine and it might now seem, at least for a few days, longer, less bearable.

"I'll get up," he said. "I saw a CD there before that looked interesting." He leaped off the couch, bypassed her body planted opposite him like a road sign, and leaned over the CD box.

He drank his second beer from a safe distance, standing by the bookcase. He pulled out a book every so often and leafed through it, asking if she'd read it and what she thought of it. Her answers sounded impatient, and he thought she was hinting that she was tired, that it was time for him to leave. He sipped the last of his beer and put the bottle down on the table. "Great table," he said. "If you ever want to get rid of it, keep me in mind."

"I don't think so," she said dryly, staring at the floor.

"Okay, I'll get going," he said, and she got up from the couch, where she had been curled up within herself while he had perused her books.

As she walked him to the door, he thought perhaps he should say something about the steaks, set up a time, but he said nothing because he no longer knew if it would even happen. He suddenly felt as if he had already given up what he had been hoping to achieve by hosting the meal, and at the door he said, "Bye, then, and thanks for the invitation."

"What invitation?"

"To the opening."

"You're welcome," she said quietly, and they lingered a moment longer between the open door and the stairwell, which had the same smell as his own stairwell.

He sniffed and said, "Someone was frying something here tonight."

"Yes, they're always frying things here. It's a frying sort of building."

"Bye, then," he said, and ran a finger over her arm.

"Good night," she said, and closed the door after him.

As he walked down the steps he sensed relief, but when he got into his car he was overcome with a sadness that was so sudden, so familiar, that he sat motionless for a few moments, staring at the key in the ignition.

When he left, she suddenly felt very alert, as if over the last few days she had been snoozing in a hammock that Yonatan had been rocking and now she had tumbled to the ground. She looked around the room, which was dotted with leftovers of what had happened between them and what might have been: his cigarette butts in the ashtray, the beer bottles, the CD case. His rejection revealed itself to her in the tiny details. She knew the signs, especially the flight, the way he suddenly got up to go home as if prompted by some secret universal cue. Idan used to do it sometimes. They would be sitting in a bar, drinking, touching each other under the table, and just when she thought he was drunk enough, he would call the waitress and order the check, and when they went out into the street he would say he was beat—that was his favorite expression, "I'm beat"— hail a cab, kiss her on the cheek, say, "Good night," and disappear.

She cleared the bottles and dishes off the table and thought perhaps she had only imagined the tension between them and that moment when he had grabbed her hand and said, "Leave it." Or perhaps she had not imagined the tension but had misinterpreted it, and when he had told her to leave it, he had actually been trying to tell her to stop making plans around him. She shouldn't have mentioned the tension, she thought. That was the turning point; that was where it all went wrong. On the other hand, she reasoned, a little fatalism wouldn't do any harm. If something was supposed to happen, it would, with or without her slips of the tongue.

She emptied the ashtray into the trash, threw away the empty beer bottles, transferred the leftover nuts back to their paper bags, and went into the bathroom to turn the washing machine on, because although it was after midnight she knew she wouldn't fall asleep and she was full of a bad kind of energy: not the kind that enabled writing but the kind that brought on a frenzy and turned to sadness. She sorted out the dark laundry from the whites and thought perhaps what had happened wasn't so bad after all, and that her sense of catastrophe was exaggerated, even slightly comical; he had a little girl at home and couldn't be expected to behave like a bachelor. Still, there was something insulting about his departure, like a man who walks into a store to examine the goods, but bolts outside when the shopkeeper approaches him; you can't tell whether he ever intended to buy anything or whether he just went in out of curiosity or boredom.

She sat on the rim of the bathtub, stared at the machine drum filling with soapy water, and reminded herself that at the beginning of the evening she had been embarrassed to be seen with him. She hadn't particularly liked his books either, which she had read a few years ago. They were full of verbal acrobatics and showing off and they lacked soul, or so she thought at the time. They lacked evidence of true suffering. She thought they had been written by an arrogant writer. She felt uncomfortable in the clothes she had worn to seduce him, and only now, sitting on the side of the bathtub, did she realize how hard she had tried. She took her sweater off, then the skirt and stockings, and remained sitting in her bra and underpants, which were also black—the sexiest items in her lingerie wardrobe. She took them off too and threw them into the sink. She sat that way awhile longer, listening to the machine spin, until her nakedness became uncomfortable; she would have thrown that into the machine too, if she could have. She thought of a line from a poem by Emily Dickinson, whom she had studied at the university: *After great pain, a formal feeling comes.* She went into her bedroom, lay down in bed, and pulled the blanket up.

The next morning, he phoned Irma Gutt and told her he thought it would be best if Dana took a break from the piano lessons. "It's stressful for her, and I can see she's not practicing. It's just a phase she's going through; she's stopped going to Scouts too," he said, as if that could soften the blow of abandoning the lessons. "Anyway, I don't want to pressure her. She's mature enough to know what's good for her. With regards to the piano, I mean."

He lit a cigarette as he waited for a response, and it suddenly seemed to him as if the conversation were not about his daughter but about him as an irresponsible parent who smoked too much, who breathed down the mouthpiece into the ear of a nice elderly American lady with an old-fashioned hairdo, entirely gentle and fragile, and now she was listening to him squirm, listening to his breathing much the way she listened to her pupils playing—pleased, but lurking for mistakes.

But Irma took the news well. She said she was sorry; she said she understood and that her door was open at any time and that Dana was a wonderful girl.

"I know," he said.

"Simply wonderful. She has a romantic soul."

"Really?"

"She likes the Romantics—Chopin, Brahms. Especially Brahms."

"Yes," he said. He felt a twinge and didn't know why.

"It's a shame, she was very much looking forward to playing him," she said.

"Maybe she will one day."

"In any case, my door is always open, Mr. Luria."

"Yonatan."

"Yonatan," she repeated. "And I wish Dana the best of luck."

"Thank you," he said, relieved.

"And to you too, Yonatan. I wish you the best of luck as well!" It was as if he were also a retiring student.

When he put the phone down, he thought of calling Rona to ask if she was coming to the parent-teacher meeting that evening, and if she needed a ride, but he decided against it. He suspected that out of a combination of hope for them and perhaps also a hidden desire to see them fail, she was monitoring him and Shira, and she would obviously have had input, especially about last night—like a sports commentator, she would be happy to analyze every move for him. The matter of the dinner might also come up, and he didn't know what to say. In his mind he could already hear her asking what she should bring and if he needed help, and himself clearing his throat and fumbling for an evasion or postponement. For a moment he thought he might ditch the meeting. He was planning to move Dana to a different school anyway, because she hated it. Tamar wanted to leave too, and Rona, who had connections at City Hall, had promised to try and transfer them both to a school in another area next year. He hated these meetings. They reminded him of cocktail parties, empty of content and full of everything that didn't interest him. When he went, he always sat next to Rona and formed a mute coalition with her, silently agreeing with everything she said, as if she were his big sister or his spokeswoman.

When Dana came home from school, she informed him she would be sleeping over at Tamar's that night. "You and Rona will be at the meeting, and we'll have the house to ourselves," she said.

"Why do you need the house to yourselves?"

"No reason, just for fun."

"Okay. So you're leaving me alone tonight?"

"Do you need a babysitter?"

"Yes." He laughed. "Should we ask Ziv to come down?"

"We could ask Shira," she said.

"You're a very devious little girl. I don't know what side of the family you get that from."

"Yours."

"But I'm curious. Why did you suggest that I invite Shira over?"

"You said you didn't want to be on your own tonight. You're chicken."

"Me?"

"Yes." She laughed, and he was glad to see her happy.

"Then you're a platypus!" he said.

"Well, you're a marmot."

"And you're a mongoose."

"A mongoose?" he said. "Now you're just making up animals!"

"No, I'm not! There is such a thing. You're an author, you should know."

"What is it, a cross between a monkey and a goose?" he asked and pinched her backside.

"That's sexual harassment," she said, and pinched his butt.

"And that's parental harassment." He grabbed her wrist, sensing her fragility.

"Sue me," she said.

"You should go over to Tamar's early, okay? Otherwise I'll drop you off on the way to the meeting. I don't want you walking in the dark, talking about harassment."

"You'll drop me off? Are you crazy? It's twenty feet away!"

"Madam," he said, "you know I don't like Allenby Street. I don't want you walking around there at any time of day."

"Then I won't go down Allenby, I'll walk through the square."

"I'll take you," he said. "I want to pick up Rona anyway."

"Okay." She gave in. "I'm going to do my homework."

"Nerd," he said.

"Mongoose."

At a quarter to eight, he dropped her off outside Rona's, and a few minutes later Rona got into the car, kissed his cheek, and said she couldn't be bothered with the meeting. "So what's happening with Friday?" she said, before she had even put her seat belt on. "Are you going to leave us all hanging? Is there a dinner or isn't there?"

"There is," he said, "just like we arranged."

"Arranged?"

"I think so. Didn't we? Didn't we make an arrangement? We said Friday night, didn't we?"

"I don't know. I thought it was left open. Did you talk to Shira?"

"When?" he asked, startled, then quickly confessed. "Oh, by the way, did you know we went out yesterday?"

"No! How should I know?" She sounded sincerely surprised, as if she did not possess the telepathic spying skills he had attributed to her.

"We went to a gallery opening."

"The photographers' exhibition? I was supposed to go too; I had an invitation."

"Why didn't you come then?" he asked.

"Give me a break. I don't have the patience for that kind of thing. So how was it?"

"What? The exhibition?"

"That too," she said and raised her eyebrows pointedly.

"Oh, really."

"Yes, really. It was so obvious that you fell for each other."

"We fell for each other? That's taking it a little too far."

"She did, then."

"You think?"

"I know."

"Why? Did she say anything to you?"

"Oh, come on!"

"Well, what do you want? I haven't done this sort of thing for ages."

They were near the school now, and he started looking for parking. He would have been glad to ditch the meeting and go to a café with Rona, or even sit with her in the car, so they could continue their conversation. There was something about her interrogation that made everything seem less scary, as if by extracting the details from him, she also salvaged them from what his mind had managed to inflict upon them during the past day and night, turning them from dry facts—he went out with Shira, she wants him, he might want her too but he fled the scene—into something completely different, into tiny living creatures, little mongooses that nibbled away at the events, consuming them like so much mongoose food.

Talking with Rona not only made everything less frightening but also newly tempting. In the past, too, he had found that talking with her— about school, about the girls, about Ilana, about cooking—reassured him. He had attributed it to the fact that she was a psychologist and listened closely, but now, as he begrudgingly squeezed into a space Rona had spotted from afar and had pointed to excitedly, he tried again to understand what it was about her that made him feel so normal—normal and foolish, but without the self-hatred—and he realized it was not that she was a psychologist but that he could gossip with her; she brought out in him the side that liked to gossip, that excelled at it.

They walked toward the school. He told himself that after the meeting he'd ask if she wanted to go and sit somewhere. He hoped the girls hadn't killed each other or burned the house down or been kidnapped; he wanted to keep gossiping about himself.

Esti, the nurse, greeted him as if she were the hostess at a formal event. "I'm so glad you came," she said, and shook his hand, and Rona left him standing at the entrance to the gym and went over to chat with a group of parents in the corner. "You look great," Esti said, as if she had forgotten that she'd seen him only a week ago. "You look really great."

He glanced at her and said, "You too," and looked at Rona, whose shoulders were now shaking with laughter. He wanted to join her, to take shelter in her shadow as he always did. He wanted to snag a seat next to her and win her company for the rest of the evening, because he suddenly felt that his entire happiness now depended upon his conversation with her; like a proportion junkie, he needed a few doses to get him through the next three days, until the steak dinner, from which he now realized there was no escape.

Esti said they were starting soon; the PTA chair was pressed for time so the meeting would probably be very short. "A quickie," she said.

"What?" he asked, because he hadn't heard her.

"It'll be a quickie today! A short meeting."

"That'll be good," he said, and smiled at her.

"Come and sit down, there's a seat here," she said, so he sat next to her in the first row of about twenty rows of chairs that had been set up in the gym. It was the last place he would ever have thought to sit. When the meeting began he could see Rona looking for him, so he waved at her.

She smiled with astonishment, like a classmate making fun of a teacher's pet sitting too close to the front.

The gym was stifling and he was restless. He craved a cigarette. The PTA chair stood in front of the rows of parents and began with an apology. "I have to go to Beersheba tonight. Some family business that can't be postponed. So I apologize in advance that we won't have very much time." Although he couldn't stand the guy, Yonatan thanked him silently. "At least we'll try to be efficient," the chair said, and invited Esti to come up and speak.

Esti got up and pulled down the hem of her blouse, something flimsy in a flesh tone that looked like silk, with the outline of her bra showing through. The chairman sat down at the end of the front row and Esti stood in his place. She said she wasn't there to try and convince the parents to pay the fees. She knew it was a lot of money. She knew it wasn't fair to saddle them with this burden. She just wanted to explain what it was all about, so they would realize that they were talking about basic essential equipment. "Critical, even," she said and looked at Yonatan, as if the word *critical* somehow reminded her of his presence. She pulled out a folded piece of paper from her pocket and read out a list of items.

"Excuse me." One of the parents interrupted; Yonatan didn't know the man, who was sitting directly behind him. "But why do you need a digital thermometer? That costs over three hundred shekels, doesn't it?"

"Yes, it is expensive," Esti explained, "but it's very difficult to take some temperatures orally, especially with the younger children."

"It seems like a luxury to me," the man said.

"Excuse me? Has your child ever been sick?" Yonatan heard Rona's voice in the back row. "You have a son in the first grade, don't you? Have you ever tried to take his temperature?"

The man turned to look at her and then turned back to Esti and spoke to her. "I didn't say it wasn't easier. At home we have a digital thermometer. But in light of the excessive demand that the school is making on us—and it seems to me that five hundred shekels from each parent is indeed excessive—we can cut corners here and there."

An argument developed among the parents, and Esti was left standing at the front of the gym with her list. Yonatan tried to figure out what he thought but he had no position, nor was he sufficiently focused to form one. He supported Rona. He trusted her. Everything she said was acceptable to him. If she were running for prime minister today, he would vote for her.

He yawned and stretched and, because it was so hot, opened the top two buttons of his denim shirt. Now he regretted wearing an under-shirt. He saw Esti looking at him, smiling, and he smiled back. After ten minutes the fuss calmed down and it was agreed that the matter of the thermometer was marginal. Esti went on reading her list, and fifteen minutes later the meeting was over. It was settled that the parents would pay half the amount this year and the second half next year. The man sit-ting behind Yonatan sighed and clicked his tongue and wondered out loud why he had bothered coming. Yonatan hurried over to Rona, who was deep in conversation with a divorcée lawyer with whom someone had tried to set him up a year ago; he had refused, claiming he knew her from school and she was too much of a yuppie for him. When he told Rona what he thought when he went to pick up Dana one day, she said he was an idiot and he had gladly agreed with her.

"Dorit is an amazing woman," she had said. "And she's beautiful."

"I know," he had said at the time. "But I can't be bothered with dates now."

"Chicken," she said, and he said yes.

Dorit smiled at him bitterly now, as if they had already had a cata-strophic date.

"We're going to get something to eat," Rona said. "Do you want to join us?"

He refused, saying he wanted to work. Rona kissed his cheek and left the gym with the beautiful lawyer. Confused, he stood in the door-way and was taking out his cigarettes when Esti came up to him and asked if she could catch a ride.

"Where to?" he asked coldly.

"Home," she said hesitantly, as if she had expected him to decide where she was going.

"Where do you live?"

"Next to Rabin Square."

"No problem," he said, and lit his cigarette.

"I'll be there in a sec. I'm just getting my coat."

He nodded and said he'd wait. She went inside and then came back out, wearing her short coat, smiling.

"You look a little troubled," she said, as they walked to the car.

"Really? No, I'm not."

"Annoying meeting," she said. "Pretty redundant, don't you think?"

He said it was no more annoying or redundant than all the other meetings. "Do you rent?" he asked, after they had driven in silence for a few minutes.

"No, it's my apartment," she said.

"Good location."

"Yes, it's really convenient. I walk everywhere."

"Don't you have a car?"

"No. I don't have a license."

"I don't believe it. You don't have a license?"

"I know. People never believe me."

"It's just so unusual. I don't think I know many people who don't drive. Did you ever learn?"

"I took two lessons four years ago. And that was enough. I have no coordination, and I'm chicken."

"You don't look like one," he said.

"One what?"

"A chicken."

They drove up Ibn Gvirol and he started to feel more relaxed, as if any small talk would calm him down, no matter with whom.

"Tell me," he said, when they stopped at a light, "who was that windbag who was being so cheap about the thermometer? The guy sitting behind me."

"Oh," Esti said, and leaned back in her seat. Now that the atmosphere in the car had changed she could also relax. "That's Avinoam Sharir. Did he get on your nerves?"

"He's a real pain," he said.

"He's also a widower."

"Really?"

"Yes. Not that I meant to put you in some niche of widowers or anything like that."

"No, it's interesting. What does he do?"

"He's a composer. He's actually quite successful."

"Yes, I think I've heard the name."

"His wife died of cancer. He has two kids. A girl Dana's age, and a boy in the first grade. Cute kids."

"When did she die?"

"About a month ago," she said. "We went to visit him from school when he was sitting shiva."

"Where does he live?" Yonatan asked, because he suddenly had an urge to know more about the other widower, and he wanted to prolong the conversation.

"Some alley near Meir Park. I don't remember the name."

"He's my neighbor, then."

After they passed Rabin Square, she asked him to turn right and then left and practically in the same breath she asked if he wanted to come up for coffee, and he agreed. When they got into the elevator they kept on talking about the widowed composer, even though there was nothing left to say. Yonatan felt that Esti was struggling to come up with things to say about him, supplying mean details about past events that had shown up his cheapness.

"Thriftiness, it's called these days," he said.

"Yes, thriftiness. But you know, it's not nice to gossip about widowers."

"Well, as a widower, I give you permission," he said, and when they reached the fourth floor and stepped out of the elevator, and he stood behind Esti while she searched her bag for the keys, he realized the tedious conversation about Avinoam Sharir was foreplay for sex that he didn't want.

(2 0)

Esti said she'd make some coffee, and Yonatan followed her into the kitchen, which was remodeled and huge compared to his own. "Wow," he said, "this is great!" even though he didn't mean it.

"Really? You like it?" Esti asked.

He nodded. "It's really very nice." He leaned against the black marble countertop. "And so clean!" He realized he had heard himself utter the same line somewhere else, but couldn't remember where.

Esti smiled shyly and said, "That's the easy part. I have a cleaning lady."

"We need one too, urgently." He scanned the ceramic floor tiles that showed his reflection, buttery and distorted like his compliments.

"Don't you have one?"

"No, we really should."

She nodded in agreement. "Of course, with a kid in the house."

"Actually, the kid is not the one who makes the mess."

She laughed and asked if he wanted her cleaner's phone number and he said he did—why not?—but knew he wouldn't call her. She asked what he wanted to drink, and he asked for Turkish coffee with milk.

"Don't you feel like something a little more stylish?"

"Stylish?"

"I can make drip coffee," she said in a seductive voice, and he said he would prefer Turkish.

"A mug or a cup?"

"Cup."

"Sugar?"

"No." He watched her pour water into the cup and stir the coffee; then she made instant coffee for herself. She stood on tiptoe to open one of the light wooden cabinets, took out a packet of chocolate-chip cookies, and placed a few of them on a dish. He thought it wasn't a bad idea, to sleep with her; she seemed like a good candidate for breaking the fast.

"Shall we sit in the living room?" she asked, and he carefully picked up his coffee and followed her down a long hallway. The floor, which was marble or faux marble, was scattered with little rugs and he slipped on one of them and almost fell. "Careful!" she said and turned to look at him. They went into the living room.

There was something touching about the room's ugliness. The couches, the drapes, the coffee table with a fruit bowl in its center, the wine-colored rug—they all looked as if they had been bought to be used by the family that would soon follow, but they remained as they had been: new, spotless, without history.

He sat on the loveseat and Esti sat opposite him, in the center of the three-seater, and wiped her glasses with the hem of her blouse. She now looked more like a mole than a bee.

"Is the coffee okay?" she asked, after he took a sip and put the cup back on the table.

"Excellent," he said, and wondered what she was like in bed. Ilana, whom he had thought at first would be boring simply because she looked so normal, had amazed him when they were together for the first time, with her absolute lack of inhibitions.

A week after they had eaten meatballs at her sister's, they went to Jerusalem and had dinner with his parents, and he didn't know which was more embarrassing, the fact that for the first time in his life he had brought a woman home or the pleading faces of approval that his mother transmitted to him all evening.

On the way home, as they drove down the steep Castel bends, Ilana said she thought she was falling in love with him. He kept quiet. She turned her head to the window and repeated, in her American accent, "I think I'm falling in love with you."

He wasn't surprised. Most of the women he went out with fell in love with him at some point, but he had never heard the words uttered with such simplicity, in the same tone Ilana had used moments ago to say she liked his mother's food.

"Did you hear me?" she said after a few moments, and turned off the radio. "I think I'm falling in love with you. What do you have to say about that?"

He said nothing, flattered, but started planning the breakup.

Then she opened her mouth again and said she wanted to sleep with him. Then she turned the radio back on because the silence must have become unbearable for her too. He still said nothing, slightly angry, and tried to concentrate on the jazz program on Channel One. He felt like hurting her, to teach her a lesson for being so bold, for her lack of respect for words.

"So?" she said. "Are you going to keep quiet all the way to Tel Aviv?"

He nodded in the dark.

"That's a shame. You know what, then? Forget what I said. Let's be friends. You seem like a nice guy."

"A nice guy?" He burst out laughing.

"Yes." She sounded hurt. "What's so funny?"

"Nothing. Just . . . nothing."

Then they were quiet again, and without knowing where the words came from as they escaped from his mouth independently, as if they were a feeling rather than its messenger, he said, "If you still feel like it, I don't mind." Now he was the one looking at her, nodding in the dark.

He got off at the Latrun intersection and turned onto a dirt road that led into a forest, and when he stopped and turned the engine off, Ilana got out of the car, opened the back door, and sat down in the backseat. She giggled and started taking her clothes off quickly, covering his reluctant body with little kisses and bites as it joined hers, unaware that she was going to be broken up with that same night.

He tried to get it over with quickly, ignoring her touch, though it was actually pleasant and new and humorous. He reminded himself that it had been a few weeks since he had slept with anyone, and so, at least from his point of view, his behavior was justified. He considered himself an excellent lover, but that night he didn't care; something in him wanted to punish this American woman who had tempted him in such a sexless, efficient way. He leaned back in the Citroën's seat and let her straddle him. He liked that position because it allowed him to be lazy, and he looked into her face, amused and slightly less angry when she came. She immediately opened her eyes and said, "Now you," and he didn't know that he was about to fall in love with her.

He missed her. Esti's ugly room contained not a single object he liked, not one that could justify forgiving the rest of them; they made him miss his old car and his old life and his wife, and the days when it was still imaginable that he would sleep with someone in the backseat of a car, and he thought that he had been widowed and grown old at the same time.

He must have smiled, because Esti asked what was funny, and he said he had just thought of something. "Something interesting?" she asked, and he said no. She asked if he wanted more coffee, because he had emptied his cup, and he said yes, why not, because he knew this was his opportunity, and that if he could only sit here long enough, he would eventually start, somehow, to want her.

She got up and took the cup and the dish of cookies, two of which he had eaten, into the kitchen. He sank into the shiny purple upholstery of the couch, and tried to calm the part of him that wanted to get up and leave. He knew he could be bad, really bad, that he could behave like a real son of a bitch—that's what Ilana would call behavior like his. "Son of a bitch," she called him in English, sometimes angrily and sometimes affectionately, but when he heard Esti rinsing out the cups in the kitchen, he told himself he was getting carried away again. Why think in terms of good and bad, when this was simply sex with an available and fairly attractive woman. Yes, he thought, she didn't look bad at all. He got up and went into the kitchen and without a second thought—without any more thoughts at all—he put his hand on her waist as she stood on tiptoe to get the back cookies out of the cabinet. *Son of a bitch,* he told himself, feeling a shiver run down her back. When she turned, he grabbed her hand and focused on her eyes, catching her with a look that said everything she thought of him was true—she didn't even know the half of it— and he was a son of a bitch.

The second he touched her she knew she was making a mistake. A mistake, her shivering spine screamed, but Yonatan pushed her back on the counter and held her face with both hands and kissed her, and the mistake took on the flavor of teeth and saliva. She wanted to ask, How long? How long has it been since your last time? She wanted to ask if she was the first since his wife, because the force of his biting kiss told her it had been awhile. It had been for her as well—too long—so that suddenly what they were about to do was not a mistake but healthy, normal; it was right. But still she hoped for a little more tenderness.

She kept on hoping even when she found herself standing facing him in the kitchen undressing, looking down at the ceramic tiles. She didn't have the courage to ask if it might not be better to move to the bedroom, as if it wouldn't count if they did it here; perhaps that was the only way he could do it, but she wanted it to count. He didn't undress but turned sideways as he pawed one of her breasts, and she leaned against the counter and tried to suck her stomach in. She kept her underpants on and reached out to unbutton his shirt and, with the other hand, stroked his cock through the corduroy fabric and didn't know which was more pleasant, the touch of the flesh or the touch of the fabric.

He studied her nipples, then her stomach; a feathery line of black hair, neither repulsive nor attractive, descended from her navel. Her panties looked like the cotton ones Ilana used to wear, but she had preferred colored ones and Esti's were off-white, like her bra, which he peeked at from the corner of his eye as it lay on the counter, one strap drooping over the side of the sink. He worried that it might fall in and get wet and told himself, I'm not concentrating.

He was suddenly embarrassed by the large mole between his shoulders, which the nurse's hands were now touching. He was afraid she would be disgusted, and afraid he would be repulsed by her touch, but he had an erection for some reason, and he kissed her again and made a note to himself that he was kissing too hard, like an adolescent, with teeth but no tongue, like he used to kiss women he didn't like. He stood across from her with an open shirt and a white cotton undershirt beneath it, and an erection that the corduroy both concealed and emphasized. He shoved his hand between her legs and pulled her panties down with the other hand, and she thought she deserved more, not this act that was slightly violent.

A compromise between violence and boredom, he thought; he was full of desire, but he didn't know what it was that he desired. Without even wanting to, he found himself noticing needless details: the tuft of black fuzz on her abdomen, the way she held her stomach in, and the goose bumps on her arms, one of which rested on the counter while the other reached forward to massage his penis. At least the sex will be wild, she thought; he thought, Get it over with as quickly as possible.

He unbuttoned his pants and pulled them down with his underwear and remained standing in them, as if they were shackles around his ankles. He felt stupid, and she moved him aside until he took one foot out of the mess of material and then the other foot, like a child undressing, and she sat on the floor and quickly took off her panties, and he sat opposite her and pushed her back until she was lying on the floor with her head touching the kitchen table leg, and he lay on top of her and kissed her and felt her mouth reaching out to the man she thought he was, to the man he could be but not with her, and her tongue traveled through his mouth while his remained obstinately stuck to the roof of his mouth. He suddenly thought of the words from the oath—*If I forget thee, O Jerusalem,* and almost burst out laughing. His lips trembled and Esti misinterpreted him again, and with her tongue still in his mouth, she mewled a satisfied murmur.

He suddenly let go of her, sat up, leaned back against the fridge, and said, "I can't, Esti. I'm sorry."

She sat up and stroked his face. "It's okay, I understand, we got a little carried away."

They sat facing each other, cross-legged, and he saw her stomach fold over her crotch, and she looked at his thin legs and at his balls that shyly adhered to one thigh, and at his penis shrinking above them, and whispered in his ear, "It's really okay, Yonatan, I understand." But the name *Yonatan* suddenly turned her on. So many times she had whispered it to herself and scribbled it on sheets of paper: dozens of times she had pronounced it nonchalantly when she called to let him know his daughter was sick. *Yonatan,* she whispered now in her heart and felt how, despite the disappointment, despite the compassion, something in her insisted on this. Although it was obviously a mistake, something demanded it insistently, because she deserved it. She realized now that his evasive shyness, the way he always said "I'll see you soon, Esti" and lowered his eyes, was directed precisely toward this great moment, which in truth she had planned quite differently—it was supposed to happen over a weekend in a hotel, or at least in a bed, not on a floor that still smelled of cleaning solvents. Still, this was the moment and she couldn't let it slip away.

She stroked his neck and whispered in his ear, "Yonatan, are you all right?"

He nodded quickly and said, "You?"

She nodded and gently pushed her tongue into his ear, and he pulled away, smiled awkwardly and looked at the brown specks dancing in her green eyes, and thought, A cross between a bee and a mole. His legs started falling asleep and again he felt her tongue in his ear, and her teeth gently tugged his earlobe. My ear is attached to her palate, he told himself, but he didn't laugh, and something moved down there against his thigh.

Yes, she thought to herself, he's starting to rouse, and she went on cautiously nibbling his ear, whispering, "Yonatan, Yonatan," and feeling how from one Yonatan to the next she could barely control herself; she was ready for his penetration as she had never been ready in her life. "Yonatan," she whispered.

He whispered back, slightly alarmed, "What?"

"Nothing, Yonatan," she said.

He thought of Yonah Wallach's poem, "Yonatan." He couldn't stand it; if she uttered one more Yonatan he would get up and leave, but he knew he wouldn't. Her lips broke away from his ear, and her head slid down between his legs, and her teeth gently nibbled at his penis, and he pulled her head away and lifted it and whispered, "Esti . . ." *I can't, Esti,* he wanted to say. She was heartened upon hearing her name and put her head down between his legs again, and he leaned back against the fridge, felt its vibrations against his back, and meant to get up, slowly, so as not to insult her, but she spread his legs and sucked him so strongly that she managed to birth a semi-erection.

She knew it was going to happen now, they were going to do it, and she wanted to suggest that they move to the bedroom, where it would be more comfortable—she was glad the cleaning lady had changed the sheets yesterday—or at least that they have a glass of wine, because there was a bottle in the fridge. But she didn't dare lift her head up, and she realized that even here, on the floor, would be fine, somewhat passionate even, like those scenes in the movies, and she even thought she might not insist on a condom. Yonatan, Yonatan, she said, silently over and over, and thought she wouldn't mind having a child by him, by Yonatan.

He couldn't stand the sight of her face, so full of love and compassion and encouragement that threatened to destroy his half erection, but he was going to come in her mouth, so when she looked up from between his legs and tried to speak, he did something he had never done to any woman, ever: he pushed her head back down.

Since it was too late to retreat—he knew it was coming and he anticipated it like pain—he told himself that Dana was transferring next year anyway and he wouldn't have to see Esti again. There would be no more winters with morning phone calls, which would now be impossible. Then suddenly he had a terrible thought: what if Rona can't transfer the girls to another school and the nurse takes revenge on his daughter, she sees her burning up with a fever, fainting in the hallway, turning blue and wheezing and choking, but does nothing, doesn't call him, lets her die because of him.

All of a sudden he saw an image of Ilana, sobbing in his arms after the ambitious cake she had made for their first anniversary had burned. She said she had wanted to make a "glamorous" cake. He laughed and wondered which English word she had thought of that had led her to use the Hebrew *glamorous*. He had meant to ask but never got around to it, and now he remembered Esti asking him if he wanted something more stylish to drink, and he felt how this fresh memory was defiling the old one with all its sadness, and so to protect it he remained with it, caressing Ilana's face and hair just as he had done then, when she had cried and he had honestly tried to comfort her but couldn't help laughing—at first a private laughter that gurgled in his stomach, then a laughing fit that eventually swept her along.

Then he imagined Shira who rode him as he held her breasts. He tried to guess what kind of breasts she had, because it was hard to tell with those bulky sweaters she wore. Mid-sized, he thought, neither big nor small, medium and perfect in their mediocrity. He had no idea where she had suddenly sprung from but he was grateful for her presence, as if they had arranged to meet here at this time on this floor in this position, and he came, sensing—through the pleasure—Esti's surprise, as she choked and stopped moving.

She rolled over on her side, with her head resting on her arm, and stroked his thigh with her other hand. He sat with his legs spread, listening to the refrigerator's hum, to the oven timer ticking, as if he were waiting for a buzz to tell him when he could get up and go. He touched her cheek lightly and said, "Should I get you a glass of water?" She shook her head. "I'll get you one," he said, because he wanted to get up, and he quickly put on his underwear and pants, and took a glass off the drying rack and filled it with water, and leaned over and gave it to her. She sat up and took a tiny, dry sip and gave it back to him, and he put the glass on the counter. She seemed to have been injured in a motor accident and was lying there, on the ceramic road, while they waited for help.

He put on his undershirt and shirt, took his cigarettes out of his pocket, and asked if he could smoke. She nodded and said there was an ashtray in the drawer under the microwave. He thanked her and took out a glass ashtray printed with a construction company's logo. He wanted to apologize to her, but didn't know what for. Esti got up and put her clothes on. She looked sleepy, thoughtful, and he put a hand on her shoulder and asked if everything was all right, and she nodded and said she was going to the bathroom.

When she came back she said there was a cake in the fridge; yesterday was her birthday and her mother had brought a wonderful cake. "Happy birthday! I wish I'd known!" It sounded stupid, mean even, because what would he have done had he known, bought her something? Tried a little harder not to come in her mouth? He hated himself—he hated himself intensely—but his body hated no one now.

"I'm not hungry," he said.

"Coffee? I'm making some anyway," she said, as if she didn't expect him to take her up on the offer. He did, to postpone his escape a little longer, to not be a complete son of a bitch.

"Esti," he said, when they sat at the table drinking their coffee, and he found himself nibbling one of the chocolate-chip cookies left on the dish; he thought they had soaked up some moisture during what had happened here in the kitchen. "I feel a little uncomfortable about what we did just now." He turned to the microwave because he couldn't look in her eyes. "I mean, it was good for me, really good, but I just feel uncomfortable with the whole situation, with the fact that I may have unintentionally made you think I was interested in a relationship." He heard himself speaking these words and refused to believe it; he never knew he could produce these clichés, that he was capable of tossing them out so easily; he was like one of those vending machines: very clumsy, very necessary, and completely unreliable. "I haven't been in a relationship with a woman for a long time. Any kind of relationship," he stressed and hoped she'd understand, but she had fixed her gaze at a large calendar hanging on the wall. "And the thing is, I don't think I'm capable of being in a relationship now. Not a real one."

"Just one-night stands?" she asked stiffly, aiming her words at March.

"No! What makes you say that? I'm really not built for one-night stands, I'm not interested in one-night stands! Really, really not at all!"

"What then?" she asked, and finally looked at him.

He took another cookie and crammed it in his mouth. "I don't know. I know it sounds terrible, but I really don't know."

"Do you need some time then?"

"No!" He panicked. "It's not a matter of time. Esti, what happened between us shouldn't have happened. Certainly not with you. You work at my daughter's school, we've known each other for years, and it would have been better, *if* I was going to have a one-night stand—if that's what you want to call it—for it not to be with someone like you."

"Someone like me?"

"But I was attracted to you," he lied, to avoid her question. "I was so attracted to you."

"And you haven't been with someone for a long time."

"In bed, you mean?"

"In bed," she said, and her eyes pierced the floor again.

"Yes. A *very* long time."

"Since your wife, of blessed memory?"

"Yes, since my wife, of blessed memory," he said, and let out a nervous giggle.

"What's funny?"

"Nothing. It just seemed funny to say 'my wife, of blessed memory.'"

"That's what one says, isn't it?" She was hurt.

"I know, I know. It's just . . . it just suddenly sounded funny."

"So really you're trying to tell me that this was an isolated thing and we're not going to see each other again."

"Yes. Well, no."

"No?"

"Because we'll *see* each other, won't we? At school. I'm sure Dana will be sick lots more times." He said this as if it offered some sort of compensation. "So of course we'll see each other." He felt loathsome. He felt loathsome and hungry and wished he'd accepted the cake, because how many more cookies could he gobble down without her thinking he was a total pig? He got up and did the opening steps of his departure dance: went over to her, put his hand on her shoulder, rubbed his nose in her hair, and said, "Smells good."

"Thank you," she spat.

"Hug," he ordered, and got her up on her feet and wrapped his arms around her and pulled her to his chest and lifted her chin up and looked into her eyes and asked, "Are you okay?" She nodded, and he asked, "Really, truly?" and hated himself again, and she nodded again. "Dana's waiting for me," he lied, "I have to go." He kissed her on the lips, a soft and long and lying kiss.

When they stood at the door Esti hugged herself, wrapping her arms around her shoulders as if she were cold. He knew that stance. At once he was revisited by pictures of women he had left standing that way, alongside doors, hugging themselves. When he was young, he had thought it was their way of clinging to him one last time before he left, but today he knew it was their way of scorning him.

"Okay, so we'll still see each other, right?" he said, and Esti nodded. "Good night then," he said, and released one of her arms from her embrace of herself, held her hand, and squeezed it in his own, a kind of comforting squeeze like the kind you give mourners. He whispered, "Bye, Esti, good night."

She shut the door behind him.

(2 1)

He left Rona and Shira virtually identical messages about Friday night's meal. He told them to come whenever they wanted—seven, eight—trying to sound indifferent, and that they didn't need to bring anything. He also left his address for Shira, just in case. Then he went out to the butcher. It had been over a year since he'd bought steaks, and he assumed the butcher wouldn't recognize him.

He was unable to erase the image of Esti curled up on the kitchen floor. Strangely, he didn't feel even a shred of guilt. When he had come home that night, he had taken three schnitzels out of the freezer and thrown them into the frying pan, then listened to the sizzling that sounded very noisy in the silence of 1 A.M. Then he washed the dishes, went into his study, turned on his computer, and wished he had Solitaire.

He went into Dana's room, which was so neat one might suspect it belonged to an elderly spinster. He found Shira's novel on her bed; between the front cover and the first page was a bookmark with pictures of Dalmatians on it. He sat on the bed and started reading, curious as to how the sentences appeared to his daughter. His devious daughter. Soon she would turn eleven. He got off her youth bed, straightened the now-wrinkled sheets, and as he brushed his teeth he thought about the term *youth bed,* which struck him as ridiculous. He walked around the apartment with its odors of frying, shut the windows, turned off the lights, and when he went into his room and undressed he told himself, Now I'm getting into my adult bed, and pulled up the blanket. His body was calm and empty.

He wondered what kind of teenager Dana would be and when she would start to hate him; perhaps she already did. When she was a baby he had often tried, never successfully, to picture what she would look like as a woman. Lately he had trouble remembering what she looked like as a baby. He saw her in his mind's eye, sleeping with Tamar in a bed that opened out to two twin beds, and he thought of Tamar, who even now, although her body was boyish and thin, was somehow sexy and standoffish in a way Dana was not, even though she was more developed than Tamar. Last week, when she had been at home sick, he had noticed that her sweatshirt, the one she liked and which she had outgrown, revealed two small fleshy pillows in the place where, until not long ago, there had been only babyish nipples, and it embarrassed him.

"You need new sweats," he said, as he handed her a cup of tea on the living room couch, where she was watching TV. "I need to get some too, so if you'd like we can go when you're feeling better." She agreed feebly and went on staring at the screen.

He must have predicted the changes before they had occurred. The fact was, he had been careful recently not to walk into the bathroom when she was there, and he knocked on her bedroom door before going in to say good night. Now he wondered if he'd have to start being careful when he hugged her. He didn't want to be one of those fathers who made a big deal out of their daughters' adolescence, embarrassing them with their own awkwardness. Although during the years of his own adolescence he had begun to disparage his father, he was grateful to him for accepting his son's exhausting transition from boy to young man without exclaiming at all the little changes—the hint of a mustache or a changing voice—as he heard other fathers do with their sons. His father was so engulfed in his study that when he noticed one day that some other man had moved into his house—taller and more depressive—he didn't ask any questions.

In four years Dana would be fifteen, and he might find her sprawled on the couch watching TV every evening. She might reply to his questions in an unfamiliar voice that he would do well to get used to now. When she was fifteen they would no longer be able to go shopping for clothes together. They would no longer hug. A moment before he fell asleep it occurred to him that when she was fifteen he would be fifty. Then he would need an old person's bed.

There was no reason to feel guilty, he reassured himself, as he walked into the butcher's shop. He had behaved as any other man would have, and while Esti had been giving him a blow job, millions of women around the world had been giving blow jobs to millions of men. The butcher did remember him and greeted him warmly, coming out from behind the counter and putting a heavy hand on his shoulder. "I thought you'd turned vegetarian!" he chided him.

"God forbid!" Yonatan said, and shrank away from the hand. The butcher slapped his back and went back behind the counter. He smelled of blood.

Yonatan asked for four pounds of steak, and the butcher disappeared into the huge refrigerator, came back, and presented him with various cuts, holding them up so he could examine them closely. Yonatan loved meat. He found it hard to believe that he'd gone for more than a year without eating a steak. Was he punishing himself for something, or was it laziness, some kind of culinary senility? The butcher highly recommended a particular cut, and Yonatan said he would take it. He looked at the huge man's chest as he sliced the beef for him, and at his palms, which looked as marbled and aged as his cuts of meat, and thought this man was the perfect stereotype of a butcher. He asked him for a few slices of bacon as well, and was suddenly overcome with a desire to buy a huge variety of other cuts, to stock up his freezer, fill up his life with meat. The butcher wrapped the steak and the bacon and Yonatan paid, thanked him, promised to come back soon, and went out onto the street.

He went to the market to look for asparagus, and when he couldn't find any at the first stall, he decided he would be better off making something else, something more original, so he wouldn't appear to be imitating Rona's meal. He bought artichokes as an appetizer and three types of lettuce, and decided on baked potatoes as a side dish—something simple and modest, so his steaks could be the star. On the way home he thought about the bacon and eggs he would make himself for a late breakfast and was filled with joy. He was amazed by the way food, especially thinking about food, made him happy, but he knew it wasn't the food itself, fine as it might be, but rather the hours of preparation and the minutes of eating that gave him some sense of normalcy, of belonging—the illusion provided by a good meal.

He was glad to have put himself in this trap of entertaining, and before he turned down Bialik he stopped at a little housewares store and bought a set of wineglasses and six straw place mats he took a liking to. Then he went up to his apartment, put the meat in the fridge, and played his messages—there was only one, from his mother, inviting them for lunch on Saturday and complaining she hadn't seen them for ages. In the kitchen, he made himself bacon and eggs and decided to tell his mother that he and Dana would come. That way he would have a weekend of activities and wouldn't even have to try and write. He stood looking at the strips of bacon curling in the pan and the eggs hardening around them and felt happy.

But Esti lying on the ceramic tiled floor would not leave his mind. As he ate, he tried to reconstruct their conversation but was unable to do so. Then he tried to remember what she had been wearing, but could only recall the bra tossed on the counter with one shoulder strap hanging in the sink. How quickly his fears—years' worth of carefully honed anxieties—had turned into one reasonable erection. How his yearnings had lost their complicated names and all flowed into her mouth. He felt a little guilty about that—she had really looked as though she had not been expecting it—and he could have at least been more considerate. On the other hand, he thought, as he bit into the last strip of bacon, he required some consideration too. He hadn't slept with anyone for almost five years and had even stopped fantasizing—five years that were, in effect, the beginning of his forties—perhaps not a man's best years but certainly not his worst. Half a decade of abstinence had concluded with one blow job, not an especially good one but not bad either.

He looked at his empty plate, dotted with grease, and lit a cigarette. It occurred to him that he himself was the perfect stereotype of a forty-five-year-old leftist widower who had a preadolescent daughter and casual sex.

(2 2)

She almost called at the last minute to say she couldn't make it: she felt she was already in enough trouble. But she decided that canceling would make things even more complicated than simply showing up for dinner in a relaxed, friendly, expectation-free way. She put the bottle of wine she'd bought in her bag, put on her denim jacket over an old unflattering sweater she had been wearing all day, and quickly walked through the park, convincing herself that it wouldn't make any difference whether she got there early or on time.

She arrived at seven-thirty. Dana opened the door for her and she heard Yonatan asking, "Who is it?"

"It's Shira!" Dana said.

"Shira?" Yonatan called out.

Shira yelled out, "Hi, it's me!" and the girl made a sweeping hostess gesture with her arm and ushered her in.

There were no smells attesting to cooking and, apart from a large table in the living room, where Dana led her, there were no signs of dinner. On the contrary, the house looked as if he hadn't been expecting guests at all. From somewhere in the apartment, Yonatan shouted that he was coming. The Voice of Music was playing the final movement of the piece she had started listening to at home.

"Dad's shaving," Dana said. "Want to drink something?"

She said she didn't. "Am I early?"

"Yes. I mean, no. I mean, I don't know."

"Nice apartment," she said, and Dana smiled shyly. Shira wondered how, in fact, a child was supposed to react to such politesse.

"You haven't seen all of it, so how do you know it's nice?" Dana asked.

"I'm guessing. I know these old apartments. I live in one too."

"You do? Do you also have three rooms?"

"Two. Do you have three?"

"Three and a half. My dad has a study that used to be a balcony we closed off. Want to see my room?"

"Yeah, why not?" Shira said, and got up from the couch. As she followed Dana down the hallway, she heard Yonatan coughing in the bathroom, a deep smokers' cough. Then he cleared his throat and spat.

Dana turned her head to Shira and smiled, embarrassed. "Dad, I'm showing Shira my room," she called out, perhaps to prevent him from making any more noises.

"Okay," he said, and she heard him turn the faucet on. "I'm coming in a minute. Sorry."

"No need to be," Shira said cheerfully to the closed door and thought about the man who for the last four days had seemed so strong by virtue of his absence. He had suddenly stopped being a sexy fable of power and abandonment, now that she saw his apartment, which wasn't nice at all but claustrophobic, now that she heard him coughing and spitting and imagined him leaning over the sink, perhaps an old sink like hers, webbed with veins of cracks and rust.

Before she walked into Dana's room, everything she had seen thus far fell into one picture—the dark entrance with the coatrack bowing under the weight of winter items, coats and scarves, beneath which peeked the pink pompom of a girl's woolen hat; the table in the middle of the living room, reminding her, in its detachment, of Passover Seder night; the living room itself, which crowded around the table and looked embarrassed and surprised by the presence of a stranger; and then the hallway and the bathroom door with frosted glass in its upper half—all these seemed to be pieces in a puzzle of despondency.

Dana's room was vast. It had a large window divided into three long narrow panes, set in old wooden frames painted dark blue. The panes were covered with Disney stickers, some of them peeling off. On the floor beneath the window was a large wooden trunk painted in the same shade of blue, on whose lid was written, in faded gold letters, DANA'S SECRETS. Up against one of the walls was an old grandmotherly bureau with keys in its locks. By the other wall was a bed covered with an Indian fabric with a procession of elephants surrounding the bed: each black elephant held the tail of a white elephant with its trunk, and they in turn held the black elephants' tails. In the center of the procession she saw her book. She looked at the colorful wool rug at the foot of the bed.

"It's from the Old City," Dana said, having followed her eyes, and sat down on the bed, holding the book. "We're reading your book now."

"Really?" She felt pangs of embarrassment for the man shaving in the bathroom.

"Yes. My dad's already finished it and now I'm reading it."

"Well"—Shira faked an amused tone—"what do you think of it?"

"I've only just started," Dana said, and opened the book to the first page. "I'm only here, but my dad finished it in two days. He reads fast."

"Do you always read grown-up books?" she asked, instead of asking what her father thought about the book.

"No. But because we know you I wanted to read it."

"That's nice. I'm flattered. So is this where you do your homework?" She pointed to a desk that looked like an old butcher's table next to the bed, and Dana nodded and went on flipping through the pages.

From the hallway Shira heard Yonatan announce that he was getting dressed and would be with them soon. They were both quiet. Through the open window she could hear Allenby: a store alarm blaring and the constant hum of pedestrians. The girl's room suddenly looked like a huge square of loneliness. A sour metallic smell spread through the apartment. Shira sniffed the air.

"It's the artichokes," Dana said. "They must be ready."

"Yes," Shira said.

"I'll go and turn them off soon," Dana said. She lay down on her side, propped up on one elbow, and started looking through the book. "It looks interesting" she said, as if to herself, and Shira heard a closet door slamming in the next room. "I think I'll like it," the girl said, and looked up.

"Hi," Yonatan said, and stood in the doorway, flushed and shaven, his hair wet, wearing wrinkled, freshly laundered jeans and the same gray sweatshirt he had worn when they first met. "I'm dressed."

He went up to Shira and ran his fingers over her arm, and she felt the shiver of someone who has sworn to herself not to feel that shiver again.

"Are you two coming to help me in the kitchen?" he asked, and when he noticed the book on Dana's bed, he smiled at his daughter and then at the speckled floor tiles, and said, "Your book is amazing."

"Really? You liked it?"

"Very much. And I'm consumed with envy."

"Envy?"

"Of your honesty."

"Thank you." She wasn't sure what he meant but didn't ask, so as not to sound too interested. "So what needs to be done in the kitchen?"

"Everything!" he said, and with a gentlemanly motion he gestured to the hallway and said he needed urgent rescuing. Shira walked in front of him, inhaling the artichoke scent that welcomed her, warm and violent, while behind her the tickling smell of shaving cream and laundry detergent lingered, and the smell of renewed hope—but this time, she told herself as they went into the steamy, bubbling kitchen, hope without expectation, if there was such a thing.

Dana was in charge of setting the table. She wanted to know how. "What style should I use?"

"Your style. That's the style I like," Yonatan said and kissed her hair. She shook him off, twisting her face, but he didn't care; he was happy.

Shira offered to make vinaigrette for the artichokes, and he said, "Vinaigrette? How could I not think of that? I've been racking my brain all day for a sauce to make."

"It's just a dressing, don't get excited."

He said anything she made would be wonderful. He took out a wooden platter of steaks from the fridge.

"Wow!" she said. "This is exciting!"

He looked at the beef affectionately, and then at her, and said, "Yes, pretty exciting. I'm actually quite good at this."

She stood by the sink and washed the lettuce, and then the potatoes he handed her one by one as he stood next to her with a dish towel to dry them. "Will seven be enough?" he asked, before putting them in the oven. She smiled, and he said, "No, I'm serious," although the potatoes were huge.

"Of course it's enough. Too much, even; look at their size." He examined one of them in his hand, nodding, as if he hadn't purposely chosen the largest ones in the market. "If you ask me, one each is plenty," Shira said.

"No, I always prefer to have too much food than too little."

"Me too," she said, and wiped her hands on the dish towel he was holding. "You know those people who always make too little spaghetti?"

"Oh, yeah! The pasta criminals."

"I hate them," Shira said.

"Me too! I despise them!"

"If you don't have any spaghetti left over in the colander, that means someone's going to be hungry," she said.

He laughed and wanted to hug her. He sat down at the table and lit a cigarette. "Want one?" he asked, and she nodded, and he lit a cigarette for her. She stood opposite him and took a drag, and her stomach was once again at kissing height.

He suddenly felt as if he had just returned from a long journey that had lasted only four days but had exhausted him. And he hadn't liked the destination. Last time he had been there he was a student, and now he felt like an elderly tourist. That morning, the image of Esti in a fetal position had finally stopped haunting him. "Nothing happened," he had repeated to himself as he drank his coffee on the balcony. "Nothing at all happened," he reassured himself, until he realized that was exactly what was troubling him: the nothing—that complex, urgent, nonrecurring nothing—they had shared.

When he went down to the store to buy some last-minute supplies and tried to guess what flavor of ice cream Shira preferred—forgetting that Rona had called to say she would bring dessert, forgetting Rona and the girls and their preferences—he realized he had fled from Shira because he didn't want that nothing with her; he wanted everything but was afraid that the nothing was inevitable, perhaps a stage he had to go through, that the nothing was still something that needed to be shared with someone.

He put out his cigarette and went to deal with the steaks. Shira sat in his place and shook the vinaigrette she had made in a jar. She watched his dance steps as he twisted the big pepper shaker, then covered the cuts of meat with crushed pepper and piled them carefully back on the wooden board. He looked for the dish towel, which she was absent-mindedly clutching, took it from her, and wiped off his bloody fingers. She realized Dana was standing in the doorway, leaning against the door frame and watching them with a dreamy, satisfied look.

The doorbell rang and Dana opened the door. Rona came into the kitchen with Tamar, holding a pan covered with foil. "I made panna cotta, and I really hope it didn't fall apart on the way." She sat down at the table and looked around. "You know, I haven't been here for years," she told Yonatan.

He tried to remember the last time someone other than Nira had been here. Tamar came over sometimes after school, but Dana usually preferred to go to her place—more and more so recently, and he wondered if she was ashamed of the apartment, of him, of the life they led here among his books and CDs and moods and cigarette butts. The idea seemed appalling but not implausible. In her place, he would also have chosen a different parent.

"Dad." She came up to him holding a wineglass with a napkin fanned out inside it. "How's this?"

Rona and Shira were impressed, but he pulled her to him and hugged her close, and she squirmed and got out of his arms and said, "Don't! You'll ruin it!" He said it was lovely, like in a wedding reception. "Good job," he said, and knew that the sudden hug he had imposed on her was not for her but for the benefit of the two women watching him: for Rona, to remind her that her daughter didn't have a father who could hug her like that—he hated himself for it, but he suddenly felt like bursting the perfect hermetic bubble she had created—and for Shira, he didn't know exactly why, perhaps to show her what a skilled hugger he was.

Dana and Tamar dragged chairs from all over the apartment into the living room and arranged them around the table. It was strange for him to see his desk chair, his torture chair, wheeled in and positioned at the head, as if it was happy to escape the study.

They ate the artichokes. Tamar said the way people put down their chewed leaves said something about their personalities.

"What do you mean?" Yonatan asked.

"Look," Tamar said. "Dana and Shira just put them on their plates in a messy way, but me and my mom and you make neat piles. See?" She pointed to his plate and dragged a leaf through her teeth.

"Yes," he said, and looked at the tower of leaves he had erected on the edge of his plate. "So what does that say about us?"

"It says we have a very good aesthetic sense, that we like things to be clean and tidy, and that we're a good match for each other."

"Who, you and me?"

"No!" She laughed and dipped another leaf in the dressing. "Let's say, you and my mom."

"And what about us? Don't we match?" Shira asked.

"You?" she said, and pretended to think about it. "Not so much."

"Why, because I don't have an aesthetic sense?"

"I don't know." Tamar shrugged her shoulders. "It's just a theory. I didn't make it up."

"It's a pretty dumb theory," Yonatan said, "considering that being clean and tidy is not exactly my strong suit." He stacked the plates and announced ceremoniously that he was going to broil the steaks. "Does everyone like them done medium?"

"No! Gross!" Tamar said. "I hate blood. Make mine well done."

"I told you we weren't a good match!" he teased.

"To be honest, I also prefer mine a little more well done," Shira said. "Medium-well, but you poor man, I'm making things difficult for you. Make mine medium too."

"No, it's okay, you're not making things difficult." For a moment he was disappointed that the woman he had seriously decided to devote himself to falling in love with liked her steaks cooked longer than he did.

He stood cooking the meat in the cast-iron skillet he took out of the cabinet. It was still greasy from the last time he had used it, almost two years ago, he recalled, on Dana's ninth birthday. It was the kind of skillet that wasn't supposed to be washed, which was why he liked it—"a lazy man's pan," Ilana called it—but he was also fond of it because it stored memories of past dinners.

He watched the juices running into the pan and thought, After the steaks we'll probably rest a little and have some coffee and panna cotta. Then the guests would leave. Dana and he would take the rarely used extension leaves out of the table and put them back in the closet. They would push the table back into its corner, close to the piano, where it was usually loaded with books and newspapers and bills and a few pairs of balled-up socks that somehow always ended up there. Tomorrow they would go and have lunch with his mother, who was probably snoozing in front of a TV talk show now, her hand with its large freckles and prominent veins resting on the remote control. They would have chicken soup or some new experiment, a recipe from the paper, something Chinese or Thai, although recently his mother had stopped trying out new recipes and stuck to the ones she knew. For a main course she would make brisket, because it used to be Dana's favorite dish. He couldn't bring himself to tell her that his daughter had since developed more sophisticated tastes and he wouldn't mind a change either. They'd have fruit salad or compote for dessert and then a marble cake with coffee.

They would sit in the living room or the garden like three stiff characters in a British drama. His mother would tell him things he'd already heard, and when she asked what was new with him he'd say nothing; what could be new? Dana would say the same when she was asked, and he would be a little angry with her for not trying harder to have a conversation with his mother, but he would understand her, although he wouldn't know if her impatience was a mirror of his own behavior or a symptom of her adolescence. Even before he told his mother they had to leave, she would go into the kitchen and pack the leftovers for them in plastic containers, which they'd bring back next month on their next visit. At the door she'd ask why they were leaving so soon. "It's early," she'd say, and he'd say he still had to write today, even though he knew he wouldn't write a single word and wouldn't even try. It was the magic excuse that no one dared dispute.

Driving the bends on the way out of Jerusalem, he would tell his daughter for the thousandth time how much he missed the city of his childhood, how sorry he was that it had changed and become religious and had sent people like him into exile. Dana would look out the window and nod, just as Ilana used to, a *yes, yes* containing some empathy but also scorn for the campaign of self-pity that was always part of these trips.

He shifted the steaks around the skillet and pierced one of them, which was cooked through to medium, and he took it and the two next to it out and put them on a plate that he covered with another plate, and left the other two in to cook. Shira stood behind him and he turned to her, wiping the sweat from his forehead with his sweatshirt sleeve.

"Is that one mine?" she asked, pointing to one of the steaks in the pan.

"One of them is. Whichever one you want. Take the big one."

"It looks wonderful."

He touched the steaks with his fork, and she thought she was capable of being his friend, she was fairly certain of it, now that she had overcome the disappointment of discovering he didn't want her.

(2 3)

He hadn't planned it and was slightly shocked to hear himself say it, but a little before midnight, when he said goodbye to them at the door, he asked his guests if they wanted to go with him and Dana to Jerusalem the next day; he was sure his mother would be happy to see them.

Rona said they were already invited somewhere, but definitely another time; she hadn't been to Jerusalem for ages, she loved Jerusalem, and she'd be happy to meet his mother. Shira said she would come. He said he'd pick her up at noon, and she asked if it was really all right and his mother wouldn't mind.

"Mind? Will she mind if we bring a guest?" Yonatan asked Dana, who was standing next to him, yawning.

"No way," she said. "She'll be thrilled."

When Shira woke up in the morning, she realized her father would be deprived of his usual Saturday visit and called quickly to ask how he was. She said she'd stop by if she got back early enough, and if not she'd visit him tomorrow. A year ago, or even a month, he would have asked who Yonatan was, where they were going, and when they'd be back. But the old man on the other end of the line didn't even bother to say what he always told her, his regular mantra that had started as a warning and a farewell and had turned into a habit: *Drive carefully, please.* He sounded as if he had lost his language.

"Okay," he said, when she told him she was going out of town and would probably not see him that day.

"Are you all right? Have you had something to eat this morning?"

"Fine, yes."

"Do you feel well, Dad?"

"Fine. Fine, yes," he said, as if he were answering a completely different question.

She went out onto the balcony to check the weather. It was warm again, and she wished it was raining. A rainy drive to Jerusalem could have been more romantic. On the other hand, she reminded herself, what was being forged between them now was friendship, and the weather had no effect on that type of relationship.

When the Subaru drove up, Dana got out and moved to the backseat, despite Shira's protestations. There was a school-trip atmosphere in the car. The last time she had been to someone's mother for Shabbat lunch was when she went with Eitan to see his parents on their kibbutz. She liked them. Being around them gave her a temporary sense of normalcy, and she couldn't understand what Eitan meant when he said he hated their arguments. At the dinner table, his parents would reminisce about trips overseas, completing each other's sentences and casting doubts on the veracity of each other's descriptions. To her, this was not arguing but communicating. Her parents had never talked at the dinner table, and their silence always sounded like a noisy fight to her.

"How sad that summer's almost here," Dana said, and looked out the window.

"I know," Yonatan said.

"Let's move to Sweden."

"Okay," he said and lit a cigarette.

"Dad, I'm serious!"

"Me too. We're moving to Sweden. Want to come to Sweden with us?" He smiled at Shira.

"Yes. But it gets hot there too sometimes."

When they got to Jerusalem and made their way to the German Colony, Shira noticed that Yonatan's driving seemed different. He drove slowly and looked very calm, almost dreamy, as he turned his head to look outside. He drove as if he were taking a walk, as if the streets belonged to him, or used to. When they reached his mother's house, a beautiful stone building behind a wall covered with climbing vines, they got out of the car and walked into the garden down a gravel path that crunched beneath their feet. She felt weak in the knees. There was something somber about this garden, something cold and secretive that reminded her of the first meeting with Yonatan, at Rona's dinner, which now seemed so distant, irrelevant, but still somehow moving, like the memory of a mundane event that emerges in one's mind as a turning point, even if nothing extraordinary happened.

Yonatan's mother heard them walking down the path and came out to greet them. Yonatan turned to Shira and said, "I already told her you were coming and she's very happy, so don't feel uncomfortable."

The old lady hugged her granddaughter first, then went up to Shira to shake her hand, and finally looked at Yonatan with a look that contained both hesitation and affection. "How nice that you came," she said to Shira. "I'm Rachel, Yonatan's mother."

Shira apologized for coming empty-handed.

"Nonsense! I would have been very angry if you'd brought something."

"Very?" Yonatan asked cynically. "You'd have been very angry?"

"Maybe only a little," she said apologetically. "But I would have been angry."

"She has nothing better to be angry about in life," Yonatan said. "If only."

The living room was the exact opposite of the garden. It was warm and colorful and overflowing with artifacts and Persian rugs and afghans, and it had a smell of fuel from the large stove that stood up against a wall. "I didn't turn the heat on today," his mother said, when she saw Shira looking at the stove. "It's warm, isn't it? Would you like me to turn it on?"

"No way," Yonatan said. "We're already sweating."

"If you want the heat on, just tell me," the old lady said to Shira, and she nodded and smiled. "Sit down in the meantime, I'll bring you something cold to drink."

The three of them sat on the couch in a row. They listened silently to the rustles coming from the kitchen—the fridge was opened and closed, a cabinet door slammed, glass chinked—and it occurred to Yonatan that he wouldn't have heard these noises if not for Shira, if he were not starting to take in his childhood house, and his mother, through Shira's eyes and ears, if he did not feel that each of these meaningless sounds said something about him. "Maybe you'd like to go and help?" he asked, and Dana got up quickly and went into the kitchen.

"She's a good kid, your daughter," Shira said.

"Yeah? And how's my mother?" he asked. When he turned to her, she saw weariness and worry in his eyes, and the embarrassment boys feel when they introduce their aging parents to a stranger.

"Your mother's great too."

"Grandma wants to know if grapefruit juice is okay for everyone," Dana asked.

"That's all she ever has, so why is she asking?"

"She says there's Coke too," Dana said.

Yonatan turned to Shira questioningly. "Apparently, we have a choice today," he said. He lit a cigarette and tossed the match into a little copper ashtray with ornate Arabic script on it, on a low table.

"Grapefruit is fine," Shira said. "Is it all right to smoke here?"

"Yes, of course it is," he said, and gave her a different ashtray, a larger one, made of colorful glass. "As you can see, here there are more kinds of ashtrays than drinks."

"Does your mother smoke?"

"She used to, occasionally, but not anymore." He got up and went over to touch the stove. "Sometimes she doesn't turn this off properly and it just keeps running on low, and then she complains that she's hot." He rapped the chimney with his knuckles, and she felt the need to protect the old lady slaving in the kitchen—the one who had bought Coke for them, which would probably remain in the fridge until their next visit—from her son's attempts to minimize her like a document on the computer.

But she found herself joining in. "My dad's been forgetting things too, lately. It's a good thing he doesn't cook. Otherwise I'd be in a constant panic about him leaving the gas on."

Yonatan appeared not to be listening. He blew rings of smoke and looked around nervously, examining the room with a surveyor's look. "She's a hoarder. Look how much junk she has here. It's unbelievable."

"It doesn't look like junk to me. There are lovely things here. Your mother has good taste."

"It's junk. Believe me, most of it's junk."

Dana came in and sat opposite them on a large leather beanbag.

"Tell me, how long does it take to pour a glass of juice?" Yonatan asked.

"She's looking for the good glasses," Dana said.

"Oh, come on. Mom! Will you come back already?"

His mother came in carrying a tray with tall glasses full of juice. As she served them, Yonatan noticed her hands shaking a little.

"You have a lovely house," Shira said.

"You think so?" Rachel asked. "There are things from all over the world here."

"Grandma was an anthropologist," Dana said.

"Really?" Shira asked, as if Yonatan hadn't lovingly told her about his mother a week ago, when they were sitting on her balcony, when she still saw him as a different man, a different son, not the one sitting tightly on the couch projecting teenage hostility, crushing out his cigarette forcefully as if to announce to everyone that, as far as he was concerned, this visit was over.

"I used to be," Rachel said, "but that was a long time ago. Before Yonatan was born."

Shira wondered what her own mother would have looked like had she still been alive. Would she also try so hard to satisfy some vague but constant desire of her daughter's? Before she died, Shira had always thought of her as an unhappy woman, but she lacked the franticness and grandeur of her father's misery. She was not happy, but she also was not miserable. There was something gray and steady about her condition, something that neither blamed nor demanded, that did not deteriorate or develop in any direction. And this was how she died: not very old and not very happy. Shira wondered if she herself was like that now, or if she ever would be.

"The food will be ready soon," Rachel said.

"Great, we're starved," Yonatan said.

"I hope you like brisket," she said to Shira.

"I love brisket," Shira replied.

"What kind of soup did you make?" Yonatan asked skeptically.

"Chicken. Today I made chicken soup."

"Thank God. I was afraid you'd experiment."

His mother looked at him forgivingly and then smiled at Shira. "Yonatan tells me you're also a writer."

"Yes, it turns out I am," Shira said.

"Lovely. It's good to be creative."

"Is it?" Yonatan asked. "What exactly is it good for?"

"The soup is hot," his mother said, and invited them to sit at the table, which was already set. Shira asked if she could help.

"Sit down," Yonatan ordered, in a voice she didn't recognize. "Dana will help."

They sat beside each other at the large oblong table, which stood by an arched window that looked out onto the garden.

"It's so beautiful here," Shira said.

Yonatan scratched an invisible stain off the edge of his plate with his fingernail. "She's getting sloppy with the cleaning." He held his plate up and looked at it in the light.

"Mine's clean," Shira said, and put her hand on his arm.

Dana came in slowly, carrying a bowl of soup in both hands. She gave it to Shira. Then she went back to the kitchen and reemerged with another bowl for Yonatan.

"Sit down, Danaleh," her grandmother said from the kitchen. "I'll bring ours."

Dana sat down opposite them, with her back to the window. She thought they looked strange, almost childish, as they sat there, close to each other, as if everything she had wanted to happen between them had already happened—that thing she did not want to name, because a name would necessarily be accompanied by embarrassing pictures—and now they were pretending nothing had changed. She wondered if Shira had purposely worn the same skirt she wore last Saturday at Rona's. From Tamar's room, where she had sat drawing, she had heard her dad complimenting Shira on the skirt. She tried to remember if he used to compliment her mother on her clothes too, but she couldn't. She told herself it would be better to think about her mother as little as possible now and was surprised to discover how easy it was.

Yesterday, as they sat on her bed together and waited for the steaks to be ready, Tamar had asked if she thought her dad and Shira would be a couple. She said she was almost positive they would, and Tamar said, "I think so too. It's pretty obvious." Yes, Dana had said, it was really obvious. "And if they get married," Tamar said, and ran her fingers along the row of elephants, "then you'll have two mothers. A biological one and a stepmother."

"No," Dana said, and went back to flipping through Shira's book, "I still won't have a mom at all."

"Yeah, I guess you're right," Tamar said, without looking up from the bedspread.

"But you know, it's not for me that I want them to be a couple. Not at all," Dana said.

"No, obviously, it's for your dad," Tamar said.

"Yes," Dana said, "only for him," and she held the book up to her nose. "Do you like the smell of new books?"

"I love it," Tamar said and looked up from the bed. "Let me smell."

They passed the book back and forth, touched it, turned its pages, and smelled it, and during those quiet moments, with the smell of steak spreading through the apartment and mingling with the scent of paper, which somehow fixed itself in her mind as the scent of Shira, Dana realized that whether or not her father found love, her mother was fading like the golden letters on her trunk, becoming more and more absent from her post by the window in that house on the hilltop, the one overlooking the road, which Dana now understood was not what had killed her because a contractor had killed her. And she realized that the familiar pain of missing her constantly was becoming smaller than the pain of missing her less.

When she thought about Shira, when she tried to imagine her living with them, she knew it was complicated, because although there was enough space in the apartment—they would make space; she was even willing to swap rooms with them because her room was larger—it was complicated. Where would Shira put her computer? How could two writers live together? What if one of them wrote and the other didn't? What if one of them closed him- or herself up all day in the little study and came out with glowing eyes and a distracted smile, as her father used to come out years ago after a good day's work—what would the other one do then?

She ate the brisket, which had mushrooms in it today, and heard her father asking, "What's with the mushrooms? You never put mushrooms in the brisket."

"I wanted some variety," Grandma said. He asked if they were from a can, and she said they were, and he looked at his plate suspiciously. Shira complimented Grandma on the brisket and took a second helping and asked how she made it. Grandma said it was very simple and gave a lengthy explanation. Her father ate quietly and looked dejected.

Last night, after they had said goodbye to everyone and washed the dishes and taken the table apart and put it back in its place, he had been in a good mood. She had never seen him like that. From her bed she heard him pacing around the house, humming something to himself; she thought it was a song from that CD by The Doors. He turned the TV on and watched an old American comedy, and she heard him laugh every so often. He didn't go to sleep until 2 A.M. and neither did she, because she didn't want to sleep away these rare moments when his happiness had a physical presence, like another person in the house.

But in the morning he was back to his old self. Before leaving they spent almost half an hour searching for the car keys. "What do I need this for?" he asked himself, as he turned over cushions and felt beneath piles of paper on the living room table and under a California cookbook, where they had looked for an artichoke recipe. Although only a few hours had passed since yesterday, she already missed him. She missed the mess that was different from the one the two of them made; she missed the piles of dishes and the table setting, which had seemed crucial to her, as if the placement of the knives and forks or the way the napkins were folded would have a lasting effect on the future of the evening, which was, judging by the happy noises her father had spread through the apartment, a huge success.

Shira was chatting merrily with her grandmother, who had brought a pen and paper to write down the recipe. Her father suddenly got up and went to open the window and said you could die of heat in this house. But the window wouldn't budge and Grandma told him to leave it, it had been stuck for years, and she felt him push her chair forward without noticing because he was trying so hard to open the window, and then he jabbed her back with his elbow and didn't apologize because he was so focused on the stuck window.

"Yonatan, leave it," his mother said. "It's stuck."

And he said, "I don't want to."

She and Grandma and Shira exchanged maternal smiles, and Shira asked if he wanted help, and he said no and rocked the handle in his hand for another minute, and then finally gave up and sat down again. Shira took out her cigarettes and offered him one, and with a sour face he took a cigarette, and she lit it for him, then lit one for herself, and Grandma stunned everyone by asking for a cigarette too, and Dana could already tell that her father was going to say something insulting, but Shira silenced him with an infectious smile, and he smoked and smiled to himself and glanced with amusement at his mother, who smoked her cigarette with the utmost gravity. Dana saw that Shira's shoulder was touching her father's and her free hand was resting on his arm, and suddenly he started laughing, quietly at first, and Grandma asked what had happened, and then the giggle turned into wild laughter and then a coughing attack, and Shira slapped his back until it subsided and he took the hand that had slapped his back and placed it on his thigh, under the table, and his mother kept asking what was so funny and blew rings of smoke into the air, and Dana looked at her father, whose eyes were watering from laughing so much, and she knew she didn't need another mother, she needed another father: this one.

(2 4)

"Are you crazy?" he said, when they'd finished eating the compote and cleared the dishes, and his mother was boiling water for coffee. "Why would you sleep over here?"

"Because I feel like it."

"But you have school tomorrow."

"So what? What's going to happen if I don't go for one day? I'm not missing anything. Believe me."

"And how will you get home?"

"I'll take a bus."

"Alone?"

"Yes. What's the big deal? I'm not five years old."

"But you don't have a change of clothes here, you don't have pajamas."

"Grandma will lend me something. It's not a problem."

"And what does Grandma say about this? Have you even asked her?"

"Yes! And I'd love to have her," his mother shouted from the kitchen.

He turned to Shira, as if she were the one who had to give her approval. "I don't know your rules," she said, "so I'm not interfering. It doesn't seem like a problem to me for her to come back on the bus. But again, I don't know what rules you have at home."

"We don't," Yonatan said. "That's exactly the problem. We have no rules. She does exactly what she wants."

"Oh, really? When exactly have I done whatever I wanted? Give me an example."

"I don't remember. But forget that. Do you really want to stay over at Grandma's? Fine, then! Have fun, the two of you, but tomorrow Grandma's taking you to the Central Bus Station. Mom, do you hear me? You're taking her to the bus station."

"All right," his mother said, and suddenly she sounded younger and stronger than she had when she was just his mother and worried only about him. She sometimes used to employ the same tone of voice when she answered his father as he barked requests from his study or reminded her to do things she'd already done.

"Okay?" he asked, just to hear her answer him again that way.

"Okay," his mother said loudly, from the kitchen. Oddly, when he left, reminding her again to take Dana to the bus station and make sure she got on the right bus, she didn't equip him with plastic boxes of leftovers this time.

When they got in the car, Shira suggested that he give her a tour of the neighborhood, and he agreed happily. It was twilight, and the old streets looked inviting, almost empty and still slightly wintry despite the weather. They drove slowly, looking at buildings and yards and the walls that surrounded them, at iron shutters that let yellowish light drip out, and Shira said she envied him for having grown up in this neighborhood, in this city. He shook his head sadly, but also proudly, and said, "Don't be jealous. You, at least, still live in the town where you grew up."

"You can come back here."

"Sure I can. Did you know that this neighborhood has become an Orthodox stronghold? It's almost entirely Orthodox Americans. My dad hated them. He hated them more than he hated the Me'a She'arim Orthodox."

"And you?"

"Me? I hate them all equally." He slowed down and stopped outside a two-story stone building.

"Beautiful," Shira said.

"Not only beautiful but historic too."

"Oh, yeah?"

"Yeah. Here, in my friend Moshe Rubin's house, we used to have parties."

"Here?"

"Here." He leaned over to the window on her side and pointed to the tiled roof. "He had an attic room. You wouldn't believe what went on in that attic."

He remembered walking down the street to the parties and back home, his clothes smelling chilly. He remembered those Friday nights as an era unto itself, as if all those Fridays had been gathered into one great mysterious proclamation about his youth. He remembered how proud he felt, arrogant and self-assured, when he left home after dinner on his way to Moshe Rubin's house—Moshe was a cardiologist now—and saw the usual crowd coming out of Friday-night prayers at the little Sephardic synagogue on Emek Refa'im Street. He would think to himself, They go out to pray and I go out to get laid. Although he was a virgin until he went into the army, he felt as if on those Fridays, as he walked determinedly from his parents' house to his friend's house, as he climbed the steep spiral staircase up to one long erection, he was fighting that handful of religious people, whom he now missed because there were so few of them, a rare landscape in his neighborhood and yet a part of it. He even missed their little synagogue, where today there was a pizzeria; on Passover, they sold pizza made with matzo meal.

"Did you go to parties too?" he asked, when they drove away from the building and headed toward the Cinemateque.

"We had lots, but I never went. It was beneath me. Anyway, I had a boyfriend when I was a junior, so I didn't need those parties to hook up. I did plenty of fooling around as it was."

"Yes. But on the other hand there's nothing quite like those hookups. It's the kind of sex you can never experience again. Not that I want to—I mean, it wasn't that amazing—but there's something about the way we hooked up back then—think about slow-dancing in total darkness— that was a kind of delightful prologue to everything we found out later. I often try to describe those hookups in my writing, and I can't do it."

"You just did."

"Maybe it's not the city I miss but the hooking up," he said, and they drove on in silence until they came to King David Street. He pointed out the YMCA building and told her he believed this was where he decided to be a writer, after falling in love with the organ music. "I sound so old, don't I?"

"No. In fact you sound very young."

He asked if she wanted to get a drink or if she'd rather go back to Tel Aviv. When she said she'd rather go back he was disappointed because he suddenly realized that he was hitting on her: This whole trip, and especially the tour of Old Katamon and the German Colony, was a seduction trip and she was rejecting him. They drove in silence all the way out of Jerusalem, just listening to the radio, and when they started talking again it no longer had the magic of their previous exchange, when they were driving around the streets of his childhood. They talked about parking problems, about the nightclubs that kept opening up all around them, about the constant noise; it seemed that the change of scenery, now flat and monotonous, had brought with it a change in topic.

He wondered if she was playing him. How could it be that for a whole afternoon her arm had rubbed against his with such ease, her hand had lain in his, on his thigh; then she wanted to see where he had grown up; and now—she wanted to go home. He hated that kind of woman, although he used to be that kind of man. And again he saw the picture of Esti, except this time she was not curled up on the floor but sitting across from him, staring over his shoulder at the calendar. He had hurt her, but at least he hadn't played her. And it wasn't too late to call her, he thought, it had only been four days; he could even call her that evening. But he didn't want her; he didn't even *want* to want her, so it was odd to him that he couldn't get her out of his mind. Maybe, he thought, he was preoccupied with her because she was the first woman he had hurt in the past decade.

Shira thought the drive from Jerusalem to Tel Aviv was always either too long or too short, even though it almost always lasted fifty minutes. The last time she had been there, six months ago, when she drove her father to a neurologist at Hadassah, looking askance at her father as he watched the scenery as if he were abroad, she felt as if she was so far from home it would take her days to get back. Now, as they passed the airport, she was sorry she hadn't taken Yonatan up on his offer to go sit somewhere and have a drink, because then they could still have been in

Jerusalem—under the influence of a few beers that would have taken them somewhere else—not the place they were at now, fifteen minutes away from their separate addresses, so quiet and sober. This friendship was confusing. Perhaps, she thought, she had refused his offer because she had never yet turned him down, because without his realizing it, she had already accepted him in a thousand different ways. Today, when he took her hand and put it on his thigh, she felt he was doing it out of alarm, to restrain her, to reject her again.

When they got off at the La Guardia exit, Yonatan sighed.

"What's the matter?" she asked.

"I'm hungry. My mother would slit her wrists if she heard me, but I'm starved."

She almost said she was full, but she asked what he felt like.

"Eating?" he asked, and she nodded. "I don't know. Everything."

She felt like asking if he wanted to stop somewhere and get some falafel or pizza, but she asked if he wanted to come over for spaghetti.

"Spaghetti?" he asked the windshield, in a tone that sounded disappointed. "I would kill for spaghetti."

"But just plain spaghetti," she said and tried to think what ingredients she had at home.

"I'm dying for just plain spaghetti. That's the spaghetti of my fantasies: just plain spaghetti."

At home she had three messages from her father. Yonatan sat on the couch and leafed through the paper while she stood with her back to him and listened to them, knowing he was listening too, wishing she had ignored the flashing light on the answering machine. In the first message, he said, "Hello, it's Dad," and then coughed deeply and moistly into the phone. She turned to look at Yonatan, and he looked up from the paper and smiled at her. "My father," she said, and he said, "I figured." When the coughing subsided, she thought she heard him drinking something, perhaps his morning coffee. Then he said "Shabbat Shalom" in a thick voice and hung up.

It didn't occur to her that the second message would also be from him. "Shira?" his voice asked, echoing as if the answering machine was a large empty room. "Shira?" Her embarrassment turned to alarm. Without turning around she knew Yonatan was listening, as tense as she was. "It's your dad again," he said softly. "I told him I was going out of town," she said. "He must have forgotten." Yonatan murmured yes.

Then his voice came again, clear and demanding this time: "Shabbat Shalom, Shira, it's Dad," and in the background you could hear the hourly news bleeps from his transistor radio, then the sound of the phone being put down, and she thought that everything she had told Yonatan about her father paled against his recorded voice. Then there were three beeps announcing the end of the messages.

When she turned around he was standing close to her, still holding the paper. He looked worried, he looked fatherly, he looked as if he wanted to kiss her.

"I have to call him," she apologized. "It won't take long."

"Of course. No problem."

"I'll take the phone into the other room," she said, and he nodded and touched her cheek with his knuckles and sat down on the couch again. When she took the cordless phone into the bedroom and dialed her father's number, which was the first number in the speed dial, she thought about all this touching between them; no one had ever given her so many small touches in one day. And when her father picked up and they started their dazed conversation, she suddenly got up off the bed and took the phone back to the living room, because she wanted him to hear her, to see her like this, so he could keep caressing her cheek with his eyes and ears.

She leaned against the bookshelf, propped the phone on her shoulder, and signaled to him that she wanted a cigarette. He got up, took the pack out of his pocket, gave her a cigarette, and lit it. He stood next to her and examined her books.

He felt sorry for her and he wanted her. He wondered if he would ever experience with his mother this terrible thing she was now experiencing with her father, and when he did, who would be there with him. He went over to the coffee table and brought her an ashtray, and she took it and nodded thankfully. He went into the kitchen and opened the fridge and took out two bottles of beer and found the bottle opener on the counter, and he went back to the living room and held up a bottle inquiringly. She nodded again, and he opened it and gave it to her. She took a sip and put the bottle down on one of the shelves and put her little finger in her mouth and started biting her nail and, without knowing where he found the courage, he gently pulled her finger out of her mouth. She smiled shyly, and he thought he had never felt so close to anyone, not even to himself, and if she had not looked so naked right now, he would have undressed her.

She put the phone down and sighed, and he took it from her and put it in its cradle and went back to stand opposite her. She kept on standing by the bookshelf, looking exhausted.

"Spaghetti?" she asked quietly, and he took her in his arms.

They stood embraced, leaning on the bookshelf, and from his shoulder he heard her sniffle and felt the damp warmth of her tears seep into his sweatshirt. He gently tried to pull her face away from his shoulder to see her eyes, but she clung to him, her nose burrowing into his shoulder, and he put his hand on her head and whispered something meaningless and stupid and deep into her hair, and suddenly he felt that all the hugging he had ever done was training for this embrace and he wanted to cry too.

The phone rang and they both tensed up. The machine answered and after the beep came the very friendly voice of a man who said, "Good evening, this is Gideon the electrician," and announced that he couldn't come the next day.

"Wrong number," Shira mumbled into his shoulder, and he whispered to her, "Some poor guy will sit in the dark tomorrow." She looked up at him and said she was sorry, and he asked what for and she said she didn't know, and he said he didn't either, and then he kissed her.

It amazed her how quickly she went from sadness to passion. When she bit his lip and ran her tongue from his mouth to his cheek and to his chin and into his mouth again, as if she were afraid of losing a treasure she had found, she realized that she had not gone from sadness to passion but was still in the familiar territory where the two are joined together, and that she had wasted too much of her life trying to separate them as if they were enemies.

He put his hand on her back and walked her to the bedroom, where a lamp with a square lampshade was lit on the bureau, projecting an orange light. She sat on the edge of the bed, and he knelt at her side and pulled her boots off her feet and set them at the foot of the bureau. Then he took her sweater off, and as she lifted her arms up to help him a strip of white stomach was revealed to him, bordered between her bra and the waistband of her skirt, which made it stick out a little. He put his lips to her navel and kissed it. Then he looked up at her and she smiled shyly and closed her eyes. He reached behind her to unhook her bra, surprised to discover how slow his movements were.

She wanted to lie on her back or on her belly, or stand up, not sit at the edge of the bed like a little Buddha, with her breasts resting on her stomach, which had been made into a ball by the tight skirt. But on the other hand there was suddenly something wonderful and reassuring about that stomach, about this truth, as if the stomach was a natural extension of her crying; she had not sensed the sobs approaching or leaving, but she now felt their effect in her body like a drug and she was no longer embarrassed. It was not the lack of embarrassment she used to feel with Eitan but something else, a sexy weakness that was like the flu, and much as she had wanted Yonatan to hear her conversation with her dad earlier, she now wanted him to see her sitting like this, on the edge of the bed, with her stomach drooping like a heavy load.

He stood her up on her feet and opened the zipper of her skirt and pulled it down along with her stockings and underwear; then he sat her down again and looked at her. He felt overdressed, but he didn't want to take his clothes off yet. He stroked her thighs and was dizzied by the warmth transferred from the nervous skin to his fingers. He hadn't thought she would be so passive, but instead of disappointment he found himself turned on, turned on from the tenderness and compassion until he thought he might come, and even though he did not want to come that way, alone, fully dressed, he wondered what kind of orgasm came from such compassion.

She kissed him, leaning forward, her stomach folding over his hand, his mouth and lips loose, almost helpless, and with her hand she held the back of his neck, half leaning on him, half holding him in place. It went on for a long time, that kiss, her mouth busy and investigating, his mouth quiet and waiting, until she got up off the bed and he straightened up too, and for a moment she held herself against him in an embrace that was both tempting and desperate. Then she turned him so his back was to the bed and sat him down on the edge, where she had sat. He leaned over to untie the laces of his green Chuck Taylors, and she pulled them off his feet, holding his feet on her stomach and tossing the shoes behind her. Then she took his socks off and looked at his bare feet; they looked pale against her skin, which he now saw was slightly darker than his.

She took off his sweatshirt and he sucked his stomach in as if he had been punched. She knelt between his legs, leaned her head on his chest, and caressed his back. Between his shoulders her fingers found a rough mole. He flinched, trying to twist his shoulders so her hand would slide down, but she held her hand against the mole as if she were trying to calm it, not him. Then she stood him up, opened the buttons of his jeans, and pulled them down. She looked at his underpants, which were exactly as his daughter had described them at the café, faded cotton briefs of a nondescript color that might once have been blue or, possibly, green.

It was strange for him to be suddenly, as if by chance, exactly in the place he had so wanted to be. But fantasies never bother with the little details, the clumsy ridiculous minutiae of sex, always leaving the unwanted parts on the editing-room floor. He felt exposed when she pulled his underwear off, as if along with them a layer of his skin was also peeled away, revealing the true him—chicken, as Dana had called him that time: a mongoose with a huge erection.

She sat next to him on the bed. They were both naked now, examining each other sideways. It was an unfamiliar angle, exciting in its clumsiness. He pressed his lips against her shoulder. He wanted to ask himself why he loved her, and whether the last few years had been preparing him, unaware, for this love, but when she lay on her side with her head resting on one arm and the other arm on her hip, he knew he needed no answers. He lay on his side opposite her.

She had never seen anyone look at her this way, and again she felt as if she wanted to cry, but this time she was afraid to lose what she had not yet gained. Tears started streaming from her eyes. He touched her cheek and pressed up against her with his body, she put one of her legs on his thigh, and they kissed quietly—a long slow haul at the end of a race.

"We've had a rough day," he whispered in her ear, and entered her.

"Yes," she said, flooded with happiness. "We've had a rough day."

PART FOUR

(1)

The anxiety attack he expected the next day, like a vexing relative scheduled to arrive on a punctual train, never came.

When they got out of bed that night, dressed, and went into the kitchen to make spaghetti, he tried to imagine how the morning would be but could not, because he had long ago forgotten how mornings were with a woman who, although his body smelled of her now and although they had cooked together and were about to eat together and go to sleep together, was still a stranger—perhaps even more of a stranger than she was before he slept with her.

So when does a woman stop being a stranger? he wondered, as he sat at the table, chopping onions on a wooden board she set before him with a kiss on his cheek. She stood by the counter with her back to him, scratching one foot with the other while she opened a can of crushed tomatoes. She looked like a little girl, with her hair disheveled and crumpled, wearing a T-shirt with a picture of Wile E. Coyote and Roadrunner. It was still her favorite cartoon, she told him, and she wished they showed it more often on TV. He briefly had trouble reconciling her with the woman on whose stomach he had come only fifteen minutes ago, letting out a long strange yell he could barely believe.

He never yelled in bed, but he wasn't in the mood to contemplate the meaning of his shouting, if it even had one. He felt quiet, as if the cry had drained him of all the words and syllables and other sounds trapped in him for years, leaving him happily mute. Shira was also quiet. They exchanged a few words about the sauce: "Garlic?" she asked, dangling a bulb in front of his eyes, and he said, Lots. When she handed him the onion and chopping board and knife, he asked if she wanted a dice or a coarse chop, and she said, "It doesn't matter." When he insisted, she said, "Something in between." After she opened the can, she peered into the fridge and turned to him with a sour face. When he asked what was wrong, she said, "There's no basil. Not even parsley." He waved his hand dismissively, and that was it. They said nothing more. Not even when they sat facing each other, eating spaghetti with spicy sauce; he had poured in some Tabasco at the last minute.

He was glad when they left the dirty dishes in the sink and went back to bed, taking an ashtray, cigarettes, and two bottles of beer, as if they were about to have a long conversation. But they kept quiet. They lay across from each other and touched each other sleepily but with curiosity. Her eyes closed and her mouth fell open and he smelled the Tabasco on her breath and gently placed his fingers on her lip as if measuring a pulse; he felt his own eyes close and a wonderful weariness descend on him. He listened to the alarm clock ticking on the bureau and remembered that when he was young, and found himself spending the night in a strange woman's bed, he would lie awake for a long time, sometimes all night. The slightest sound took on great meaning back then—a dripping faucet in the kitchen, a car honking, a TV echoing from a neighbor's apartment, the call of a crow or a breath or a clock ticking—as if all these were parts of the body and schedule of the woman asleep next to him. These were things that did not belong to him, and never would, and made him miss his bachelor home and his bachelor bed and feel so lonely and hostile that in every drip or honk, every TV laugh or crow squawk, and every breath or tick he heard the words *Go home.* But Shira's clock ticking, although very loud, reassured him now, as if it were his own alarm clock beneath the orange light of the lamp, which he now switched off, reaching carefully over Shira's head. I'm either falling in love or getting old, he thought, and decided to let the morning decide.

(2)

When she woke up, she heard him washing the dishes. She listened to the water running, the dishes chinking, sounds of a pan being scrubbed, spoons and forks dropping in the sink, and closed her eyes again. There was something calming about those sounds, the noises made by someone who has risen first and is keeping himself amused, trying not to disturb the other person but hoping she'll wake up. When she heard the faucet squeak shut, she yawned loudly. She smiled at him when he appeared in the doorway, wearing a sweatshirt and underwear, drying his hands with the dish towel. He asked if he'd woken her and she said no. She asked how long he'd been awake. "About two hours," he said, and sat on the edge of the bed and stroked her cheek with the back of his hand, which was cold from the water and smelled of detergent. He does that a lot, she thought, the cheek stroke. She couldn't think of any other men who did that and wondered if it had anything to do with his being a father, accustomed to pinching cheeks or wiping tears away, and she thought, I've never before slept with anyone's father. She took his hand and kissed it. She thought her own touch had softened too, turned from fearful to devoted. With him, she was learning unfamiliar movements, or ones that had long been dormant, too timid to come out. She liked herself this way, passive in movement, passive in thought, someone who wakes up second rather than first.

She glanced at the clock and was alarmed to see that it was only eight; if he had gotten up so early he may not have slept well—perhaps he never fell asleep at all and was just waiting for her to wake up so he could leave. She thought about the ten years that separated them. She hadn't thought of their age difference all week, and in bed she had forgotten about it, but now she wondered if the fact that he was older had any significance—a reassuring significance, like the sound of dishwashing, which only a moment ago had made her feel safe.

He asked if she wanted coffee and she said yes, in a sleepy, indulgent voice, although she was no longer sleepy or indulgent but rather alert and extremely nervous. "With the pot?" he asked. She said it was complicated, and he said it wasn't and that he already knew where everything was. "But did you buy any coffee?" he asked, and she wasn't sure what he meant. "You ran out last week," he said.

"I bought some, it's in the freezer," she replied, and tried to gain confidence from the knowledge that he remembered such things, knew his way around her inventory, had studied it as he had studied her body.

When he got off the bed, she asked him to open the blinds and the balcony door to let in some air. She lay on her side and watched him struggle with the door's stubborn handle. It reminded her of how he had tried to force the window open at his mother's the previous day. She missed that day, and thought about clothes and how they made different puzzles of the same person. Last night, when they ate and he wore only his jeans with no top, he had looked like a boy. Now, without his jeans, wearing only a sweatshirt that reached down to his thin hips and a pair of underwear, which in the light of day she saw was pale blue, he looked almost old.

"I want to call my mother," he said from the kitchen, "to find out if Dana's already on her way. What time is it?"

"Eight. Exactly eight."

He said it was still early, they were probably only just getting up. He knew his daughter, she liked to sleep late. "Did you know you have to pierce a hole in the coffee container before you open it, otherwise it spurts out all over the place?"

"Yes. I learned the hard way."

"It gives new meaning to the term *caffeine explosion.*" He stood in the doorway again, holding a spoon in his hand, and she laughed and thought there was nothing to be afraid of. He was in a good mood, and her interpretations—of yesterday, of his clothes, of his shout when he came, which had scared but also flattered her—were redundant and exhausting and could very well blow up in her face just like the vacuum-packed coffee.

He went back into the kitchen, and she wondered if she'd be able to hear the coffee percolating from bed, and what kind of sound it would have this morning. She needed to pee but didn't want to move, wary of spoiling this photograph of their morning-after scene, still damp from developing chemicals: he making coffee in the kitchen, she lying in bed, half relaxed, half paralyzed with terror.

"Should I heat the milk for you?" he asked from the kitchen.

"No need. I like it cold." She got up and went to the bathroom after all, smiling at him when he watched her pass by in the hallway.

"Should I bring your coffee to you in bed?" he asked, and from the bathroom she shouted no; she would come to the kitchen.

She brushed her teeth and looked at herself in the mirror and thought of all the mornings she had brushed her teeth and looked at herself in the mirror, when on the other side of the wall was a man for whom she had ambivalent feelings and whom she might not even like but was still afraid might leave. But she did like this man. She had had all week to take comfort in various definitions of him, and to treat her disappointment as regret over something that shouldn't have happened anyway, and perhaps it was better that it hadn't. As long as the physical aspect was absent she had had room to maneuver, but now she felt trapped, as if this new three-dimensional form of their relationship had erected fences around it.

They drank their coffee in the kitchen. She looked outside through the balcony door, and the sun shone a white triangle on Yonatan's cheek. He said he was warm, took off his sweatshirt, and put it over the back of his chair. She considered saying something about the weather but feared that trivial conversation would disclose a failure, as if they no longer had anything to say to each other.

"Looks like there's going to be a heat wave today," he said as he looked out.

"The nerve. Considering it's only March."

"So another week begins," he said, and stared over her shoulder.

"Yes," she answered and was suddenly hit by a sense of loss. "Another week."

"So what are you going to do today? Write?"

"Maybe." She knew she wouldn't write a word, because she would spend the day mourning him. "And you?"

"I hope I'll be able to do a little writing. Although even saying that is a lie. I mean, I don't write at all."

"No?"

"No." He shook his head and lit a cigarette. "I stare. I stare into space and feel sorry for myself. That's what I do best. I excel at it."

"But everyone has those phases, don't they? I'm going through one too."

"Does five years sound like a phase?"

"Five years?"

"More or less."

"But you started a new book."

"I started one, so what? How many first pages are on your computer?"

She smiled. "But you said you had about fifty pages. That's respectable."

"That's the opposite of respectable."

They smoked quietly, and she conquered the urge to go up to him and kiss his chest, as she had done at night, because she was afraid it would seem like a cheap effort to comfort him over his writer's block or prevent him from leaving.

"It must be nine by now." He got up abruptly. "I have to go. Dana's supposed to call from the bus station for me to come and get her." He put his cup in the sink, went over to her, and stroked her cheek again, but this time she thought his touch was condescending and she told herself that the whole thing was hopeless anyway. There was something about Yonatan that was as evasive and misleading as his yell, something that pierced her heart and then disappeared.

He went into the bedroom and came back with his shoes and jeans. She was sad to see him get dressed in front of her, every item of clothing increasing his strength. He tied his shoelaces, stood up, made sure his wallet was in his back pocket, and motioned with his head that he was leaving. She walked him to the door and felt suddenly very naked, despite her T-shirt and underwear. She thought her legs had grown shorter and thicker, and that even her toes, which she now looked down at so as not to meet his eyes, had swollen and were slightly distorted. He turned the key in the lock, opened the door a crack, and touched her cheek again, a touch she suddenly thought was neither soft nor condescending but final.

"Want to come over to see us this evening?" he asked.

She said nothing. She stood quietly staring at her toes and ankles and knees and thighs, which had now gone back to looking normal, rehabilitated, as if her panic were a growth that had turned out to be benign. She stretched, arching her back and pushing her chest out, and Yonatan leaned down and kissed her nipples through her shirt. Then she reached her arms out to the sides, truly sleepy and indulgent this time, and said, "Yes, I'll come over."

3

It seemed odd, she thought, as she climbed up the stairs, but she missed the girl. After they said goodbye that morning, she suspected that missing her was a mask for missing him, but when Dana opened the door with her hair still wet, wearing brand-new blue sweats, she could hardly hold back from hugging her.

"Dad's in the shower," Dana announced, and Shira was struck by a sense of déjà vu. She had been here only two days earlier, but it was a different home.

"Did you have a good time at your grandmother's?" she asked and went into the living room with Dana, where they sat down together on the couch.

"It was okay." Dana bounced the remote control in her hand, and Shira thought she had grown up a little since yesterday.

The TV flickered with the sound turned down, and there was piano and orchestra music playing. "That's nice," Shira said. "What is it, Tchaikovsky?"

"I'll tell you in a minute." Dana went over to look at the CD cover. "Rachmaninoff. But you were close. They're both Russian."

"Do you play?" Shira pointed to the piano.

"I quit. You?"

"No, but I wanted to learn."

"Then why didn't you?"

"At first, because we didn't have a piano. And later, when I was twelve and my parents said they'd buy me one for my bat mitzvah, I didn't feel like it anymore."

"I can understand that," Dana said, examining Shira with a look aimed at locating further points of similarity. "Did you have lots of friends at school?"

"No. How about you?"

Dana shook her head.

"But you have Tamar. She seems like the best friend you could ever have."

"Yes. She likes you too."

They sat and watched the news on Channel 2, which seemed surreal against the Rachmaninoff backdrop.

"Do you always watch the news with classical music in the background?" Shira asked and took her cigarettes out.

"No. Dad put this CD on before he took a shower. He said you'd be here soon. Did you eat yet?"

"No. Why?"

"We haven't either. We waited for you. We didn't know if you'd eaten."

"I'm not very hungry," she said, but when she saw the disappointed look on Dana's face she said she'd be happy to join them, because she could always eat.

"Me too. Unfortunately."

"Why unfortunately?" She had another urge to touch the girl.

"Because it makes me fat."

"And what's wrong with that?"

"I don't know." She flipped through the channels until she got to MTV. "Most of the girls in my class are skinny. They're always dieting."

"Tamar too?"

"No, Tamar's actually a big eater. But she's lucky, she's always been thin. She has good genes. Do you like MTV? I hate it."

"Me too."

Dana flipped over to the Science Channel. "I like nature programs."

"Me too," said Shira.

"My dad does too. Do you want something to drink? Want a beer? We bought some beer. Do you prefer Tuborg or Goldstar? My dad got both kinds because he didn't know which one you liked."

"I like them both. But I'll wait until we eat." Then she complimented Dana on her sweats.

"They're new. We bought them today. We went shopping for clothes for me, and Dad ended up getting stuff too."

"Really?" Shira lit a cigarette. "What did he get?"

"T-shirts. He bought about ten. We found a place where they sell Gap seconds. And jeans, dark green ones."

"And what did you get?"

"This," she said, pulling the sleeve.

"That's all?"

"They had jeans too, but I couldn't be bothered to try them on." She went back to watching the news. "I hate trying things on."

"Me too."

"Really?"

"They always have this sickly, unflattering light in the changing rooms, and it's crowded and sweaty, and I always look ugly and it depresses me for days."

"Me too. Do you like tomato soup?"

"Yes, I love it. Why?"

"That's what Dad made for dinner. I love it."

"Excellent."

"And I think he also bought some kind of fancy bread."

"Fancy?"

"At the bread store. Something with rosemary. Do you like rosemary?"

"I like everything."

"Me too." Dana smiled at the screen. "Are your parents alive?"

Shira said her father was.

"When did your mother die?" Dana asked.

"Almost fifteen years ago."

"How old were you?"

"Twenty-two. I was a student."

"Oh," the girl said.

"Not the same as in your case," Shira said.

"No. Not the same as in my case." She seemed to like being considered a case, as if the loss of her mother were a medical condition, something that, with proper treatment, might be cured.

Yonatan appeared in the room. "Hi," he said, and leaned over to Shira and kissed her lightly on the lips, picking up Dana's look out of the corner of his eye. He kissed her too, and she squirmed on the couch and said he smelled like toothpaste. He was wearing his new green jeans and T-shirt.

When he got home that morning and was waiting for Dana to call, he had decided not to hide his relationship with Shira from her. He knew that would also make it more difficult to conceal it from himself. He was afraid of his escape patterns, which only Ilana had managed to break, precisely because she had never tried—patterns that this morning, as they drank coffee in the kitchen, he had sensed rousing inside him, prickling. When he picked Dana up from the Central Bus Station, he informed her dryly that Shira would be coming over that evening and that she might stay over. He expected, even slightly hoped for, a flurry of questions that would help him clarify matters for the two of them. But Dana didn't ask anything, as if she knew that when she got back from her grandmother's she would not be coming back to the same home, as if she had traveled much farther than thirty miles on her first intercity trip alone—a trip that had not started that morning but long ago.

They sat in the kitchen and ate their soup. Shira wondered what they'd do afterward, whether they'd sit and watch TV together, impersonating a family. She wasn't sure if she was supposed to go home or stay over and cuddle quietly with him in bed so the girl on the other side of the wall wouldn't sense her presence.

That morning, after he left, she found the stain of semen that had congealed on her stomach, and touched it with her fingertips, afraid to crumble it. All day she kept feeling it under her shirt, pinching her skin in a comforting way, until she took a shower in the evening. Now she spread butter on the bread, which had taken on a special status because it was from the store where they had met, and asked herself if they might already be a couple to him, and if things were perhaps far simpler than she thought.

Yonatan asked what she did today, and she told them she had visited her father. But she did not say how scared she had been when she rang the doorbell over and over again and no one answered, although she had sensed his presence beyond the door and had eventually used her key to enter the apartment. It was afternoon and the sun was strong, but the apartment was dark and nocturnal because all the blinds were drawn. She expected to find him lying on the floor somewhere, passed out or dead, and she kept standing in the hallway, calling out, "Dad," at first in a whisper and then loudly, until she heard sheets rustling in the bedroom and hurried in there and turned on the light, and saw him lying on his side with his cheek crushed against the pillow, eyes half open, squinting at the sudden light. On the rug at the foot of the bed was a large plastic bowl, which used to be a salad bowl, and when she got closer she saw it contained a murky fluid of an indistinct color. She asked what had happened, and her father mumbled that he had food poisoning and had been vomiting and having diarrhea all night. She asked what he'd had for dinner and he said nothing, maybe just a piece of quiche. "Which quiche?" she wanted to know, as if it had some significance. "From the deli?" Cauliflower, he said and closed his eyes. She leaned over him and touched his forehead, which was cool and damp, and she picked the bowl up and emptied it into the toilet and flushed the toilet and washed the bowl in the sink and didn't know where to put it, because it could never go back in the kitchen, so she put it back on the rug in his room, in case he needed it again. She asked when he had started feeling ill, and he said he couldn't remember, in the middle of the night. His speech was slow and hoarse, more exhalation than speech, and she said they had to open the blinds and windows to air the room out a little, was that all right? He didn't answer.

She darted around the apartment, opening blinds and windows, and then went into the kitchen and washed the dishes. When she finished she looked for the dish towel and couldn't find it, and remembered she'd seen it on the bathroom floor; her father must have taken it in there at some point during the night. She wiped her hands on her pants and thought about the life he lived here when she was gone: What happened to him? What did he do? What were his nights like? It occurred to her that the dish towel that followed him around from room to room knew more about him than she did.

She went out onto the living room balcony, lit a cigarette, and wondered what to do. Last time she had phoned their family doctor, Dr. Rimon, three months ago, when her father had flu that lasted for weeks, she had detected impatience in his voice, even hostility. What did she want him to do? he had asked. Her father was an old man and couldn't manage on his own anymore. He needed a suitable framework. When she had put the phone down and looked at her father, who was lying in his bed in the same pajamas he wore now, with the coil heater lit at his feet, reminding her of elderly people who burned to death in their sleep because of those heaters, she had rolled the words *suitable framework* through her mind and pictured him sitting inside a wooden square, as if the old man lying on his side were a hyperrealistic picture, not her father.

She stood on the balcony and stared at the street and put her cigarette out in a planter that used to house a miniature orange tree, which Emmanuel Herman had brought as a gift on one of the holidays. She tried to reconstruct her sex with Yonatan. All day she had avoided it, satisfied with the fleeting touch of her fingers on her stomach, because she was afraid of the replay, of the emotions it would awaken. There was something heart-wrenching, something injured about the sex, she thought, and wondered briefly if she had enjoyed it. She knew she hadn't. Even when she came, giving in to his fingers but shutting her eyes as his look followed her facial expressions, intense and worried, she knew they were not making love or fucking but contending with a state of emergency, administering first aid to themselves and to each other, like two medics who find themselves on the same battlefield, hit by the same shrapnel.

She heard her father sigh. When she went into his room she found him sitting on the edge of the bed, feeling around for his slippers with his feet. "Where are you going?" she asked, and he gestured with his chin toward the bathroom. He got up slowly, stood on his feet, and left the room, holding his hands out to the wall to guide him. She followed him, ready to catch him if he fell, until they reached the toilet, and in each of those steps, his and hers, she felt as if she were accompanying him to a place where he was someone else, someone she didn't know and had never met, who would never again be her father.

Dana asked what her father's name was. "Max," she said, and felt a lump in her throat.

"That's a nice name," Dana said.

"You think so?" Shira asked, and sopped up the rest of her soup with some bread.

"Yes. I really like that name. If I ever have a son, I might name him Max."

4

They sat in old wicker armchairs on the balcony. Through the open kitchen window, they heard water run down the sink as Dana washed the dishes, humming a Doors song to herself. There was a sudden sound of glass shattering. "What happened?" Yonatan shouted, and Dana said a glass broke.

"Are you okay?" Shira asked.

Yonatan thought, So this is how a relationship begins: with soup, idle talk on the balcony, a girl dropping a glass, and two adults. It was as if last night was a fiery prologue to all this serenity.

"She inherited my clumsiness," he said.

"You're that way too?"

"Are you?"

"I break things all the time." She raised one leg and put her foot on the railing, exposing a small scar beneath her knee. "That's from the first glass I ever broke, at the age of four, I think. When I bent down to pick up the pieces, my mother yelled for me to be careful, so I slipped and fell on the glass."

He looked at the scar and smiled and wondered how he hadn't noticed it last night. He wanted to say he was falling in love with her, but instead he asked what the last thing she broke was.

"A jar of sun-dried tomatoes at the supermarket, on Friday. Imported ones! It was really embarrassing."

"Were they angry?"

"No. Not at all, actually. They didn't even want me to pay for it. But I felt bad for whoever had to mop up all the oil from the floor afterward."

He had several big things to say to her. That she was the first woman who had sat on this balcony with him since Ilana died. That he thought his daughter was already very attached to her. That at night, when he came, he felt as if he were emptying out and filling up at the same time, which was why, perhaps, he had walked around all day with an almost physical feeling that he hadn't actually come. He wondered how he would tell her these big things without scaring her, and how he would keep saying the little things he had said all evening without boring her, and whether, when they went to sleep—and he suddenly had the alarming thought that she might not stay—his body would know how to calm itself.

Dana came out and said she was going to bed.

"So early?" he asked.

"What do you mean, early? It's eleven."

"So you're leaving us?" Shira asked.

"Yes. Leaving you in the lurch."

"In the lurch? Who taught you these phrases?"

"You did. Good night."

"Give me a kiss then," he said, and when Dana told him to stop putting on an act for the guest, he said, "Come on, don't be that way. Give your old man a good-night kiss."

Dana conceded and put her lips to his cheek. "At least you shaved." She looked at Shira. "It was for your benefit; you should appreciate it. Are you staying?"

"I don't know." Shira tried to fake disinterest.

"You're invited," said Yonatan.

"Just be careful, he snores," Dana said.

"That's enough out of you, snitch. Go to bed."

Dana retreated with backward steps into the living room, waving goodbye and blowing kisses.

"So, are you staying?" he asked, after a few moments of silence, and she said she would. "I hope you'll be comfortable. The bed sags a bit in the middle."

"I sag a bit in the middle too," she said, yawning.

"Are you tired?"

She nodded and put her hand on his, and he squeezed it and asked what side of the bed she liked, because he personally didn't care.

She said, "Your side," and they got up and took their empty cups and the ashtray into the kitchen, and in the kitchen they stood and kissed, and he lifted her shirt and kissed her belly button. "I missed this," he said, and for the first time since they met she did not feel passion and sadness but simply happiness; and as they walked down the hallway to the bedroom together and he turned off lights as they went, he suddenly realized that the tension that had spread through his limbs after sleeping with her, and had stayed with him all day, was merely the result of an internal misunderstanding: his body thought the sex was the decisive final cord of almost half a decade, but his heart knew that what had happened between them was the first quiet sound of the decade just beginning.

(5)

Tamar wanted to know if they walked around the apartment naked, if Shira cooked for them, and if Dana thought they were doing it. She said her mother said that the second she saw them together she knew they'd be a couple, a blind man could see it, and she was happy for both of them that something good was finally happening because they both deserved it. They were sitting at the round table, eating leftover onion quiche heated up in the microwave. Tamar said it had too much onion and picked at her plate and said sometimes she wished her mother had a boyfriend and sometimes she was glad she didn't, because who needs a stranger walking around the apartment naked, with his thing out.

"That's not the way it is," Dana said. "My dad doesn't walk around naked with me."

"Of course not, because he's your dad. But if he wasn't your dad it would be a different story."

Dana said she didn't know about that.

After a few thoughtful moments, during which she might have still been roaming her and her mother's apartment with the naked intruder, Tamar asked again, "So what do you think? Are they doing it?"

Dana said they were.

"You mean you heard them?"

"No way! They do it quietly."

"You mean no moaning and shouting, 'Yes, yes; more, more; rip me open'?" Tamar asked and took a tub of ice cream out of the freezer.

"No," Dana said, and blushed, because she didn't know what Tamar meant but she was embarrassed for Shira.

"Then how do you know they're doing it? Maybe she's just sleeping over."

"Are you a moron? She has her own place, doesn't she?"

"Well, maybe you're right," Tamar said grudgingly. "But don't be so sure. There is such a thing as a platonic relationship. Have you heard of that?"

Dana hadn't, but she didn't want to give Tamar the satisfaction of explaining it to her, and anyway she knew her father's relationship with Shira was not platonic. Shira didn't sleep over every night. She had counted only sixteen nights out of the twenty-one since the first night, and there were times when she wondered what Shira did when she wasn't with them, and whether her dad was sad on those nights or if, like herself, he was a little glad to be back in their old routine, even though it was a routine she didn't like.

She had expected that immediately following Shira's first night at their place, her father would go with her and pack her things up and bring her over. She thought there would be immediate changes at home—that instead of the drapes made of Indian fabric that her mother had sewn for the living room, which were faded and fraying at the edges and looked like an old theater set, there would be new ones, like the ones Rona bought on Herzl Street, made with off-white jute and hung on wooden rods—and she expected they would have a talk with her. But none of those things happened. Shira didn't even bring a change of clothes, just a toothbrush, which she took back every morning, wrapped in a plastic bag from the big roll they kept in the kitchen. She put it back again every night—not in the glass by the other two toothbrushes but on the sink, face up.

They were careful when Dana was around, permitting themselves only small touches and pretending they were accidental, especially in the kitchen, where she sometimes caught them giggling and tickling each other and kissing when they thought she wasn't there. And facing the TV—where the programs she was used to watching now seemed different, and she found it hard to concentrate on them—her father's arm would hang over Shira's shoulder, or Shira's hand would encircle his thigh when she leaned over him for something, cigarettes or a bottle of beer or the TV guide. On Friday afternoons they took the *Ha'aretz* supplement into the bedroom and did the crossword together, and it was during those moments, which involved no touching or tickling or kissing, just the folded newspaper and a pen and a closed door, that Dana felt betrayed.

"Would you like them to get married?" Tamar asked, and heaped another portion of chocolate-chip ice cream in their bowls.

"I don't know. Maybe."

"Would you like to have brothers or sisters?"

The idea of a baby squeezing into their three-and-a-half-room apartment seemed so implausible that she didn't know what to say. "Would you?" she asked Tamar, who seemed to want to be asked, judging by her taut expression.

"So badly. But my mom's too old to have a baby. She says she wishes she'd had another one when she still could have. Did you know we're thinking about adopting?"

"Adopting?"

"Yes. Maybe a Chinese girl."

"So you'll have a Chinese sister?"

"That would be so cool! I hope I get a Chinese sister. I'll teach her everything I know. It will be fun. She'll be half my sister and half my daughter."

"But don't you like being alone with your mom?"

"I do, of course I do, but there's something screwed up about being an only child, don't you think? I once read about it in the paper. I read that only children get screwed up."

Dana had never thought about it. Her father told her that when she was three or four she had begged for a brother or sister. Her mother had promised that they'd start working on it and that within a year or two there'd be a baby in the house, but after the accident she couldn't remember ever wanting a brother or sister. It was as if her mother was the only woman in the world who could have brought that baby home and, when she died, not only the potential sibling went with her but the idea itself. Now she tried to imagine what a half brother or sister would look like. She licked her teaspoon and looked at the palm trees in the yard and pictured the baby; she gave him her father's eyes because they were her eyes too, and Shira's nose and her skin tone and smoothness, but when she tried to give it her own mouth and chin, which were exactly like her mom's, she realized that was impossible, and she suddenly wanted a baby of her own, the kind that would have a chance to inherit some of those lost features.

"I look like my dad," Tamar said suddenly, as if she had read her thoughts.

"How do you know?" she said, slightly embarrassed. Tamar's father was a subject they spoke of freely, but there wasn't much to say about him.

"Because I don't look anything like my mom, so who else could I look like?"

Rona came home and said she'd had a horrible day. "How's the quiche?"

"Yummy," Dana said.

"Gross," Tamar said, and her mother kissed her hair. "Mom, when are we going to adopt a Chinese baby?"

Rona threw the empty ice-cream tub into the trash and said, "I see you've already taken care of dessert."

"Well, when?"

"Why does she have to be Chinese? What's wrong with a Romanian baby?"

"Come on, Mom," Tamar said, and Rona said it wasn't the right time to talk about it. Then she asked if they had homework and Tamar nodded and made a sour face.

"Go and do it together, then," she suggested, but Dana said she had to go home. Rona asked how her dad was and she said he was fine. "And Shira?"

"She's fine too."

"It's about time we had a meal together," Rona said.

"Yes." Dana headed to the door.

"I'll call," Rona said. "Say hi to Dad and Shira."

Dad and Shira, Dana thought, as she went down the steps. As if they were two first names. On the way home she became agitated about her future brother or sister, as if Shira were already in the delivery room with her dad. She turned toward Allenby and stopped at the pedestrian crossing, and tried to decide whether to cross the street or turn back and go home. It was late afternoon, not yet dark, and although it was early April, it felt like summer. She wondered if she really hated summer so much, or if it was another of her father's pet peeves that she had adopted so as not to hurt him.

She crossed the street, but before the light changed she turned around and ran back the way she had come. She didn't know what she wanted, but she knew it was something urgent. She hoped that walking down the bustling street, which, unlike her father, she was fond of, would clarify her desires or at least distract her from the longing that now filled her eyes with tears. She went into a clothing outlet and rummaged through piles of T-shirts. They were soft, as if they had been worn and laundered thousands of times, but they had the chemical scent of fabric dye. Then she went through the women's lingerie and stacks of men's underwear, and had a sudden impulse to buy underwear for the three of them. The store clerk asked what she wanted. She said she was just looking and the clerk said this wasn't a place to look, this was a place to buy. She left the store and walked toward the market. Her father always warned her about terrorist attacks, but now she squeezed her way through the shoppers and thought not about bombs but about herself and about the sadness that had overcome her, which was unlike any other kind of sadness she had known. It was nice to walk through the crowded market. The crowds carried her along in all sorts of directions, as if she were in the ocean. What was he so afraid of? she wondered. Of Allenby and bombs and drowning. He was always trying to protect her, not realizing that he could not shield her from the internal catastrophes she lived through at every moment, especially recently, because some of them were his own fault. She hated the way he hugged her. She hated feeling her chest crush against his and the way he pretended not to notice that something was growing there, like a partition between them. Above all, she hated what was growing there. At night in bed, she would examine the two protruding breasts under her reading lamp, afraid to touch them so as not to encourage their growth, not to feel from the outside what growing up was, because feeling it on the inside was enough.

That morning, in the kitchen, as she watched Shira stretch, she saw her large breasts beneath her shirt, rising and sagging heavily, her nipples not dark and erect, like the ones she saw on models, but pointed toward the floor. She tried to imagine how her father felt when he touched them, how a baby would feel when it suckled on them, and how her own would look, because her mother had small ones; she could tell from the pictures. One thing was clear: She didn't want breasts. The feeling was so strong she wasn't capable of even uttering the word.

Tamar had no problem with it, and at school she was always whispering to Dana and pointing at girls who were more developed. She would say things like, "Look at that one," or "How did *she* suddenly get breasts?" and she liked to guess who was already wearing a bra. Dana cooperated and always added her own comments, but she wished she were as flat as Tamar was. She hated the feeling of not knowing so many things—like what a platonic relationship was—and yet living with the sense that she knew too much. Lately, she hated so many things that now she wondered if she hated her father too.

When she got home she found a note from him on the kitchen table. He said he'd gone with Shira to the ER because her father hadn't felt well. He had tried to get hold of her at Rona's but she had already left. He hoped she was all right, and there was fruit salad in the fridge. He signed the note *Love, Dad,* which was strange: he always signed *Bye* and usually didn't even bother adding *Dad.* She sat down on the couch in the living room and thought about watching TV. She went over to the stereo system and took out the Doors CD. She was curious to know if they had listened to it together, and how it sounded when she wasn't at home. She put her feet up on the coffee table. The ashtray was so full it was overflowing; she took it to the kitchen to empty and then wiped the table thoroughly with a cloth. When she went to wash her hands in the bathroom, the tub was full of water with bits of foam floating in it, little bubbles that made a sound when they burst. She touched the water. It was still warm. She pulled the plug out and suddenly felt scared, wondering if Shira's father was going to die. She walked toward her room to do her homework, but instead she went into her father's room and looked around to see if anything had changed in recent weeks. The bed was messy, but no more so than when he had slept in it alone.

A few months after the accident, her nightmares had begun. According to Dad and Nira, they lasted almost a year. She would wake up in the middle of the night crying, but not remember what she had dreamed. Her father would carry her in his arms to their bed, where she would fall asleep immediately. But once she heard Nira reprimanding him, telling him that once she got used to it, it would be hard to stop. Her father replied that he didn't have much choice.

Nira always knew what was best for them, but lately, even before Shira, Dana thought her father was rebelling. A few weeks ago she had heard him say to her on the phone that there was no point in bringing them Michal's hand-me-downs, because Michal was thin and tall and they didn't fit. She heard him pause for a minute, and then he said impatiently that he was grateful, but it was a waste of time and energy for her, and there was no point shortening and widening jeans that would only be good for one season anyway. When he admitted it wasn't only a question of sizes but of different tastes, she could hear her aunt's hurt feelings on the other end of the line.

Last week, when Nira came to visit, she sat down in the kitchen and asked what was new, not expecting an answer. Her father said there was some news and told her about Shira. "Someone I'm seeing," he called her, and said she should be coming over soon and they could meet.

Nira said she'd be happy to, but after a few minutes, even before she'd had her coffee, she said she had to run. Dana heard her say to her dad at the door, "I hope you know what's good for you, Yonatan. More important, I hope you know what's good for the girl." When he said not to worry, she heard Nira whisper, "Because to tell you the truth, I no longer know what's good or not for anyone." Her dad was quiet then, and her aunt sighed and said, "Well, ask us over sometime, so we can see who she is," and he said okay.

She heard the door shut and he came into the kitchen and said, "Your aunt's getting to be a real kibitzer." She asked what a kibitzer was and he told her, but she disagreed, because she knew Nira was simply getting older, just as he himself was, although he didn't realize it, and that he was a kibitzer too, with his hugging and his pretending he was a different father, especially around strangers; especially around Shira.

Now she sprawled on his big bed and was happy to hear its familiar creaks, which hadn't changed over the years. She curled up under the blanket and dislodged from under her back a rolled-up cotton shirt that Shira slept in. She shut one eye and looked at the sheets. Her grandparents had sent the bed linens from the States and, like all the sets they sent, it was too big for the Israeli-sized bed and the fitted sheet didn't fit very well. She looked at the dark sheet, following an almost invisible striped pattern, and noticed that it was covered with white stains that looked like moisturizing lotion. On the floor, she saw her father's underwear in a human position, as if the man wearing them had lain down on the floor and evaporated. She knew she would never be able to fall asleep here again. The bed no longer belonged to her parents or to her dad, but had become undefined, a bed in waiting, hovering, like she was, in no-man's-land.

She went into her room and sat down at her desk, took her notebooks out of her backpack, and tried to concentrate. Shira's novel lay on her bed with the bookmark still shoved between the front cover and the first page. Every time she read the first few lines, something prevented her from going on, a superstitious conviction she had developed—she was becoming like Grandma Rachel lately—that the farther through the book she got, the more her dad would fall in love, and eventually his love would become irreversible, like being carried away by the plot of a suspense novel. She knew it was stupid but she couldn't control it, and she wondered if her old fears were coming back and if she might become addicted to strange bedtime rituals again. She knew that avoiding the book was pointless, because Shira and her father had become a couple regardless of the rate of her reading; and while she was stuck on the first page they had overtaken her, leaving clouds of dust in their wake.

She thought of her father sitting next to Shira on a bench in the ER—although she couldn't recall if they had benches in the ER—perhaps holding her hand, and Shira resting her head on his shoulder, maybe crying, and perhaps they were kissing; but something was wrong with the picture, because if they were both sitting together, then where was Shira's father? They wouldn't leave him alone, after all. So she imagined them standing over the bed of an old man she didn't know, and then she felt as if she herself were the old man, as if her life had already happened and now she was just recollecting it. She felt extremely tired, and a sour sense of anger rose in her throat, but she didn't know what she was angry about.

She got up and went into her dad's room again and picked up his underwear with her fingertips. She took it into the bathroom and tossed it in the laundry hamper. Then she went back to her desk and tried to concentrate again, but she couldn't. She glanced at the clock, saw it was already after eight, and wondered when they'd be home. She went into the kitchen and took out the fruit salad and ate straight out of the bowl with a spoon. Shira had obviously made it, because her father didn't have the patience to cut fruit into such small pieces. His fruit salad always got stuck in her throat; he never bothered to peel the bits of pith off the orange segments, and they would lodge themselves in her mouth and almost choke her. She finished half the bowl and put it back in the fridge. She wondered if tonight, when they got back from the hospital, they would make the baby who suddenly seemed so certain and no longer preventable. She sat at her desk again and listened to the noise from Allenby flooding her room through the open window. The street always sounded noisier, more invasive, when she was in a bad mood. She wondered if you could grow old without living through at least half a lifetime, because she felt as if she had already experienced enough, and she asked herself, Why not? If people can die young, what's to prevent children from growing old? She shut the windows and sat on her bed and picked up the book, but then she got up, went into the bathroom, took her father's underwear out of the hamper, went into his bedroom, and put it carefully on the floor, exactly as she had found it.

(6)

He punched the vending machine, but not a single can came out. He'd already wasted ten shekels trying to get a drink. The first time, he put his money in and pressed the button for mineral water, the light started blinking precisely at that moment to indicate there was no more water. He tried to release the change, but the machine had swallowed it up. He put some more coins in and this time chose apple cider, but the machine was still adamant. He wondered if he should make a third attempt—he now suspected the whole machine was broken—but then he saw Shira coming out through the doors. "I came out to have a cigarette; he's fallen asleep," she said. He told her about being robbed by the vending machine, but she seemed uninterested. She stood with her back to him and smoked, and he kept hitting the buttons and jostling the lever that was supposed to give him back his money.

The doctors had decided to hospitalize her father in the Internal Medicine department, and she said she was relieved. This way, at least she would know he was being cared for, if only for a night or two. As Yonatan had listened to the doctor report that Max's blood tests were irregular—his potassium levels were very low, or very high, and something about white blood cells—and he had to stay in the hospital for observation, he had also sensed relief. Now, as he kicked the obstinate machine and realized it was not responding, while Shira remained unaware of this struggle, he realized it was selfish relief: She didn't want to take care of her father; he didn't want to take care of her.

He touched the back of her neck and she looked at him, gave him a small unfocused smile, and turned back to the ER doors again, as if she feared that taking her eyes off them even for a moment might cause an alteration in her father's condition. He might deteriorate, or perhaps show sudden improvement and be sent home after all. He looked at her ass and thought about their sex, which over the last few nights had gone from slow and hesitant to extremely wild but soundless, because of Dana sleeping in the next room. He found there was something exciting in that combination of passion and silence. He gave up on the machine and sighed.

"What's wrong?" Shira asked, as if she had only just noticed that something was going on behind her back.

"Nothing. The machine robbed me."

She touched his cheek and asked him to put her cigarette out and said she was going in, and he wanted to ask how much longer she thought they'd need to stay. Three hours in the ER was enough for him and he was hungry, but he said nothing.

"You can go," Shira said. "I'll stay here until they admit him and then join you. Dana must be waiting at home."

He said it was all right, he'd stay a little longer, and thought about the bath they were going to take together and how they had fucked on the couch in the living room that afternoon, with the Doors CD that had become their sound track over the last few weeks playing at full volume, swallowing up their silence. He followed her into the ER and stood next to her by her father's bed. The old man looked calm and angelic as he slept, and Yonatan thought of how his own father, in his final days, had still looked angry and busy even in his sleep.

She sat down on the chair Yonatan had dragged over from a nearby bed and waited for the doctor to arrive with the admittance forms. The chairs seemed different from any other, but she didn't know why. Perhaps because they were heavier and less comfortable, as if hardened by years of being positioned at this particular angle around patients' beds. Her whole body ached—the same body that had tensed up as she stood naked in the living room and dialed home to check her messages, one ear listening to the bathtub filling with water, and the other to Mrs. Binder, her father's neighbor, informing her that her father had fallen down the stairs and was at her place now but she didn't know what to do; his knee was cut and he seemed confused; and she should please phone as soon as possible. She didn't say what time it was.

She had dialed the neighbor immediately, as Yonatan came in and announced that the bath was ready and hugged her from behind. The neighbor said they'd taken her father to the ER an hour ago. She apologized over and over again and said she didn't know what to do, the wound on his knee wasn't serious but he seemed apathetic. "Such a poor man," she said, and started sobbing. Shira tried to reassure her and felt Yonatan's body pressing against her ass, rubbing up against her, and she asked who took him, and Mrs. Binder said, "An ambulance. An ambulance came." Shira, whose imagination transported her quickly to the ER, parked her car in the lot, ran all the way inside, and found her father sprawled on a bed behind one of the screens or in one of the hallways, suddenly felt as if two women were having the conversation with Mrs. Binder, twin sisters: the devoted daughter who had already positioned herself by her father's bed and was waiting with him for the doctor, and the one who now, practically paralyzed by guilt, started rubbing her ass against Yonatan's second, surprising, erection.

Now Yonatan leaned on her chair, looked at her watching her sleeping father, put his hand on her shoulder, and remembered the day of the accident. Zvi had gone to identify the body because he said he couldn't do it. When the police had called, he phoned Zvi and Nira and waited for them to come, and when they arrived he collapsed, because it was important for him that they see him collapse. He knew there were difficult days ahead, and he wanted to set the bar of his neediness very high. But before that, he took Dana upstairs to Ziv's parents, who said, "Of course, of course, no need to ask," when he told them what had happened and asked them to watch her for a few hours. When Nira and Zvi rang the doorbell, he opened the door and, without saying a word, lay down on the hallway floor and started sobbing. He lay in a fetal position and Nira leaned over him, also sobbing and caressing him, while Zvi walked around the apartment with the cordless phone and made the necessary arrangements. Yonatan wasn't sure how long he lay that way; many things happened around him while his soul was absent. Nira came over to him every so often to tell him, gently at first and then firmly, to get up. People came and went, the phone rang constantly, and once he heard Dana's childish voice in the stairwell and panicked. But now, when he thought about it, two things stood out in his memory: his warm cheek on the cold tiles and the strange pleasure of collapsing.

They accompanied her father to the Internal Medicine ward, squeezing into the elevator with an orderly, who skillfully maneuvered the bed. "Is this your father?" he asked, looking back and forth at the two of them. Shira said, "Mine." The orderly asked, "Are you the husband?" Yonatan said, "Boyfriend." The orderly gave them a knowing grin, and they both smiled politely. Shira pulled the blanket up around her father, and Yonatan took her bag and slung it over his shoulder.

When they transferred him into another bed in one of the ward's rooms, Shira's father woke up and looked blankly at Yonatan, who said, "I'm Yonatan, remember?" and her father held his hand out and Yonatan shook it, and that combination of limpness and determination reminded him of his own father again.

"Who is this?" Max asked Shira.

"This is my friend Yonatan." She explained to him that they were going to do some tests, and in the meantime the doctors had decided to hospitalize him for a few days. Tomorrow, she promised, she would bring him some things from home: his slippers and robe, his toiletries and shaving kit, and the transistor radio. She asked if he needed anything else. He closed his eyes and it was hard to tell if he was snoozing or pondering her question. "Dad?" she asked, and he opened his eyes with a start. "I'll bring you a newspaper, and I'll bring your cookies."

"Glasses," he mumbled.

"Yes, thanks for reminding me. I'll bring your reading glasses. Do you want us to rent a phone for you? So you can phone if you need anything else?"

"A phone?" he asked.

"Yes," Yonatan said. "You can rent a phone for the room here. I think you can also rent a television."

"Television?" He opened his eyes.

"Should we rent you a TV, Dad?" She hated herself for her tone, that hospital tone that had too much cheerfulness and restrained alarm. But her father didn't answer. He closed his eyes again and fell asleep, his mouth falling open as a kind of fishlike response to her question, and her heart shrank in pain. "Shall we leave?" she asked.

Yonatan nodded. "Don't you want to tell him you're leaving?"

"What good will it do? He keeps falling asleep anyway." Still, she leaned over and kissed his cheek, and when his eyes opened for a moment, she whispered that she was leaving now and she'd come the next morning, and he should sleep well.

Yonatan said, "I hope you feel better, Mr. Klein," and put his hand on her shoulder, and they left the room and went down in the elevator and quickly crossed the parking lot, almost at a run, and said nothing until they were out of the hospital area, leaving behind a kind of twilight zone or prison, as if fearing that someone might notice them sneaking out and order them back.

With summer in full swing, Shira finally found the courage to go back into the little shop on King George Street and buy her father the onion bread he liked. For five months, since the day they first met there, she had viewed the store as a road sign that signaled the beginning. Every time she walked by, and glanced inside or examined the selection of breads in the window, a thrill went down her spine, which, over time, turned to alarm; if this is where it all began, she thought, as she moved away from the window and the sales clerk's questioning look, this is also where it all could end.

The past five months had been too good to treat as routine. If she had had any close girlfriends, they would probably have told her she was crazy; it was her fear of losing Yonatan that would eventually drive him away, and five months was plenty of time to determine with certainty that he was her partner now. *Yours,* they would say emphatically, over and over again, to drill it into her. But she didn't have that sort of girlfriend, and now of all times, as she experienced this fearful happiness, she wished she had someone to share it with.

A renewed burst of writing had surprised her one morning when she went home to pack up a couple of cardboard boxes, no more, with a few essentials. There were some clothes and cosmetics that she needed, and Yonatan wanted to know why she didn't bring them over, instead of wearing the same T-shirt almost every night. And their shampoo wasn't right for her hair. She complained that her hair was dry and wished she had her moisturizer and facial cleanser, and tampons; she always brought only two or three of them in her purse, never bold enough to leave a box in their bathroom. The same fear that prevented her from going into the bread shop warned her not to leave traces in the apartment on Bialik.

One morning after Dana left for school and they were sitting in the kitchen, he asked again why she didn't bring her things to the apartment. "You're right," she said. "I'm just lazy." She hoped he would take advantage of her lie—she could tell by his amused expression that he was on to her—to tell her finally that maybe she should move in with them, it was a pity to waste money on rent when she spent most of her time here anyway, he was glad she was here and it seemed natural to him, even though it had only been five months since they met—five months that had made him forget his previous life, a life he didn't wish to remember.

He smiled and said, "You *are* lazy." She said she'd pack up a few things that morning, and he asked if she needed help and she said she didn't, it was just a few bags.

"What are you going to do this morning, write?" she asked. He said he wouldn't, that he would go and price some air-conditioning units, and maybe even order one if he found something cheap. She said it was about time, and he said summer was almost over. "You can use it next summer then," she said.

He repeated her words, humming. "Isn't there a song that goes like that? Something about 'next summer'?"

She said she thought the lyrics were "this summer."

"Really?"

"'This summer you'll wear white,'" she said.

"Oh, yes. I hate that song."

She said she did too, but still found herself humming it as she crossed Meir Park, after they had parted with a kiss on the corner of Allenby and he had wished her luck with the packing, and she with the air conditioner.

She hadn't written for five months either, although, unlike Yonatan, who claimed he must not have anything to say now that he was happy, she felt she did have something to say. But she held back, not even turning on her computer, out of some strange sense of loyalty, afraid that what she had to say would threaten his silence. But that morning, after she stopped at the corner shop for some cardboard boxes, she sat down at the computer and opened the abandoned file that contained her new novel. She read through all twenty pages of it—pages that represented her life until five months ago—and found she did not despise it. It wasn't bad at all, in fact, and it depicted, with chillingly prophetic precision, her relationship with Yonatan, minus Dana. She kept on writing for three or four hours, and when she was done she saved the new pages, unsure whether this sudden inspiration was the result of her happiness or if she was motivated by her suspicion that the past few months, which she had just described, were a gift mistakenly given to her.

When she went back to the apartment that afternoon, carrying two boxes and giving Yonatan the car keys so he could go down and bring up the other two, she felt guilty, as if she had spent the morning betraying him. She asked what he had done all day, how things went with the air conditioner, and he said it hadn't worked out, they were too expensive, and tomorrow he'd drive out to a place he'd heard about in Rishon Lezion, where they had cheaper units. "Want to come?" he asked.

"Tomorrow morning?" He nodded and she didn't know what to say, because she wanted to keep writing. "We'll see. I have a translation job to do."

He asked what she had done all morning, and she said not much; it took her a long time to pack—another lie, because she had filled up the four boxes in minutes, having packed them in her mind thousands of times.

"Did you talk to your dad today?" he asked, because ever since he had been discharged without diagnosis yet again, she called him every morning, sometimes twice a day. She said she had. "How is he doing?"

"Same as usual." She was disturbed by her lies and wanted to confess that in fact she had spent the morning writing. But she knew that if she told him, she would do so with such matter-of-factness, in a way that would so belittle its importance, that the nonchalance itself would be a huge lie. "He's starting to get used to the idea of having some help at home," she said.

"Really?" Yonatan took some eggs out of the fridge. "Do you want an omelet?"

She nodded. "He hasn't exactly agreed yet, but when I talked to him yesterday, all of a sudden, without my even bringing it up, he asked how one goes about getting a Filipino, and I told him to leave it to me."

"And that's it?"

She nodded again and said it was a big step, because up until a month ago he wasn't prepared to hear about having help.

"That's true. I wonder what happened."

He asked how many eggs she wanted, and she said one. He called out to Dana, who was in her room—she had been shutting herself up in there for weeks now—and asked if she wanted an egg, and Dana said she wasn't hungry. He cracked the eggs into the frying pan and said lately she wasn't eating and he was worried she'd become anorexic like half the girls in her class; it was exactly the right age.

Shira said she wouldn't.

"How do you know?" he asked.

"Because she's kind of like me, the way I was at her age."

"So what? What does that have to do with anything?"

"She'll find more sophisticated ways to torment herself."

"Such as?"

She sensed the confession bubbling up inside her, and said, "Oh, she might decide to become a writer."

Yonatan smiled and turned the gas off and slid her half of the omelet onto her plate.

"I'll slice some tomato," she said, and got up to get one out of the fridge. Standing by the counter, she said, "Actually, I did some writing today."

"You did?" He cut a few slices of bread from yesterday's loaf.

"Yes. I just sat down and wrote all of a sudden, for about two hours straight. I don't even know where it came from."

"Great."

At night, before they fell asleep, without knowing whether it was to ingratiate herself or calm her fears, she told him about her bread shop complex, how for five months she hadn't been able to go in there because that was where they had met. "Remember?" she asked, and he nodded as he lay in bed reading the paper, without looking at her. "I know it's idiotic, but that moment, when we met, even before we *really* met, when you were horrible to me, remember?" He nodded again. "Well, for some reason that moment has taken on mythic proportions, and I'm afraid that if I go there now something will go wrong and we'll break up." She looked at him, but he seemed unmoved by the confession. "I feel guilty because I know my dad loves their onion bread, and I go by there at least once a day. But I can't go in."

"I'll buy it for you then," he said, still not taking his eyes off the paper.

"You don't understand," she said, and he said he did. "What do you understand?" she asked, and held back an urge to touch him, to strip off the new underwear she and Dana had bought him when they'd gone shopping together. She wanted to put an end to this silly disclosure, which instead of relief had brought her to a dead end. "Come on, what do you understand?" She snatched his newspaper away and threw it to the floor.

He turned around on his side and pulled the sheet up to his neck and kissed her shoulder and closed his eyes. "That you're silly. That's what I understand."

(8)

In the mornings, after she went back to her apartment to write, he would go downstairs and wander the streets like someone who has been abandoned and is looking for amusement. Later, and the closer winter got—and although you couldn't feel it yet, you could already hope for it—it became something he enjoyed; he took comfort from his regular route, which was his and his only, almost intimate, like a new book, the one he would never write. For the first time in his life he did not feel paralyzed but liberated, and hoped he could learn to enjoy the freedom he gained by not wanting to write.

His daily walks took him first to the square, then down the steps by the old City Hall, and from there to Bograshov, whose usual traffic and ugliness always surprised him after the beauty of the old buildings on Bialik, all of which were being renovated and preserved, one by one, except his own, which apparently had no historic value. From Bograshov he would go up to King George, where he would decide whether to turn left and keep going to Masaryk Square and then back, across the street and up Ben Zion Boulevard to meet Rothschild Boulevard, where he would continue to pepper his excursion with impressive architecture, or turn right toward Allenby and the market. The Allenby option always made him feel cowardly, as if he were heading home when his walk had barely begun, and yet he almost always chose it.

Near the corner of Borochov, he would slow down or come to a stop and think about her. Even though it had only been an hour since they'd parted, he thought of her as if she were someone who had left his life long ago, although he knew he would see her again in a few hours, when she came back from her morning of writing and unlocked the door with the key he had copied for her, and which she had attached to her key chain, a big silver lucky charm, a *hamsa*. When he thought about the *hamsa* he was flooded with love for her and her superstitions, her annoying and touching fears, as if they were physical defects: moles or scars that he sometimes wished weren't there and other times wanted to touch, to hold and protect from himself, from his critical gaze. When he left Borochov behind, he felt free again, as if that corner were only a small obstacle on his course, something that needed to be bypassed, like the large rocks the city had placed on the sidewalks to stop drivers from parking on them, and which pedestrians always walked into.

When she had a bad day—she gladly shared the bad days and spared him the good ones, though if the situation were reversed he would do exactly the same—he consoled her by saying that at least she was writing. Anticipating her reaction, he would hurriedly add that he wasn't saying this because he felt sorry for himself, quite the opposite: He was fine with not writing, he had never felt so free and light, as if years of dieting were finally showing results. When she looked at him skeptically he would say he was so fine with the situation that he wasn't sure whether he wanted it to be temporary or permanent. When she dared, once in a while, to include him in a good day, she invited him to join her in the wonderful dreaminess—"wakeful dreaminess," she called it, and he agreed—that takes over after a successful day of writing. He felt no frustration from watching the dreaminess from the sidelines—that reward he knew so well from his own writing days—but was only happy for her. His happiness surprised him; he never imagined he would feel so supportive toward someone who should have been threatening, which suggested a clear line where his career ended and hers began.

Every so often, like a man pausing to tie his shoelaces, he would stop to ask himself why he loved her. He would stand outside a store selling hardware, bathroom fittings, or cheap shoes, and wonder, *Why her?* How could he have found room in his life for her so easily, even though it had seemed too crowded to contain a single other item like an air conditioner? Then he would keep walking, slightly confused or sometimes the opposite, determined to continue on his route without further disturbance, to think only of what he needed to think about: what they would have for dinner that night, or what would happen with his daughter, whom he hadn't been able to transfer to a different school after all, and who had been leaving the house depressed and defeated every morning for two months now, so different from the girl she had been last year, from the girl for whom he used to have answers.

Once she had asked him what happened to people when they died. She was four and they were spending the afternoon together, waiting for Ilana to get back from a daylong symposium in the English literature department. She sat on the rug in the living room and chattered with her dolls, held their heads near one another, leaned over, and whispered secrets in their ears. He played her some classical music, one of his favorite pieces, which he now could not remember—perhaps it was the Schubert quartet he listened to so often in those days. But he remembered how he had watched her from the couch as he read the paper and had tried to hear the music through her ears. As she knelt, she seemed focused on her low, crowded world on the rug, the world where she made the rules, and she hummed something that sounded like a song from one of her videotapes. Then suddenly she raised her head and asked him what happened to people when they die. He remembered what his mother had told him when he had asked the same question as a boy: "Nothing," she had said dismissively. But he hadn't believed her; *nothing* seemed impossible.

"What happens when people die?" He repeated his daughter's question, looking at her inquisitive eyes.

She nodded.

"You mean, what happens to *them*? What do *they* do?"

She nodded again.

"Lots of things."

"What things?" she asked.

"All kinds."

"Yes, but what?"

"Everything! All the things they did when they were alive, except they do them differently."

"Different how?"

"Quietly. For example, they don't speak."

"Why? Aren't they allowed?"

"They are allowed, but they don't feel like it," he said.

"Do they think?"

"Of course."

"And do they sleep?"

"All the time."

"All the time?"

"Well, not all the time. Sometimes they're awake."

"And what do they do when they're awake?"

"Whatever they did when they were alive."

"Do they eat?"

"A little. They don't need much."

"Do they play?"

"Yes. They love playing," he replied.

"Do they have toys?"

"Yes, I suppose they do."

"Dolls?"

"Could be."

"Do they watch TV?"

"I don't know. Maybe."

"And do they listen to music?"

"Yes, all the time."

"Like the kind we listen to?"

"This kind?" He pointed at the stereo system, unsure which answer she would prefer, afraid that perhaps his mother's reply was wiser after all, more reassuring.

She nodded eagerly again.

"That kind too," he said. "They have lots of CDs. They can pick whatever they like."

"So they aren't bored?" she inquired, clearly troubled, as she walked a naked Barbie whose wardrobe was lost toward another, larger doll, which she held with her other hand.

"No, of course not."

"So they have fun?"

"Yes. I think so."

She bashed the two dolls together, let out a whistle, and then said, "Boom!" She looked at him, smiling, and waved the Barbie in the air. "Look! I killed one! Now she'll have fun."

For her eleventh birthday, which they celebrated at a Japanese restaurant with Rona and Tamar, Dana had asked for her own television set. "It can even be a used one," she said. She had already found out how much it would cost to get a second cable connection, and she would pay for it herself, from pocket money she had saved up.

"She wants privacy," Shira said. "I can understand that."

Even though he also understood her, and even though he bought a small TV set, he felt as if the two of them were abandoning him, that the fantasy he had recently started nurturing—that they would soon become a family—was being ridiculed by his adolescent daughter and the woman he loved.

It occurred to him that he wasn't truly happy for Shira. Not because he was afraid to see her succeed while he was completely forgotten and his books disappeared from the shelves, but because he was used to being the axis around which the household turned: the creaky, moody axis, the one you couldn't make noise because of. Now Shira had usurped this indulged spot. She was the one whose face was scrutinized curiously after a workday, as they tried to guess what she had written. Then, perversely, he realized that unexpectedly, in a way that defied all logic, he actually was happy.

Sometimes he missed Ilana. She was his first love, except that now he began to suspect that perhaps Shira was his first true love and he had loved Ilana but in a quiet, comfortable, arrogant way, because he always felt stronger and was never afraid to lose her. But he *had* lost her. That love now seemed like child's play compared to what he faced now, every morning at the end of his route, when he went upstairs to his crowded, empty apartment and cooked complicated dinners that his daughter disdained, preferring to eat a bowl of cornflakes or half a pita in her room—meals that his beloved happily devoured after her hard day of work. Or he would tidy the house or masturbate, as if all the years during which he hadn't dared touch himself had now erupted like a disease, bursting out at night or early in the morning on Shira's various body parts: her stomach or her breasts or her thighs or the small of her back—he absolutely refused to come inside her—or the palm of his hand. This is my new career, he told himself, amused, as he tossed the evidence of his activities into the laundry hamper—a soiled pillowcase, dish towels dirtied while he cooked. He would soon be forty-six and he was in love like a child, masturbating like a teenager, and cooking like crazy.

But mainly, he was old, he told himself, as he went into a big record store and bought a Doors anthology. Shira and Dana both complained that they were sick of the one CD he played over and over again. The anthology was on sale because it must have been popular only among aging widowers. Every three months he went to the money changer and redeemed the check his father-in-law had sent, wondering if he would keep sending them if it weren't for Dana and feeling he no longer deserved them, because not only had he found another woman, he had also stopped pretending to be writing. As he deposited the shekels into his account, he thought about how he had relieved himself of two jobs at once: widower and artist. The idea amused him, but he soon sank into depression, and then he would sit in a nearby café and watch the passersby on Allenby, feeling for his wallet every so often. He remembered the Saturday at the end of last winter when they had met at the pedestrian crossing, and how the three of them had sat here, and how childish Dana had been then when she sat between them and planned out the picture she would later draw for Shira. He wondered where that picture was now, if she had kept it or thrown it in the trash. He missed that tension between them, not only because it was gone, but because it had signified two possibilities: that something would happen between them and that it might not.

On the first rainy day of the season, which had finally arrived in November, she was stuck in a traffic jam, listening to the windshield wipers squeak and the radio announcer report faulty stoplights, slippery roads, and accidents in a cheerful and forgiving tone, because it could all be blamed on the first rain that everyone had been hoping for. That afternoon, she had stood with her father on the balcony, watching the sky grow dark and the clouds roll in from the west, and had wondered what he thought about when he stood there like that, in his flannel robe, leaning his elbows on the railing. He looked full of thoughts—about clouds, about the beginnings of other winters. And yet he also seemed utterly vacant.

For months she had been trying to persuade him to let a foreign worker into the house to help out. She made inquiries, talked to some agencies, and told him about a Filipina candidate who sounded suitable. When he said there was no space for anyone else in the apartment, she said she would empty her old room, which had become a storeroom; it was about time she sorted it out and threw away whatever he didn't need. When she saw how the idea horrified him, she suggested that they just pack everything in boxes and store them, perhaps in paid storage. Would he like her to find somewhere? He shook his head. He no longer claimed—as he used to when she suggested they clean up the room— that these were important documents and maps whose fate only he could decide and he didn't have the strength right now. He simply shook his head slowly, thoughtfully, as if he knew something no one else knew and wouldn't disclose it. Only later, when she said goodbye and went down to her car, feeling the first heavy drops of rain on her head and hands, did she understand his refusal, and it scared her. She tried to imagine what it was like to pack up your things, knowing you would never see them again.

The radio announcer's exuberance annoyed her. Even the first rain, which she always looked forward to, seemed like a nuisance; maybe she was getting old. She also wondered if her father would remember, before he went to bed, to draw the blinds and close the windows she had opened. For the first time in her life, she was glad to live in a city where there was so little rain, where there was no need to worry that a forgetful old man might drown in his bed at night because of an open window. She asked herself if she loved her father and knew she did, but she also knew it was sometimes hard to differentiate her love for him from her fear of not loving him.

She and Yonatan had been talking about moving to a different apartment for weeks now: somewhere larger, maybe even in the country-side. Not because the apartment on Bialik was too small for three people—it had housed three people before—but because it seemed too small for these particular three people: her and her writing, which had taken on a physical dimension, like a sublettor; Dana, whose seclusion and attempts to diminish herself, perhaps even to disappear completely, took up a vast amount of space; and Yonatan, who looked lost in the small area the two of them left him.

A few days ago, when she went down to buy cigarettes, she saw him on King George Street. He was standing near her street corner, on the opposite sidewalk, looking in the window of a toy store. She knew he went out walking in the mornings and did his shopping and errands, but when she saw him standing with his back to her, his hands in the pockets of his corduroys, his gaze fixed on the display window, he did not look like someone running errands or shopping but like someone killing time. He was staring at the old globe in the window—she knew the shop and its permanent displays well—or at the inflatable beach balls, or perhaps what drew his attention was what always attracted her own: an inflatable yellow duck that had been hanging there for years. Its underinflated neck looked broken. She stood hidden by a bus that had stopped at the corner and wondered if Yonatan had discovered the handicapped duck. She wanted to cross the street, run over to him, and surprise him from behind, wrap her arms around his waist, kiss him deeply in front of the store, as if they were lovers taking a stroll down the street together, but she knew that right now there was much distance between them.

When the bus drove on, she saw that Yonatan had broken away from the window and had stopped at the nearby kiosk, where she had planned to buy cigarettes. He bought a pack for himself. He went on toward Allenby, and as he walked he unwrapped the pack and threw the cellophane into a trash can, took out a cigarette, and put it between his lips. Then he stopped for a minute to dig through his pocket for a lighter, one that used to belong to her and which, incredibly, was still working. He shielded the cigarette with his hand, tilted his head, and lit it. She wanted to turn herself in again, to call him from the other side of the street, wave innocently, happily, as if she had not been standing there watching him for five minutes. She pictured herself coming home in the afternoon, showering, taking clean clothes out of the closet, knocking on Dana's door and peeking in to ask how she was, then going up to him in the kitchen as he stood at the stove or washed the dishes or leafed through a cookbook, wrapping her arms around his waist and kissing him as if nothing had happened. But she kept standing there, and she no longer cared if he turned around and saw her, because she knew he wouldn't, he was so immersed in his morning. He tossed his cigarette on the ground, crushed it with the sole of his shoe, and went into the wine store that had opened recently next to the kiosk. She could already savor the red Chilean wine they would drink with dinner, as well as the sour taste left by secretly observing her lover, and she crossed the street, bought her cigarettes, and hurried back to what used to be her home and had now become what you might call a writing studio but was in fact an excuse.

She had promised him she would give up the apartment soon. "You can work in my study," he offered generously. "I'm not using it." But she said she wouldn't feel comfortable. "All right then," he said, and she thought he was slightly relieved, "we'll find you a corner somewhere. Besides, we're moving to the country, aren't we?"

"Yes," she said. The thought of life in the country filled her with happiness but also a certain degree of fear.

"We'll find something with enough space for you to have a whole studio."

They were planning to drive out that weekend to look at rental houses on a few moshavim in the area. The real estate agent had addressed them as a married couple and referred to Dana as *the daughter*. "There's a separate unit for the daughter," he said, praising one of the houses. When they asked him about schools in the area, he asked what grade the daughter was in. Then he asked if they had a dog and Shira said they didn't, they had no room for a dog in the apartment. The agent said they could raise as many dogs as they liked on the moshav and asked if the daughter liked dogs. Shira said she did and was suddenly excited at the idea of finally having a dog and being treated like someone who already had a daughter.

When she reached Bialik and started looking for parking, the rain stopped. She circled the block and the nearby ones over and over again, as if her car were some sort of urban shark. She knew it was a matter of timing and patience. Eventually someone would have to move. She drove slowly, her eyes scanning the parked cars, looking for signs of life. The radio played a jingle advertising an old-age home. Two singers, male and female, mimicked children's voices and sang a rhymed verse about Golden Meadows Residence, an assisted-living center only ten minutes from Tel Aviv, as if they were grandchildren back from visiting a grandparent and were thrilled about the place. Their voices sounded familiar; they also advertised cereal. She changed the station but kept hearing the commercial, which had scared her, and she was impatient to get home. She circled Bialik several more times, driving with the window rolled down, inhaling the postrainfall air, until she quickly slid into a spot that opened up on Hess Street, silently thanking the old man who had vacated the spot in a large old Volvo, leaving her so much room she didn't even need to maneuver.

(1 0)

On Saturday, when they went to look at houses with the agent, Dana said she didn't feel like going.

"But what will we do if we see something we like?" Yonatan asked.

"We can't take something without your approval," Shira said; Dana said she trusted their judgment.

"Are you sure you don't want to come? Don't you feel like getting some fresh air?" Yonatan asked. She said she didn't, she had homework to do.

"We can always go back and see the house again," Shira said, "if you feel like it." Her father said that was true, and asked what she thought. She shrugged her shoulders.

"First find something you like. You'll probably hate everything anyway." He pretended to be insulted and asked why she said that, if she really thought they were so picky. "Because you're not serious," she said.

Shira had been living with them for nine months, during which time Dana had monitored her movements, her clothes, her makeup, and her moods. But despite her hopes that if she observed Shira thoroughly enough, she would become like her, she remained who she was. Yet at the same time she changed rapidly, with near-violent speed, and was convinced that there was no woman in the world—not her mother, not even the perfect woman—who could save her, who could arbitrate between the person she was now and would be in a moment and the girl left behind, even perhaps reconcile them. Lately she felt like she did in gym class, which started with a jog around the playground. Her body got in her way and felt heavy inside, leaden. She always straggled behind, trying to catch up with the other girls, who looked so light and feathery; it amazed her that they could chat with one another as they ran.

Tamar was starting to bore her. Not because anything had changed about her—on the contrary, it seemed as if nothing had—and just as her body had remained the way it was a year ago, thin and supple and lacking the threatening hint of breasts, she also still had the same cheerful, bouncy mood she had always had. And even though she had started showing an interest in boys—they would spend hours talking about this boy or that who had invited her to a party, danced with her, given her a French kiss that was gross—there was something about her that rejected heaviness, as if she were coated with a layer of Teflon. Tamar said sex was disgusting. She said she would never do it, except maybe once or twice just to have children, if she ever wanted children, and she wasn't so sure she did. But Tamar didn't know anything about sex, and Dana did. The whole apartment reeked of it, and even though it wasn't a smell but an atmosphere, it had the force of a smell, the kind they tried to remove from the air before she came home from school.

It embarrassed her to see her father come out of his bedroom on Friday afternoons, their time for resting and doing the crossword. He never had his shirt on, and his chest, with its curly graying hairs sticking damply to his skin, the chest she knew so well and which had comforted her so many times, looked suddenly indecent. Shira always wore her shirt but she walked around without her pants on, and her long T-shirt covered her underwear but not her thighs. When she sat down you could see hairs, also curly and sticky-looking, as fascinating and scary as her father's. The more they exposed themselves, the more Dana was careful to cover herself up. Her dad called her a nun when he saw her walking around with a sweatshirt zipped up to her throat, even though it was warm outside and she was really hot walking around like that. But she removed her layers only in her room. "Have you gotten religion?" he teased her, and every so often he grabbed her arm and tried to pull her in for a hug or a tickle, but the idea of him touching her, pulling her against his bare chest, shocked her so much she couldn't even smile or dismiss him with a cynical remark. "You used to have a sense of humor," he said, and then not only her body but also her sense of humor felt raped. She couldn't stand to see him sprawled on the couch or sitting in the kitchen with his shirt off, his damp skin glowing dangerously. He would look at her briefly, amused and worried, unaware of his new monstrousness, and say, "Come here for second. Why are you always in such a hurry? Sit with us for a minute." Shira would say, "Stop it, Yonatan. Leave her alone," and smile at her understandingly. Dana would strain to smile back and her eyes would stray to Shira's thighs. She wondered if some of those curly hairs might have stuck to her father's chest, and if that was the reason he was stroking himself so affectionately.

One night, when she had a cold and got up to get a tissue from the bathroom, she heard Shira sigh heavily. She wanted to go back to her room, but kept standing by their door, listening but not knowing what she hoped for: to hear something or not to hear anything. Her knees felt weak and her thighs ached with a fluey chill, and then she heard that sound again, like a call for help, as if Shira were ill. Then another sigh came, louder this time, and her father whispered *shhhh,* but Shira couldn't stop, as if she was in so much pain she couldn't hold back. She sighed again, firmly this time, as if angry at being ignored, and she heard him whisper *shhhh!* again. It annoyed Dana, but she didn't know if she was annoyed for Shira's sake or for her own, as if he were trying to prevent her from hearing more and more of these sighs in case she might finally decipher them. Reading her mind, Shira sighed again, but this time she sounded slightly relieved, and Dana stood by the door and was reminded of the scales Irma Gutt used to make her do on the piano. She classified the last sigh as a descending scale and it suddenly sounded like a game: her father's *shhhh,* accompanied by laughter, and those sighs. She stood close to the door and tilted her head and swallowed, and her throat hurt, but suddenly it was quiet and she was disappointed: it was over without her knowing what had happened, whether it was something good or bad, and for a few moments all she could hear was her own heavy, congested breathing. When she was about to turn back to her room, she heard an ascending crescendo scale, but instead of her father saying *shhh* he also sighed a descending scale, and their duet of sighs went on like that, with increasing frequency, as if they were competing. She felt her entire body tensing up expectantly, but it wasn't clear what she was expecting. She felt that even if the door suddenly flew open and they discovered her standing there, she wouldn't be able to escape. The sighs were coming quickly now, scales going up and down, chasing each other, and she felt that she too was part of the chase. She was so tense she didn't feel her nose running, snot stinging her upper lip, and then she heard Shira give one long sigh, decisive but also surprised. Her father replied with his own sigh, neither decisive nor surprised, not even musical, but brutish, something that sounded like a bellow—a sound she hadn't thought her father capable of producing. But after all, her father was no longer really her father; he was a stranger who walked around the house half naked and stroked his chest.

Now she sat at her desk and tried to do her homework. She hated that desk. She hated the room, the rug from the Old City, the bureau that Nira said was worth a lot of money, the bed, even the elephant cover her mother had sewn for her. Everything looked so childish, belonging to a different world, but when she tried to imagine what she would prefer instead of these things, she couldn't think of anything. She went into the living room, lay down on the couch, and turned the TV on, but she switched it off after staring for a few minutes, without even noticing what channel she was watching. She hated watching TV in the mornings—it reminded her of sick days—so she took some leftover cauliflower quiche out of the fridge and warmed it up in the microwave Shira had brought from her apartment. Her father had protested at first, claiming microwaves were a needless invention and emitted dangerous rays. But he soon fell in love with the machine and would heat up the half-full cups of coffee he found all over the apartment, and she thought, How quickly he falls in love! How different from her he was! She scraped the leftovers into the trash, washed her plate, and went back to her room. She remembered their conversation last night at dinner—she had agreed to join them because it was Friday—about the houses they were going to see today. She had eaten in silence and listened to them enthuse. Her dad talked about all the things he would plant in their garden, listing names of plants and herbs as if he were a gardener, and Shira looked at him lovingly, as you look at a child excited by some nonsense. They asked her what kind of dog she wanted, and she said she didn't care and was flooded with guilt because she hated the dog before it even existed.

In the spring, she would turn twelve, and the idea of going to the beach on her own, as her father had promised she could when she was twelve, no longer seemed like an accomplishment. The joint bat mitzvah party Rona was planning for her and Tamar—they had set a date in May, exactly halfway between their two birthdays—seemed superfluous now. She wondered if this was how depressed people felt: so angry that nothing interested them, as redundant as the things they thought about, as redundant as the thoughts themselves. She got up off the bed and went to the trunk under the window. She hadn't opened it for years. She sat on the floor and ran her finger over the gilded letters that had almost completely faded: DANA'S SECRETS. How innocent they all used to be, she thought, and missed the days when the trunk was big enough to contain all her secrets. Her finger was covered with dust, and she wiped it on her pants and thought, We need a cleaner, but we'll never have one, just like we'll never move. Then she opened the lid and glanced inside. There were some stuffed animals that she touched and felt nothing for and old children's books in Hebrew and English. She stared indifferently at them, as she had stared at the TV before, and then she knew what she was looking for.

She pulled out a large brown envelope from the bottom of the trunk. It was folded in four and contained a tape, which she now removed. It was the old answering-machine tape with the message her mother had recorded. Even a year after she died, her father didn't have it in him to record a new message, so everyone who phoned them would hear her mother's cheerful voice announcing, in a faint American accent, *Shalom! You've reached the Lurias. We can't answer the phone right now, but if you leave a message we'll call you back.* She remembered how the word *call* disclosed the heaviest accent. When her father asked her permission to change the message—she was seven then, and he consulted her about everything; it occurred to her now that the older she got, the less important her opinions became—she agreed, and he suggested recording a message with her own voice. She asked him not to erase the old tape, and he took it out of the machine—she remembered the *click* the tape made when it popped out and the chill it had given her then, as if they were digging someone out of a grave—and she put it into the brown envelope, folded it in four, and buried it deep in the trunk.

Now she took the tape to the living room, popped the new one out of the machine, put the old one in, and hesitated for a moment, unsure of which button to press, afraid she might erase the message. She thought of going out and calling home from a pay phone but knew it would be strange, even a little perverted, to hear her mother answer. Then she found the right button, pressed it, and immediately heard the *Sh* in *Shalom* whistle through the room like a misfired bullet. The message sounded a little blurred; her mother's voice was vague, half erased, as if time had taped another message over it. She listened over and over, at first trembling at the voice, but from one replay to the next she became indifferent, as if, along with the tape, her emotions had also faded. She took the tape out and put back the current one that had her voice on it, recorded when she was seven, addressing the caller with confident childishness. They should change that message too, she thought. She tried to think of the right wording for their new situation. *You've reached the Lurias* was true but imprecise. *You've reached Shira and Yonatan and Dana's house* sounded silly. She thought that *Hello, we're not at home; leave a message,* would be a reasonable compromise. She went back to her room, put the tape into the envelope, and put it back in the trunk, knowing she would probably never listen to it again. Or perhaps she would play it for her children one day, so they'd know how their grandmother had sounded. She would show them her pictures in an album, point to her face, and ask, "Do Mommy and Grandma look alike?" And the children—she imagined them three or four years old, a boy and girl, maybe twins—would nod eagerly. When she asked if Mommy and Grandpa looked alike, they would hesitate, unsure of the correct answer.

(1 1)

As they stood with the agent outside a low derelict house with a tiled roof, walls coated with yellowing stucco, and two little front windows with torn screens, Shira knew without doubt that they would never leave Tel Aviv. They smiled at the earnest agent as he talked incessantly, perhaps sensing he was about to lose these clients. Like the previous two they had visited, this moshav was too quiet for her; it seemed to be wrapped in boring secrets, even hostile, as if it were making a mockery of her and Yonatan, this urban couple with their bucolic fantasies.

They had followed the agent's car all morning. He was in his mid-twenties and made a point of driving slowly and using his turn signal often. When they parked behind him outside the first house, he got out of his car quickly, stretched as if he had been driving for hours rather than twenty minutes, looked up at the sky, spread his arms out to the side, and said, "Breathe! Breathe in this air!" They did, still optimistic, and looked at the large sweat stains spreading under his arms. He took a huge bunch of keys out of his pocket and strode quickly down the path, through a disused, fenceless yard that blended into the road. When he leaned over to put the key in the lock, his cell phone dropped out of his pocket and Yonatan hurried to pick it up. "Thanks," said the agent, embarrassed, "that always happens."

His name was Ofir; they didn't know his last name. Shira thought perhaps they should rent a house just to make him happy, because she suddenly felt sorry for him, even though she had made fun of him only a few moments before in the car. She had laughed at his elegant slacks, which were so heavily pleated in front that they looked like a balloon. There was a little sticker on the back of his leg that said ISRAELI APPLES over a picture of a grinning sabra wearing a silly hat. She considered saying something to him, or maybe peeling off the sticker without his knowing, and she wondered if he had kids who had stuck it on his pants as a joke before he left that morning. "Are you married?" she asked, when they walked into the musty house. Yonatan looked at her in surprise. "I was just asking, because you look so young."

"Yes," Ofir said, and quickly started to pull up the blinds on the only window in the room.

"Do you have kids?"

"Not yet. But God willing, we will."

The blinds wouldn't open and Yonatan said it didn't matter, but Ofir struggled with the blinds and said the house was flooded with sunlight and it would be a pity for them to miss it. He finally gave in and went over to the light switch. He flipped the switch but the light didn't come on, and he concluded the owners must have cut off the power.

"They sprayed here too," Yonatan said, sniffing the air.

"Yes, I think they must have."

Yonatan kept making polite inquiries, even though they had already agreed, with a quick look, that they hated the place. Ofir answered eagerly, opened and closed cabinets in the bathroom and bedrooms, and promised to find out from the owners if they would put a fence up around the yard, or at least share the cost. He agreed with them that a fence was essential. "Otherwise the dogs will get out," Yonatan said.

"What kind of dogs do you have?" Ofir asked, when they left and he bent down to lock the door.

"None yet," Shira said.

"Oh, that's right, you told me," he remembered. "But you will."

Shira nodded and said, "God willing."

Then they went to the second house, which was on a nearby moshav and looked very much like the first one, and they struck that one down even before going inside. Ofir said he understood and he was only showing it to them because it was so close, but he knew they wouldn't like it. Then he gave them directions to the third moshav, in case they lost him on the way, and in the car they tried to guess what kind of husband Ofir was and what his wife looked like and what he was like in bed. Yonatan thought, We've become a couple of gossips; he enjoyed the feeling. He liked going out for a drive on Saturday with his partner to see houses on moshavim, and he would have been happy to keep doing it every Saturday as a hobby, forever or at least until they grew old.

He wondered what Shira was thinking about—about the houses they'd seen and the moshavim they might live on or about her writing. He said, "He's probably a lousy lay," and she said he shouldn't be so sure, sometimes that type was full of surprises. "Have you ever slept with someone like that?" he asked, and she said when she was a student she had had a few dates with her father's insurance broker. "Really?" he said, and she nodded. "That's like sleeping with a cliché," he said.

She smiled to herself. "Maybe, but this specific cliché happened to be amazing in bed."

He was flooded with jealousy. She had never said *he* was amazing in bed, at least not to his face; he doubted that she'd said it to anyone, because she didn't have any close girlfriends. But he reassured himself with the thought that he'd never told anyone she was amazing in bed either. He did say that when she was gone, when she went to her apartment to write—and obviously if they rented a house on a moshav she would have to give up her apartment—he fantasized about her. He wanted her to ask what happened in his fantasies, but she just said, "Really?" and he nodded, full of secrecy and lechery. He wanted to tell her that in between cooking and doing the laundry and drinking coffee on the balcony—which he had now tidied up, planting mint and verbena and basil in the old hanging planters—he masturbated while he thought about her: standing, lying, sitting opposite the television, distractedly watching *National Geographic*. But she didn't ask, just as she had never told him what she thought about his books, but he knew.

When they stood outside the third house, which was built in what Ofir called "a Mediterranean style," with elegant arched windows and flecks of stucco on the front like whipped cream, she glanced at Yonatan to exchange another look of rejection. They were not going to leave the city for a rustic joke like this. But he looked as if he had fallen in love with the house and forgotten her. This time, his questions sounded serious, as he fingered the stucco, seeming truly impressed, and disappeared into the house with the agent, leaving her standing outside, worried. How could their tastes be so different? How could this man, who had been lecturing her ever since they'd met about architectural styles in Tel Aviv—high ceilings, Bauhaus, clean lines—how could this Jerusalemite, who had grown up in one of the most beautiful Arab buildings she had ever seen, be considering, even for a moment, living in this Mediterranean monstrosity?

She followed them inside and found them standing in a little room next to the bathroom. Yonatan turned to her, grinning, and said, "Look, it even has a pantry!" She wondered if his vocabulary contained any more of these terms that disclosed the fact that he was nothing more than a little closet bourgeois—that the apartment on Bialik, the furniture, the books, the CDs, the clothes, his relationship with his daughter, were all a kind of ongoing neglect rather than a way of life. Ofir expected enthusiasm from her, and when she didn't respond, he kept talking to Yonatan and did not address her again during the tour, investing his efforts in the real client, the one whose wife was too picky. Except that she had stopped feeling like his wife. Only once before had she seen Yonatan so cut off, so independent, ignoring her in what seemed not a hostile gesture but an attempt at survival as if she were the one threatening him and not the other way around. It frightened her to discover this new strength of hers, the strength of someone who is wanted, whose loss is feared; it was a strength she could not rejoice in.

They had recently gone to the wedding of her old neighbor, Dalit, which took place in an outdoor venue somewhere between Herzliya and Netanya. As they drove over, she fantasized about their walking up to the reception embraced or holding hands. It was silly, but she had never found such pleasure in so minor a fantasy. But they didn't hold hands when they walked down the gravel path lit with paper lanterns.

She had sensed he was moody in the car. That afternoon, she had brought up his writing for the first time. She said she was worried about him; he seemed restless. He told her not to patronize him. She said it didn't make sense for him not to have a problem with the fact that she was writing every day, that she was so prolific and might even finish the novel within a year at this rate. If the situation were reversed, she said, she wasn't sure if she would be able to be as supportive of him as he was of her. He said that was because she was incapable of being supportive of someone else, someone she loved, and had nothing to do with writing but with personality, and maybe that was why she had never married. She said he was a child, and he said, Apropos children, someone who's never been a parent doesn't know what it means to make a sacrifice. She asked what exactly he was sacrificing; he had just claimed that for him, not writing was a choice, a great relief, something brewing in him for years that the relationship with her had finally legitimized. "'Because I'm happy,' you said. That's why you don't feel like writing."

He said, "Yes, and you are writing *because* you're happy."

She replied, "So where's the sacrifice if we're both happy?"

And he said, "Never mind, forget it."

"Tell me," she said. He said there didn't have to be sacrifice for there to be a *feeling* of sacrifice, and the feeling didn't necessarily have to spoil their sense of happiness. She said, "Bullshit, those are just words." He said if that was how she felt, it didn't matter. "It does matter," she insisted.

"Maybe you don't know what it means to love," he whispered, and she said maybe, and they kept standing in front of the closet, trying to decide what to wear to the wedding.

He dressed with obvious unwillingness, slowly buttoning the shirt she chose for him when he said he had no idea what to put on. Perhaps she should have told him not to come instead of picking out his clothes, she thought, as they drove the whole way in silence. But she knew she needed him there, even his hostile self, much as she needed his presence—the one that planned their meals and fantasized about her and roamed the streets in the mornings—to write. She felt selfish, but there was also a lightness and absence of guilt in the selfishness. It's simply a by-product of our love, she thought, a kind of refuse, or bonus.

This selfishness—and any child in love knows this, so why shouldn't she enjoy it too?—is power.

When they arrived at the reception, she introduced Yonatan to Dalit, who came up to them glowing in her wedding gown and makeup and high hairdo, squeezing her groom's hand. Yonatan nodded politely, and Dalit asked if he was Yonatan Luria, the author. Shira quickly answered for him that yes, he was the writer, and Dalit said she was a fan of his and wanted to know when his next book was coming out. Before Shira could answer, Dalit said, "I'm so happy you came!" but the groom dragged her to another table where his friends were sitting. They looked very drunk and very young, and she flashed them a smile that said, What can I do? My husband is forcing me, waved coquettishly, and disappeared.

On the way home, he was impenetrable. At the beginning of the evening she had tried to placate him; then she got angry; but as they drove home, the silence became even more combative than it had been on the way there. She began to feel scared; he reminded her of herself. She remembered how she used to clam up with Eitan, acting on some indistinct sense of insult, and how he desperately tried to make her happy. Now she tried to soothe Yonatan, who pretended to be focused on driving, as if the traffic were heavy. She reminded him that Rona had invited them for dinner the next evening, and said she would go past the store on King George tomorrow, and asked what kind of wine to get. He said dismissively that it didn't matter to him. "Chilean, Italian—I really don't care."

Now she waited for Ofir and Yonatan outside the Mediterranean house, leaned against the car, and swore she would never live in this moshav. But when they came out and she saw Yonatan's face shining she decided to relent, to give him this house as compensation for her writing. He came up to her with worry spreading over his brow, as if seeing her leaning against the car with her arms crossed had wakened him from a dream. He asked what she thought, and she shrugged. Although she had decided to give in, she couldn't do it with words. He said, "You hate the house, don't you?" She shrugged her shoulders again, and he said, "Forget it, then. Let's go home, I'm starved."

She felt tears well up in her eyes and said, "But you like it."

"So what? We both have to like it." He put his hand on her shoulder and pulled her to him. He whispered in her ear, "What's up? What's this mood?" She said nothing, and he said, "We'll find something we both like."

Choked up, she asked, "And what if we don't?"

"We will," he said, and she repeated her question. He said, "Then we'll stay where we are. Is that so bad?" She shook her head. "Then why are you in a bad mood?" he asked, and she said she didn't know, maybe because she was getting her period. "Do you have cramps?"

"A little," she said, and he kissed her hair and they both stood and looked at the house.

Ofir looked at them sheepishly and asked if everything was okay. Yonatan said, "She's not feeling very well."

The agent said, "I hope you feel better," and she could tell he hated her, and they promised to think about it and let him know and got into the car. He asked when they'd let him know, because there were other clients who were interested, and they said, Today or tomorrow.

As they drove off, Ofir honked at them, and Yonatan put his head out of the window and Ofir asked if they wanted him to ask about the fence. Yonatan said, "What fence?"

"At the other house," the agent said, and Yonatan said there was no need. When they left, she turned and saw Ofir's car driving behind them back to Tel Aviv, defeated.

(1 2)

Sometimes, when he woke up first and looked at her curled up on her side with a blanket pulled up to her chin, feet poking out at the bottom—and especially when she slept with her socks on and they slid down and hung limply off her feet like a baby's pajamas—he would tell himself that he had experienced a miracle and his occasional suffering was simply a natural attempt on the part of his body and mind to adapt to it. Sometimes, when she stirred in her sleep or rolled over, or her foot suddenly kicked out reflexively and he wondered if she was dreaming that she was falling or dreaming about him, or when she opened her eyes for an instant and he wasn't sure if they registered his look before shutting again, he was afraid he was going to lose her, because he wanted her but didn't want the things she wanted.

She wanted a child. When she asked what he thought, now or in the future—but not too far in the future, she said; she was already thirty-seven—he answered that the idea seemed scary. He said that if a baby were to suddenly land in the apartment he would probably get used to it, but to be responsible for bringing a baby into the world in a planned, thought-out way—no, he didn't think he could do that. Dana, he said, was older now and too preoccupied with herself to be happy about a brother or sister. In fact, that was the last thing she needed. But you? she would ask. What about you? He would say he really didn't know. He loved her, he loved him and her together, even the three of them together—although his daughter had become intolerable lately; had she noticed how much Dana hated him?—but no, he didn't want a child. Or rather, he would say, trying to soften the blow, he didn't know what he wanted, and you can't have a child if you don't really want to, can you? She would nod, disagreeing, distant, and he would reiterate, feeling condescending and cruel, that he understood her need for this child whom he, personally, did not need, did not want. At least that was how he felt now, although he didn't know how he'd feel a year or a few years from now; he knew they didn't have all that time, but still, if she was asking him about now, his answer was no, not now.

When he watched her sleeping, he asked himself if he were a miracle for her too, or perhaps more of a catastrophe. Or maybe—and this thought sent shivers down his spine—he was neither a miracle nor a catastrophe but rather something that she referred to, when she told him about past relationships of hers—particularly about someone called Idan, who must have been especially traumatic or beloved—as "an ongoing fling." He tried to reassure himself with the thought that he had never been anyone's fling, that they had all loved him in the end. But he also knew there was always a first time, and the fact that he was forty-six did not mean he could not be a fling. In fact, it might make it all the more likely, he thought, as he reached out to touch her, trying not to wake her but hoping she would wake, because watching her became unbearable at these moments. And once, when he put his fingers close to her lips to feel her breath and she woke up and blinked at him, he tried to give his voice a playful tone and said, "Hey, is this a fling?" She said, What? and closed her eyes. He asked what he was for her, if he was a fling, and she mumbled into the pillow, Of course not. Are you crazy? He said, "Are you sure?" She said, Sure, and fell asleep.

Later, when they drank their coffee in the kitchen, she asked what the early morning interrogation had been about, and he said, "Nothing. Anxiety attack."

That winter, which turned to spring almost before it had even begun, they went to look at houses on moshavim almost every Saturday. They got to know the greater Tel Aviv area well, and even broadened their search to the coastal plain on some weekends. But from one Saturday to the next, they realized they were not going to move to the country. They kept going, though, and debating, with or without agents, and here and there they fell in love, separately or together, with some house that seemed full of potential, that had always been rented by the time they decided they wanted it, until Yonatan got a call, one day in May, from an old student friend who was now a professor of literature at Hebrew University, asking him to teach a course there the next year.

"But what exactly would I teach?" Yonatan wanted to know.

"Whatever you want," his friend said.

He said he'd think about it and wasn't sure which made him happier, the job offer or the fact that he was still considered a big name. He liked the idea of being able to go up to Jerusalem once or twice a week, to make a gradual return, symbolic and noncommittal, to the city he so missed, the city that had a winter, where you could sometimes wear a coat without sweating. He could see himself roaming the drafty hallways of the Mount Scopus campus, the eternal wind whistling outside, rattling the windows. He would wear his favorite corduroy pants and soft sweaters, but not give up his Chuck Taylors—not conform completely to the respectable professor look. His students would be required to read his books and give them serious thought, and as he stood before them, he would summon up his cynicism and humor—all but forgotten since the anxieties of being in love had left him humorless—and would turn into an improved, more likable version of his father.

When he told Shira about the offer, he could tell she was relieved and even happier than he was to be rid of his burden of continuous idleness, and for a moment he was hurt, but he was too happy to be truly insulted. "I'll feel less guilty about writing," she said, with candid simplicity.

It surprised him, but he suddenly heard himself say, "I really do need something to do." Yes, she said, and he thought she wanted to get up and hug him, but she restrained herself. "But I've never taught before," he worried.

"So what? You'll be there as a famous author; you can do whatever you want."

And he said, "The pay's probably lousy," and she said it might not be, and wanted to add that he wouldn't be doing it for the money, but said nothing.

She could tell he was already there on Mount Scopus in his imagination, far away from her, and she said, "They'll love you." And he said, You think? "Especially the coeds," she said, and he smiled and she hated herself for her patronizing tone, too encouraging, which she knew from conversations with her father. Then she heard herself say, "Who knows? Maybe we'll end up moving to Jerusalem."

He had often fantasized about the house in the German Colony. The idea that he would one day inherit it both excited and scared him; his mother was already eighty, but he could not imagine the day when she would no longer be alive. When he inherited the house, he would become a wealthy man, a man with options. He would have to decide if he should sell it—with the money it would bring, plus the sale of the apartment on Bialik, they could buy an estate—or if perhaps—and this was such a revolutionary and improbable idea that he enjoyed amusing himself with it—he should renovate it and move back in, as a family. In this fantasy, he was already planning to send Dana to the Music Academy high school—maybe she'd want to take up playing again—and he would put Shira in his father's study, build himself a flourishing academic career, and get a dog. He had always wanted to see the overly manicured garden, which, like the city itself, reminded him of a depressive beauty, turned into a different place—a place where it would be nice to raise a child one day. He didn't really want a child; he preferred to keep fantasizing about what he would do with his life as a millionaire and only regretted that this required the death of his mother. One step at a time, he told himself, after he called his friend and said he would be happy to accept the offer. No need to hurry. First he would get reaccustomed to the city and make sure his love for it was real.

(1 3)

On the day Shira was supposed to bring the young Filipino for an interview, her father was hospitalized. She had arranged to pick up Sam in the afternoon, from the southern part of town, and had already planned what to tell him on the way. She would explain how to make her father like him, and she imagined him answering, "Okay, no problem," in his cheerful English. But that morning, when she called her father to make sure he remembered they were coming, there was no answer. She reasoned that he must have just gone down to the store or the deli, or perhaps he was in the bathroom shaving for the meeting, but she knew he wasn't, and as she drove there, one clear picture flashed in front of her eyes: her father lying on the hallway floor. She couldn't get rid of the image; it gained control the way her parents' telephone number had taken over during her exam on the morning her mother died.

She didn't even bother to ring the doorbell. She opened the door with her key and found him lying on the floor in her old room, which she had worked all week to clear so it would be ready for Sam to live in. Her father had spent the week sitting on the youth bed, mumbling and gesturing as she transferred documents and maps into boxes. She taped the boxes up and wrote each one's contents on it with a black marker, following his mute instructions.

He looked unconscious. She shouted, "Dad! Dad!" but he didn't move, and for a moment she wasn't sure if he was breathing. He lay on his stomach with one knee hunched up to his chest and one arm bent backwards, as if he had jumped off a rooftop. He wore his slippers, and a robe was bunched up around his hips, exposing not the familiar pajamas but a pair of smart gray slacks she hadn't seen him wear for years and an elegant thin leather belt around his waist, still unbuckled. She wanted to phone Yonatan, but he had gone to Jerusalem to meet his friend at the university and she didn't know how to get hold of him. She called an ambulance, then sat on the floor next to her father and waited. She tried alternately shaking and cradling him, and eventually managed to pry out a sigh. The paramedics came quickly and she opened the door and led them to her father. They laid him on a stretcher and rolled him out and took him carefully down the stairs, and in the ambulance he suddenly woke up. They even had a conversation, but she could never remember what they talked about, as if the conversation was composed not of words but of the codes she would later use to file it away in her brain.

He was suffering from kidney failure. No one at the hospital was talking about depression or exhaustion anymore, nor did she receive the kind of looks of accusation she usually got from social workers and orderlies, who generally made it clear that the main suspect in a parent's dismal condition is always the child. Now they had a diagnosis: Her father was a genuine patient, as if within seconds he had been upgraded and no one would now try to send him home. He was admitted to one of the Internal Medicine wards, which was full of mostly elderly people. His two roommates looked as if they had spent most of their lives there. One sat on the edge of his bed, reading Psalms. There were framed photographs of babies on his bedside table. The other man was rinsing a glass out in the sink, lathering it with slow ceremonial motions, and then he went out to the hallway, came back with his glass half full of Turkish coffee, and stood drinking it by the window, which looked down on the hospital laundry.

As she sat next to her father, who stared ahead indifferently, she tried to think what she could do for him, what she could bring to make him also feel at home here, some pictures or belongings, and then she remembered Sam, who was supposed to wait for her on the street in half an hour—Sam who had suddenly become irrelevant. She hurried to call him from the pay phone at the end of the hallway, and a woman with a foreign accent answered and said, "Sam no here." She left a message, enunciating every word and knowing the woman hadn't understood a thing, despite her "No problem" assurances. She put the phone down and went back to the room, taking in the geriatric patients sprawled in wheelchairs, scattered around the hallway like environmental sculptures and walking in slow motion. She wanted to be Sam or his heavily accented wife, to belong to a different world, one full of foreign scents and colors and sounds, a world where old men like her father were a way to make a living.

When she got back to the room, she saw the old man standing at the sink again, soaping his glass and trying to strike up a conversation with her father. She was happy to think he might make new friends in this place, the same happiness she felt every time Emmanuel Herman came to visit. But her father was silent, failing to acknowledge his roommate even with a nod or a sign. Shira thought she saw disdain, for the first time in many years. She remembered the disdain with which he looked at the prostitutes on Allenby when he took walks there with her as a child, and how she pitied the prostitutes on the one hand but also liked seeing her father strong. Now, though, there were no sparks in his disdain, only weakness. His roommate gave up and went back to his window, where he stood with his hands linked behind his back and rocked on his heels to the rhythm of a tune he hummed to himself. She thought about Emmanuel Herman, who must have given up too, as he hadn't been to visit her father for months. Or perhaps he had become frightened, because he had started to sense an illness which, unlike his own, had no name.

She remembered what Yonatan had told her about his father, how at the end he was full of indiscriminate disdain for everything and everyone, especially the religious orderly who took care of him. She wondered if that was what was happening to her father now, if it was a final eruption of volcanic hatred. She missed their walks, when she was able to be, for an hour or two, just the daughter of a conservative man who was afraid of prostitutes and tried to protect her from them. She missed those walks because she knew that her father's look had also involved curiosity and perhaps a little pity.

A nurse came in with folded pajamas and placed them on the bed. "Will you help him?" she asked, and Shira nodded. She hoped he would refuse her help, that he would suddenly jump up, take the pajamas to the bathroom, and get dressed in there. She took off his slippers and put them on the floor. His ankles were swollen. She still hoped he would protest that he didn't need her help, but he said nothing. She wondered who had helped the other two men with their pajamas. They looked healthy, as if they could get dressed on their own, as if they were here because there was no room for them at the old-age home, and they were patiently waiting at this temporary stop. The relief she had felt only a short while ago about his hospitalization disappeared as she began to grasp that she and her father had entered a place where time had no meaning. The nurse came back with an IV drip hanging from a pole and asked why the father wasn't in his pajamas yet. Shira said she didn't want to wake him, and thought of how his status had changed instantly from *her* father to *the* father. The nurse looked at his chart and called out, "Mr. Max, time to get up!" When he opened his eyes in alarm, she kept using the same tone while she set up the drip. "You have to get your pajamas on. The daughter will help you." The nurse said she'd come back in a few minutes to hook him up to the drip, and before she left she patted the folded pajamas, drew the curtain around the bed, and said, "Let's go, we don't have all day."

She supported his back and helped him sit up. "Would you like to get dressed on your own?" she asked, but he didn't answer. He reached out to the pajamas and felt them with his fingertips, as if evaluating the quality and condition of the fabric, and she hoped he was about to send her out, but he rocked back and forth as if he were on a ship deck, and then lay on his side and sighed. "Come on," she said tenderly, "I'll help you," and sat him up again. She spread the pajama top on the bed and said it might be too small. Then she looked at her father lying on the edge of the bed, leaning forward, his eyes fixed on the floor, and said maybe it wasn't after all. She untied his robe and pulled it down off his shoulders, carefully holding his elbow and trying to extricate his arm from the sleeve. "Help me a little," she whispered, and he obediently lifted one arm and then the other. The robe slid down around his waist, and she unbuttoned his white shirt—she thought of Sam again and wondered if he'd got the message on time or if he was waiting for her on the street—and asked if she should take off his undershirt, and he shook his head. He had not one drop of energy left, she thought, but he knew what he wanted. After she put the pajama top on, she asked him firmly to get up, in an attempt to dull the spreading panic. He held her arm and stood up, and she swiftly opened the button and zipper of his pants, pulled them down to his ankles, and told him to sit down. She held the pajama bottoms and looked at his legs. She knew he was thin but didn't know thinness could look like this, helpless and aggressive at the same time, a thinness that assailed its observer with pleading and defiance: Look how low I've sunk. Look how low you too will sink one day. And when she saw his hips, which seemed to have the same circumference as his knees and calves, she thought, We are protected from our parents' aging until the moment we have to undress them, and then they actually undress us, strip us of everything we know about ourselves and about them, crumble the walls we have built, walls that collapse in a moment, with a violent kick, at the sight of such thighs. Neither human nor birdlike, they seemed to belong to no familiar person or creature; even his white underwear looked empty.

She put his feet into the pajama bottoms and pulled them up over his knees, and asked him to stand up again, which he did, his trembling hand digging into her shoulder. She pulled the bottoms up over his waist and helped him lie down on his side, covered him with a sheet and the thin woolen blanket, and told him she was going out to get something to drink and she'd be right back. She asked if he wanted anything and didn't wait for an answer. She quickly crossed the hallway until she reached the elevator area, where there were several large ashtrays. She lit a cigarette and took a deep drag, and even before she finished smoking she knew she'd want another, one wouldn't be enough—all the cigarettes in the world wouldn't be enough now—and she lit the next cigarette with the first one. Outside, two workers were unloading crates of vegetables from a parked truck, stacking them on the asphalt. She put her face to the window, and waited for someone to come and take the carrots, and thought about the colorfulness of the vegetables against the backdrop of the gray building and the black asphalt, spotted with oil stains. The orange of the carrots, the red tomatoes, the green peppers, and especially, she thought, the lettuces and bunches of parsley sticking out from the gaps in the crates, all looked strange against this background, as

if the delivery had arrived at the wrong address. But then two men wearing aprons and rubber boots came out and took the produce inside. On
the way back to her father's room, she stopped at the vending machine
and bought a chocolate bar and sat on one of the orange plastic chairs
and ate slowly, knowing there was no reason to hurry back, knowing that
this time her father wouldn't leave this place. A quiet, foreign, official
voice told her: This is the end.

(1 4)

Jerusalem behaved like an old betrayed lover that morning, alternately flirting with him and spitting in his face but also willing, under
certain conditions, to make up.

The meeting at the university finished early, and before going to eat
at his mother's, he decided to walk around downtown. He hadn't been
downtown for years, avoiding it as if it were the hub of the noise that had
taken over the town, the area where the deepest and most dangerous
cracks were revealed. He left his car in the parking lot at Independence
Park and started walking toward Nahalat Shiva, planning to continue on
through Zion Square to the Ben Yehuda pedestrian mall. It was late
morning, and the streets looked busy and happy, and he remembered
how he always used to think that Jerusalem was a town that preferred
mornings, out of some inner knowledge that afternoons would bring a
certain sadness. Like an experienced manic-depressive, it hurried to
recharge with healthy urbanity before its self-imposed curfew.

My love, he whispered in his heart as he walked along Yoel Salomon
Street, amused by the nostalgic wave that had swept over him. My pale,
sickly love. He looked on without anger, with compassion even, at a
noisy group of American kids sitting outside a café that must have been
new. It had an American name, and when he glanced at the menu hanging by the front door, he read that they served bagels with cream cheese
and lox and that the place had a *glatt* kosher certificate, which hung at

the entrance like another menu. On his right was another unfamiliar café, with a menu identical to the first one.

By the time he reached the pedestrian mall he felt depressed. Huge plastic signs, shockingly colorful, hung on the sooty stone walls over storefronts, bazaars, falafel and *shwarma* stands, and pizzerias that displayed kashrut certificates instead of menus. Some of the stores he remembered had become souvenir shops. I'm ugly, his ex declared, enjoying the pain she was inflicting upon him. I'm loud and vulgar, and I'm not yours anymore.

He missed Shira. Precisely because she did not know the city the way it used to be, she could look at it as a tourist, and perhaps through her eyes he would be able to fall in love again. He drove away from the city center as if escaping someone but when he reached the German Colony, he calmed down a little. Emek Refa'im Street looked like an extension of downtown, but the narrow side streets, which were now crowded with cars parked on the sidewalks, still had a certain lush green beauty. He drove in and out of them, taking the long way to his mother's house, lingering over the houses with their beautiful stone walls, as if they were a dam against the fundamentalist torrent that had flooded the town. He was proud of these houses and walls for not changing all these years, for being steadfast and arrogant, cold Jerusalemites, like his mother's stone house, which would one day be his. When he turned onto Rachel Imenu, he thought, Perhaps, after they settled in here, after the three of them shut themselves up behind their wall, he might consider starting a new family. He wanted to call Shira and wished he had a cell phone—she had already got one, but he still resisted—because he urgently needed to make sure she hadn't changed over the course of the morning, that she still wanted him, his city, his child, and he could barely stop from pulling over by a pay phone, even though his mother's house was around the corner. He parked by the house, got out of the car, and went in through the iron gate.

His mother looked slightly startled when he hugged her. She came out to greet him as usual, and he hurried to her and enveloped her in his arms, pressed her to his chest, and then quickly let go when he realized he was hugging his mother and that the last time he had done this was when his father died. Once inside, she asked what had happened and he said nothing, that he had to make a phone call, and he went into his father's study. He tried the apartment on Borochov—he rarely called her there because he didn't want to disturb her—and when there was no answer he tried at home, but she wasn't there either. He sat at the desk for a few more minutes, stroking the shiny oak surface, wondering where she could be. The large dining table was already set, and as soon as he sat down his mother put a bowl of soup in front of him. He asked what it was and she said it was something new, cream of spinach. He asked, "A recipe from the paper?" When she looked defensive, he said, "It looks wonderful," and ate the soup heartily, complimenting her several times.

She sat opposite him with her back to the big window, her gray hair lit up by the sun, and he could tell that she was eyeing him suspiciously. She clutched an old dish towel that had a print of cows on it, part of a set that Ilana's parents once sent them. His mother had seen one of the towels at their place and loved it, and Ilana said, "Take them all." His mother protested, but it was clear that she had fallen in love with the cows, and Ilana packed the set up for her: six towels, an oven mitt, and matching apron.

He felt a wave of generosity toward his mother, and when she took the empty soup bowl to the kitchen and asked if he wanted a leg or a breast, he said, "You mean you don't remember what I like anymore?"

She said, "You're always changing your mind."

He said, "You're right," and smiled. "I'll have a leg." And when she came back with a plate of chicken, new potatoes, and the cauliflower with tomato sauce that he had consistently liked all these years, he said, "We're thinking, maybe, of moving to Jerusalem."

He could see her struggling to contain her joy. Not only was her hair glowing now, her entire face seemed lit up from inside, as if a flashlight were roaming beneath her skin, and he thought he also noticed the little tremor in her hands that attacked her when she tried to disguise stress or excitement. He sipped the grapefruit juice she poured him—she knew he was coming and had bought fresh juice—and when he realized that with his sudden generosity he had given her something that did not belong to him—he had never seriously discussed moving to Jerusalem with Shira or Dana—he said, "But it's just an idea, so don't get too excited yet."

She shook her head eagerly and said, "No, no, I understand." After a pause, she asked, "But what made you decide to move back?"

"We haven't decided anything yet, Mom. It's just an option for the future; it's not even relevant now."

"Why not? Because of her father?"

He remembered Max, whom he had failed to take into account in his Jerusalem fantasy. His mother got up to bring him a dish of compote, and he heard her open and close the door of the cabinet where she kept the little glass dishes, the ones he had eaten out of as a child. It always amazed him that she had managed to keep them in one piece all these years. She came back, and only then did he notice that she was dragging her leg. She sat down again and sighed to herself, and since he didn't want to completely divest her from the gift he had given, he said, "For now it's just an idea, it still needs to be thought through."

"It's a good idea."

He asked if she still had the whole set of dishes or if any had broken.

"The whole set," she said, and asked if he wanted some more compote.

Although he was full, he said he would love some more, because he wanted to flatter her, and when she went into the kitchen again he wondered if after he inherited the set he would also manage to keep it intact, and he knew he wouldn't. He could already see the little dishes breaking one by one, shattering on the floor or in the sink, dropped by clumsy hands, until not a single dish remained.

(1 5)

No one was home when she got out of school. The nurse didn't ask any questions when Dana lied and said she was sick; she let her go without even calling her father, who in any case was in Jerusalem and couldn't be contacted. "Just promise me you'll go straight home," Esti said, and Dana promised.

When she went up to the classroom to get her backpack, she met

Tamar, who asked where she was going. "I don't feel well," she said, and Tamar asked what was wrong, and she said she had a sore throat.

"I'll call you later then," Tamar said.

Dana ran down the steps and out into the street through the gate and heard the bell ringing for recess. She felt free and a little excited, as if she were setting off on a great adventure.

She tried to decide where to go—to hang around Sheinkin, or maybe Dizengoff Center, or the market; it occurred to her that she could also go to the beach if she wanted—but her feet carried her to Allenby, and within minutes she found herself close to home, and she sat down at the café on the corner. The waitress gave her a menu as if she were a regular customer. She dug around the inside pocket of her backpack to count her money and ordered a lemonade. Even though she had enough money to get something to eat, she didn't dare, afraid she might have counted wrong and would get stuck with a check she couldn't pay, and the owners wouldn't believe her when she swore she lived a few houses down and her dad would come and pay them that afternoon, and they would call the police. On the other hand, she thought, everyone had believed her today: Esti, Tamar, the waitress, and her father, who was at his meeting in Jerusalem now and was certainly unaware that his daughter had cut class for the first time in her life.

She drank her lemonade and counted her money again, but she still didn't have the courage to order a piece of cake or a sandwich. She was sorry she wasn't the calm person she had hoped to be; she wasn't the opposite of her father; even with the huge distance that separated them now, you could still see how similar they were. She suddenly had no idea what to do with her free morning. She wondered if this was how unemployed adults felt—free and confused and vaguely guilty—and if this was how her father felt. He had looked so happy before leaving this morning, relieved that he finally had somewhere real to go. She suddenly missed school and thought perhaps she had made a mistake, because her excitement and freedom had been overcome by fear, by a feeling that although her home was only a few yards away, she had left it very far behind.

She had never sat in a café on her own before. She watched the passersby who filled the street. No one looked at her as she sat at the outside table, sucking the last drops of lemonade through a straw, a backpack on her knees. She wondered if a few years from now she would remember this morning and say to herself, That was the first time I sat in a café alone. She didn't know whether this morning was important. She asked for the check, and when the waitress put it down on a little dish in front of her, she calculated the tip; her father left ten or fifteen percent, depending on his mood, but she left twenty. The check was so low she was afraid to leave less. Then she got up, disappointed at the hollowness of this adventure, heaved her backpack onto her shoulders, turned onto Bialik, and went upstairs to the apartment.

It was strange to be home without them. Despite the heat wave, there was a coolness inside, as in a cave or an abandoned ruin, both pleasant and troubling. Usually, when she came home from school, all the windows were open, the music from the living room blaring down into the street, as if a sixteen-year-old lived there rather than her father. The apartment always smelled of the dishes he cooked, which she refused to taste on principle because that represented reconciliation with someone who had no idea how to fight with her.

She went into her room and lay down on her bed. Now she wished she had found the guts to order something to eat at the café. Their sandwiches, which came on big platters with lettuce and arugula salad, looked very good. She was hungry, but she knew what was in the fridge: leftovers from a Shabbat lunch with Rona and Tamar. She was sick of these communal meals, sometimes at their place and sometimes at Rona's. "I'm sick of it!" she had hurled at her father once, when she refused to go with them to Friday-night dinner.

"You're sick of everything," he replied indifferently, as if stating a fact, as if he weren't angry.

She yelled from her room, "That's right, I *am* sick of everything. Especially of you!" and pictured him rushing to her room from the bathroom, where he was shaving, and standing in her doorway and asking firmly what was up with her lately, demanding that she tell him everything, sitting on the edge of her bed with bits of shaving cream on his cheeks, looking at her tenderly—not his new tenderness, which was fearful and demanding, but the old kind, the automatic unsophisticated kind. But her father just yelled from the bathroom that he was sick of the way she talked, and then she heard him wash his face and spit into the sink, and Shira knocked on the door, which was ajar, and came in and stood opposite her, drying her hair with a towel, and asked what was wrong, what was *really* wrong.

"Can we talk?" she asked.

Dana said no, and when Shira asked why not, she said, "Because there's nothing to talk about."

Shira said, "Well, when there is, will we talk?" She said no again, because there wouldn't be anything to talk about ever, and Shira smiled and said, "Okay," and left the room.

She didn't want understanding, she wanted anger. She remembered the terrible fight between Rika Kahane and her eldest daughter, Liat. It was at the slumber party last year, which now seemed far away, impossible—how could she have wanted to join the team? It was still going, rejecting some girls, accepting others, and Tamar, despite her repeated proclamations, was still part of it. The others had all been asleep when Liat came home late from a party. Rika, whose nervous pacing on the ground floor had kept Dana company in the too-quiet room, followed her daughter upstairs. She whispered something, and then a door slammed, and then there were more whispers. Then she heard their hushed voices in the next room, and the door opened, and there was the sound of Liat's bare feet running down the stairs, then her mother's high heels clicking after her. They kept on fighting in the kitchen. Dana could hear every word, as if the stairwell served as a megaphone. Liat called her mother evil, a castrator; Rika told her to watch her mouth; her daughter told her to watch her husband. Rika asked what exactly she was implying and that if she had something to say she should come out and say it, without playing games. Liat shouted, "Don't play innocent. You know exactly what kind of games Dad is playing, and you know who with!"

"Who?" Rika screamed, and then she repeated her question quietly. "Who, Liat?"

"Come on, Mom!" Liat screeched, "don't make out as if you don't know!"

"I don't," Rika said, and she sounded like a child. "You tell me."

"Boys!" Liat screamed, and her scream turned to a wail midway. "Dad's screwing boys—"

Her mother broke in. "Shut your mouth, Liat. I'm warning you."

"I won't!" Liat sobbed. "You may be willing to keep quiet, but I'm not. I'm calling him in Germany right now and telling him we're not having him back."

"You will do no such thing," Rika said firmly. "I'm warning you, you shut your big mouth."

"It's Dad who should shut his big mouth, if he could stop giving blow jobs for one minute!" Then she heard a shriek, different from the previous ones, and Liat sobbed, "Are you crazy? What are you hitting me for? Are you nuts?" Then she heard the fridge door open and close, and the microwave bleep, and the sound of a chair being dragged across the marble floor. Dana had been astonished to discover that people could fight and eat at the same time.

After a few minutes of silence, during which Dana tried to guess what they were eating, she heard Liat yell, "Stop it, leave me alone! Get away from me!" There were sounds of crying, but she wasn't sure whose until she heard Rika declare, "Liati, you're high. You've been smoking something, that's why you're so hungry. You never come home hungry." Then Liat's voice again, sobbing with her mouth full, "Leave me alone!" The chair was dragged across the floor again; she heard water running in the sink, and Rika told her daughter this was the last time she was going to any parties, that she was not having a fourteen-year-old girl smoking drugs, she wanted to know what the other parents thought of it, and she was calling to ask them tomorrow, but tonight she didn't want to see her face anymore.

"Go to your room and stop stuffing yourself like a stoned cow," she said. Liat started wailing again, the desperate wails of a little girl. "Mom," she cried, "Dad's a homo!"

"So what?" her mother said. "He's your dad. It doesn't matter what he does, whether he's gay or straight; it shouldn't make any difference to you. Liati, he's a wonderful man and he's a wonderful father, and that's what matters, do you hear me?" She heard her voice coming closer to the stairs. "Come here, where are you going? Liati?" "I'm going to throw up!" the girl screamed.

At that moment Dana asked herself why none of the girls in the room had woken up from the noise. She heard footsteps running up the stairs again, and the door of the bathroom Liat shared with Lilach slammed shut. Dana couldn't tell if the sounds coming through the wall were vomiting or sobbing, and when she heard the toilet being flushed she realized it was both, and then she heard Rika coming slowly up the stairs, and the door to the master bedroom slammed too.

That was the anger she wanted, the kind that leaves cracks in the walls, which then seem to keep standing as if nothing had happened: the next day there was no trace of the fight, and at breakfast—which they all ate on the patio, and which was described by Rika, who looked serene and smily as always, as "brunch"—you couldn't guess what the two of them had been through that night: the daughter, who pushed her spinach-ricotta omelet around the plate with her fork and said she felt nauseated, and her mother, who with loving, perfectly made-up eyes, begged her to eat. Dana wanted someone to beg *her* to eat too, but no one did.

Now she lay on her bed and felt a lump in her throat and tried to remember the last time she had cried. It was over a year ago, in the kitchen, on the day she stopped piano lessons, when her father started going out with Shira. She couldn't remember why she had cried, but she remembered he had hugged her, and even though she had already felt uncomfortable at his touch, there was something wondrous about his arms. That must have been their last hug, she thought.

A few days ago, Tamar told her she needed a bra. "You need a size zero," she determined, eyeballing her chest like an experienced lingerie saleswoman. "If you'd like, we can go together. I don't need one but I'll go with you." Dana agreed. "Or we could ask my mom to get you one," she continued. "Or Shira, ask Shira, or you can get one on your own, and if you go on your own, ask for size zero, remember." Dana said okay and prayed for Tamar to shut up.

She lay on her stomach, swallowed her tears, and felt the two lumps on her chest crushed against the mattress. Lately she felt like a collection of lumps. Her brain felt like a lump, and her stomach, and in her heart was a permanent lump of insult; she also sensed the presence of a lump between her legs, smaller and harder than the others. I have cancer, she thought, teenage cancer. She pressed her thighs together and her stomach into the mattress, and suddenly there was something pleasant about that hard tension, as if she could see the precise location of the lump, feel it with her fingers, break it open. She moved carefully, almost impercep-tibly, on the bed, and held her breath. Something told her to stop, the same something that filled her with shame, but something else made her continue. She rocked back and forth on the mattress, which was soft, submissive, lessening the tension instead of focusing it. She slid her hand under her stomach. Now she moved on her fist, flinching at first from the pain caused by her knuckles, as if her fist was trying to punish her for what she was doing; it occurred to her that her father or Shira could come home any minute and maybe she should put her key in the lock. But she couldn't get up; she was afraid she would never again find the precise location of that lump which was waiting, full of expectation. She kept moving rhythmically on her fist, taut inside but keenly aware of every external noise, knowing instinctively where she was going but not getting there. It was the most wonderful frustration she had ever experi-enced.

All sorts of thoughts went through her mind, so many that her head started to feel empty: empty of thoughts but full of scenes and fragments of sentences. *Size zero,* she told herself, over and over again, but this time with no pain or anger; she saw her father and Shira touring a lovely coun-try estate, surrounded with lush greenery, the kind you see on British television shows. *Size zero*—the words flashed before her like a banner ad trailed by an airplane on the beach, and in fact they did make her angry but in a pleasing way, as if they had come especially to distract her body a little longer from the destination it was seeking on the mattress. Then she started to feel warmth spread through the small of her back and the folds of her stomach. *Size zero*—she saw herself sitting at the café, looking at the menu, but she couldn't read what was on it and she knew she had to concentrate now but not think. Disjointed pictures and words blended with the heat waves that turned into chills and a bodily hum. *Size zero*—she could no longer feel her fist or the mattress, only the lump between her legs, which had become everything, consuming the pictures and words, the country estates, the cafés, the bras and the menus, and her, and the girl she left behind.

They sat embraced in the car, in the hospital parking lot. Her ear was against his chest and she felt his heart beat rapidly and thought, So much strength from such a frightened man! But with the word *frightened,* she thought of her father, who today, for the first time since being moved from Internal Medicine to the nursing ward, had looked truly alarmed, as if he realized he would not be getting out, that he would never again see the hospital's lobby, the parking lot, the guard at the hut who always said goodbye to him with a sorrowful nod.

Yesterday she had told the landlord at the apartment in Borochov that she was leaving. "Thank God," Yonatan had said, with a look of victory. "Now we can find something on a good moshav." She said yes, knowing they both knew they would never leave the city, that looking for a house in the country was a way to preserve a shared fantasy that would distract them from other things: her father, for example, or the child they wouldn't have.

Dana still had not joined the search. On Fridays she would emerge from her room after dinner and put the weekend papers down in front of them, where she had circled various classified ads with a purple marker. "This sounds big enough so your dad could come and live with us," she said once, and pointed to an ad for a rental on a moshav between Tel Aviv and Jerusalem. They both looked at her with surprise; they had never discussed Max with her. She had met him only once, on Passover, when they took him to Jerusalem for her grandmother's Seder, a few days before his first hospitalization.

It was a strange drive. Shira's father was very alert and talkative and tried to make Dana laugh several times. She sat next to him and politely answered his questions about school and her hobbies. Then Max asked if she missed her mother. The car fell silent. Shira didn't know if she was embarrassed by his question or surprised by the realization that he remembered the things she had told him at various opportunities about Yonatan and Dana. She was unsure how to handle the discovery that, during all these months, when she had been convinced she was having one-way conversations with him for his amusement, to pass the time and dull the pain of spending time with him, her father had been listening and recalled every word, and now he asked Dana if she missed her mother. It occurred to Shira that the question might not be addressed to the girl but to her.

"Yes," Dana said. Max nodded and asked no more questions, and it wasn't clear if he was quiet because he had grown tired and had retreated again or because he had obtained all the information he needed. During the meal, when Yonatan's mother tried to engage him in conversation, he answered with nods and feeble smiles, but his foggy eyes looked very alert, both defensive and longing as they followed Dana.

"You were so nice," Shira told her later, after they took Max home. Dana said, "Your dad's a sweetie," and although she had never thought of him that way, the description seemed apt for his performance that evening—a virtuoso recital never to be repeated. He was not a sick old man or an alien, and not her father either. He was a sweetie.

Dana asked what he had, what exactly his illness was, and Yonatan said, "He's just old."

His daughter gave him a look full of teenage disdain and said he wasn't that old, and Shira said, "He's seventy-seven." Dana said, "That may have been considered old once, but not anymore." Shira felt as if the girl was trying to tell her something, forgive her for something. When-ever they were alone, Dana came up with questions, as if she had pre-pared a list and was waiting for the chance to ask them, in a businesslike incidental tone, ostensibly uninterested in Shira's responses. But her movements, the way her body tried to show disinterest, revealed not only curiosity but great urgency. One day she asked if Shira thought about her father's death, if she thought he would die soon. Shira, who was washing dishes, turned off the faucet—the occasion seemed to demand silence— and looked at Dana—who sat at the table and dipped her finger in a now-cold cup of instant coffee, putting it in and out of the cup, her eyes watching the drops drip on the tablecloth—and said, "Yes."

"And what do you think? That when he dies things will be harder for you or easier?" Dana asked.

"I don't know. Why do you ask?"

"No reason."

Shira turned the faucet back on and continued washing the dishes, although she no longer saw the plate she was holding under the water but rather the question that hovered in the air. They were both quiet until the noise of the water and the cutlery clanging became unbearable to her, and she turned the faucet off again, wiped her hands and sat down across the table from Dana and lit a cigarette and said, "I'm dead scared, Dana. I'm absolutely terrified."

"But your mom's already dead. So it's like you've experienced it, isn't it?"

"Not at all," Shira said. "It's not something you gain experience in. And anyway my mother wasn't ill; it was different."

"Mine wasn't either. My dad told me she died on the spot." She looked up, smiling, and said, "Give me a drag, okay?"

"A drag? Are you crazy?"

"I want to try it."

Shira said it wasn't a good idea to start smoking, at her age or ever, and Dana asked when she had started. She said, "In high school, when I was fifteen."

"I'm twelve."

"But what do you need it for? You'll just gag and cough."

"That's better then, isn't it? I'll hate it now, and I'll never want to smoke. Think about it as something educational."

"Yeah, sure."

"Seriously," Dana said. "You'd be doing me a favor."

"Okay, but don't tell your dad, promise?"

"Of course." Dana reached eagerly to take the cigarette Shira offered her, and said, "You neither."

"Of course not. Are you crazy? I'm not going to snitch on myself."

"Not about this," Dana said, and held the cigarette gingerly between her fingers. "About what we talk about."

"What about?"

"Death and all that."

Death and all that, she thought, as she watched Dana hold the edge of the cigarette up to her lips, take a short puff, and try not to cough. With her mouth full of smoke and her cheeks puffed up, she waved her hand as if asking what the next step was. "Blow it out already!" Shira said, but Dana seemed to be stuck with the smoke. "Blow it out!"

Dana started to cough and Shira got up to get her a glass of water, and when she gave her the glass she took the cigarette and put it back between her own lips. When Dana kept coughing, squirting water out of her mouth all over the tablecloth, she slapped her back until she heard the choking turn to laughter, and she also started laughing and kept slapping Dana's back, gently this time, until her fingers ran into a bra strap, and almost stopped there. The kitchen was quiet again, with only the sounds of Dana's breathing and the soft rubbing of Shira's fingers on her T-shirt. Dana was no longer a girl but not yet a young woman, and when Shira looked at her hunched back, her head drooping between her shoulders, and her hair, which was neither straight nor curly and reminded her of her own, as tangled as her inner being, she thought Dana was like a chrysalis.

She tried to remember herself at that age but could not. She could only remember what came before and after, and she thought about her father in the nursing ward—he was also a kind of chrysalis, but the kind from which nothing would hatch. She could only recall the time when she worshiped him and the time when she hated him, but not what came in between. Yesterday she fed him with a teaspoon. She had managed to avoid doing it, trying not to visit him at mealtimes, not to imagine him opening his mouth for the spoon proferred by a nurse's hasty, expert hand, convincing herself that if there was still any space where she could permit herself not to be the daughter of someone terminally ill, meals, and bathing, and visits to the toilet were that space—visits she made with a wheelchair that had a big circle cut out of the seat, which the orderly would position over the toilet bowl and then encourage her father, with a firm voice, to do his business. At those moments she would go out to the hallway, to smoke or make a call from the cell phone she had purchased. She would talk to Dana, ask how she was and what she was doing, trying to prolong their chat, or have practical conversations with Yonatan, mainly about what they would have for dinner, what needed to be bought, what should be thrown away. When they finished talking and she turned the phone off and went back into her father's room, she would tell herself bitterly, but also with a certain degree of relief, that she had become one of those people who sit on hallway benches and have loud conversations with their relatives right under signs prohibiting the use of cell phones.

One morning, she came back to her father's room after a cigarette and phone break and heard him shouting from the bathroom. Unable to find the orderly, she went in and found him lying on the floor with his pajama bottoms down at his knees, clasping the cord attached to the buzzer, the wheelchair tipped on its side with two wheels in the air, like a car in an accident. With an efficiency that surprised and saddened her, because she knew she would go back to it again and again, she lifted her father up, pulled up his pants, sat him carefully in the chair, and wheeled him back to his bed. Then she went to the nurses' station and said, "My father fell in the bathroom. The orderly left him there and he fell. I want the doctor to come and see him right away." Then she returned to the bathroom and flushed the toilet. As they waited for the doctor, she stroked her father's hand as he stared at her with foreign eyes that welled up constantly. After the doctor had examined him and found no injuries, she went out for a cigarette and sat down on the bench. The images had acquired a sound track: some shouting from the bathroom, one long complaining "Aaaagh," a soft and grateful "Shiraleh" when she picked him up off the floor, and the sniffles that followed his tears.

(17)

Alon the handyman, who came to give a quote, had read Yonatan's books. "It's a shame, no?" he said, as they stood in the study. "Where will you write?" He was a philosophy student; Rona said he had good hands and was honest and reliable. "It's a shame, no?" he repeated, and looked at Yonatan and ran his hand over the condemned wall.

"It used to be a balcony anyway," Yonatan said, as if that were a worthy excuse, and Alon said he understood. "And I understand the wife also writes?" Yonatan nodded and the handyman persisted and asked where she would write now, and where would he write? "Have you thought of that?" he asked, as if he were not the builder but a concerned publisher.

"We'll figure something out," Yonatan said, and rushed him out to the living room and the kitchen. Alon soon started scribbling sketches in his pad, pacing back and forth between the rooms, rapping on the walls with his knuckles, until he gave an estimate and immediately lowered it, even before Yonatan had time to haggle. "A special discount for artists," he said, and told Yonatan he also did some writing. "Not for public consumption," he added, and they agreed he would start work next week and shook hands.

Yonatan liked the man's name and thought if he ever had a son he would name him Alon. Dana and Alon, he said, and liked the combination, but he would have preferred another daughter, although he couldn't think of a name for a girl, and reminded himself that he would prefer not to have any more children at all. He wondered whether thinking about another child was evidence that he was sick of his life, or if in fact he was so content that he was ready to include another person.

Yesterday he took Shira with him to a parent-teacher meeting. It was the first of the new school year—the first he had ever gone to willingly, not just to participate in by expressing his opinion about matters concerning his daughter but to share his affairs with the world. No one would dare pity him now or hit on him. He knew he was thereby giving up his two favorite aspects of widowhood, and doing so happily. He was so caught up in excitement over the launching of his new life that he forgot they would probably run into Esti. When he saw her in the gym, sitting with her back to them in the first row, he felt a brief chill and quickly put his hand on Shira's shoulder, protecting her from a danger of which she was unaware, but then he removed his hand and shoved it in his pants pocket. He led her to the last row and they sat down. He searched the gym, habitually looking for Rona and praying Esti would not turn around and see him. Shira asked what was going on. "You look tense," she said; he denied it and hoped Esti would turn around now, so he could give her a little smile, with lips as tight they had been when he had kissed her—he couldn't now imagine kissing her, and in fact he hadn't really kissed her, not like he knew how to kiss, he reassured himself—so he could get it over with now instead of suffering all evening.

Esti turned around and saw him. Then she saw Shira. He smiled and waved and felt relieved, but then Esti started walking toward him and he chided himself for sitting at the edge of the row. A mole and a bee, he remembered thinking of her once, but when he looked at her making her way toward them—her hair was longer, tied back in a playful ponytail—he thought for some reason of a boomerang and didn't know what he would say or how to introduce Shira, and whether Esti's "nice to meet you" would give away their one-night stand, the one that hadn't happened.

She said, "Hello, Yonatan," and he remembered her whispering "Yonatan, Yonatan" on the floor and how it had annoyed him until it started turning him on and he came, and he remembered his bare back against the fridge and Esti huddled on her side and the dish of cookies, and he suddenly felt humiliated. He was already planning to ask how she was, but Esti now smiled at Shira and said, "You're Shira Klein, right?" Shira nodded, and the nurse said she was a big fan, her number-one fan, and Shira said she was very flattered.

Esti said, "Honestly, I've never met an author I like face-to-face." Yonatan remembered that woman from the mall, he couldn't recall her name or what she looked like, but he saw himself pushing a shopping cart, aware of her presence behind him, excited by the possibility of late-morning meaningless sex. Shira said, "Thanks so much, really, that's so nice to hear." She asked for the nurse's name and her fan told her, Esti, and Yonatan was suddenly alarmed by the idea that he might still find himself wandering around a DIY store alone one day, with a huge cart and a small erection, and he grabbed Shira's hand and demonstratively put it on his thigh.

Esti asked, "Are you working on something else now? Please say yes!" Shira said she was, and he felt her fingers squirming uncomfortably between his own, which gripped them like a vise.

Esti said she couldn't wait, that she would be her first customer, and he suddenly heard himself say, "You don't need to buy it, we'll send you a copy."

The word *send* sounded violent to him, and the *we'll* even more so, and Esti smiled at him—it was suddenly inconceivable that those lips had once sucked him—and said, "Thanks, Yonatan, that's really nice."

As usual, it was Rona who came to the rescue. She walked up to them and squeezed into a vacant chair next to Shira, smelling of perfume and haste, and asked what had happened and if they'd already started. Esti said goodbye and went back to her seat. Later, when the three of them went out to a café, with Shira and Rona sitting facing him, exchanging gossip, he wondered whether Rona had ever been interested in him, if she had tried to hit on him and he hadn't noticed, and he asked himself, if he could fall in love with her, or sleep with her, and he didn't have an answer, and then he watched them share a pasta dish and asked himself, Why Shira, why not Rona? and again he had no answer. "Give me a bite," he said, and they both handed him their forks. Even if there was an answer, it didn't really interest him, and he took Shira's fork and put it in his mouth. He had never enjoyed such bad pasta so much. It was strange, he thought, as he asked the waitress for another fork and ate off their plate, that it didn't annoy him, and that this café, which until not long ago he had looked down on, now seemed fine—as if it had gone through some major renovation, although nothing about it had changed—and it was all because of the Pettuccine Alfredo.

(1 8)

She hated school trips. At first she was going to get out of it, ask her dad to send a note saying she couldn't go—he liked drafting these notes, enjoyed hating school for her—but a week before the trip she changed her mind. She decided to join in, and moreover she decided to enjoy herself, a decision that filled her with new anxiety.

She sat on the floor in Tamar's room and watched her pack a duffel bag, although it was too early to pack. Tamar stood in front of her closet wondering what to take, even though she knew, as always, what she wanted. Dana looked at her thin legs, her thighs that didn't stick to each other, her round little bottom, which boys would love, of course, unlike her own, which was big and shapeless and—when she dared study it, standing on a chair opposite the bathroom mirror—looked like unbaked dough. Recently, she was more cautious when getting down off chairs, and did so slowly, holding on to the edge of something, because jumping shook her breasts, which were swelling rapidly despite her prayers—she hated these lumps of flesh with all her heart and thought they hated her too, they had picked the wrong girl to grow on.

Perhaps that was what had made her become a vegetarian. She hadn't touched meat since the beginning of summer, and as if to spite her it turned out to be a very carnivorous time; her father cooked meat for himself and Shira almost every day. They no longer tried to convince her to join them, did not protest when she helped herself to some fruit or yogurt and withdrew into her room. They accepted the fact that she was living as their lodger and were perhaps even relieved.

She looked at the small of Tamar's back, at her prominent shoulder blades, her hair tied up in a ponytail, so smooth and well-defined— simple hair, she thought, and dreamy—and at the back of her neck with its soft, feathery down. She watched Tamar open and close the doors of the beautiful closet her mother had specially ordered for her from a carpenter, as a bat mitzvah present, and when she thought about the party they had had in the spring, she felt as if the event belonged to the distant past, to the days when she could still conceive of something making her happy in the future. Next spring she would be thirteen. Now, in October, that seemed far away, but she was hoping that by then something would happen to change everything: she would turn into a different person, or die.

But she didn't want to die. That was the problem. She wanted to live, but differently, without the transparent filth she felt clinging to her with every movement, every breath and thought—awake, sitting in class or walking down the street; asleep, rubbing up against the mattress, guilty and addicted. To be her was to be a downer, flawed; the blemish, she thought, had spread from inside and was seeping out. She would have given anything to be smaller and cleaner, to go back to that winter night of the accident, when her father came to get her from the neighbors and she went downstairs with him to their empty apartment, which suddenly belonged only to the two of them. She would have given anything to be the girl who knew nothing and who could be lied to, who *should* be lied to because she was only a girl.

Ziv and his parents had taken her on an outing. They went to a little amusement park inside a mall on the outskirts of town and were very patient when she asked to ride the bumper cars over and over again. Then they went to a movie, and although it seemed strange that both Ziv and his parents were taking care of her, she happily dedicated herself to having fun. When they came back in the early evening, Ziv carried her up the steps on his shoulders, and as they passed her apartment door she banged on it with her fists, but Ziv's mother quickly held her little hands and said, "Shhhh, Mommy and Daddy are sleeping." Dana knew she was lying because they never went to sleep before she did, and she burst out laughing. Ziv's father, who looked distracted and had not said a word all afternoon, hushed her, putting his finger to his lips and then to hers, and when they sat her down in the kitchen and gave her dinner—orzo and salad—Ziv's mother suddenly burst into tears. Dana asked, "Ziv's Mommy, why are you crying?" She said she wasn't crying, that it was because she had been chopping onions, and Dana told them that her mother also cried when she chopped onions. Ziv's mother said, "Does she? Really?" and started crying again, and Ziv's father put his finger on his lips again, but this time it wasn't her he was hushing. She laughed, and Ziv's parents also laughed, but their laughter sounded exaggerated, like when evil cartoon characters laugh, and she got scared because she suddenly realized there had been something strange about this whole day. She asked where her parents were, and they looked at each other. Ziv's father said they were busy right now and had asked them to take care of her. "So you're taking care of me now?" she asked, and the three of them nodded. "Until Daddy comes," Ziv's father said. Their names were Alice and Reuven, but at the time she only knew their titles. "Is Daddy going to come?" she asked, and Reuven and Alice said he would, soon, and through the kitchen window she saw it was already dark. "But why not Mommy?" she asked and pushed her plate away. "Because Mommy is very busy," the man said, and the woman stood with her back to them and sniffled. "More than Daddy?" she asked, and Reuven said yes, much more, and she was proud of her mom for being busier than her dad for a change. She heaped more orzo onto her spoon—it was the tastiest orzo she had ever had, better than the kind her mom made. She ate and watched Ziv's parents watching her, and thought she was lucky that her parents were so young, because Ziv's parents were very old and not as pretty as hers. "Ziv's Daddy," she asked the old man who sat across from her eating orzo, "when will my daddy come?"

Her father showed up looking old. There was something gray in his face, and his eyes were large. He didn't say anything when he saw her, and the other grown-ups were also quiet. Ziv went to his room. Dana got off her chair, went to her father, and wrapped her arms around his thigh. He leaned down and picked her up. "She ate well," Alice said, and her dad thanked them. When they left and started going down the steps, she tightened her grip around his neck and leaned her head on his cheek, because she suddenly knew with certainty that this day, which had been wonderful, was actually not wonderful but terrible, and the stubble on her father's face was not the kind she liked to rub her cheek against, and the cigarette smell coming from his skin was not the usual smell but something sour and unpleasant. They went down step by step, only one floor but a very steep one, and in her heart she wished they could keep going down, that the steps would go on forever, because as long as they hadn't reached home, it was still possible that nothing had happened and she was just tired. After all, while she was eating dinner in Ziv's kitchen, she had heard the weather report jingle from the TV in the living room—the same jingle that followed her and her mother on their way to the bathroom at night—so she realized it was very late and something had gone wrong with this day. Although her eyes were closed and her head was buried in his neck, she knew they had reached the door, because behind her she heard her aunt and uncle's voices. But she didn't hear her mother, and she suddenly opened her eyes and turned her head, and with one fleeting look she immortalized all they had left behind: the stairwell and the hope that the nice day would end with a normal evening—a normal bath, a story, and two kisses. When her father put his hand on the door handle, she asked, "Is Mommy home?" He shook his head and pushed the handle down, but before opening the door, he let go, pressed her head to him and kissed her cheek hard, and she thought she could hear a strange animal sound coming from his mouth. "Is she busy?" she asked, and he shook his head again and opened the door. It was not her mother she missed, but the hope she had during those terrible minutes in the stairwell.

Tamar asked if she thought two sweaters, three T-shirts, and four pairs of jeans were too much. Maybe she didn't need a sweater because it might not be cold, but it was better to have one, although maybe two was too many. She would just take the one that some boy had complimented her on last year, a boy she sneered at now but whose compliment was still valid. "So what do you think?" she asked, and turned to Dana. Dana said she didn't know and looked at Tamar's tanned knees, her stomach that peeked out under her tight tank top, and her perfect flat chest, and then she looked at her face. She wasn't a pretty girl, but at least she was still a girl. She must have looked like her father, the dark young man who may have been a medical student, Tamar said, or maybe a law student, who had donated his sperm. Even though it wasn't really a donation because the women paid for it, Tamar said, with the same matter-of-factness with which she talked about the man whose identity was concealed from her, as it was from her mother. Perhaps, Dana thought, that was what made Tamar and her mother so close, such good friends: they were equals because neither of them had the key to the door behind which that man was hiding. Dana envied her for that. All these years of their friendship, she had wanted everything Tamar had: her home, her mother, her body. She suddenly also envied her for not having a father.

She tried to imagine her father without an identity but could not. She tried to give him the qualities of a different man, a made-up stranger, but he shed them like baggy clothing. She couldn't peel away who he was from him. She couldn't peel him away from her. She tried to imagine what it was like to grow up knowing that one of your parents was neither living nor dead, and that was the way it would always be for you, one less parent to grieve over. She envied Tamar's freedom, the genes that someone had given her for money without being there himself to love her, to fight with her, to pick her up out of bed when she had a bad dream, a sliver of his identity shed from his skin like paint that stuck to her each time he carried her in his arms.

"It's really too bad you're not coming," Tamar said, and sat on her duffel bag. "You're missing out." Then she added softly, "It's really too bad you won't lighten up a bit. It's too hard for you."

They had hardly seen each other all summer. There was tension between them, which along with the heat and humidity had made their meetings especially oppressive. Sometimes they hung around Dizengoff Center together and went into clothing and CD stores or to a movie, and a couple of times they met at Tamar's, where there was air-conditioning and it was more pleasant, in every way, and there was no smell of meat-balls and cigarettes and sex.

"I *am* coming," she said.

Tamar leaped up and said, "Yes!"

"I think I am. I'm not sure." She tried to imagine herself having fun, sitting in the bus all the way to the Galilee with her classmates. She saw herself sitting next to Tamar, almost stuck to her, so Tamar would infect her with her laughter, her ease, the darkness of her skin, her boniness and suppleness. And she would stay close to her for the remaining five days of the trip and would insist on sleeping near her in the bunk beds they had been promised the hostel would have—either above or below her, as long as she was close enough to her.

Tamar said, "It's so awesome that you're coming!"

Dana wondered how someone could even want to be with her, and she mumbled, "Yes, I really hope it will be fun."

"I'm on top!" Tamar declared, and Dana asked what she meant.

"In the bed!" Tamar slid off her duffel bag onto the floor, leaned her back on it, put her legs up, and started cycling in thin air. "Let's work out! I have a tape." Dana said she didn't want to. "Oh, lighten up." Tamar sighed and spread her legs in the air, opening and closing them while she supported her hips with her hands. She said it was an excellent exercise for the thighs and stomach. She said it made your stomach flat. "So is it settled?" Dana didn't know what she meant. "That I'll be on top?"

"Yes, I don't care." She looked at the little slit Tamar's leggings made between her legs.

"Come on, do it too!" Tamar encouraged her, but she couldn't imagine lying on the floor in these clothes, which were purposely too large, and she couldn't take her eyes off that innocent slit, which opened and closed like an eye every time Tamar scissored her legs. "Come on!" Tamar said breathlessly, but Dana's eyes still refused to part with the blind eye that winked at her, and she suddenly understood something Shira had once told her about the danger of observation.

It was long ago, it seemed now, although she knew that a year and a few months were not enough to be considered long ago. Still, that late-night conversation seemed very distant, as if it belonged—like her bat mitzvah party, like the hope of growing up—to another era. It was just after Shira moved in with them, when there still was a *them,* when she and her father were the impenetrable, crowded entity they had been. Although perhaps they never were, she now thought. Perhaps she had deluded herself about their joint gloominess, just as she had deluded herself that Shira's arrival would banish it. They both had insomnia that night. They met at 1 A.M. in the kitchen, and Shira suggested they have some herbal tea. Dana hated herbal tea, but she agreed because Shira said it was calming and would help them fall asleep. They went out to the balcony and sat in the wicker chairs, resting their feet on the railing. Shira asked why she couldn't sleep and Dana said she didn't know. "You?"

"Thoughts," Shira said and lit a cigarette.

"About what?" Dana asked, and hoped she would talk about her dad, about love.

But Shira sighed and said, "About nothing. I'm just like that." It wasn't clear if she was addressing Dana or the darkness surrounding them. "I'm screwed up. My head is like a computer out of control, spewing out needless files, and I can't make it stop."

"I'm like that too."

"Really?"

"Yes." Dana sipped her tea, waiting for the calm.

"Yes, you look a bit like the suffering type."

That flattered her. "You too," she said, because she wanted to return the compliment.

"Oh, you have no idea. But I'm trying to change."

"Why?" Dana asked.

"Because it comes with a price. Cumulative damage, like smoking. How many years can you spend in constant suffering, without becoming worn down, without getting sick of it?"

She looked at Shira and tried to find signs of wear on her face, on her body, but she couldn't. She wondered if she was talking about the same kind of suffering—a constant longing to be someone else, someone other people would want to be. She glanced at Shira again and took another sip of tea, which was neither helping nor calming her, and knew their suffering wasn't the same. Shira looked so complacent, so serene in her plump body, beneath her smooth skin, in her T-shirt and underwear. Dana wanted to be her. Then she noticed Shira quickly wiping her eyes.

"Sorry," she said and put her cigarette out. "It just came out." She got up and went inside and came back with a roll of toilet paper and blew her nose. Dana saw that her cheeks were damp with tears and she had a small apologetic smile on her lips. Shira sat down again, lit a cigarette, and blew the smoke out toward the trees in the yard, the ones nobody took care of and yet they kept growing, satisfied with the rain that came or not in winter. Shira said she smoked too much. She was crying because she suddenly remembered her mother's funeral. It was one of the hottest days they'd ever had, she said, worse than a khamsin; they even talked about it on the news. She walked next to her father down the long path through the cemetery. Relatives and a cluster of her mother's good friends walked behind them. In front the Chevra Kadisha people carried the stretcher on which her mother's body lay, wrapped in a white sheet.

"One of them had a limp," she said. "He was in the back, right in front of me, holding one of the stretcher handles. They were walking too quickly for him. He was wearing a black suit and a black hat with a black yarmulke underneath, and he was sweating terribly. I remember walking next to my father, with my mother on the stretcher, and behind me I could hear crying and whispering, but all I could see was that undertaker, or whatever he was, hobbling along like a madman, almost running, and my heart ached for him." She quietly blew out her smoke. "Do you understand?"

Dana tried to imagine the breathless undertaker's limp. She wondered if it was the same as one of her teachers, who had polio as a child, or maybe he was like the beggar on Allenby, whose pants were always rolled up to his knees, exposing one healthy leg and one that was swollen, reddish-purple, and covered with blisters. Or maybe it was like the slight limp she herself once had, when she was three and stepped on a nail. She knew many kinds of limps, and she suddenly saw herself there with Shira at her mother's funeral, in the merciless heat, on the path in the cemetery where her own mother was also buried.

"Do you understand?" Shira asked again. "The saddest moment of my life—my mother was dead—and what was I doing? Feeling sorry for the undertaker. But that's not what bothers me, the fact that I felt sorry for him, because he really was pitiful. But it's that I somehow always find myself outside, observing rather than participating, as if I'm above life and death, even though I know I'm not. Sometimes I remember my mother's funeral and feel as if I wasn't even there."

Dana looked at her and said she hadn't been at her mother's funeral.

"You were little. They wanted to protect you from it." She wiped her eyes and said she was sorry. "I don't know where this outburst came from. It's hardly your fault."

"It's okay. You don't need a reason. Life is a horrible thing, isn't it?"

Shira smiled at her and said, "Not life. Observing it."

They both looked into the dark, at the survivor trees, which stood quiet and alert, and Shira leaned back and the wicker creaked, and she said that the world, in her opinion, was divided into two groups: those who observe and those who are observed, and she didn't know which group she wanted to belong to, or whether it was even up to her or was something you had at birth.

Dana didn't understand what she was talking about, but she liked the words. They sounded so serious, precise, and Shira asked if she understood again, and Dana nodded and continued to stare into the yard. Shira yawned and said, "Serious stuff, no?" Dana nodded again and kept sitting silently. She wanted to be a serious person, like Shira. "Nothing we can do about it," Shira said.

Even though Dana still didn't understand, she said, "Nothing at all."

Shira said she was tired and yawned again, and said, "Do you really think so?"

Dana said, "Nothing."

Shira got up and said she was going to sleep. "How about you?"

She said she wasn't tired yet and would stay up awhile, to think.

"But not too long." Shira stood behind her and put her hands on the chair's armrests, and for a moment Dana thought she was going to lean over and kiss her. Her body tensed up, trying to decide if it was interested in a kiss from an almost strange woman. It had been a long time since she had been kissed, she wasn't sure how long; her father embarrassed her with his hugs, but he rarely kissed her. She didn't see many relatives, and her grandmother Rachel wasn't the kissing type. It's been a long time, she thought, looking straight ahead and feeling Shira's breath on her neck; it smelled like lemon verbena and cigarettes. If she were a dog she might have also picked up her father's scent in there, she thought. Yes, she told herself, she wanted this kiss, from this woman, she wanted to be kissed by her so she could become her, and her skin bristled and her breath stopped, and the wicker creaked again, and she closed her eyes, and Shira said, "I'm beat," and went inside.

She heard Tamar breathing rapidly. She got up slowly and went over to the large window with its multiple panes, which looked out onto the backyard with the strange palm trees—everything was so beautiful in this house that you could sense it like a physical pain. "Well, what are you waiting for?" Tamar yelled from the floor. Dana went over, stood looking at her from above for a moment, and then lay down beside her and joined in.

(1 9)

Without noticing that it had happened, his dying became routine. She spent a few hours by his side every day, feeding him, arranging his things in the little cabinet. The nurses called them *personal items,* which amused her because, after spending so much time in this place, almost everything he touched became one of his personal items: the pale blue plastic cup he drank coffee from (and recently only a few sips of water here and there), the oxygen mask that hung over him and was occasionally held over his face when he had trouble breathing, the chair next to his bed—all these had become his own, and sometimes they struck her as more personal than the items stored in the cabinet, which no longer had any use: a leather wallet, a transistor radio, a wristwatch, a comb, a few handkerchiefs, a shaving kit, and reading glasses that broke her heart every time she saw them.

She parked the car in the mall's massive parking lot. Yonatan had gone to Jerusalem for a faculty meeting and she had promised to go grocery shopping, which she was now looking forward to like a night out. She left the hospital, the afternoon sun dazzling her pupils, which had been under flashing fluorescent lights all day, and said goodbye to the guard, who asked after her father. She was impatient to get to the mall, which she usually hated because it made her feel she was in a maze, and every time she went inside she had to take a mental photograph of the exit signs.

That morning, when she and Yonatan had said goodbye next to their adjacent cars—amused by the fact that, for the first time since meeting, they had both found parking spots right outside the building— she told him she loved him.

"Me too," he said, and looked at the cars' bumpers kissing. "Maybe we shouldn't move them?" He held her hand and she waited for him to say something—something momentous, as he always did when he held her hand. But he kept looking at the cars.

Finally she said, "It's your birthday next month."

"Don't remind me."

"You really are getting old. So what do you want?"

"As a present, you mean?" She nodded, and he said he didn't know. "Nothing. Don't get me anything."

"I'll get you something anyway, so you might as well tell me what you want; otherwise I'll get you something you don't need."

"Get me something I don't need," he said. "That's what I want."

Last spring he hadn't given her anything. They had been together for a year, but she assumed he didn't consider that long enough to justify buying a present. So she had ignored his birthday several months later. They were both slightly embarrassed to discover that Dana had bought each of them gifts: a Bugs Bunny T-shirt for her, and a CD of Dinu Lipatti playing Chopin for him. "We don't have this one," Dana said, and he thanked her. In the morning, after she went to school, he listened to the CD and told Shira he couldn't stand Chopin.

"How can you not stand Chopin?" she asked.

"That's just it," he said smugly. "He's canonical, that's why. All the aunties like him."

She told him he was a snob, he told her she was plebeian. She told him he was a know-it-all; he said she was unsophisticated. She said, "You are so childish," and he said, Yup. "By the way, what exactly are you rebelling against, at your age?" she asked, as they drank coffee in the kitchen while a mazurka played in the background.

"Old age, of course," he had said. "And talking about rebellion, she did this to me on purpose, my daughter. She knows I prefer Glenn Gould."

When she got into her car now and watched him get into his in her rearview mirror, she had thought about what she had just told him, how quickly the words had been removed from the shoulder of the road, as if swept up by the municipal cleaner's huge brushes, or perhaps they had metamorphosed quickly into a discussion of birthdays.

She went into the mall, inhaling the smell of pizza and air-conditioning. She stood by the escalator and tried to decide if she should go down to the supermarket or sit in one of the awful cafés on the upper floor. Her mother had liked those cafés. She enjoyed the menus, the large portions, the waitresses' uniforms, the bustle. When Shira would turn her nose up and say the coffee was bad and the prices were outrageous, her mother would say that coffee was coffee, and the cafés had a nice atmosphere.

"Atmosphere?" Shira would hiss. "You call this atmosphere?" She was in her early twenties and mocked her mother for her popular tastes, her lack of criticism, her joie de vivre. She seemed to mock her for everything back then, as if the mockery were both a form of communication and a silent plea.

"Then where do you suggest we sit?" her mother would ask. "Is there somewhere here you'd prefer? We can go wherever you want, I don't mind." Shira would say she was missing the point.

Now, as she sat at one of those cafés, beneath a green-and-white-striped umbrella, perusing a huge laminated menu, she could no longer remember what the point was. The disdain had since gone, making way for envy of people who lived from one moment to the next, from one bad café to another. She had fallen in love with Yonatan because he was like her. She had fallen in love with him because she thought he also longed to be a part of the thing he disdained. But their love had given her the strength, or at least the requisite indifference, to rid herself finally of the disdain.

Two young women sat at the table next to her, one rocking an infant in a stroller and the other in an advanced stage of pregnancy. They were drinking lemonade and paging through a catalog of baby furniture, talking very loudly, enthusing over the pictures and trying to choose between two different children's furniture sets, natural or peach colored. "The peach is more special," the woman rocking the stroller said.

The other one said, "You think so?"

"Of course. The natural looks ordinary. Everyone gets the natural. You should definitely go with the peach."

"But it costs twice as much," said the pregnant woman, who looked a little younger than her friend.

"Forget the price. What are you worried about? Your parents are buying it, aren't they?"

"Yes," the other one said, still hesitant.

"So go for the peach, don't think twice!"

The younger woman took the catalog, held the picture up to her face, sipped her juice, and said, "I do love this one, but Eli will say it's for girls; he won't go for it."

"What do you mean, for girls?" She took a pack of cigarettes out of her purse, lit one, and said, "It's unisex, can't you see?"

"*I* know that. I'm not the problem, I like it. But he'll say it's for girls. I'm telling you, I know him."

"Tell him this is what everyone's getting now. . . . I swear to God, this kid is driving me crazy." She leaned over the baby, whose crying was getting louder. She picked up the baby—he was very large, with strange features. He fell silent and looked at Shira over his mother's shoulder.

"He's driving me crazy today. So, what do you say? You think Eli will flip out over the peach? Then get the natural. The natural's nice too." The strange baby smiled at Shira.

After paying the check, she went down the escalator to the basement floor, but instead of going into the supermarket she turned into a large home-appliance store. She hated these places. They made all the appliances, even fridges, washers, and TVs, seem completely unnecessary. A salesman who was too young and too courteous, wearing black pants and a white shirt that had the chain's logo embroidered on its pocket, asked if she needed help. "I'm just looking at air conditioners," she said. The salesman seemed thrilled. He walked her over to the air-conditioning department, lecturing at length about BTU's, wall units and floor units, and central mini systems, one of which was on sale, but she didn't listen. "How big is your apartment?" he asked, as they went into a little display room that was separated from the rest of the store and was freezing cold.

"What?" she said.

"Your apartment. How big an apartment do you and your husband have?"

"I have no idea. Medium, I suppose."

"Okay, never mind the footage, I'll show you our most popular model. It's on sale now. You've come at a great time, it costs double in summer."

When she left the store she felt dizzy. She would have gladly sat down at the café upstairs now. She'd paid 5,300 shekels, in eighteen installments, for an air conditioner that would be delivered that weekend. When she told the salesman she'd take it, he looked stunned. She had never spent so much money on an electrical appliance but what astonished her was the fact that it was clear they would still be together next summer and the next. This air conditioner, she thought, as she went into the drugstore instead of the supermarket, was the true meaning of the words of love she had offered that morning. Or perhaps it was a revolt against the apartment's unbearable heat, against the idle talk of change, against an eternally undecided lover.

She pushed a shopping cart around and had no idea why she'd come in here. Every time she visited these shops she emerged with dozens of products she didn't need: soap, shampoo, fancy toothbrushes—they all carried some promise of a cleaner life. She put a packet of the soap Yonatan liked in her cart and kept going. She had spent so long in the mall that she had no idea what time it was, or even if it was dark yet. She started to make her way to the checkout, stopping to pick up some fabric softener and passed the pharmacy, coming to a halt by the home pregnancy tests. Her eyes scanned them, one by one, until they rested on a larger oblong box that said *Know your fertile days.* She touched it but pulled her hand back quickly, as if it burned. Then she reached out, took the box, and started reading the text on the back.

"You can pay here," the pharmacist said, and pointed to her cart.

"For this too?" Shira asked and waved the box.

"Yes," the pharmacist said, "for the ovulation kit too."

(2 0)

The first day of the semester was also the first day of winter. The weather had changed overnight, and he sat on the balcony, unable to fall asleep, watching the sky, which appeared damp and heavy. He couldn't sleep, but felt no distress or fear; in fact he was excited at the thought of facing a classroom the next day. He enjoyed staring at the sky and drinking his tea with a few leaves of mint from the planter and didn't mind if Shira did not wake up and join him. They had spent many nights on the balcony, as if it were a transfer station between wakefulness and sleep, chatting, sitting quietly, or trying to solve the remaining crossword clues. Sometimes he hoped they would both have trouble sleeping, so they could sit in the night air on the wicker furniture. But now he wanted to be alone. It felt like the first time he had been alone for years. Completely alone, without missing or craving anything, without thinking about his daughter or his wife or the book he wasn't writing, without anger; alone out of choice, alone as only someone can be who is loved by the person sleeping in the next room.

Yesterday he took the car to be washed, as if it also were starting a new career. When he got home, he decided to tidy the glove compartment, which had served, ever since he bought the car, as a holdall for little items and documents he was too lazy or afraid to throw out. Each time it was opened, it became more difficult to close. He left the engine and the air-conditioning running and emptied the contents onto the seat beside him. He pulled out a crumpled map of the city that he sometimes used when he had to find an unfamiliar address—though he hadn't had to do that for a long time—and put it back in the compartment. Then he picked up a flashlight and a cardboard box with a spare bulb. He wasn't sure if it was burnt out or not, but he put them back too. He found two old plastic lighters, tried to light them, and, discovering they were empty, tossed them into a plastic bag he found on the floor. He had purposely tackled the objects first. He was afraid of the paperwork.

He stuffed a pile of advertising pamphlets and old receipts into the bag. On a piece of ruled paper torn from a notebook, he found some ideas that now seemed ridiculous, yellowing from the sunlight, yellow to begin with.

The male character should be the ideal cross between me and other men. Intellectual and arrogant but also kind of tawdry. Likes music and cars. Childish. Women love him, gossip about him, try to hit on him. He looks unattainable. Loves eating, great lover. Has no children. (In fact, maybe there shouldn't be any of me in him.)

On the other side of the sheet he had written a big heading—THE FEMALE CHARACTER!!!—and, underneath, *I have no idea.* These were notes for the novel he had started writing just before Ilana was killed, his abandoned novel. He used to have a notebook where he wrote down his thoughts every day. He liked that notebook—it was one of Dana's, and the wide rules gave him a sense of freedom, of being uncommitted. But when it disappeared one day, he was relieved. He didn't know how this single page had ended up in the glove compartment. The sentences sounded foreign and cheap—the thoughts of a relatively young and haughty writer—and the handwriting looked as if it did not belong to him. He had crushed the page in his fist and thrown it in the bag.

Now he sipped his tea and thought about the morning, which was already there, pregnant in the night air. He thought about the drive to Jerusalem, the ascent to Mount Scopus, and his course, which he had been told twelve students had registered for, a number that seemed satisfactory to him: intimate but not too intimate. He thought about his course title: "The Author in Search of His Voice," and about the writers he had decided to discuss, which included no one living and no Israelis. He turned to the courtyard, to the trees whose leaves rustled in a wind that had grown stronger, and tried to stifle the fear that had been simmering in him all day, that he might be a charlatan.

"If you're a charlatan, then so is everybody else," Shira said, when he confessed to her that morning that he didn't think he had the talent or the guts to talk about other authors. "And do you know how I know you're not?" she said, standing with her back to him as she fastened her bra—the one that made him feel like a real family man when he hung it up or took it off the laundry line—more than any other item of clothing, this old bra enchanted him because of its soft tatteredness.

"How?" he asked, desperate for some persuasive comfort.

"Because charlatans have no idea that they're charlatans. They don't even entertain the possibility."

She was completely on his side. She was on his side like parents are on their children's side, and sometimes he wondered if he were on her side in that same blind and eternal way. She told him dryly that she only had a few chapters left to finish her novel, which was still unnamed and which she wouldn't let him read, claiming that his criticism, even if enthusiastic, would completely unbalance her. At first he was hurt, then relieved. He didn't want to find out that this novel was particularly good or bad, he didn't want to go back to that moment, which now seemed distant, when he had finished reading her first novel and realized she was more talented than he was and yet he still wanted her—a moment of maturation, he thought, and he didn't want to mature anymore. Sometimes he hoped she would never finish, that she would get stuck, as he had, that she would get lost in her book as in a yellow and infinite desert, and possibly give up and decide one book was enough, one success was enough, and she had no need for yet another triumph in an arena from which he himself had disappeared. Sometimes he hoped she would fail, and when he imagined her failing, he imagined himself consoling her. Then he felt so guilty that he would interrogate her about her work, how it was going, what she had written, if she was sure she didn't want him to read a few lines—he knew how it went, he remembered the satisfaction, he knew the frustration—because he was afraid that his very thoughts had jinxed her writing and he wanted to remove the jinx. But he didn't have to ask to know what kind of day she had. Her desk was in their bedroom, next to the window that looked onto the path leading up to the building next door. The window was always closed, but one day he found she had opened it and the room was flooded with light, and instead of the wooden blinds he was used to, he saw a wall covered with yellowing stucco, crisscrossed with sewage pipes, and suddenly their bedroom looked very vulnerable.

When he couldn't find anything to do and it was too hot to walk the streets, he would sit in the living room or the kitchen, quietly listening to music or preparing his course, which gave him an excuse to reread his favorite authors: Faulkner, Joyce, and García Márquez. He would guess by her movements around the house, by the number of times she went to the bathroom, her trips to the kitchen, the distracted smiles she gave him when he smiled at her too warmly from the couch, whether she was having a good day or a bad day. Since her father had been moved to the nursing ward, she had hardly written. She spent mornings in the hospital, and in the afternoons she was too tired and depressed to write. She only had a few chapters left, she said, perhaps three or four, but she felt very far from finished. When he asked if he could help in any way—anything, he said, hoping she would want physical comfort, something that would distract her from her father and her unfinished book and remind her of him, the person who could make her forget these pains—she would smile politely and say, "No, but thanks."

At the bottom of the glove compartment he found an old drawing of Dana's that she had brought home from school when she was six: a three-legged green dog standing under a black tree and a red sky. He remembered her getting into the car, which still smelled new, and putting the drawing on his lap, not proud but rather businesslike, but he couldn't remember what he had told her or what he thought of it then.

He knew the dog symbolized something, death probably, but he wasn't sure, because the sky didn't look optimistic either. He looked at the drawing now, shuddering in memory of the period when it was drawn and missing the child who had drawn it. For a moment he thought of giving it to her as a souvenir: perhaps she would have an explanation now. But since he didn't know how she would react, if at all, he gave up on the idea, folded the paper carefully, and put it back in the glove compartment.

He was afraid of her, he realized. During the past year he had searched for the words that would best describe their relationship: a father with his adolescent daughter, a widower and a child who had lost her mother, an aging man and a young woman. He tried soft and curvy words like *complex, ambivalent,* and *claustrophobic.* But now, as he leaned back in his seat, the Voice of Music and the air conditioner working together in harmony, he realized it was fear. He had never been so afraid of someone he loved so much. It was clear to him that Dana was revolted by him, and he understood. Through her eyes, the ones that were so like his own but that had avoided meeting his for so long, he saw his old age: the current one, which everyone could see, but also the one ahead of him, a pot simmering quietly on a low flame. Sometimes, when he was busy and caught her looking at him, he saw himself lying in a bed in some ward, like his father, like Shira's father, like all parents not fortunate enough to die elegantly in their sleep or in an accident, and he imagined his skin could feel her shivering in a way his flesh recalled easily, when she saw the person she had never truly known becoming someone she did not want to know.

He sat in the car and thought about the morning she was born. He had been certain it was going to be a boy and that he would be born at night; he constantly envisioned the crazy nighttime drive to the hospital. But his daughter came into the world at eight-thirty on a spring morning, and he wasn't there. He was meeting a TV director in a café on Sheinkin, where they discussed the possibility of *Passion* being made into a movie. He had met with interested directors before, all very young and excited, and he had never heard from any of them again. They all said *Passion* was a very cinematic book. They even said—and hoped he wouldn't be insulted—that it read like a screenplay. He said he was flattered, but he was hurt: Truly great authors, he thought, not only do not write books that read like screenplays but there is something in their work that despises the cinema. The director he met with that morning was the youngest and most enthusiastic of all, and had flattered him so much on the phone that when Yonatan arranged their meeting he forgot that Ilana had an ultrasound appointment. She was in the thirty-eighth week of her pregnancy, and it was a routine exam. When she heard he was to meet with a director, she insisted that he not cancel the meeting. "What do you want to schlep to the doctor's with me for?" she said. "It will only take two seconds, and anyway there's no parking. I'm better off taking a cab." And since he had accompanied her loyally to all her exams during the pregnancy, and had even sat waiting with her at the clinic for a whole morning when she had a glucose-loading test, he felt entitled, this one time, to miss it.

In retrospect, it amazed him that, contrary to what the books and movies depicted, he had no premonition that morning. In fact, he was very relaxed when, toward noon, the director glanced at his watch, apologized and said he had to run, and thanked Yonatan, who said the coffee was on him. He stayed outside, enjoying the clear air that reminded him of a foreign country. He knew he would never hear from the young man, who had lectured him, before leaving, about how difficult it was to get funding for these projects. Yonatan didn't much care whether or not *Passion* became a movie; he met with directors primarily to bask in the glory of their praise. In a week or two he was having a baby, and he had been warned by everyone who had children that his perspectives and priorities would completely change. But he wasn't afraid of that. On the contrary, he was counting on it. He was impatiently awaiting the day when he could wear his new identity. He fantasized about the moment when he would look into his child's eyes and manage to catch in them something new and encouraging about himself, a scoop that would be both amazing and obvious.

He felt somewhat betrayed when he came home, expecting to find Ilana sprawled on the couch with her swollen feet up on the table, reading one of the baby books her parents had sent, and instead found a message on the machine from a nurse at the maternity ward, who said Ilana was hospitalized after having an emergency C-section, and that everything was all right. An hour later, he was sitting by her bed, wetting her lips with a damp cotton swab. When she opened her eyes and saw him coming in, she had uttered such a dry, hoarse "Hi" that for a second he thought she was dying. During the ultrasound, the doctor had discovered that the baby's pulse was weak. "You did say you hadn't felt it very strongly the last couple of days," Yonatan said, and she said yes and, in the same hoarse voice, alarming and pitiful, said it hadn't seemed like a big deal; Nira had the same thing with Evyatar, remember?

He didn't but said he did, of course he did, anything to make up for not having been with her.

So the doctor, Ilana told him, had sent her to the ER. "And what a stroke of luck," she whispered, "because when I got there, there was no pulse at all, and then it came back, but very weak. It was scary, Yonatan." She sucked on the swab. "And then they took me into surgery. I asked them to phone; did they phone you?"

He nodded. "I was at that stupid meeting."

"How was it?" she asked, as if they hadn't just had a daughter four hours before.

He watched her catheter bag filling up and said, "Never mind, that doesn't matter now." He asked if she was in pain, and she said she wasn't but she probably would be later.

"Have you seen her?" she asked, and he said not yet; he had come to see Ilana first. "They said they'd bring her to me this afternoon, but I have to see her now," and she burst out crying. He wiped her eyes and kissed her forehead, and said he'd be right back with their daughter. She turned aside and started sobbing that she was so thirsty, and he didn't know if she was crying from thirst or because she missed the baby she hadn't yet seen.

He rushed to the nurses' station and told them firmly that he had to take the baby to her mother. He expected a battle, but there was none; one of the nurses called the newborn room and announced that the father was on his way. He ran over and followed another nurse to his daughter's bassinet. "Congratulations," she said, and left him there. He stood over the baby and looked at her: She was lying on her stomach with her face turned sideways and her eyes closed. Her hair looked reddish and wet, one of her fists was near her mouth, and she was wiggling her little pinky finger, which was also red. *The father is on his way:* He repeated the nurse's announcement and his heart shrank. Since getting married, and perhaps even before that, he had been trying to prepare himself mentally for becoming a parent but unsuccessfully, like someone packing a suitcase but not knowing what to put in it. And now, a few simple words uttered matter-of-factly into a phone had turned him instantly and without complication into a father. Maybe, he thought, the change does not occur within but from outside, when in the eyes of the world you become a parent. Because now he was the father of this redheaded baby, who had barely come into the world and did not yet have a name, and he hadn't even asked Ilana how much she weighed. He looked at the little note stuck to the edge of her bassinet: 7.91 pounds. His eyes strayed to the notes on nearby bassinets: 5.95 and 6.83. His heart filled with pride, as if his daughter's impressive weight was his first accomplishment as a father. He looked at the wiggling pinky again, which seemed to be trying to tell him something. Daddy's here, he told her silently and wiped his eyes, which had started to tear, and swallowed his saliva, which still tasted like the two double espressos he had drunk at the café.

Cleaning out the glove compartment in the car, he had no sense of time passing. Then he suddenly felt restless, as if the project he had undertaken was infinite and unnecessary. He quickly gathered some shreds of paper and tobacco into the bag and a few puzzling screws left on the seat, turned off the engine, and got out of the car. He threw the bag into the trash can on the sidewalk and started walking home, but then he turned around, went back to the car, opened the door, took out the drawing from the glove compartment, and put it in his back pocket.

(2 1)

She didn't like any of the backpacks. They had looked at several dozen, all of which were too big or too small, too childish or too old-fashioned, and all, in general, not right. After the fourth store, Shira suggested they go and rest at a café before continuing the search. Dana agreed and thought maybe it would be better if she didn't go on this trip; perhaps the fact that she couldn't find a bag was a sign from above. But Shira, who had read her thoughts or perhaps knew them from her own past, said, "We're not going home without a backpack!" and sat down with a sigh at a table outside the little café on Allenby, their café.

"I have something to tell you," she said.

Dana's heart skipped a beat because she thought Shira was going to say something important.

"You're going on this trip even if you have to carry everything in plastic bags like a bag lady." She asked the waitress for iced coffee. "And not only are you going," she said, lighting a cigarette as she squeezed the words out of her pursed lips, "but you're going to have fun. You're going to love it. That's what's going to happen." Dana looked at the sidewalk and smiled one of her cynical smiles, and Shira said, "Do you hear me? It's going to be an awesome trip, and you're going to have an awesome time, with or without the stupid backpack. Wait a minute, why didn't you order anything?"

"I did," Dana said quietly. "I ordered lemonade."

"I didn't hear you." Shira sighed again and told her about one of her own high school trips, and how she had broken down the first day and called her father in tears to come and take her home. "And just so you know, unlike you and your dad, we were enemies."

It was strange to picture Shira's father driving along the southern Arava highway on a Saturday morning, in a big car with a long name. "Would you like to be that age again?" she asked.

Shira looked at her and said, "Fourteen, fifteen?"

Dana nodded.

"No. Not if you paid me." After a few moments of silence, while they looked at the people passing by, she said, "Well, maybe." She told Dana her mother always used to say, "If only I could be sixteen again, but with the experience I have now." She said she used to belittle her and say that was something only an old person would say. "But now I know she was right. So right! And I know that if I tell you that now, you'll think the exact same thing about me, that I'm a withered old lady and I don't know the first thing about life, especially not your life."

But that's not what Dana thought. On the contrary. Shira seemed young, younger than her, because even without the plastic bags she felt like a homeless bag lady, and when she looked at Shira she wanted to be her age and to be full, like her, of the confidence and serenity of someone who already has half her life behind her. She watched her put her cigarette out in the ashtray and dig through her handbag for her purse, and she felt guilty at having rejected all the backpacks they'd seen, even the khaki canvas one that she had liked. "It's gorgeous," Shira had said, fingering the bag and feeling all its compartments. "If you don't want it, I'll take it myself, even though I don't really need it. So what do you say? Do you want it? This is my treat, so don't even look at the price." But Dana had twisted her face and said it was horrible, it was for old people. Now, as they got up to leave, she was filled with regret.

They walked toward Ben Yehuda Street, where Shira said there were some more stores. They walked side by side, examining the shop windows, and Shira pointed to various clothes and asked Dana's opinion. Dana said she had no opinion about anything and felt she was having trouble breathing. On the radio they said the heat wave would end that night and it would rain the next day, but it wasn't the heat that bothered her but the image of the canvas backpack dangling in front of her eyes reproachfully, and her heart that suddenly wanted to confess.

Shira stopped outside a shoe store. "Look at those sandals," she said and pointed to a pair of colorful flat thongs that looked Indian. "They'd probably make me look really short. But look at the price! It's a steal. Let's go in for a minute."

Dana rambled in behind her. They sat on the low bench and Shira tried on the sandals. "I have wide flat feet," she complained to the saleswoman.

The woman said, "What nonsense! They look lovely on you." She offered to bring her some other styles to try on.

"Do you mind?" Shira asked Dana, who shook her head. "At least there's good air-conditioning in here," she said, and sat down again, stretched her foot out, and wiggled her toes in the sandal. "Look how horrible my toes are. I'd put on nail polish, but your dad hates it."

Dana said they weren't horrible at all but hers were.

"Oh, please!" Shira said. "Show me your toes." Dana held her foot out; she was wearing Teva sandals. "What are you talking about? They're really cute, I wish I had toes like that. Mine look like sausages."

"Well, mine look like Cheetos." The saleswoman brought new boxes, and Dana took one pair of sandals out and handed them to Shira.

"Better Cheetos than sausages," Shira said, and put the sandals on. "Does my dad really hate nail polish?"

Shira nodded. "On toes, yeah. He says it's vulgar."

Dana remembered the old bottles of nail polish with the congealed tops and wondered if they were still in the medicine cabinet.

Shira walked back and forth from the bench to the mirror, and Dana noticed that when she walked, Shira pulled her shirt down just like she did herself, to cover her behind. "I hate trying on shoes," she said, and sat down again. "Not as much as I hate trying on clothes, but even with shoes you have to look in the mirror, which is extremely depressing."

They walked out into the heat and Shira lit a cigarette. "I need to go on a diet. Even my feet are fat."

As they quickly crossed the street to the luggage store, Dana heard her breathing heavily and wanted to ask if her dad minded her being chubby and if he was the reason she wanted to lose weight. But instead she asked why she didn't stop smoking.

"Why?" Shira said, and put her face against the window of another shoe store. "That's a smart question with a stupid answer: self-destruction. It's simple. It's simple and disgusting and pathetic." She pointed to a pair of platform sandals and asked what Dana thought.

"Aren't they too high?"

"Yes, but they'll make me tall."

"But you're not short."

"What are you talking about? I'm a midget! I'm not even five-three."

Dana looked at her; Shira was a couple of inches taller than she. "You're average, then."

"Thanks for the compliment. That's all I need now: average."

"I didn't mean it that way," Dana said quickly.

"I know, I'm just kidding. Don't take me seriously. I'm really messed up."

Dana didn't believe her, but she wanted to. Shira was perfect, even more perfect than Tamar, who was enviable only because she was still a child. She stood behind Shira as she peered into the window to examine another pair of sandals and looked at her big behind, and thought, Maybe she really does hate herself—and the thought made her envy seem more manageable, hopeful.

Shira turned to her. "Do you mind going in so I can try them on for a second? Just that pair, I promise."

"No problem," Dana said, and they went in.

"We set off to buy a backpack and look what it's turned into," Shira said, when they left the second store with no sandals. She pointed north and said she thought there was a nice store near Bograshov, but Dana said there was no need and maybe they should buy that other bag after all.

"The khaki one?" Shira asked happily.

"Yes. It was the best one."

"Great. And it doesn't look old-fashioned at all."

They turned back and hurried to the store, which was the first one they had visited, and suddenly Dana began to fear that someone else had bought the backpack—someone with good taste, like hers, but no hesitation.

"Hey," Shira said breathlessly, "you're walking too fast for a fat old smoker like me."

Dana slowed down, and when they waited at the pedestrian crossing she tried to calm herself. It will be there, she thought. They crossed and turned onto King George, and she didn't know what she would do if it wasn't there, how she would forgive herself, so she sped up again and heard Shira panting behind her.

"No one's going to snag it."

"How do you know?" Dana looked at her.

"Because I do."

"But how?"

"Because it's yours, that's why. You and that backpack were meant for each other."

When they left the store with the backpack—which had briefly looked pathetic again, simply because it had waited for them—in a large plastic bag swinging from her arm, she was struck by an embarrassing urge to hold Shira's hand. They stood close to one another, their hips almost touching, waiting to cross the street on the way home, but she didn't want to go home. From her point of view, the afternoon had just begun, and the purchase, the relief, the heat that had started to ease up, and the coolness entering the air filled her with happiness. If they went home now, the spell would be broken. They would each go into her own territory, each back to her role, and she was sick of that and of her room, which had become a large cage, and of her life, which seemed old and tiresome and maybe a little too small for her.

As they walked toward Bialik, she wondered if her father loved Shira for the same reasons she did: because of her brain; because of her beauty, which was so round and soft and sad and ever-changing in front of your eyes; because she hated herself; because he saw himself in her. She hoped not; she hoped he loved her for different reasons, ones that she did not know and could not guess, men's reasons, because she didn't want to share this love with him or steal it from him. Because he did deserve to have love, just as anyone did, her sense of justice told her as they turned onto their street, but he especially, because he had suffered, because he had lost his wife, because he had a daughter who tortured him. She could see a light on through the drawn blinds and wondered if he was home. Although it was a little after six, the clouds had darkened the sky and a huge downpour was clearly brewing and would arrive tonight or tomorrow, and she thought that yesterday at this time it was still fully light, a violent summer light. The three of them hated the sunlight, the three of them shared the same hatred—and when she looked at the light flickering between the slits of the blind as she walked toward it, she wanted to confess to him: I hate summer too; I hate the sun and the sea and the market, just like you.

"Do you feel like getting something to eat?"

She heard Shira's voice as if it were very distant. "What?"

"What to eat or what did I say?"

"I didn't hear."

"I asked if you wanted to get something to eat."

"At home?"

"No, out. All this talk about dieting has made me starved."

"Should we get my dad?"

"No. I don't think he's home. I think he went out to look for a book for his course."

They stood at the corner of Allenby and Bialik and Dana wondered if she should tell Shira she'd seen the light on at home, that her father must have come home and might even be cooking something for them. She purposely avoided looking at the house so Shira wouldn't see, and said, "He'll probably be home soon."

"So what? He's not a child. Well, actually he is." She dug around in her bag for her cigarettes. "But for now let's say he's not." Dana watched her fingers as they fiddled with the lighter that refused to work, and thought it was a sign from above, that maybe she shouldn't smoke this cigarette, because just a moment ago she had heard her wheezing. "And anyway," Shira said, as she took a book of matches out of her bag, "he's probably sitting on the floor in some bookshop now, forgetting we even exist." The book of matches was empty. "So do you want to?" Her unlit cigarette dangled between her lips. "They opened this diner-style place around here, where you can get hamburgers. But you don't eat meat, so that's no good."

Dana said a diner sounded good; she could get fries or something. She stopped a young man wearing baggy pants and an embroidered shirt, who was smoking a cigarette, and asked him if he had a light. Before Shira could protest, the young man pulled out a lighter from his little leather bag and lit her cigarette. Shira took a relieved drag, looked around, and said she couldn't remember if it was left or right.

Dana said it was to the right. "I saw it on the way. It's on the other side of the street."

"Are you sure?" She looked from side to side again, squinting, and Dana prayed she wouldn't turn back and see the apartment, which now seemed to be illuminating the entire street as if it were Allenby's sole source of light: the pedestrian crossing, the stores, the beggar by the bus stop with his healthy leg tucked under his body today and the diseased one stretched out.

"Yes, I'm sure. Come on, the light's green." She took hold of Shira's hand, and they crossed the street.

She was expecting the phone call, but still it surprised her. She was distracted, sitting on the bathroom floor waiting to see if a blue stripe would appear in the little window on the ovulation kit's plastic stick. Like a ray of light in a dull sky, she thought, as she carefully monitored the white background that had turned gray when her urine touched it. But there was no stripe yet, and it was now of all times—now, when for a brief wonderful moment she had ceased to be the usual tired observer, watching her body from the outside—now the phone rang and she stood up quickly, careful not to kick the stick, and hurried to the bedroom. She knew what it was even before she picked up the phone, yet was still surprised to hear the nurse telling her they had found an infection in her father's blood and she should come to the hospital soon.

From that moment on, everything was technical, like the phone call to the secretary of the literature department, asking her to let Yonatan know he should call Shira's cell phone urgently; technical like the efficiency with which she threw underwear, a toothbrush and toothpaste, a book, two packs of cigarettes, and a lighter into her bag; technical like the thought: Why the book? And technical like the panic that waited for her to finish her business before making its dramatic appearance; technical like her quick glance, a moment before she left the apartment for who knew how long, at the stick lying on the bathroom floor just as she had left it but completely different, with a dark admonishing stripe in its window.

In the car, which started immediately without its usual morning hesitation, as if it had also been expecting this day, she continued to feel nothing. She sat in traffic on Bograshov and tried to decide which way would be quickest, because, although she took this route every morning and knew the roads well, she had never left at rush hour; everything looked different, alien, the buses and the cars, the drivers and the pedestrians, even the stores and the buildings, as if she had accidentally wound up in someone else's daily routine. Still in a traffic jam, far from the stoplight, she thought about her sudden efficiency, how she hadn't forgotten to remove the evidence from the bathroom floor, how she had put the stick back in the package and thrown it into a trash can outside the next door building before getting into her car, how another woman would probably have forgotten, perhaps intentionally—another woman, she thought, would have taken the opportunity to cleanse herself of guilt, confessing without saying a word. She remembered a particular look on Dana's face, how she had suddenly darkened like the afternoon sky. She had been in such a good mood yesterday, such a rare mood. Now Shira felt guilty for failing to restrain herself from sharing something several sizes too large for Dana, something unclear even to herself.

They had sat in a red booth in the diner. As Dana read the menu, one hand on the Formica-topped table, the other on the bag next to her, Shira thought, She'll never be beautiful. She had her father's eyes, but they looked better on a man than on a girl. Her lips were thin, almost erased, and there was something vulnerable in her little nose and chin. This is his daughter, she told herself, as if it were a sudden discovery. This is the result of one of his cells encountering another cell. This is what one possibility of Yonatan looks like; other ones perhaps were now inside her.

"What are you getting?" she asked, and Dana said she couldn't decide. "What are your options?" she asked helpfully.

Without looking up from the menu, the girl said, "Hamburger or cheeseburger."

"But you're vegetarian. What happened?"

"I don't know. I really feel like a hamburger."

"Then get one! I'm getting a cheeseburger."

"Me too, then."

"And fries?"

"Of course." Her face had the same look of relief as when they left the luggage store.

"And onion rings?"

"Do you even need to ask?"

Shira asked, "What else would you like?" and when Dana started looking through the menu again, she said, "Do you feel like, maybe, a brother or a sister?" Dana put her menu down, and Shira continued without looking at her or waiting for an answer. "Because I want to get pregnant. In the near future." Seconds after emerging, the confession smelled like burnt oil. "Because I'm not young, I'm thirty-eight, but your dad's not really into it; I mean, I think he does want a child, in principle, someday, but it's not urgent for him, and I know that if I don't confront him with established facts it will never happen, do you see?" But Dana was staring at the Formica. "So I've been thinking about this a lot recently." She stopped talking when the waitress came to take their orders, and when she left she lit a cigarette. "At least it will be a good excuse to quit smoking."

"What?"

"A pregnancy."

"Oh, yeah," Dana whispered.

"Listen. I know this is really unfair of me to tell you all this, because he's your dad and all, and maybe you feel your loyalty should be to him, but I felt it wasn't right not to tell you there's a chance that this might happen, that I might get pregnant, maybe soon. Or maybe not, maybe it won't work at all, I don't know, maybe I'm infertile, maybe I'll chicken out in the end." When Dana looked at her with sad, inquisitive eyes, she said, "Maybe in the end I won't do it, you know."

Now she couldn't decide if Dana's gloom had indicated knowledge, lack of knowledge, or a complete unwillingness to know. All night she tormented herself for telling her, not because she was afraid Dana would tell Yonatan—she might have even hoped she would, and in fact maybe subconsciously was using her, which depressed Shira even more. She drove through the intersection and turned onto Dizengoff and remembered how the confiding atmosphere, the tightening friendship, had instantly been replaced with something sticky and rubbery, like the cheeseburgers, and even the near-wintry chill of the evening could not revive their afternoon or lessen her error, because she had committed the crime and made the girl her accomplice.

"Facts on the ground," she remembered saying, although she hadn't known the expression was in her vocabulary. Facts on the ground—like the air conditioner that arrived a week ago, a little too late, she thought, as she looked out the window at the darkening sky.

At first he was angry. The two technicians rang the doorbell and she hurried to the door, whispered to them that it was a surprise—her partner didn't know about it yet—and the three of them stood in the living room doorway, secretive and triumphant. One of them asked where she wanted to install it, and she said the wall between the living room and the bedroom. Yonatan was sitting in the couch reading *The Sound and the Fury*.

"What's that?" he asked.

"An air conditioner, sir," one of the technicians proclaimed. "Your wife got you a surprise."

"She's not my wife," he hissed, and put down his book.

"Your girlfriend," the younger technician said. "Your girlfriend."

"Have you lost your mind?" he said quietly, restrained in the presence of the two strangers, who rushed to her aid.

"No, sir, she's very smart, your girlfriend," the older one said. "It was on sale, half price."

"How can you live without air-conditioning these days?" the other one said. "It's awfully hot in here. How can you live like this?"

"You can," Yonatan said. "Believe me, you can." He put the book on the table and went over to the huge box they had put down near the doorway. "How much did this cost?"

Shira said she'd tell him later. "Is it all right if we put it here?" She pointed to the wall between the two rooms.

"What do I care? You decide! You make decisions without consulting me anyway." He left the room, and she was suddenly embarrassed in front of the two men.

The younger one said, "I guess he doesn't like surprises."

His friend checked the wall and said, "No big deal. It caught him unprepared. I'd be mad too if my wife pulled a stunt like this."

"Shelly would get her ass kicked," the young one agreed, and when Shira looked at him, he said, "Just kidding, just kidding. She'd get her ass kissed, not kicked."

"Yes," the older one said. "He'll thank you later. You'll see."

She heard Yonatan slam the bedroom door and suddenly felt sorry for him; he wouldn't be able to hide there either. The technicians had already taken out their tools and the young one was banging on the wall with a hammer. "Excellent, it's plaster," he said. "This is going to be a piece of cake."

She picked up the book on the table and grew angry at herself at having invaded this den full of books and music and dust with her air conditioner. She wanted to change her mind, but the sound of a drill shook her out of it, and she suddenly felt Yonatan's hand on the small of her back. "Move away," he said and pushed her aside and went over to the technician who had started drilling in the wall. "Where are you putting it, at the bottom or the top?"

"Bottom," the man said, slightly afraid. "It's a floor unit. She chose the floor one."

"And we'll put the motor here, outside the window," the other one said.

Yonatan asked how much horsepower the unit had, and the older one, relieved that the ice was broken, told him happily about the unit's merits. "Does it run quietly?" Yonatan asked.

"Quiet as a baby!" the man said.

"How much did it cost?" he came close to her and pushed her away again, gently this time, a little smile hovering on his lips. "How much did you spend, you nut?"

"What do you care? It's a gift. Don't ask questions."

"But I want to know."

"Why?"

"Because I'm nosy." He went up to the technician with the drill. "Are you sure it will cool the bedroom too?"

"One hundred percent!"

"With the same power?"

"Sure with the same power. Even stronger. You'll see, you'll sleep like a baby tonight. Just make sure you cover him." He winked at Shira. "You don't want him catching a cold."

"We'll have to move the bureau," Yonatan said to Shira. "It's standing just where the outlet will be. Should we put the bed there?"

"Yes. I'll help you."

He turned his back to the technicians and came close to her. "Only if you tell me how much it cost."

"No. You'll never know."

"Okay," he said and encircled her waist. "Then don't be surprised if I'm a little cold in bed tonight." He went into the bedroom and she heard him dragging the bureau across the floor, making a screeching sound that was like yelps of happiness, as if the furniture was giving away his feelings. She wondered if the technicians had heard what he'd said to her, and if they saw him sneak his hand under her shirt before he left.

"See?" the older one said. "In the end he was happy."

It seemed sweet now, to replay that afternoon, which seemed distant enough to be rightfully considered a memory: the noise of the drill, the coffee Yonatan made for the technicians with the pot—they hadn't used it for a long time and it was dotted with white spots of mildew—the launching of the air conditioner, which within minutes cooled the living room and the bedroom, and then the sex under a blanket in the freezing cold. She stopped at the light to turn into the hospital parking lot and felt nostalgic for that afternoon; it belonged to last week. One choice afternoon out of the previous life she had lived before the phone rang, so expected and so sudden, as if for years her father had been on a waiting list for a flight and a seat had suddenly opened up.

She went into the parking lot, got out of the car, passed by the guard, went into the elevator, and up to the nursing ward. It was eight-fifty, and although there would be more monumental moments today, far more difficult, she knew she would remember the time as if it were when her life was reset.

Her father wasn't in his room. She stood by his bed, where the sheets and thin blanket were folded on top, and her heart sank but stopped for a moment, opening with ease: It's over. She stood where she was, wondering if she should open the cabinet to see if his things were still there or look for the nurse. Then the roommate, who had been admitted a few days ago and looked healthy and energetic, came out of the bathroom, pulled the tie on his pajama pants, and said, "They already took him."

"Where to?" Her voice sounded tight.

"I'm not sure." He sat down on his bed. "Intensive Care, I think. The doctors came in this morning, and then they took him. I think I heard them say Intensive Care." He sighed and shook his head. "Poor man. I talked to him yesterday."

She went out into the hallway, feeling like a stranger in this place she knew so well. Since when did her father talk to his roommates? She stood outside the room hesitantly, pins and needles prickling her lower back.

"They took Father." She heard a voice behind her; it was Olga, the nurse she liked, coming out of one of the rooms. "Come with me," she said, and put her hand on Shira's arm. "The doctor's still here; he wants to talk to you." She felt like a chastened schoolgirl late for class. "Father's in Intensive Care. It's one floor up." Shira asked if he was conscious. "No, honey." The nurse held her hand, swinging it from side to side. "He lost consciousness this morning." She thought of the word *morning,* of the meaning it had here, how her father's morning had begun long before hers. "Come, sweetie," Olga said, and led her to the physicians' room. "Dr. Amir wants to talk to you. He'll explain everything." She peeked into the room and told the young doctor sitting at the desk drinking coffee out of a paper cup, "The daughter is here."

Dr. Amir was a handsome man. He had a square face, smooth black hair, and green feline eyes. He took short sips of coffee, as if it were medicine, and told Shira that her father was in critical condition.

"Judging by your voice I'd say it was worse than critical," she said.

He raised his eyebrows and smiled sadly. "Yes, I suppose it is."

"And I understand he's no longer conscious."

"He's hazy."

She thought about the difference between the way the nurse had phrased it and what the doctor said—she didn't know if Amir was his last or first name—and he, as if reading her mind, said, "You could say he's no longer conscious."

He seemed tired. She had seen him around the ward before—he had examined her father a few times—and she wondered what made such a young person want to specialize in geriatrics. "I'm sorry," he said. He leaned back in his chair, tossed his empty cup into the trash can with perfect aim, and explained that yesterday one of her father's kidneys had stopped functioning, and this morning he had developed a blood infec-tion. "Sepsis," he called it, and when she looked at him questioningly, he said, "An infection. A severe infection."

"It happened very quickly," she said. "Yesterday he was all right. It's a little odd, isn't it?"

"No. It's not odd."

"It's as if his organs conspired against him. Or, in fact, *for* him, because what kind of a life did he have here anyway?"

"Yes." He smiled. "That's exactly what it is: a conspiracy. With people of your father's age, that's exactly how it happens. It's unexpected but also predictable."

"I see." She thought that if it weren't for Yonatan she could easily fall in love with Dr. Amir.

"Which doesn't make it any less sad," he added.

"On the contrary," she said, and suddenly wanted some coffee, although she had already had two cups this morning before urinating on the stick. "The fact that it's predictable is what makes it tragic."

"I agree with you," Dr. Amir said.

"You specialize in a pretty tragic area." She was troubled by the thought of her father with his fading consciousness one floor above them. "Why did you choose it?" She hoped he would admit to an affec-tion for the elderly, a beloved grandparent, or say he was obsessed with death, confess he did not like to fight, say he was a kind of pacifist in the world of medicine. But his beeper went off and he glanced at it, put his hand on the phone, and, in a new impatient tone of voice said, "I have no answer to that question."

She didn't know if she was supposed to get up and leave now and go upstairs or wait until the doctor finished his phone call. When he saw her hesitating, he motioned for her to wait, and she was grateful for the extension. She felt she couldn't make that journey up one steep floor without first having a layover in a place where she could sit and chat with a young doctor, who might or might not be an idealist, talk to him about old age in general, as if she were interviewing him for a book on the topic, as if they were on a blind date: a young doctor specializing in geri-atrics, and a writer whose elderly father was dying. The room, with its sparse furnishings, the windows on which drops of rain slowly trickled down, the trash can that was empty except for the paper cup, the telephone, the beeper on the table, the closed door—the room looked like a play area in a mall, padded with rubber mats, a place where children could play without getting hurt.

He put down the receiver, looked outside, and said, "Winter's here."

"Yes." She started to sense the panic crawling down her back like a frozen drop of water.

"It's about time," he said, and she nodded. "Anyway, concerning your father, the next twenty-four hours are critical. At the moment he's breathing independently, but I expect that will only last another few hours. He's in Intensive Care so we can monitor him, and he's getting intravenous antibiotics, but he's not hooked up to a respirator. Do you understand?"

"I understand."

"There's already massive damage to his system, both prior damage and damage resulting from the kidney failure. So even if we can help him breathe, I'm not sure what quality of life he can expect if he comes through this."

"I know. He had no quality of life before, either."

"I suppose it's all relative. Subjective, anyway."

She nodded but didn't know what he meant—whether by subjective he was referring to her father or to her.

"And if he does come through," he said, his voice tender but his eyes firm, "it won't necessarily be ideal. Do you see?"

The rain was audible now. It slammed down on the window and on the tiled square outside, accompanied by echoes of thunder that sounded dim and far off, as if they were coming from someone's stomach, and she thought about the meatball her father had yesterday for lunch, how it now had the honor of the final meatball, and her eyes welled up.

Last week, when she went to his apartment to look for some childhood pictures to show Dana, who was curious to see what she had looked like as a baby, she passed by the deli where he bought his meals and her heart sank. She was suddenly filled with love for the place, unpleasant love, with a touch of something cold and damp. She went inside, and when she came out she had no idea what she was going to do with all the food she had bought. She climbed up to her father's apartment, put the bags on the kitchen counter, and went into the room that had become a storeroom to look for the photo albums. Since his hospitalization she had been there a few times, but the windows and blinds were closed, and now the smell of food filled the apartment like a ghost scampering around the rooms, and her father's absence became an oppressive presence. She returned to the kitchen, placed the albums she had found on the counter, opened one of the plastic containers, and hesitantly tasted a stuffed pepper.

It was the most delicious stuffed vegetable she had ever eaten. At first her mouth refused to admit it, looking for aftertastes, aggressive spices, hints of staleness, but when it found none she took another bite, and another, until she had finished the whole pepper. Then she tried a stuffed zucchini, which was also surprisingly wonderful. She felt that some truth had been concealed from her; had she known, she might have been able to change her father's destiny, or the past, or at least eat his meals with him, compliment his taste, make him happy in some way that was not so condescending or desperate. She took a plate out of the cabinet, arranged the containers in a row, and opened them all. She heaped portions of rice and lentils, Jerusalem kugel, and cucumber and beet salad onto her plate and ate standing up, looking around at the kitchen and knowing that the next time she saw it would be when she came to pack it up. Then she took in the half-empty containers in a row on the counter and burst into tears. It was a short dry sob, a cry that knows it is merely prologue. She packed up the leftovers, took the photo albums, went downstairs, and threw the bag of food in the trash can.

Dr. Amir asked if her father had any other children and she said, "No, just me."

"I see. Hard to be an only child?"

"It is now."

He smiled.

"Are you an only child too?" she asked.

"No, I have three siblings."

"Boys?"

"Boys."

"Are they all doctors?"

"No, only me."

"Why did you ask if I had siblings?" She felt a chill.

"I asked because I want to know if you have someone you can talk to about what's going on with Dad." *Dad,* he said, as if her father belonged to them both.

"What *is* going on with my dad?"

"He's not artificially respirated at the moment."

"Yes, I know. You already said that."

"Well, that's it."

"What do you mean, that's it?" she asked, and suddenly realized she was in the midst of negotiations.

"Do you want us to resuscitate him, if necessary? I can tell you with certainty that it will be."

"No," she said firmly, and when she realized what she had said, that she had uttered the small word in a voice that was too large, she said, "He wouldn't want it. It's unfair to keep torturing him."

"I agree with you one hundred percent," Dr. Amir said, as if she had given the correct answer on a quiz.

She felt cold. She rubbed her arms, leaned back in the chair, and asked what happened now.

"Nothing. We wait." He asked if there was someone close, a friend she would like to have with her; she could call from here. He pointed to the phone, but she said she had a cell phone and had already left a message for her partner. Dr. Amir got up and said he would go up to Intensive Care with her, and as she followed him down the hall to the elevators, Olga, who was standing by the nurses' station, blew her a kiss of the sort you give a child with an injured knee.

She stood in the elevator next to Dr. Amir and suddenly noticed that he was very short; his pants were too big, the fabric bunched up like a curtain, and he wore childish gym shoes. She looked at her watch and saw it was ten o'clock; she had sat in his room for only an hour but felt as if she was coming out of a long movie, blinking in the light, her eyes covered with movie cobwebs. At eight-fifty, she thought, when she had first got into this elevator, her clothes had still smelled of cigarettes and autumn.

Just before the end of class, the storm began. He was in the middle of a sentence about Faulkner when lightning lit up the classroom—during the past hour, the sky had blackened and the room had grown dark but no one had bothered to switch on the light—and the students turned to the window and then back to him, hypnotized, waiting for him to continue. From the moment he had walked in and seen the twelve students, seven women and five men, trying to guess who would drop the class and who would fall in love with him—from the moment he had sat down behind his desk and said, "I'm Yonatan Luria; I'm your lecturer; I was an author but I'm not anymore, and I'm really, really happy about it"—they were his.

"I'm going to talk with you about a few truly great authors and about how they found their voices," he said, looking at the eyes that examined him, still skeptical. "Our basic working assumption is that a literary voice acts exactly like a human voice. At first it's high-pitched, like a baby's cry, spewing out all sorts of nonsense, imitating other voices. This is the stage when what matters are the sounds the voice makes, not necessarily the content. Then we have adolescence, a very difficult age. You know how teenage boys' voices start to crack and they sound like toads? Later, the voice matures and stabilizes—this is its apex; this is when it's at its best. Finally, over time, the voice becomes hoarse, weakened; the vocal cords develop warts and all kinds of other afflictions, until it can barely be heard and sometimes even starts to sound babyish again, but without the charm this time, without the magic, without the wonderful innocence that is the turbocharger of any debut work." He examined the twelve pairs of eyes, their skepticism gone. "And every so often there is one last cry, sometimes pathetic, sometime exquisite. We will look at these things during this course, as if we were—and forgive me for the comparison, but it seems appropriate—these authors' ear, nose, and throat specialists. Any questions so far?"

A handsome young man with curly brown hair and a long sharp face raised his hand.

"Yes? What's your name?"

"Yonatan," the student said, and a rustle of laughter went through the class.

"Yes, Yonatan," he said, smiling.

"Why did you stop writing?"

"Why did I stop writing?" he repeated. He picked up a piece of chalk, although he had no plan to write anything, and leaned against the blackboard. "You're asking why?"

His young double nodded.

"Because I lost my voice," he said, and the class giggled. *I lost my voice,* he wrote on the board, and soaked up the pleasure on his students' faces. It was clear that no one would drop his course; perhaps there would even be a few new students next week, once word spread about the best show on campus. "That's the way it goes," he said gleefully, and scribbled some more words on the blackboard: *I now speak in the passive voice.*

"But at the top of your voice," said the young Yonatan.

"Nice!" He wrote the sentence on the board. "Anyone else?"

"And with a voice of reason?" a student with glasses sitting near the window suggested cautiously.

"Excellent!" Yonatan said. "What's your name?"

"Ma'ayan," she said, and he repeated her name back to her.

"The voice is Jacob's voice, but the hands are the hands of Esau," offered the girl sitting next to her, whom Yonatan had noted as a beauty when he came into the class, hoping not to develop a crush; he wanted to be a professor, not a caricature of a professor.

"And you are?" he asked.

"I'm Noa."

"Noa," he repeated.

"The voice of a generation," said the boy sitting on her other side, who looked a lot like her.

"Great! What's your name?"

"Itamar."

"Are you two related by any chance?"

"We're twins," Noa said.

"Really?" He wasn't sure whether to believe her.

"Yes," Itamar said. "But we don't speak with the same voice." Yonatan laughed with the class and felt that the love he had hoped for, and had not known how he would do without, could be taken for granted.

"I'm glad to see you're a creative bunch," he said, and hated himself for using the word *bunch,* which made him sound old. He rapped his chalk on the board. "Anything else?"

"Dissenting voices!" someone called out from the back row.

"Thank you. With whom do I have the pleasure?"

"Dana."

He smiled. "My daughter's name is Dana."

"We know," Noa said.

"You do?" he asked, flattered and slightly afraid.

"Yes," her brother said. "You're a public voice, after all."

A white light flashed through the already electrified room, just as he started to say something about Faulkner—later, driving down from Mount Scopus in the pouring rain, he realized he'd never finished his sentence, that the glorious introductory lecture he had spent weeks drafting in the living room had been discarded along with his fears—and when the lightning cut off his train of thought and he fell quiet and faltered for a moment, looking at his admiring class, he heard the young and cynical Yonatan, who had quickly become his favorite and who had confessed to writing a novel, asking, "Is your writing influenced by Faulkner? Do you imitate him?"

"No. I was always too arrogant to imitate anyone." His heart soared. He was standing there lecturing them about a genius, but they wanted to know about *him.*

When he turned onto the road going into the center of town, he remembered what his friend from the literature department had told him when they'd sat in the cafeteria a few weeks ago and Yonatan had asked for his advice. "You could get a great class or a terrible one. It's the luck of the draw." He felt lucky. He had an excellent class, a class worthy of a talented teacher, a class that would happily function as confessor. He felt that his confession of being a failed writer, of the loneliness of failure, the freedom of failure, a tiresome confession heard by so many in so many versions, had through these young ears become meaningful and free from bitterness.

The rain was falling so hard that he considered stopping on the shoulder. The wipers jerked over the windshield and he couldn't see the road, but he kept driving. He couldn't remember ever having seen such a harsh first rain. It usually stuttered, a celestial warm-up, but this downpour had begun over two hours ago. It was self-confident rain, he thought as he watched the water cascade down the windshield and saw that the sky still looked far from empty. He only wished Shira could have been there to see him in action, not because he wanted to boast—he knew that had she been in the room he would have been quieter; he would have stuttered and talked only to her—but because he thought she had fallen in love with the man he was this morning, that she had guessed who he truly was. In his anxiety, she saw generosity; in his acquiescence, courage; in his cynicism, an invitation to his playground. It was as if she held his negatives in her hands. She was not, as he had once imagined Ilana, the left-hand solo to his right-hand accompaniment; that image now seemed distant and childish. She was not someone playing in the next room, not an audience or a teacher, but someone who could read his score, see his black notes before her eyes, the swirling instructions, and hear the music in her mind.

He wondered if she was home now, if she had come back from visiting her father. He drove down the road leading to the Hinnom Valley, passed by the Cinemateque, and stopped at the light at Hebron Road. His mother was expecting him for lunch. After class he had been planning to go by the department office, hand in some material to be photocopied, and meet his friend, who wanted to hear how his debut performance had gone, but he was so excited when he left the class, and so engaged in talking with Yonatan and Itamar and Noa, that he forgot.

He decided to take the long route to his mother's. He continued south on Hebron Road, to his left the narrow winding streets of Abu Tor, which in his childhood had seemed mysterious and perilous and now looked romantic, until he came to the Talpiot intersection and turned right into Baka. At the bus stop on the corner of Bethlehem Road, a woman in a long coat and head scarf got off a bus, and a girl helped her carry a stroller down to the sidewalk; he wondered if she was one of those American religious women who had taken over the neighborhood. But he had stopped caring. He had never loved the city as he did now. The screen of rain distanced him from the streets, which seemed hallucinatory and powerful in the way Jerusalem streets can. He loved the place of his birth as someone who knows he will never go back to live there. He wanted a city, just a city, not a constant fantasy or a continuous disappointment, not a femme fatale, who might suddenly slap her lover's cheek, out of coquettish neurosis rather than true insult. He wanted a real imperfect lover, one who hugged him with heavy arms and whose breath was warm and smoky, but when he was with her his steps were light and he breathed easily and did not miss a beat.

(2 4)

In the Intensive Care unit, she met a stranger. He did not look like her father, did not resemble in any way the man she had left in his bed yesterday, sleeping on his side with a blanket pulled up to his chin. The man on the wide convoluted bed looked soft and subdued under the mess of rubber tubes that came out of his nostrils and squirmed over his arms. His mouth, which was always tight, was now hidden behind an oxygen mask covered with misty breath, as if it was winter inside the mask too. This man was not her father. He wore different pajamas, which looked fresh and crisp; there was no bedside table and no personal items, even the slippers that always sat at the foot of his bed (although he no longer needed them) were gone. The man lying in Intensive Care was nothing more than a patient, with no accessories or roommates or consciousness.

When she came up to his bed and leaned over him, as if called to identify the body, she found he had no smell. The previous father had

had a rich repertoire of scents; his hands, neck, and cheeks smelled of aftershave, his mouth gave off the whiff of fasting, his thinned hair smelled like grease and skin, and the pajamas gave away the events of the day: a test he had undergone that left rust-colored iodine stains on the top or bottom, an IV needle that had come loose and squirted drops of blood on his sleeve; or breakfast, bits of which always remained on his collar. But this old man was pure, completely new, as if his life were just beginning. The stains and the sounds, the sorrow and the stench—all these had vanished; her father looked so much like a baby that, for the first time since she was a child, she wanted to touch him.

"We'll be transferring him to Internal H soon," said Dr. Amir, whom she had forgotten was standing behind her.

"Why?" she asked, worried: This new father looked peaceful and at home.

"He'll be monitored there, he'll get fluids and oxygen to make it easier for him, and we'll continue the IV antibiotics, just like here."

In the elevator she had asked if Amir was his first name or his last. "First," he said. When the doors slid open to the Intensive Care unit, he gestured gracefully and waited for her to step out. Like a doorman at the gates of hell, she thought. Now she turned from her father to him. He wasn't just short, he was practically a midget. She wondered if other children used to make fun of his height. She wondered if he had a wife who loved him. His square face now looked rigid and mechanical, like a robot's. "The Internal Medicine wards are your cemetery," she said, violating the pleasant silence, the monotonous tranquillity of the beeping machines.

Dr. Amir smiled. "That's not true."

"It is," she insisted childishly. "And the higher the ward letter, the more like a cemetery."

"I don't know what your name is—" he said, and she quickly told him, as if it were vital information needed to save her father. "Shira," he said, with a friendliness in which she now detected anger. "There are excellent doctors in the Internal Medicine wards, in all the wards, in all the letters. We'll make sure your father gets excellent care and that he does not suffer needlessly."

"What is needless suffering?" she asked, and her voice sounded screechy again. "All suffering is needless."

"Shira," he said calmly. "May I call you Shira?"

"Of course you may. What sort of a question is that? What else would you call me?"

"I apologize. I didn't mean to hurt your feelings."

"No." She was rocked by waves of numbing confusion, waiting for them to carry her out to the parking lot, to the guard she missed. "I don't understand the meaning of all this sudden politeness. And if I said no, you can't call me Shira, what would you call me? Ms. Klein?"

"Yes. I would call you whatever you asked me to call you."

"I notice the nurses call you Dr. Amir."

"Yes. So what?"

"Doesn't that strike you as ridiculous? It's your first name. Either you're formal or you're not, make up your mind."

He said nothing.

"Can't we leave him here?" she said, as if suddenly struck by a brilliant idea.

"No, we can't."

"Why, because it's more expensive?"

"That has nothing to do with it."

"What do you care, then? Why schlep him around again? You yourself said you wanted to prevent needless suffering."

"Shira," he said quietly, and now her name sounded pornographic coming from him, like a lecherous whisper. "I understand you're having a difficult time, and I repeat my recommendation that you ask someone close to be with you here. You have to understand that in Intensive Care we pull out all the stops, so to speak, and we're not going to pull out those stops for your father unless you want us to."

"Can't you just pull out some of the stops?" Tears started streaming down her face, but despite the relief it was not yet the crying she had anticipated. "Look at him," she said, and hated the young doctor who was about to abandon them. "How can you even think of moving him? He'll die on the way, he'll die in the elevator." Because after agreeing to let him go, she had to change her mind in some way, to protest, or at least put a few obstacles in his final path.

The doctor, as if considering her words, went up to her father, looked at the monitor that was measuring his blood pressure, glanced at his watch, and wrote something on the chart. He turned to her. "He won't die in the elevator, Shira." His feline eyes had turned satanic.

"I wish he would," she mumbled to herself. Everything seemed to have changed. Her father had gone from being a patient whose life was being fought for to a nuisance they were deciding where to store for a few hours.

"What?" the doctor asked.

"Nothing. I was talking to myself." She remembered her trip to Greece with Eitan, a few months after they met, and how furious she had been when they were seated separately on the airplane. She had demanded that the airline seat them together, and had addressed the ground crew in the same tone she now used with the doctor. Eitan had tried to calm her down. "It's only a short flight," he said. But she insisted, planting her elbows on the counter, where they had just checked in their duffel bags, clutching the boarding passes and threatening to sue. "What exactly would you sue us for?" the attendant asked. "For separating you for an hour?" Some of the people standing in line behind them giggled, and she knew there was no chance of her enjoying this vacation, there had never been a chance, and her scene at the airport was a last-ditch effort to cancel the trip.

"Come on, someone will switch with you on the plane," a girl behind her grumbled. "Why are you being such a fussbudget?" When she saw Eitan nodding in agreement, she said she wasn't a fussbudget, it was a matter of principle. Finally, a more senior attendant showed up, smelling of expensive aftershave. He glanced at the computer screen, hit a button, and, without saying a word or looking at her, reached out for their boarding passes and replaced them with new ones.

She wondered how Eitan was. She hadn't thought of him for two years. How many children did he have, three? She knew he was a wonderful father.

"What about his things?" she asked.

"What things?" Dr. Amir asked, and his beeper went off.

"Personal items," she said quietly, tasting the strange, chalky quality of the words.

"You can bring them to the ward; the nurse will give you a bag." He touched her arm and said he would receive updates on her father's condition throughout the day and would try and go down to visit him every so often.

"Down? It's downstairs?" she asked. He nodded and left the room. "What time is it?" she asked the nurse who came up to her father, as if she didn't have a watch, or as if it wasn't displaying the correct time for this ward.

"Twenty to eleven," the nurse said without looking at her, as she changed one of the IV drips.

"What's that?" Shira asked.

"Fluids."

"And that one?" She pointed to the other bag.

"Antibiotics." The nurse wrote something down on the chart.

"What does he need that for?" she asked angrily.

"He has an infection," the nurse said. She was much younger than Nurse Olga, and not the type to blow comforting kisses in the air.

"I know. But what does he need it for?"

"I don't know," the nurse said, about to leave the room. "Ask the doctor."

"But the doctor left."

"Ask in Internal H, when you go down."

"Now?" she said, as if their flight had been announced.

"Soon. I'll call the orderly." When she turned her back and walked to the door, Shira saw a ladder running down her stockings, from the back of her knee to her ankle.

"Excuse me!" she called after the nurse, her voice piercing the civilized foreign silence of the room.

"Yes?" The nurse turned her head.

"The doctor said you'd give me a bag for his belongings, his personal items."

"Ask in Internal. We don't have any bags here."

His mother came out to greet him in a state. "The house is flooded!" she announced breathlessly. "The whole kitchen is flooded!" She clutched her coat collar. He had been here only two weeks ago, but now he saw how much she had aged, and although she was never a small woman—he always thought she had masculine shoulders—she looked fragile, faded. "A flood!" she said. "Everything's flooded!" She made sounds that could have been water or wind, as if it weren't enough to hear the noise of the storm slamming down on the ground, crashing against the gravel path they both walked up quickly, he holding her elbow, leading her home.

A drainpipe over the kitchen window was clogged. She stood behind him as he put his head out the window into the rain and told him it had happened quickly. "I couldn't do anything," she apologized, as if she could have prevented the flood had she acted faster. He clutched the window frame and stretched his neck out to find the source of the leak, the rain drowning out his mother's voice as she kept talking to him from the kitchen. He pulled his head back into the kitchen and caught his mother saying something about taking her coffee into the study, where she was sorting through paperwork—"Paperwork," he said, "what paperwork?"— She said, "All sorts of old things that belonged to Dad and me."

"To you?"—now he noticed she had taken off her coat and hung it on the back of a chair and was wearing a wine-colored robe he didn't recognize. "What do you mean, you?"

"I'm putting things straight, so I may as well tackle everything."

She stood on tiptoe and tried to dry his hair with a kitchen towel, but he shook her away—there was fear in his heart—and said, "Why did you suddenly decide to tackle your paperwork?"

"No reason," she said. "I was just taking advantage of the time while I was waiting for you." When she went from the study into the kitchen, she continued, after maybe an hour, even less, everything was flooded—everything! She spread out her arms and indicated the floor, which still had little puddles where the tiles had sunk, even though she had dried the flood. It would cost a fortune to fix this house up, he thought, and as he looked over the floor, he noticed that the edges of his mother's slippers were damp.

"Do you have a stick or a broom?" he asked. "I think the drainpipe's clogged with leaves; there's a leak right at the joint, above."

She said of course she had one and handed him the mop that stood behind the fridge, quickly and too gratefully. "Will a mop work? I just used it to clean up in here."

He nodded. "I think I should do this from outside, I don't have good access from here," he said, in the authoritative tone of a son who knows how to fix things.

"But it's raining. Maybe you should wait a little."

"We can't wait, Mom. If everything's clogged up, it will keep dripping and you'll have a big mess in here again." He walked decisively to the door, holding the mop, with no idea of what he would do with it. He had never dealt with drainpipes.

His mother pulled the umbrella out of the stand in the entrance; it always held just one, his father's. He said he didn't need an umbrella, and she said he did. "Go on, I'll come out with you."

"Put your coat on," he said, and she said she didn't need to, it wasn't that cold. They walked down the path leading to the backyard, he in front, she holding the umbrella high above his head, as if he were a foreign dignitary whose airplane had landed on a rainy day. "You're getting wet, Mom," he said, without looking back.

"Just a little, it's all right, the rain won't kill me." She kept holding the umbrella over him as he shoved the mop handle into the opening of the drainpipe and tried to push it up.

"It's completely clogged," he said, struggling. "I don't know if I can open it."

"You don't?" Her worried voice came from behind the umbrella.

"No. It might not even be leaves."

"But what else could it be?" Her question was punctuated by lightning.

"I have no idea, Mom." He felt the edge of the umbrella poking his neck.

"What a storm!" she said, as he held the mop with both hands and tried again to force it up the metal sleeve, making strenuous sounds. "They didn't say it would be like this on the weather forecast," she complained. "They said it would drizzle."

"Mom, move the umbrella, it's just getting in my way."

"But you'll get wet!" Along with the familiar worry, he detected in her voice a gleefulness, as if they had both gone camping and were caught in a storm.

"Stop it, Mom! You're stabbing me."

"Sorry, sorry, I didn't mean to."

"Move. Move back; I don't want you to get hit." From the fixing son he had become the policeman son.

"Sorry, did I hurt you?" Her cold fingers touched the back of his neck.

"Mom, stop it; really, I can't work like this."

She retreated, and he turned to look at her and saw an old lady with broad shoulders standing under an umbrella in a wine-colored rain-drenched robe, which now looked like a furry wet animal. He made fists with his hands, and hit one fist with the other and whacked the drainpipe, letting out a battle cry, and suddenly felt something dislodge. The mysterious blockage had burst, the mop went up easily, and a dead bird fell to the ground.

He felt the umbrella tickling his neck again. "What is that?" his mother whispered.

"A bird," he said.

"What kind of bird?" she wondered, leaning forward with the umbrella, which now scratched his cheek. "A pigeon?"

"I don't think so. It's the size of a pigeon, but that's not what it is."

They both looked at the wet pile of feathers, which had a small yellow beak peaking out from one side and two claws on the other, straight up and frozen.

"But how did it get into the drainpipe?" his mother asked, and her voice sounded apologetic again.

"I haven't a clue," he said, and his wet clothes clung to his body coldly. "Maybe it had a nest under the eaves and the nest fell."

"But why didn't it fly away?" his mother asked, suddenly childish and angry.

"Maybe it was struck by lightning."

"Lightning?" she said, and he said it happened. "Of course, it happens in the movies, but to people, not to birds. How could it happen to a bird? I saw a movie where it happened to a person, but a bird?"

In the feathery mess he saw an eye, open just a crack.

"It'll start to smell bad," his mother said, as she leaned over the tiny corpse. "We have to throw it away."

"Later. Before I leave. Let's go in, you're soaked." He took the umbrella, held it over her, lowered his head, put a hand on her shoulder, and walked her down the path, his eyes staring at her wet slippers, made of velvety fabric decorated with a golden embroidery that was unraveling. Through the rhythmical squishing sounds that accompanied her steps, he heard her mumbling that she didn't want a dead bird in her yard, and he promised again to clear it away later.

"But you'll forget," she said, when they went inside.

"I won't forget, you'll remind me."

His heart swelled, as if it too were drenched with rain, as he watched her put a pot of soup on the stove, dressed now in a different robe, a more familiar yolk-colored one, and thick woolen socks; he was afraid she would slip in them. He moved the toes of his bare feet on the floor and looked at his shoes and socks, drying opposite the seldom-used space heater he had once bought her, her own slippers keeping them company. He leaned back in his chair—she had wanted to eat in the dining area, but he preferred the kitchen—and stretched out the sleeves of his father's old sweater, which he wore instead of his own wet one. It was a soft sweater, a couple of sizes too small for him, that he remembered his father wearing a few times.

"Did Dana go on her school trip in this rain?" she asked, worried.

"No, it's tomorrow."

"Thank God. Let's hope it clears up by then."

"Of course it will." He realized suddenly, as if for the first time, that his mother had only one son and one granddaughter; that was all. "It will clear up soon. This isn't typical rainfall for the season."

"It could keep raining, though."

"It'll stop, don't worry."

"This kind of rain, where they didn't say when it would start, there's no way to tell when it will stop," she said, and he smiled. When had she become so fearful? When had her logic become so hermetic that you could not argue with it? Was it possible, he wondered with alarm, that his real mother was gone? That the broad-shouldered woman with the well-groomed faded honey hair, now flattened in separate strands on her head like doll's hair, had already gone without him on that journey everyone talked about?

"Poor thing," she said, as she stirred the soup.

"Who?"

"The bird."

"Yes." He sighed. "Poor thing. . . . You know what? I taught my first class today."

"Oh, yes!" She turned to him with a guilty look on her face. "I forgot to ask you how it went, because of all this chaos. So, how was it?"

"It was all right." He listened to the rain, to the lid dancing on the pot, and then asked, teasingly, "So what kind of soup do we have today?"

"Chicken," she said apprehensively. "Because of the rain. I defrosted a chicken I had in the freezer. Is that all right?"

He smiled, his heart, damp from compassion, broadening: If she had a chicken in the freezer, that must mean she hadn't gone too far. He nodded and barely held back from getting up to hug her. "Don't you know I love your chicken soup?"

"Really?"

"Come on, didn't you know that?"

"Of course I did. But maybe I forgot." She ladled soup into a bowl and asked if he wanted a piece of celery in it.

He thought to himself, Why not? Why shouldn't I get up and hug her? Nothing big that would demand an explanation, just a little hug.

"Yes. Put some celery in. Put anything in." He watched her trembling hand holding the ladle and fishing out some celery for him.

"Carrot?"

"What's the matter with you today, Mom? Are you going senile?"

"Well, for all I know you don't like it anymore."

"I like it," he said, and got up from his chair. "I like it a lot." He was going to walk up to her and wrap his arms around her, but he went to the window and touched the frame. "Dry."

"Good job." She carefully put the bowl of soup on the little table in the corner. "The way you knew exactly what to do right away. I wouldn't have known."

He stood close to her and raised his hand to put it on her shoulder. "I just guessed." But his mother turned to him and suspiciously eyed his hand, which had now dropped to his side. "What's wrong?" he said.

"I forgot to buy oyster crackers."

He said it was all right, he didn't need any.

"Wait, I do have some! I just remembered, I bought some last week! They're in the cabinet up top."

He said he'd get them, and went to the cabinet over the fridge, and the phone rang and she hurried to the living room. "Don't slip!" he called after her. He poured a handful of crackers out, tossed them into his mouth, and stood inspecting the window with satisfaction.

"It's Shira," his mother said, when she came back. Then she whispered, "I think she's crying."

(2 6)

It was still not the crying she was hoping for but something close, and she thought she could hear, in its hiccuping sobs, the beginnings of the question: Was there some other kind of crying, massive and wild, the great crying of her fantasies, or perhaps this was it—there was no other.

When the doctors made their visit, they asked her to leave the room for a few minutes, but the minutes turned into an hour and a half, and she stood in the hallway of Internal H, leaning on the wall, her cell phone in one hand and, in the other, a large bunch of keys she had distractedly taken from her bag and was now holding as if she were on her way out.

Her father used to hold his keys too. His wallet had its regular place in his back hip pocket, his reading glasses and pens always peeked out from his shirt pocket, but he could never find a place for the keys—as a child, she believed they had preferential status, like her own—and when they walked down Allenby he would clutch both the keys and her hand in his own, the serrated edges sticking through the patchwork of their fingers. Sometimes she wondered why he didn't use his other hand, why he preferred to hold his two most precious assets with one grip, but she never asked, and she never told him that the keys dug into her flesh and pressed on her knuckles.

The pride she felt on those walks with her busy energetic father, who, with his disdain, tried to banish the whores and beggars from her field of vision; the admiration she felt when she sat across from this handsome, introverted man in the café that no longer existed and which had been replaced with a bustling hovel that sold pirated tapes, reduced the pain to a pulsating spot in her palm. She adapted her walk to his hasty pace, looked where he did, became friends, in her heart, with the people he stopped to chat with, holding her hand the whole time. She held her breath when they went into stores because she hoped he would find what he was looking for. Their intimacy, which did not yet have a name, seemed so fragile, like a spiderweb that could be ruined with one touch, however light and curious. She said nothing because she loved him. If he loved her too, she reasoned, he couldn't be hurting her. The pain was not real. What was real were the magical afternoon hours that hung like a rope bridge between the mornings, which he spent far away from her at work, and the evenings, when he came home and became distant. The pain, she thought with childish heroism, was worth it all.

She stood in the hallway, guessing by the time the doctors were spending in his room that her father's situation had deteriorated. She wondered where his keys were now. She couldn't remember seeing them in the cabinet with his things and couldn't remember what he had been wearing on the day he was hospitalized. Perhaps she had put the keys in his jacket pocket; perhaps she had put them down somewhere in a safe place now forgotten. She tried to remember if she had seen them the last time she visited his apartment and thought of how, in an instant, the one thing he had been so afraid to lose had disappeared—the thing that had been part of their skin, his and hers. When the door opened and two young doctors came out, passing her and ignoring her questioning eyes, she thought, Maybe it's better that they're lost, because with the other items, even the reading glasses, she could somehow cope, but what did one do with a bunch of keys for doors that would soon—in her gut she knew how soon it would be—become irrelevant?

A few minutes after four. She had no idea what had happened to all the hours since they brought her father down here. She had the sudden sensation that time was passing quickly and yet also standing still, leaning, as she was, on a wall and waiting. She tried to remember when she had talked to Yonatan. It was an hour or two ago, but those were normal hours, whose dimensions matched the outside world; here, at 4 P.M. in this hallway, they were a foreign code. "Hi," she had said, when he'd picked up the phone and said Shira? in a worried voice, full of munching sounds. "What are you eating?" she asked and realized she hadn't had anything to eat all day. He said he was having some soup and she heard him swallow and ask what was going on, and in a stifled sob she told him about her father. "He's going to die," she said, and the words, like time, lost their meaning. He said he would leave right away, and she asked if it was raining there, and he said it was pouring; was it raining where she was? As if they were in two different countries. She said it had rained earlier but now she didn't know, and she searched for an outside window, not one that faced another hallway, like the one next to her father's new bed, which was covered with a light-blue curtain and looked onto another closed window, covered with the same curtain. "I don't know," she said, and he said he'd be there in an hour or an hour and a half and hung up. She remembered the stick in the neighbors' trash can, with its fading blue stripe, and saw herself sitting on the bathroom floor. She had hidden the kit in her bag for two weeks, and every time she reached for something, her date book or cigarettes or keys, her fingers met the outline of the cardboard box. Just out of curiosity, she had told herself this morning when she took the box out of her bag, and now it seemed impossible that she had done the test today, that right now an egg was moving through her body and had been with her all day, going up and down in the elevators, waiting for orderlies and doctors, and now leaning on this wall, opposite her father's room; perhaps it would be with her later, perhaps it wouldn't—this egg that knew no guilt or terror, or what it meant to miss someone.

The nurse came out and said, "You can go in now. The doctor wants to talk to you." She looked at her and saw a body in uniform and a face without features, as if her eyes had tired of giving detailed reports or had realized there was no point in details anymore; this strange, quick, and static time in which she was now located was like those afternoon hours with her father, a rope bridge connecting two times—the one in which he existed and the one in which he didn't—and they were both the same. She disconnected from the wall and wiped her eyes with the back of her hand. "But please turn off your cell phone," the nurse said, "there are instruments in here." Shira said it was off, looked at it to make sure, and threw it in her bag. But she kept holding the keys as she went into the room.

The doctor now seemed irrelevant too. She glanced at him and then looked at her father. The doctor said there had been a deterioration over the last hour, the antibiotics hadn't stopped the infection from spreading, his blood pressure was very low, his breathing was shallow and irregular, and there wasn't much time left.

She looked at her father and said she thought he wasn't breathing anymore.

"He is breathing." The doctor had a foreign accent, but she no longer cared where he was from. "It's hard to see, but he is breathing."

She was overcome by anger, tired and grumbling anger. They had just taken the elevator down here; she knew the orderly who had taken them down from Intensive Care and had even been happy to see him. "How is the father?" he had asked, his big stomach pushing against the foot of the bed, his arms leaning on the steel rests on either side of it.

"Not good," she had said, and looked at him pleadingly, as if he were a new doctor who had come to give a diagnosis in the elevator.

"Everything will be all right," the orderly said. "What's his name?"

"Max. Max Klein," she said, as if he couldn't be saved without his last name.

"Everything will be all right, Mr. Klein," he said, looking at her father's white face. He hadn't been shaved that morning, and gray stubble covered his chin and cheeks like a soft layer of moss. "Everything will be all right." His voice echoed between the service elevator's metal walls. "And where is the boyfriend?" he asked.

"He's at the university."

"Studying?"

"Teaching."

"Very nice. What does he teach, computers?"

"Literature."

"Literature is interesting," he said, and the doors opened to the hallway of the Internal Medicine ward. "Literature is important."

When the nurse instructed him to take the bed into this room, which had three empty beds in it, she had stood deliberating over which one to choose until the orderly determined unequivocally: next to the window. In the middle was no good, he said, too crowded, and by the entrance there was a sink, no privacy. Best is by the window. All that couldn't have happened today, she thought, and when she glanced at her watch she desperately missed eight-fifty, that first trip in the elevator, in the previous time. Right after they moved her father into the bed, the doctors came and asked her to leave, and since it was only for a few minutes, she decided to put off going to his old room for his things. Later, she thought, she'd go and also get something to eat. The croissants had looked reasonable but she had never been hungry enough here to try them, and she pictured herself drinking café latte in a huge glass, the kind that would be suitable for her current thirst, and smoking a cigarette or two and then going up to the ward and reorganizing her father's things. She had stood for an hour and a half outside his room until she was suddenly called in, and from that moment on there was no *later*.

"Look," she said to the doctor. "He's not breathing."

"He is breathing. It's weak breath, I know it's hard to see, but he's breathing."

"But how will I know when he stops?" she said, panicking, as if her father were planning a trick: slipping out of the room on his tiptoes, exit-ing the world in absolute silence, with that same quiet elegance in which he used to get dressed. He would be sucked out all at once and leave his sloughed body on the bed, so she would keep looking at him without ever knowing if he was there or not.

"We'll let you know," the doctor said and looked at her watching her father. She did not take her eyes off him for a second, as if her look were respirating him. "We'll let you know," he repeated, and she thought she could hear true sadness in his voice, in his foreign accent. "But I think you'll be able to tell."

(2 7)

Just after leaving Jerusalem, he realized he'd forgotten to remove the bird. Even though he told her he had to hurry because Shira's father was in critical condition, his mother had insisted on pack-ing a lunch for him, and he had put on his socks and shoes, still wet, and watched her rummaging through the kitchen cabinets, looking for plas-tic containers—the normally neat cabinets were chaotic—and said he really had to run. "One second," his mother had said, breathing heavily as she poured his soup into a container and pressed the lid down firmly. "Be careful, it's hot."

"It'll just spill in the car," he protested.

"No, it won't, you'll drive slowly." She filled another container with brisket and potatoes. She kept clicking her tongue, and asked, "But what does he have?"

"An infection. He's lost consciousness. I think this is it, Mom."

She walked him to the door, and he asked her not to come out but she insisted. "It's stopped raining," she said, and held her palm out to the sky.

He told himself he would call her later, and then realized that, before going to the hospital, he would have to go home and put the food in the fridge—his mother was delaying him again, he thought, putting tasty obstacles in his way. In any case, he would have to go home to make sure Dana had everything she needed for the trip, give her some money, and have a little talk with her—he wouldn't see her for five days. He might suggest that she spend the night at Tamar's because he didn't know when he and Shira would get home.

He listened to the three o'clock news. There had been record rainfall that morning all over the country, even in the Negev Desert and the Arava, the announcer said, but the sky had cleared now, shreds of clouds were hovering in deceptive laziness, and if not for the glimmering road dotted with puddles, one could imagine that the dramatically reported storm had been a collective fantasy.

He thought about Shira, about her crying, how she had cried the first time they had been together too, in her apartment—only a year and a half had passed, but that time suddenly seemed sweet and almost collegiate—how he had looked at her leaning against the bookshelf, talking with her father, who was only a telephone presence at the time, a generic father, a disturbance; how he had examined her tense body stretched over the phone cord like a splint and wanted to interrogate it, to rape it, to comfort it—that body, like her father, was now a part of his life.

He felt guilty for having had a wonderful morning. While she had been running back and forth between hospital wards, he had basked in the glory of his students' admiration, much as he had bathed himself in spring sunlight that morning at the café on Sheinkin with that director. How was it he was always absent when needed? He hit the gas pedal hard and the speedometer needle jumped up, but even before he had time to chastise himself for speeding dangerously, his foot had to move to the brake, the other joining in listlessly and pressing down on the clutch; the traffic was backed up to just after the Latrun intersection. He didn't know if it was because of an accident or the rain, or if it was one of those traffic jams that had no reason, as if a supreme power had decided to amuse itself and put the road into a coma, freeze the drivers, and then suddenly wake them up, without having any idea of what had happened to them. Something told him this was a serious holdup. He looked around at the cars on either side of him, trying to decide, as he always did when he was stuck, if he should move to the outside lane, where traffic seemed to be moving faster. But he decided to stay where he was, calm down, and give in to the passivity enforced upon him, which was somehow pleasant, excusing.

He had been crawling behind a truck for twenty minutes, memorizing its license plates and the sound its brakes made, which reminded him of a peacock's scream. He had not moved more than a mile or two and was already feeling his enforced calm dissipating, aware of its unreliability, how the passivity moved impatiently inside him and made way for restlessness, which became, when traffic came to a standstill again, true anger. He listened to the traffic reports on two stations, but neither one mentioned his holdup. He thought about Shira and wondered where she was now, if she was taking her father for a test, listening to a doctor's explanations, or sitting in her usual corner by the vending machine, smoking a cigarette. How lucky he was that he had been saved from having to watch his father die; the phone call had come afterward, so he could only imagine the final moments, do with them as he wished, write hundreds of scripts, rewrite, develop, and then reject them all. He looked at a luxury car with diplomatic license plates that was now positioned between him and the truck and knew Shira was not in any of the places he had pictured; even if he could position her somewhere, she would always be somewhere else. She had told him once, a few weeks after they met, when they sat on the balcony one night drinking beer, that she no longer believed in absolute unity, in that fusion that had existed between her first novel's protagonists.

"That totality: I used to want it so badly. Not just to be with someone but to simply *be* someone else, who would also be me," she said.

And he said, looking at her with a love that was, at that moment, more complete than anything she had ever written, simpler than any phrase he had ever used in his books, "Then it's not someone else."

"Who isn't?" She looked at him with those sad eyes, which were new to him then and fascinating.

"That someone. If it's you, it's not different."

"No, I suppose not." Then she burst out laughing. "We sound like the commercial for that yuppie American perfume, do you know the one I mean?" He said he thought he did, but he didn't, and she looked at the sky and quoted a few lines sardonically: "'Am I touching you, or are you touching me? Am I you, you me? How will we know who is who?'" She whispered the name of the perfume in his ear, her lips cold and wet from the beer, and he laughed and said yes, that was it. But he wondered if he was that someone she had once written about, the someone from the commercial, the someone she no longer believed in.

Now he tried to remember how her lips looked, as if he hadn't seen her for years. Their image appeared instantly, a human file called up on the screen, and flickered on the windshield, standing between him and the luxury car. He saw them move in conversation, open and close as they ate, drank, kissed, remained silent; then he imagined her eyes and saw them closing and opening, blinking, smiling at him, angry at him, huge and half open when she came, like her lips. He summoned up feature after feature and projected them on the windshield, stuck in a traffic jam that, from one moment to the next, seemed more and more infinite. When did that Palestinian taxi wind its way into his lane? He looked for the luxury car, which had disappeared, and now he saw her hands, small, indelicate, unbeautiful, miming. They joined the eyes and lips in their various actions, all of which, he suddenly realized, were connected to him. He tried to imagine her sitting on her own, smoking by the vending machine, thinking about her father, imagining his death, and could not. Then he thought of himself hugging her and saw each separate quality of the embrace—the intensity, the temperature, the dim fullness of her limbs as they were gathered up in his—and he was filled with longing.

But it was not only her he longed for, he missed his mother. The bag on the seat next to him filled him with compassion and fear, because he knew the day was not far off when he would try to reconstruct the flavor of his mother's cooking in his mouth and would fail, and other flavors would come instead, the flavor of missed opportunities, for example. What did he know about her, this woman who had had a life before him, while he had had none before her? What did he know about this old lady, who had probably given the kitchen a cursory cleaning after he'd left and then gone to rest in her room or back to sorting her mysterious papers until she too had remembered the bird? He stared at the green Palestinian license plate, which looked as beat-up as the orange taxi, and his head began concocting political slogans to amuse himself: *Stuck together forever,* he thought, and crawled so close to the taxi that his bumper was almost touching it. "Up each other's ass," he said out loud, and almost extricated himself from the sadness that had descended upon him, but then he saw his mother leaning down to take the dustpan out of the cabinet beneath the sink, retrieving the broom from behind the fridge, going out into the yard in her robe and slippers to clear away the little corpse, and the sadness became panic, and he knew that anything his mother did in his imagination would now appear to be her last act in life.

A little before four, he was encouraged to see the sign for Ganot interchange. This was the point where traffic usually eased up or became less claustrophobic. Then, finally, there was a report of a disabled vehicle in the left lane, but it was unclear if the vehicle was the cause of the jam or its result. In any case, he was hopeful that soon he would see the big sign, WELCOME TO AYALON HIGHWAY, that he loved and hated so much, because when the highway was wide open it made him feel as if he were in America, and when it wasn't it reminded him he had nowhere to run to. "Strange Days" came on the radio, and he was happy that his favorite song, his sex song, would accompany him through the moments of deliverance, when he would finally be able to put his foot on the gas. But Jim Morrison's voice, with the special effect that had been added to it, a kind of dim metallic quality of someone singing from inside a can, suddenly made him fearful, as if Morrison had recorded the song after he was dead. The cars seemed to be crawling along even more slowly. He went underneath a cement bridge, and he remembered a bridge that had collapsed a few years ago, killing three people. He put his face to the windshield and looked up, searching for cracks in the structure, then looked left and right at the complacent drivers on either side and wondered how many victims the disaster would claim: who was likely to survive and who, like him, was stuck directly underneath. He drummed nervously on the steering wheel and stayed close to the Palestinian taxi in front, which, like him, still remained faithful to the middle lane.

When he passed under the bridge he considered switching lanes. Perhaps a change of scenery would help, he told himself. It was four-twenty, and he knew there was no way he would be home before five. Now he wished he'd left Dana a message before leaving. She had probably been home for ages and may have even called his mother about him, and now his mother would be worried. On the other hand, maybe instead of going home Dana had gone off to wander the streets, at odds with herself and with him. What did he even know about her? She must have an entire secret life, as he had had when he was her age, and still did, and always would. And how lonely that life was, he thought. He was filled with sympathy, not for himself—he was an old fox by now, who knew how to steal into the chicken coop he himself had fenced off and get away unscathed—but for his daughter, for whom everything was just coming into being. How many scratches would she get? How many injuries would she suffer as she crawled under the fence? If only he could guide her: You can get in this way, not that way; there's food over here, over there there's a trap; here you'll find love, don't look over there.

On a sudden impulse, he decided to move to the left lane, which looked as if it was starting to pick up speed. He put his turn signal on and waited for a driver to let him in. He thought about the three of them, about his daughter and his mother and Shira, and wanted to save them but did not know from what. He counted twenty-three cars, twenty-three drivers who ignored him, defending their territory, until he heard a friendly little honk, looked in the mirror, and saw a woman driving a little Subaru Justy like his on his left, gesturing to him, and he waved a thank-you and quickly merged. Curious to know who the woman was, he strained to catch sight of her face in the rearview mirror, but he couldn't see her clearly. She looked younger, in her thirties, a normal woman in a normal car. Then he noticed that she kept turning her head to the right and her lips were talking or singing, and every so often she leaned so far over that her head disappeared from his field of vision and then reappeared; now he could clearly see that she was making faces, and when her hand joined in the pantomime act, opening and closing like a beak, her fingers moving opposite some invisible entity, he realized there was a baby next to her. He kept looking at her in the mirror as he moved slowly with the traffic, looking ahead every so often so as not to hit the car in front of him, and all the time he had a big grin on his face, as if he were the baby she was trying to amuse. He wasn't even angry when someone cut in front of him and charged down the lane, which had suddenly cleared without warning. The cars in the lanes to his right also began to move quickly.

The traffic jam is over, he thought, cleared in one second of inattention. Soon he'd get off at La Guardia; he hoped the woman would too, because she seemed like a fairy godmother who had lifted the curse from the road. But the Subaru driver was so busy with her baby she didn't even glance at him when he moved to the right. She kept on driving and he got off at his exit, which was completely clear, as if he were the only person using it, and when he stopped at the light, the five o'clock news came on the radio, announced by a series of beeps that penetrated the car like a distant alarm clock ringing into a dream, and he remembered driving with Dana, when she was a baby.

She would sit next to him in a huge car seat with teddy bears and bunnies on it. She always looked so small in that seat, a tiny copilot, the padded straps hiding her shoulders, her bare feet turned in different directions. She would fall asleep with her chin on her chest, and he would look at her and his heart would flutter: here he was driving her now, here he was driving her into his life. Once, when she was three months old, he looked at her and saw she was awake, looking at the window, and he wondered what she could see from her position, facing backward. He tried to catch the images out of the corner of his eye but could not, until he realized it was not images that she saw but pure motion, something basic and fascinating that no longer existed for him. Her face seemed distant, almost old and private; she seemed thoughtful in a way he never imagined a baby could be, and he was alarmed by the idea that she might be sad. Even though he knew it was his own perception that was painting her look with sadness, his own loneliness extracting calmness from her eyes and replacing it with shreds of contemplation, and although he knew he was not watching a sad baby or a happy one, or a tranquil or troubled one, but a person with a life of her own, a three-month-old life, compact and secretive and denying interpretation, he could not restrain himself and his lips let out a whistle. For a moment, her little body in the huge seat was shocked, and he thought she was going to cry. He reached out and tickled her under her chin, and she looked at him and smiled, and her face glowed.

As if someone had been following her around with a huge eraser, the entire day disappeared, the hours distilled into single, horrifyingly clear moments, as cold as her father's hand, which, alone among all his limbs, was still large and manly. She held it to her lips, tasted his skin, and thought, I am going to see my father die. She felt neither sadness nor fear, only anticipation. She leaned over him, caressed his cheek, and felt her straight back, her tense shoulders springy, her neck and head stiff, as if she were a scarecrow banishing birds of prey from his bed, and she imagined that the room was also anticipatory, emptying its air out and waiting to absorb her father like a substance, a spray released from its container. What, then, would she find in the emptiness left behind his consciousness? Could it be replaced by her own consciousness, snapping into place like a cube? And what was her father's final thought and what was its precise timing? Was it the thought that passed through his mind a second before he sank into a coma, or one that would fly like a lost ball between the walls of the empty room, which only this morning had been filled with the furnishings of his consciousness, when he took his final breath?

His skin tone had changed. His face and arms had taken on the color of ash or clouds. She didn't know if it was still raining outside—it seemed quiet and full of expectation behind the closed window blind, a gray she had never seen before, anywhere, not even in her dreams, which always included strange color combinations that could not be reconstructed in the morning, only feared and missed. So this is what death looks like, she thought, and heard herself say silently, *So this is what death looks like.* She wondered where that place was inside her that always knew how to phrase things. So this is his color, she thought, and her hand reached out to touch the fingers of her father's right hand, which suddenly trembled and danced on the sheet as if a train had passed beneath his bed, and then they stopped—like the rumble of an engine, she thought, after the ignition key has been turned off—and she didn't know if the trembling was a delayed response to what she had whispered in his ear just after the doctor had left, the statement, a shiver of words, that she loved him.

She put her face to his, trying to pick up hidden motion behind the oxygen mask, which no longer alternated between clouding over and clearing up but had also taken on a grayish tone, as if coated on the inside by a murky layer of used breaths. Leaning one hand on the plastic chair and the other on the bed, her breath caressing the mask from the outside, she suddenly felt the familiar pain of a metallic pinch in her right hand and realized she was still gripping her keys. She sat down on the chair and fanned them out on her lap: the house key and the mailbox key; the car keys, bigger and more impressive than the others, hanging on a separate ring; the key for the apartment on Borochov, which she had forgotten to return; the key to the deadbolt lock on her father's apartment door; and the small simple key to his mailbox, which looked like hers.

Once, when she was five or six, he had rushed to make it across the pedestrian crossing before the light changed and pulled her behind him, grasping her hand firmly, and when they got to the other side, she burst into tears. He looked down at her, surprised, and asked what happened, and she jerked her hand away from his and showed it to him, palm down. He asked again, "But what happened?" She pointed to the red grooves his keys had made in her flesh, and wailed, "It hurts!"

"But what hurts?" he asked, smiling awkwardly at the passersby who stopped near them. She pointed accusingly at the bunch of keys in his hand—"That!"—and her crying got louder, as if the confession had only added to her sorrows. "The keys?" he asked, and looked at them as if seeing them for the first time. "These?" He dangled them in front of her and she knew she had lost him; he would disappear and leave her standing alone on Allenby, rubbing her hand, surrounded by strangers, regretful.

He pulled a handkerchief out of his pocket and wiped her eyes. Then he took hold of her hand, which was still held out in the air, demanding justice, took his reading glasses out of his shirt pocket, put them on, and examined her closely. Then he closed her hand into a fist, finger by finger, and hit himself on the cheek with her fist, waiting for her to laugh—"Here. Now Daddy hurts too"—and said they would go to a café and have some ice cream. "You too?" she asked, because she had never seen him eat sweet things. "Me too. Would you like that?" She dried her eyes and through her post-crying hiccups, murmured yes, and the knowledge that her father liked ice cream was so sensational that she forgot her pain and insult. He put the keys in his other hand and took hold of hers, which now felt very light and free, and orphaned.

She put her keys in her bag, got up, and went to the window but didn't have the courage to open it or draw the curtain, because she was afraid that the outside, which over the last few hours had been moved far away, like a violent protester who might endanger them, would infiltrate the room—the outside that she missed, knowing that when she met it again, when she went out into the night or the morning, into the air that smelled of rain or of whatever had erased it, she would be a person who had no parents. She tiptoed back to the chair, sat down carefully, and then noticed the catheter bag lying on the floor at the foot of the bed, with its tube visible under the sheet. It was empty, unnecessary, she thought, like the IV and the feeding tube—so he won't inhale the contents of his gut into his lungs, the nurse had told her when she asked why he needed it—even the oxygen mask looked ridiculous now. She wanted to get up and pull these rubber toys off, one by one, but when she looked down again she saw the bag start to fill with fluid, also of a dreamlike color, something reddish and rusty and thick that did not look like urine but like the fluid from a machine. She watched the bag and thought about that dog, not the puppy they almost adopted on the beach but the one they found one summer evening, when she was ten, with the other kids on the block, lying on his side beneath a shrub in the building's backyard, panting—the dog she preferred not to think of, because he was always there, shuddering in her imagination.

The children surrounded him, arguing among themselves over whether he was dangerous, what breed he was, and how old he was, until her father, who had stood on the balcony watching them play, noticed the commotion and came down. "He has rabies," he determined, and told them to move away, and the kids dispersed begrudgingly, protesting that Shira was allowed to stay. "She's not allowed either," he said, and put his hand on her shoulder, and at that moment her mother came back from the pool, and her father asked her to go upstairs and call the municipality and tell them to come urgently to remove the lethal danger. Her mother said they should call a private vet: Dudi, her friend's son, who was doing veterinary studies. A private vet might try to help the dog—Dudi wouldn't even take money for it—but the municipality would kill him on the spot.

"Yes, Dad." Shira held his hand and swung it. "Please! Let's call Dudi."

But her father said, "Are you mad? Can't you see he's rabid?"

The city vet arrived, pushed past the neighborhood children who had disobeyed her father and come back out, and said it wasn't rabies but distemper. He said it wasn't dangerous but there was nothing to be done, it was a fatal disease; the dog was two or three months old at most and would have to be put to sleep. Her father looked pleased, as if he had been proven both wrong and right, and the vet went to his car and came back with a syringe and two glass vials, one of which contained a small amount of white powder and the other some clear liquid. Riveted, her father and the kids had watched as he emptied the powder into the liquid and shook the vial, jabbed its lid with the syringe, and siphoned in the magical substance that would help the dog sleep, as he explained what he was doing to the two children from next door. Shira looked at her mother, silently pleading for her to do something, and her mother wrapped her arms around her and crossed them over her chest, and she could feel her damp swimsuit under her dress pressing up against her back, and smelled the beloved scent of chlorine mixed with coconut oil.

The vet knelt by the dog, stuck the syringe into his fur, and stood up. "How long does it take?" her father asked, and she hated him.

"A minute or two," the vet said, and went back to his car.

"Is he asleep yet?" the little children asked, and the vet said, Soon. Her mother's arms tightened around her chest, the dog stopped breathing and trembling and looked very calm. "Now?" the kids shouted. "Now is he asleep?"

The vet yelled back from his car, "In a minute," and she slammed the back of her head repeatedly against her mother's collarbone and tears streamed down her face.

Through them she saw her father go up close to the puppy and ask the vet, who had returned with a black plastic bag, "Tell me, is he suffering now?"

"No," the man said, "he's already dead"—and at that second a stream of urine had erupted from beneath the dog's tail, and the kids from next door burst out laughing.

She wasn't sure if she should call the doctor. Perhaps the filling bag of urine indicated a change in his condition, a deterioration—but what deterioration could occur in the condition of someone who was now breathing his final superficial breaths? Someone who, since this morning, was not really there and whom no one was trying to bring back? She glanced at her watch: five forty-five. As she had walked behind the orderly who wheeled the bed in here, she had glanced into the rooms along the hallway, and they looked bustling, even happy, full of patients and visitors, food carts parked in the doorways. It occurred to her that they had purposely put him in this empty room, purposely left them alone, as a gesture of consideration, an act of abandonment, and as if her father had heard her thoughts, his chest rose and fell like a bellows and the mask covered over with vapors, and she thought she heard a sigh trapped under the rubber dome.

She wondered how his death would have been had he not had a child. No one would have looked at him this way, as she was, delineating him within the fences of her consciousness, dismantling and reassembling him, painting his body inside and out with nameless colors. She sat on the edge of the bed and put her head on his chest, and her cheek felt his sunken, spiky ribs, and a pleasant sensation spread through her body, as if he had placed his large hands on her head to bless her, had stroked the back of her neck to calm her, as if his chest had broadened and no longer looked like a cage with bent bars—as if her father had finally, for the first time in his life, been able to contain her. She sat that way, with her head on his chest, and thought that if not for the tension in the air, her body waiting for a sign from his, if not for the silence that was so complete you could hear the footsteps of the seconds escaping, she would have fallen asleep and woken up once he was gone, and in his place they would put a pillow beneath her cheek, and she would say to the doctor or nurse, whoever came to wake her, in a sleepy, indulgent voice, Is that it? They would nod sadly, and say, "He passed away." And her guilt at falling asleep at the wheel would be mingled with relief: She was with him when he died, but not completely. They were both in the room and they were both unconscious, and neither of them suffered.

Within the sacred silence, she heard her stomach grumble, at first just a dim, hesitant noise that sounded like a question. She sucked her stomach in to silence it, but the sounds kept rolling out into the surprised room, loud and persistent, as if her stomach were trying, in impolite baby language, to protest at having been forgotten, at having spent an entire day—twenty-four absolutely real hours—without being fed. She wondered if he could hear it, because she thought she saw his eyes flicker. She put her hands on her stomach to dam the torrent of rumbles emerging, leaned her head aside to examine his face from below, as she used to do sometimes as a child when she wanted to see if he was asleep, and thought his eyelids were quivering. Perhaps the final thought was darting behind them: a tornado, with fragments of furniture, momentary colors, a down of words, breezes, and sounds swirling within its eye, blending and colliding with one another: the ironed smell coming from his pajama collar and *I love you* and the salty smell of her cheek and a few stomach noises.

A decisive but amputated inhalation sucked the mask in. She held his hand again, caressed it encouragingly, and waited for the exhalation, for the half-breath to find its way out, but it seemed the air had been lost inside him and was sinking, defeated, in his chest like a yellowish haze. Perhaps now she should call the doctor; the doctor had said she would be able to tell, and he was right—she knew, on her own, and now she was completely alone with this knowledge, which was sharp and full of life as if it had sucked the oxygen her father's fearful lungs had wanted for themselves. She interlaced her fingers with his, crushing them farewell, put his hand aside, and took the other, which seemed lonely and deprived, its blue veins intertwined like the roots of an ancient tree beneath his skin. She kissed it and put it aside too, then got up to look at him, taking a few steps back.

From where she stood at the foot of the bed, her father looked like a tree on a winter day, small and gray and struggling. Perhaps not like a tree, she then thought, but like the winter day itself. She kept looking at him, waiting for one more breath she knew would come. The doctor was right, possessed of some prior knowledge about death, as if he had predicted a thousand deaths and had learned their mechanics. Sobs began to escape her throat, little coughs of fear, dry, unlike her eyes, which shed huge tears, wetting her face, her hands that held the bed railing and trembled, because what she had seen was still surprising, different from what she thought she knew, at once insulting and comforting.

There had been no trace of the complexity of his life in the elegant simplicity with which it had collapsed. The machine had shut down so simply and smoothly: every switch, every conveyor belt, each cogwheel taking a final bite out of the next one, all the pistons rising and falling, curtseying goodbye to each other. How clear was this moment that ended decades of vagueness, as if death knew the material it had to work with and did its work precisely, and modestly, and did not squirm with infinite wordings, did not contradict itself, did not hate itself—death, she thought, was not an artist but an artisan.

Her father's throat suddenly emitted a damp sound, a kind of gargle or clearing of the throat, something that sounded like a flood, like the tide, and within the crackling sound she also heard a soft thud and a flutter of wings, as if his final breath were a moth caught in a lampshade. And then it came, responsible and punctual, and was inhaled into his waiting mouth, and from his throat came a call of surprise, as if this were not his final breath but his first one, and his eyes opened briefly, devoid of any look, their egg-whiteness murky and muddy, already flooded with other bodily substances. Dotted with clouds of blood, they moved like the ocean surface after a storm, threatening to swallow up the two dots that floated on it, sole survivors of a shipwreck—his brown pupils, in which she now saw no tree and no winter day but simply her father, and his eyes shut and his mouth opened slightly, and she suddenly felt a breeze on her back, and a freezing cold flooded the room.

A large clear plastic bag with the hospital logo imprinted across it sat between them in the car like a passenger, rustling under their interlaced fingers, a pair of brown plastic glasses sticking out of its opening.

He had found Shira sitting on the floor in her father's former room in the nursing ward, taking his things out of the cabinet and putting them in two piles, one on the right and one on the left. He arrived out of breath from climbing the stairs, after watching the doors open and close on several full elevators. "Busy day," said a potbellied orderly who was wheeling an elderly lady in a wheelchair, talking as if he had known Yonatan for years. "It's visiting hours now, so it's busy. How's the father?" He parked the old lady in front of him, her knees almost touching his.

"Mine?" he asked, slightly amazed but eager to correct the nosy stranger's mistake.

"No, the wife's," the orderly said. "He wasn't doing well at lunchtime, not well at all." He shook his head. "He'd already lost consciousness, poor man," he whispered into the old lady's ear, and Yonatan suddenly felt rebuked and exiled: strangers had taken part in this day, his part, whereas he had arrived at Internal H just after seven, holding a little bag with a homemade sandwich—cheese and pickles—because they had talked about it once and he wanted to re-create the flavor she missed.

He went to the nurses' station and asked which room Max Klein was in, and a doctor with a foreign accent, who was standing there looking at medical charts, said, "He passed away an hour ago; the daughter went to get his personal items." How superfluous the sandwich now seemed, which only a moment ago had looked so festive. How pathetic the comfort he had tried to reconstruct for her seemed, wrapped in a napkin, when he saw her sitting on the floor with her back to him, putting the little transistor radio he knew so well from his visits on the left pile—the old transistor held together with masking tape—and then changing her mind and moving it to the right, where she had placed handkerchiefs, a wristwatch, and reading glasses.

"I don't know what to do," she said softly, turning to look at him, and held out the transistor, as if she knew he was there the whole time or perhaps had not noticed his absence all day. "We have to throw out some of these things but I don't know which ones." He went up to her, waiting for her to realize he had finally arrived and she didn't have to sit on the floor sorting through her father's things anymore; this was neither the time nor the place. He was grateful that his mother was the one who had been left with his father's things. *First you need to break down,* he whispered to her silently. *First we hug; then you can start talking about his things.* As if reading his mind the way she had guessed his presence at the door, she got up quickly and fell into his waiting arms, and puppyish wails escaped her throat into his T-shirt.

He smelled clean, like the new laundry detergent she had bought at the SuperPharm, as if he had brought with him scents from the world she felt she had been absent from for so long. She wanted to return to it now, like this, with her head buried in his shirt, to be led out like a suspect who emerges from the courthouse with a shirt over his head, under cover of this fragrant darkness, and in her eyes, shut tight against his chest, she saw the picture of her father being removed from the room.

The doctor with the foreign accent had determined his death at twelve minutes past six and had asked her to leave the room, and she had found herself once again leaning on the wall and waiting. But when he came out with the nurse, and the nurse said, "You may go in now," she said she didn't want to. "To say goodbye," the nurse said. "Go in to say goodbye." But Shira shook her head and kept standing there, until two orderlies went into the room and wheeled her father out on a rolling stretcher, with a sheet covering his face. She turned aside and closed her eyes, as if blinded, and listened to the sounds the stretcher wheels made as it receded. She opened her eyes and watched as her father traveled to the end of the hallway, where one of the orderlies pressed the button for the service elevator, and the other leaned down to tie his shoelaces.

Yonatan sat her on the bed and said, "Later, later we'll decide what to do with the things. Is there anything else you need to take care of here?"

"I don't know," she said, sinking into passivity as into a hot bath, and he gathered the things into the bag she gave him and told her he would ask the nurse what to do. "Tomorrow," she said. "Let's do it tomorrow. I don't have the strength now."

"Of course." He put the bag on the bed next to her. "Wait here a minute, don't leave."

She looked at him, exhausted: Where could she go? She had been in all possible worlds today.

He went to the nurses' station and told the young nurse that a patient of theirs had died this evening and his daughter wanted to know what to do, if there were any forms to fill out.

"Where did he die? Here in the ward?" He said no, in Internal H. "Then you have to go there."

He went back to the room and found Shira sitting on the bed in the same position in which he'd left her. "I'm going down to Internal. Are you all right?"

She nodded. "I'm dying for a cigarette."

"Come on then," he said cheerfully, "let's go and have a smoke."

She got up and started looking for her cigarettes in her bag, and before they left she pointed to the bed and said, "But what about that?"

"The bag?"

"Should we leave it here?" she asked, troubled.

"Sure, no one will take it."

"No. But someone may think it's trash and throw it out."

He took the bag and said, "Come on, we don't need to come back here anyway."

She started crying again and said, "It's awful, that bag. Couldn't they come up with something less transparent?"

Once again, she sat in her regular corner by the vending machine, next to the big ashtray, which was overflowing with paper cups and empty cans. She nodded feeble mourners' gestures at the passersby who waved to her, sons and daughters visiting their parents, accustomed to seeing her there. But now she felt like an impostor. There was no longer any reason for her to sit here, on the hard chair, her shoulder squeezed against the rattling machine, flicking ash into muddy remnants of Turkish coffee; she was free, at liberty to go and smoke at home like a normal human being.

"How long has it been since you had a cigarette?" he asked.

She tried to think how many hours had gone by since she had smoked her last cigarette in the car. "I think it was at eight. Something like that."

"Wow. When did you get here?"

"Ten to nine," she said, and the words dispossessed the time from its great insignificant importance.

"It happened really quickly," he said, and she said she didn't know, she had no sense of time. When she put her cigarette out she said she felt like another one, and he said, "Go on, then. I'll have one too."

After great pain, a formal feeling comes. The line echoed through her head again, but now she understood what Dickinson meant.

Later, after he made the arrangements for her and they went out into the parking lot, he remembered he'd left the sandwich on the cabinet in her father's room. Like a stone placed on a grave, he thought, and suddenly felt as if his soul was also connected to those items, that when he had seen them on the floor, separated into piles of less important and more important and then once again unified into the classless mixture that now rattled in the bag he carried, he felt he was watching old age itself, a simple pile of things. He felt sorry for these things that were destined to look so meager only because they belonged to an old man. He thought about the battered transistor radio. If it had belonged to a child—to Dana, for example—it would have looked completely different. He would have praised a child who had decided to repair it, instead of feeling sorry for the old man who refused to buy a new one.

The night air attacked her face with warm kisses, as if it had missed her too. "It's really like summer," she said. "Hard to believe it was raining this morning."

"Raining? It was a squall."

"Really? A real storm?"

"You have no idea." He was happy to tell her something she didn't know, something refreshing. "You can't imagine what the roads were like today; that's why I was so late."

Then she remembered he'd taught in Jerusalem that day, and asked how it went.

"Amazing," he said quickly, as if he had been waiting all day to tell her, and she looked at him questioningly, with eyes still wet from tears. "Simply amazing."

Although she didn't think she could feel anything but pain now, she was overcome by a great sense of relief. Yesterday she had feared he would fail, that he would come home defeated, loathing his new career, loathing her for her success in the old one, and before falling asleep she had tried to think of ways to encourage him.

"You should have seen me," he said, and put the key in the car door. "I was incredible!"

"Really?" she asked, and felt a lump in her throat. The funeral would be the next afternoon, he had told her, after talking to the Chevra Kadisha. As an expert in these matters, he had made the arrangements for her while she sat by the vending machine and smoked one cigarette after another, listening to him talk on her cell phone as he paced back and forth. She tried to imagine where her father was, because she knew the movie that kept running through her head had not ended in the hallway, by the service elevator that took him somewhere—it had gone down, not up—and when she tried to picture the refrigerator where he would spend the night, without being part of it, the place where there was no night or day but only a twilight full of blinking fluorescence, when she thought about tomorrow, about the first morning when he would not be alive, a pain cleaved her spine and pooled in her knees.

She felt Yonatan's arm around her shoulder and heard him say, "But what am I telling you all this for now? Your father died today."

"But I want to hear about it," she mumbled.

"You will, but not now." He ran his hand down her back.

"Now," she protested. "Tell me now. Life goes on."

Yonatan smiled. "Yes, but it can go on tomorrow."

When they drove out of the parking lot and contended with drivers who wouldn't let them merge into traffic, trying to trap them eternally within the confines of the hospital, she remembered her car and said they should go back and she would drive it home.

"No way. You're not driving in your condition."

"What condition am I in?" She lit a cigarette and inhaled as if she hadn't smoked for days.

"You're not driving now. You need to unwind a little," he explained patiently. "You can't be in control the whole time. In fact, it's pretty annoying, to tell you the truth." He held up her hand to kiss it.

"What's annoying?" she asked.

"That you won't let me take care of you, that you're unwilling to give up control even for a second."

"I am willing," she said, and tears ran down her cheek again. "I just don't know how."

"I'll tell you, then. Just do nothing. We're going home, and I'm going to make you something to eat. By the way, I brought you a sandwich, but I left it at your dad's—I mean, in his room. It had cheese and pickles. I remembered how we talked about that once." She smiled. "And unfortunately I can't make you another one, because they only had one roll left at the store."

"You took forever to get there," she remembered, as if she had only just begun to reposition herself in time, like a traveler back from a trip overseas. "When did I talk to you at your mother's?"

"Around two. But I told you. There was a traffic jam from Latrun all the way to La Guardia."

"What happened?"

"I have no idea, but forget that; tell me about your day."

But she couldn't, because when he died, her father had taken with him the words describing his departure. She looked out the window, at bustling Ibn Gvirol, alive with a thousand kinds of lights, at the café dwellers crowding the outside tables, at the passersby quickly crossing the street, carrying their late-night shopping. She looked at Yonatan's watch; it was almost nine, and for these people another normal day was just coming to an end. A young woman walking a dog bent over to pick up his poop, with a plastic bag covering her hand, and threw it into the trash can.

"That's so good of her," she heard Yonatan say. "A righteous woman in Sodom."

"Yes," she said thoughtfully, although it was not Sodom on her mind but Tel Aviv. How normal it seemed now, how like itself, persevering in its collective disregard of private suffering. And yet it did not arouse anger but rather gratitude, for being a kind of deaf metronome, ticking quickly and cheerfully to the sounds of heavy music.

"Where were you when Rabin was murdered?" Yonatan asked, as they passed by the square where it had happened.

"On a blind date. And you?"

"At home with Dana. It was a year after Ilana died."

"Where's Dana?" She suddenly remembered her, as if there were some fixed order of activities that accompanied her return to the world: first air, then time, and eventually people.

"She's at Tamar's. She's going on the trip tomorrow."

"I know. Does she know what's going on?"

"I didn't actually see her today. I wanted to ask her to sleep over at Tamar's because I didn't know when we'd be back, but she'd already gone there this afternoon and left me a note. I talked to her before I came to the hospital and said we'd let her know what was happening."

Again she saw Dana's crushed look, their new friendship collapsing like the onion rings the girl broke up with her fork, and although a lead screen already stood between her and that fresh memory, new life was breathed into her guilt. Perhaps when she heard what had happened, Dana would forget the silly, unnecessary confession. Death was dramatic and impressive next to a vague future pregnancy.

"She looked a little uneasy yesterday, didn't she?" he said, and honked angrily at a pizza-delivery guy on a Vespa who cut him off on the right.

"Dana?"

"Didn't you notice? When you came back from that restaurant."

"She always looks uneasy." She hated herself.

"That's true. How are you? Are you okay? I mean, I know you're not but, you know, I'm just checking."

"I'm okay right now. Didn't you say you wanted me to unwind?"

"Yes," he said, and gently nibbled her fingers, which he was holding in his hand. "But I want to manage your unwinding." His teeth gave her a pleasant chill, different from the consolation of his hugs, a chill that teased her grieving body and whispered to it: You will have joys. And tears filled her eyes again.

They parked on the corner of their street, near Allenby, and she waited for him to say that he hated parking there because of the partiers; he was afraid they would break into the car or scratch it. Perhaps tonight he would forget to say what he always did when he begrudgingly parked on the corner, knowing it was too late to find any other spot. Perhaps this night was too big for trivial statements.

He turned the key in the ignition and turned the lights off. "I hate parking here." She tried to smile but burst into tears. "What?" he said, alarmed, and then remembered that tonight she did not need a reason, and he turned to her and kissed her cheeks, his lips meeting hers from habit, not knowing if they were allowed, and she put hers against his.

This is part of the unwinding, she thought, letting it all blend: a little passion in the sorrow, secular tickles taunting jabs of sacred pain. Like a fastidious girl trying to separate different foods on her plate, looking fearfully at the piles threatening to touch each other, to contaminate each other, until she finally gave in and, with great relief, crushed everything with her fork; her tongue traveled in his mouth, and his tongue happily wound around it.

"I have a hard-on," he said, when their lips unlocked. He smiled. "I'm sorry, I know that's not appropriate now."

Dana was leaving the building just as they arrived, wearing her new backpack. "I called the hospital," she said excitedly. "First they wouldn't tell me anything, but I lied." She looked at Shira. "I told them I was his granddaughter, and then they told me he had died. It's so awful." She rushed over to Shira and wrapped her arms around her stomach. The backpack made her embrace clumsy, and Shira felt her tremble so she put her hand on the girl's head and stroked it. "I'm so sorry," Dana said. "Did he suffer?" She looked up at Shira with tearful eyes.

"I don't think so. I don't know."

"Were you with him?" She took a step or two back, rearranged the straps on her shoulder, and heaved the heavy pack up higher on her back.

"Yes."

Yonatan held her hand again.

"You mean, right until the end?" the girl asked, suddenly curious.

"Yes, I was with him when he died."

"Then at least he wasn't alone," Dana said, and Shira nodded. "It's good that you were with him." She looked at her father, who smiled sadly at her. "It's really good. That way, at least he knew he wasn't dying alone."

"Yes," Shira said. "I suppose that's true."

"Of course he knew," the girl decreed, and wiped her eyes with the back of her hand. "I know he did."

"Where are you going?" Yonatan asked.

"To Tamar's. It's better if I sleep over there."

"Are you sure?" Shira asked.

"Yes, so you can be alone for a while. We have to leave early anyway."

"What time?" Yonatan asked.

"We have to be at school at six-thirty. I talked to Rona. She knows your father died; she'll call later."

"I'll walk you there," Yonatan said, and turned to Shira. "Is that okay? Will you be all right for a few minutes?"

"I don't need an escort, it's not that late," Dana said.

"But it's dark. I don't want you walking on your own."

"But Dad—"

"Go with her," Shira said, and went toward the building. "I want to take a shower anyway." Then she called after Dana, "Hey! You're going to have fun on this trip, right?"

"I'll do my best." Dana smiled, and Shira wondered if she'd forgiven her.

"Promise?"

Dana nodded, and Shira watched the two of them walk away.

How strange the apartment looked. The usual mess in the kitchen was different today: An open jar of pickles stood on the counter, and the cheese stuck out from its transparent package. She sniffed it out of habit, to make sure it hadn't gone bad, and put it back in the fridge. She sat down and held a mug on the table that held a cloudy remainder of the morning's coffee. She got up and filled the kettle and turned it on and went into the bedroom, where she looked at their bed, at the sheets and pillows that always found themselves tangled in one pile in the morning, and at the clothes he had put on before leaving, tossed on the floor. She sat down on the edge of the bed and took her sandals off and noticed her own clothes, what she'd put on after the call came—how irrelevant that phone call now seemed—an olive-colored T-shirt and broad black pants made of soft fabric, the same clothes she had worn yesterday and had left hanging in the bathroom because she wanted to wash them; what had stuck to them today could not be removed. She took these clothes off and put on her favorite T-shirt, with the faded coyote print, threw them into the laundry hamper, and then remembered the plastic bag that Yonatan held as he walked down the street with Dana, talking, and she felt a chill again and then the phone rang.

"Shira." She heard Rona's voice, molecules of condolence clinging together to form her name. "Shira. So it's over, yes?"

Shira heard the TV on in the background, and the girls arguing about something. "Yes, it's over."

"It's difficult, but I understand he didn't suffer."

"No, but I did." She took a cigarette out of the pack on the living room table, and thought, How different the reporting of pain is from the pain itself, like two unrelated events.

"Do you want to come over?" Rona asked. "Yonatan just left to come back to you, but it only takes two minutes. Come over, both of you, I'll make you some comfort food. There's schnitzel and mashed potatoes, or maybe you're not hungry."

"I'm starved, but I don't have the strength to leave the house."

"I understand. Will you be able to sleep?"

"I hope so."

"You should try, okay? The funeral is tomorrow?"

"Yes." She sat down on the couch, suddenly weak.

"Yonatan said at three."

"Yes, at three."

"I'll see you there, then. Should I come over in the morning, just to be with you for a while?"

"We'll see. I'll call you."

"I'm taking the girls to school early, and then I'll be home. Wait a minute, Tamar wants to talk to you."

Then she heard Tamar's sweet, childish voice. "I'm sorry about your dad, Shira."

"Thanks. Have a great time on the trip, okay?"

"Okay."

"And take care of Dana."

"Okay."

When she put the phone down, she heard Yonatan's key in the door and the kettle switch flipped.

He was very quiet making spaghetti sauce, his movements efficient, his back turned to her, not revealing a good mood or a bad one. "They're really excited, Tamar and Dana." When she saw him dripping Tabasco into the bubbling tomato sauce, she remembered the first time they ate spaghetti together and how spicy it was, practically inedible, but so tasty. "Is there any Parmesan left?" he asked, with his head in the fridge.

"In a bag on the door," she said, tired indifference filling her head. "What time is it?"

"Ten-fifteen or so."

"It's late." She tried to picture the funeral, something she had imagined dozens of times over the last few months. "Which newspaper is the notice going to be in, in the end?" she asked, as if she hadn't heard him dictate it over the phone only two hours ago.

"*Yediot*. That's what you wanted, isn't it?"

"Yes. How much did it cost?"

"Forget it. I paid with a credit card."

"But how much did it cost?"

"It cost whatever it cost."

"I'll pay you back." She looked down, and her eyes were heavy with tears again.

"Okay." He squatted on his heels next to her, with his hands in her lap. "Is that what's worrying you?"

She shook her head. "I'm crying so much now, I won't have anything left for tomorrow."

"And is that what's worrying you? How you'll be at the funeral?"

"No. No one will see me anyway, because there won't be anyone there."

"I'll be there, but I don't care how you are."

"I'm dying to take a shower."

"Go ahead."

"Later, I don't have the energy now."

He put his head against her stomach, listening. "I can tell you haven't had anything to eat all day."

"Really?"

"Yes." He rubbed his nose against her belly button. "Sounds like a whole coop of angry chickens."

Her father would have died in any case, whether or not she had found love, and she tried to imagine herself now sitting in the apartment on Borochov or a different apartment, wearing this T-shirt or a different one, cooking spaghetti for herself or something else, alone. She could not.

When she got into the shower, she soaped herself carefully, unsure of what she wanted to do: remove the layers of filth or keep hold of the remnants of smells she would never smell again. Through the open door, she heard Yonatan talking to his mother, and then he came in and said, "She insisted on coming to the funeral tomorrow. See? It won't be just the two of us."

"Rona's also coming."

"And Aunt Malka."

He looked at himself in the mirror, holding his chin and turning his face from side to side. Then with a sudden thought, he quickly put his hand into the back pocket of his jeans. He hissed a curse and pulled out a mass of shredded paper.

"What happened?" she asked.

He said he forgot to take something out of his pocket before he threw his jeans into the washing machine yesterday. "An old painting of Dana's I found when I cleaned out the car."

"That's too bad," she said, and started washing her hair.

"Yes." He thought about the picture drowning in the washing machine, being spun and wrung over and over again, then drying slowly on the line, crumb by crumb, in the back pocket of his jeans.

"Will she be mad?" Shira asked, and turned her back to him to adjust the shower head.

"No, she doesn't even know about it. I wanted to surprise her. Well, I don't know what I wanted, really. You have a great ass, did you know that?"

"Yeah, right."

"No, I'm serious."

"Me too."

"I'll convince you. But not now."

"Convince me now."

"No. When the shiva is over."

"It's over," she said, and stood defiantly in the shower.

"Stop it," he said, and started brushing his teeth. "Don't tease me now. You're in mourning and I'm horny."

"Do you think I need to sit shiva?" She now stood beside him, wrapped in a towel.

"I don't know. What would your father have wanted?"

"I have no idea. I don't think it would have made much difference to him."

"I don't want you to sit shiva over me, by the way." He spat into the sink.

"Why not?"

"Just because. I don't want people traipsing all over the house."

"Anyway, what gives you the right to die before I do?" she said, as she put her T-shirt back on.

"I'm older."

"Your mother's older than your father, and he died first."

"That's true. But it's common knowledge: Men die first. Doesn't matter how old they are."

"Not in my dad's case."

"Not in mine either."

Suddenly the talk of death brought some joy into the bathroom and they lingered there, afraid to go out into the gloominess creeping through the rest of the apartment, sniffing the walls and furniture, digging into the dusty rug in the living room like a big dog looking for a spot to spend the night. "I'm not going to sit shiva," she said, and took a box of cotton swabs out of the medicine cabinet. "Not in any official way, at least. I'll grieve with myself. And with you."

"That's fine with me. Whatever you want." He slowly flossed his teeth.

They spent awhile longer in the bathroom before going to bed, devoting too much time to trivial hygienic tasks, prolonging their shelter in this refuge full of steam and chatter and sweet soapy smells.

She fell asleep quickly, but woke up at five into a chill that at first seemed to have seeped into the room from her dream about morgues. They had gone to sleep on what felt like a summer night, but yesterday's storm—it was now possible to think in terms of yesterday—had softened something in the air and broken the heat. She heard the pile of papers with her notes for the novel rustling on the desk beneath the open window, and was about to get up and make some coffee, as she always did out of some great urgency: to put an end to the negotiations her body had every morning with her brain, which was the early riser. But this morning she let her limbs win and kept lying on her side, her cheek against the pillow, her exposed toes rubbing against one another, tasting the cold. A pale light began to paint the room, softly unveiling furniture and objects: the white of the computer keyboard on the dark wooden surface of the table, the pink towel used last night to dry her hair, hanging on the back of a chair, the deep color of the armoire, its doors gaping from the opposite wall, the glimmer of the old bureau's copper handles, the crisscrossed plastic cover of the air-conditioning outlet over Yonatan's head, with dust bunnies stuck to the grooves, their color blending with the merciful democratic light and with the color of his hair, the floral sheet wrapped around his back and shoulders like a shawl, exposing his bare feet and the faded color of his underwear, gray like the light.

Her hand landed gently on the small of his back, waiting for the slightest motion, surprised but not completely, by his sleeping body. She rested her head on her other hand and looked at his two parts: his head, facing her, and his behind and legs facing the ceiling, a cheerful field of flowers between them. Her fingers fluttered over his skin. Her head was empty, a dump truck that had unloaded the verbal trash of yesterday and not yet stowed the new day's language. His back tensed at her touch, and she heard him sigh with sleepy pleasure, and felt the warmth of his sigh on her face. "Are you okay?" he asked. "Go back to sleep," she whispered. Even in his sleep, he thought to console her. She kept stroking his back, but now the flutter had become a caress, her head was reloaded, the words were lining up for morning inspection, so punctual, awaiting orders. She sighed, and he opened his eyes and asked what was wrong. "My stomach hurts. I'm getting my period." He made a sympathetic sound and asked if she wanted a painkiller. "No, you sleep." "What bad timing, to get your period today," he murmured into his pillow. "Yes, go back to sleep." He wrapped his arms around her, the lie curling up between them shyly, surprised at itself. Her hand wandered on his back, stopped briefly between his shoulder blades, touched the large mole, climbed to the back of his neck, burrowed through the roots of his hair, flowed back to the small of his back, and rested on his behind, which tensed up, waiting with an erection pushed against her stomach, to see where it would go now.

Now he sighed, indulging himself, one sleepy hopeful eye open, the other closed against the pillow. His fingers caressed the back of her neck, his lips roamed from her forehead to her cheek to her chin and lips. She lay on her back and pulled him on top of her and tugged his underwear off. Now he was wide awake and looking at her with amused surprise, and, squirming, she took off her own underwear. She thought he was about to say something, and she touched his lips with her finger to stop him and closed her eyes to let him know she could not be negotiated with, and he entered her and moved inside her with thoughtful slowness, and she could feel the little currents gather in her body and make their way to their usual meeting point. She opened her eyes; pleasure had softened his face and turned it boyish.

"Devious," he whispered, and fear flashed between the currents of pleasure. "Waking me up and raping me."

She felt relief. "Yes, I'm sorry."

"You should be, you're exhausting me. I'm an old man. What about your stomach?"

"What about it?"

"You said it hurt."

"Not anymore," she whispered. She felt him starting to disconnect, like a boat untied from its docking post, carried away on wavelets. How could she have once believed, as everyone did, that sex was the ultimate merging, when in fact it was the opposite? She looked at his child face growing distant, at his closed eyes, at the tiny pearls of sweat glistening on his forehead, and she set off alone on the path of electricity charging her body. "Come inside me," she said. He watched her silently. "Okay?" she whispered. "It's all right, I'm getting my period." Before he could refuse, she said, "I want to feel, for once, what it's like with you." She tightened her thighs around him, transferring to his hesitant body the currents that continued before she relaxed, the aftermath of her pleasure, and when he started to rouse inside her again, searching for his lost rhythm and finding a new one, extremely determined and private, she suddenly saw him making her a sandwich, and before the picture became words—*the man who loves me made me a sandwich*—she froze the image: his forehead furled in concentration; his tongue licking the butter knife as it always did; his hands, which now held her breasts, wrapping the sandwich clumsily in a napkin. Here is the love of my life, she thought and tried to rise up onto her elbows.

"No, I've changed my mind," she whispered, before it was too late. "No, we shouldn't," she said, but he went on. "Yonatan, it's not a good idea." But he didn't seem to hear and she shouted, "No!" and her hands pushed his stomach away and he said yes, and his eyes opened as a yell escaped his mouth, the same as that first time, which they now both understood. Yes. The word preceded his shout of pleasure like a colon. Yes. It danced in his velvety brown eyes, in which her own were now drowning, warm and enveloping like the current she felt inside her, responding, building. Yes, why not? Indeed, yes.

(3 0)

Instead of bunk beds, there were eight regular cots arranged in two facing rows. Dana put her backpack on the one next to Tamar's, took out her toiletries, and walked down the hallway, where the walls were decorated with framed posters of Israeli flora and fauna. The other girls were already huddled in the bathroom to freshen up before getting back on the bus; they were going to have a tour and eat lunch at a goat dairy. It was hard to find any free space at the mirrors. The girls crowded around the sinks, jostled one another, and rummaged through their cosmetic bags, passing around eyeliners and lipstick.

"Hey," Tamar called out to Dana; her face was up close to one of the mirrors. "Can I borrow some zit cream?"

Dana went up to her. "I don't have any."

"You don't?" Orit exclaimed. She was holding a towel up in front of Lilach, who was undressing by the wall. "You really should get it."

"I don't have any zits."

"You will," Lilach said, from behind the towel.

"No, I won't. My parents never had any."

"You're such a retard," Orit said. "It has nothing to do with parents. It has to do with hormones."

"You're the retard," Tamar said, sadly examining her nose in the mirror. "Where do you think hormones come from?"

"I have zits and my mom didn't," Lilach said.

"Then your dad must have had them," Tamar said. "Ask him. Is he abroad at the moment?"

"No, he's in Israel. You have them, don't you?"

"A little. I just got a really nasty one."

"And did your mother have them?"

"I don't think so."

"Then your dad must have."

"Could be," Tamar said, and walked away from the mirror. Her towel was slung over her shoulder and she held a small transparent zipper bag.

"It's too bad you can't ask him," Lilach said, and emerged from behind the towel in tight stretch capris and a purple padded bra. "Which one?" she asked Orit, holding up two tank tops.

"That one, definitely." Orit pointed to the black top.

"But won't it be cold?"

"No way. It's boiling today," Orit replied.

"But they said we'd only get back in the evening."

"Then take a sweater. Didn't you bring one?"

"Of course I did, what do you think? I brought two, the peach and the white."

"The peach goes better," Orit said. "Should I get it for you to try on?"

"Yes. But bring the white one too."

Orit went out into the hallway.

Liat, Lilach's older sister, had recently started modeling. Her pale face, with its prominent cheekbones, sunken eyes made up in smoky black shades, and lips slightly parted in rehearsed, infantile passion, had appeared in a few issues of youth and fashion magazines. She could be seen on almost every talk show on TV, sitting erect with her legs crossed, rocking the upper one nervously, providing serious answers to questions that were possibly cynical and possibly sycophantic. Something about the way she spoke was sticky and sleepy. Since her sister had become a star, Lilach seemed to have turned uglier. She had never been a pretty girl, but there had been a certain claim to beauty in her face: her eyes, shooting out commands behind an arrogant veneer of indifference; her fair straight hair, tied up in a ponytail that she whipped every time she turned her head to listen to a secret whispered in her ear or to whisper one of her own; her lips, which she had started to leave slightly parted and kept wetting with her tongue, moving exaggeratedly, separate from the words, as if she had no need for them, as if she were a pantomime of royalty.

She rearranged her bra straps and complained that Orit was taking too long. "I don't understand what's so hard about finding a sweater." She examined her breasts; the padding only emphasized the fact that they were, for now, nipples with potential. Dana watched her tighten the velvet ribbon around her ponytail and pitied her. Her reign was coming to an end. The team was on the verge of collapse, four of the girls having dropped out, leaving in pairs. When the school year started, Tamar also left, taking her defiance as a partner. The remaining girls found themselves abandoned, bored, while Lilach and Orit carried on like a husband and wife who no longer loved each other but were too afraid to part.

"What is that bag?" Lilach pointed to Dana's toiletries bag, which was made of plastic in shades of brown and yellow. She giggled. "My grandmother has one like that."

"This *is* my grandmother's," Dana lied.

"She bought you that for the trip?"

"No," Dana said, and from the corner of her eye she saw Tamar looking at her, amused. "Of course not, she lent it to me. It's silly to spend money on something you only use once in a million years."

It was actually her father's and always sat in the bathroom cabinet, covered with a layer of talc, full of scents of aftershave and shaving cream, its inner lining slightly greasy. "It's my one-night-stand kit," she heard him explain to Shira when she had cleaned out the cabinet, not long after moving in, and had asked if he still needed that ugly thing. "Don't you dare throw it out," he said. "My whole student life is in that bag." A few days ago, Dana took it out of the cabinet and cleaned the talc off, but did not touch the inside, afraid to remove an ancient geologic stratum, the person her father was before she was born.

"So what exactly did you keep in your one-night-stand kit?" Shira had teased him.

"I'm not telling."

"Why?" she asked.

"It's a secret. Can't I have any secrets?"

"You can, you baby."

"Let me see." Lilach came up to her, clutching her tank tops to her chest. "It's cute, actually. Kind of seventies. You probably can't get these anymore."

"Yes, you can," Tamar said. "They have them at any drugstore."

"At the SuperPharm?"

"No. On King George, though, or on Allenby. Anywhere."

"It's lovely." Lilach touched the bag, and for a moment Dana felt as if she were touching her father, hovering with her thin nervous fingers, the fingernails bitten and surrounded with red, injured skin. "I might get one of these too."

"Are you serious?" Tamar laughed. "It's an old ladies' bag. My mom has one too."

"So what?" Lilach said, and looked at the bag, mesmerized. "That's the whole point. That's what makes it cute."

When they crowded into the bus outside, Dana almost asked Lilach and Orit, who sat together on a bench looking gloomy, like two aunts, to join Tamar and her when they ate lunch. The tour guide had told them over the loudspeaker that the restaurant was owned by a lovely family with three daughters. "And please be on your best behavior. I've known the owner for years, he's a good man. A nature lover. And he makes great cheese."

She felt Tamar's elbow digging into her ribs. "Look at the guide," Tamar whispered to her. "He has a hard-on."

Dana peered over the seat in front of her at the guide, a man around her father's age, short and chubby, with flushed cheeks, wearing cut-off jeans and a Nature Preservation Society sweatshirt. "Idiot. It's his cell phone."

"No, it isn't! Take a good look, he has a hard-on. How much do you want to bet?"

"I'll bet you a million dollars," Dana said.

"Chicken."

"But how will we know?"

"I'll find out," Tamar said, and she got up and walked to the front of the bus, looking back at Dana and stifling her giggles with her hand. She went up to the guide, who smiled at her, and when she whispered something in his ear, he leaned down, put a big hand on her shoulder, and then nodded and took a cell phone out of his pocket. Tamar turned around and grimaced disappointedly and then she dialed, had a quick conversation, thanked him, and came back to her seat. "You win. If you'd had the guts to make a real bet, you would have won some money."

"But who did you talk to?"

"No one. I said I had to call my mother because she didn't feel well, and I asked if he had a cell phone."

Dana felt an unfamiliar lightness in the air, which still held the memory of yesterday's storm. She was looking forward to the evening, when they would get back to the hostel and lie in bed and chatter and gossip, like they used to, but it would be even more fun. The bus had turned off the highway onto a narrow road and was going uphill.

She had woken up that morning long before Tamar and Rona and had dressed quickly so they wouldn't see her in the old shirt and sweats she slept in, baggy and comfortable but showing up the impossibilities of her body: her breasts, which shook in her shirt without the simple cotton one-size bra she had bought one afternoon, on her own, in the factory seconds store on Allenby; and the two folds of fat on her stomach, which she wasn't sure were still baby fat or a hint of how she would look when she got old; and her backside, which did not stick out, was not round, not anything, and yet so present—all her contradictions moved freely in those clothes. She changed into the clothes she had brought for the trip—jeans and a T-shirt, with her dad's old sweatshirt that she had shoved into the backpack at the last minute, his beloved gray sweatshirt, which had been waiting at the bottom of the closet for a new winter to start—and sat in the kitchen at the big table, drinking a glass of water. The sun started rising in the east, beyond King George, the light trapped in the yards between the buildings. A pleasant breeze blew through the window, rustling the notes pinned to the fridge with magnets. She had never seen an urban sunrise, a partial sunrise, which the buildings blotted out, leaving it semi-mysterious. She preferred it to the boastful extreme sunrise she had once seen on a school trip to Masada—and then she heard a door open and bare feet padding down the hallway and Rona's hoarse voice whispering good morning.

A different Rona stood before her, not one she had encountered before. The Rona who now leaned on the counter, wearing a short, sleeveless nightgown and waiting impatiently for the kettle to boil, did not look like a psychologist or a hostess or a cook, or like anyone Dana had ever hoped her father would fall in love with. This Rona looked like a forty-eight-year-old woman, the same age as her mother, if she had lived. Large freckles and a reddish rash covered her shoulders and the triangle of skin revealed by the deep V-neck of her nightgown, which hung over heavy, uneven breasts. Rona stretched, poured water into a mug and threw an herbal teabag inside, turned to Dana and gave a big yawn, and then put her hand up to her mouth as if she had just noticed she was not alone. She stretched again, and this time she held the collar of her nightgown up and walked around the kitchen that way, hiding.

Dana drank her water and kept stealing looks at Rona. The morning snitched on some discomfort she felt; in the white light spilling in from the yard, a light so clean it seemed to have been laundered during the night, Dana saw colorless shoulder-length hair, sometimes brown, sometimes gray, similar to the scrawny hair that peeked out of Rona's armpits.

Her thighs seemed to have been painted with a purple marker, covered with a network of veins whose vivid color looked surprising against her pale skin. This Rona was neither young nor old, neither beautiful nor ugly, but something in between. In every movement, Rona's body expressed its awkward opinion of itself—an opinion that nothing in the world can change. Dana saw its signs in Tamar too, who appeared in the kitchen wearing underwear and a tank top. When had she acquired the habit of sucking in her stomach and her cheeks and distractedly pulling down the hem of her top?

"Mom." Tamar clung to her mother, her face turning yellow as if she were about to cry.

"What is it?" Rona asked indifferently, her voice still sleepy.

"Mom," Tamar said again, and wrapped her arms around Rona's neck.

"Did you get out of bed on the wrong side?"

"No." Tamar's voice seeped out in an indulgent whimper. "Yes. No. I don't know." She rocked against Rona's back.

"Make up your mind, because we don't have all day."

"I don't want to." Tamar pinched her nose.

"That's enough, honey. You're strangling me." Rona pulled Tamar's arms off her neck and stood up. "I'm going to get dressed."

Tamar stomped her feet and huffed. She sat down in her mother's chair.

"Have something to eat," Rona said from the hallway. "You too, Dana."

"We don't want to," Tamar said, and although she was hungry, Dana was glad to be included in this indulgent refusal. "She's getting on my nerves," Tamar said and rubbed her eyes.

"Why?"

"I don't know. I don't need a reason." She got up and put two bowls and two spoons on the table. Then she took the milk out of the fridge, and gathered up three different cereal boxes from their place on the shelf.

"That makes you look fat, Mom," Tamar said, when Rona came in wearing an off-white linen suit.

"Always a compliment for your mother." Rona stood by the mirror in the hallway and put lipstick on. "This is a new suit and it cost me a fortune and I think it's lovely. Does it make me look fat, Dana?"

"No. You look good in it."

"Mom, you look like a couch."

"And you need to get dressed now," Rona said, and poured the rest of her tea into the sink.

Dana washed the dishes and watched Rona walk around the living room, turn off the radio, raise one of the blinds, and gather various documents into her bag. Every so often, she went up to the mirror, turned her back to it, moved her shoulders from side to side, patted herself on the behind, straightened her collar, and opened or closed the jacket button. "It's really beautiful," Dana said.

"Really?" Rona asked doubtfully.

"Definitely."

Tamar came out of her room, dressed, with her big backpack on her shoulders. "Come on, Mom, it's six-fifteen; we'll be late."

"You go down, I'll be right there."

They went downstairs and waited for her on the street, until she came down in black pants and a knit top, and Dana thought, Shira was wrong: Observation brings not only sorrow but sometimes also comfort.

The bus window opened on to a dimming valley with squares of fields: a quilt of greens, browns, and grays.

"I'm bored." Tamar sighed.

"We'll probably be there soon." Her voice, like her thoughts, sounded happier, as if it belonged to someone who had felt a great relief.

"Aren't you hot with that sweatshirt on?"

"A little." She rolled the sleeves up to her elbows.

"Take it off, then," Tamar said.

"Soon." She stared out at the view. It looked familiar, as if she had been here before.

"I really can't be bothered with goats now." Tamar leaned over her, also looking outside. "I'm starved."

"We'll eat soon."

"But I hate cheese."

"I like it."

"Yes, but you like everything. Is this the Galilee?" She stared indifferently at the rocks alongside the road. The bus seemed fearful as cars and trucks passed downhill on the other side.

"I think so. Why don't you ask your friend?"

"Who?" Tamar's bored eyes lit up.

"Him." Dana pointed her chin at the guide, who was standing with his back to them, talking to the driver.

"Gross!" Tamar said, shocked.

"Why?" Dana faked surprise. "He's cute. Look how his pockets are coming out at the bottom of his shorts."

"That's disgusting," Tamar whispered, pressing up against Dana protectively.

"No, really. Look at his cheeks, they're kind of red, like apples. It's so sexy."

"Stop it." Tamar giggled. "I'll throw up."

"And look at that cute roll of fat on his neck, like those dogs have, the wrinkled ones. Don't you feel like petting him?"

"I swear, I'll throw up on you!" She buried her head in Dana's legs and stifled a scream, and then the guide breathed into the loudspeaker.

"Can you hear me?" he asked.

"Yes!" the class answered.

"We'll be there soon. You'll see it in a minute; it's just around the bend. Are you hungry yet?"

"Yes!" everyone screamed cheerfully. Dana was surprised to hear her own voice amid the shouting.

"But are you *really* hungry?"

"Yes!" they all answered.

"And do you feel like a fantastic meal of cheese?"

"No!" Tamar shouted, as Dana once again yelled, "Yes!" with everyone else.

"And will you be well behaved?"

"No!" her voice mingled with Tamar's.

"So what do you say? Are we going to have fun?"

"Yes!" the class screamed.

"What's that you say?" he shouted into the microphone.

"Yes!" she heard her voice reply, as if she were alone in the bus.

"I can't hear you!" the guide said, and she felt hot and raised her arms and peeled her sweatshirt off. "Whaddaya say?"

"Yes!" she yelled, her voice louder than any other, as if she too had a loudspeaker. "Yes!"